What Others Are Saying

"Terence Harkin's novel brings the reader into the hidden world of Buddhist monastic life with such skill that you get to live it.... The wisdom, kindness, and compassion of the Thai forest monks permeate this book, as does the healing power of meditation."—**Jason Siff**, author of *Unlearning Meditation and Seeking Nibbana in Sri Lanka*

"*In the Year of the Rabbit* captures the soul of an American Combat Cameraman...whose life is overtaken by the most controversial war in America's history. Must reading."—**Colonel Frank A. Titus** (USAF, Retired), former Instructor of International Humanitarian Law with the United Nations-New York

"*In the Year of the Rabbit* deftly manages to deal with a number of disparate issues with power and precision.... An odyssey involving the brutal violence of conflict, the pain and guilt of lost love, and the tranquility of life as lived by a Buddhist monk. Highly recommended."—**Dean Barrett**, author of *Memoir of a Bangkok Warrior and Kingdom of Make Believe*

"Vividly portrays the cost emotionally, physically and morally to any of us who experience war—whether or not a direct participant—and points out so well that what we tell ourselves about events in our lives effects our response as much as what actually happens to us, (how we) need to come to terms with that, (and how) despite the challenges we face or endure we are ultimately designed to survive."—**Nellie Harness Coakley**, RN, 7th Surgical Hospital, Vietnam, 1968–1969; Head Orthopedics Nurse, Walter Reed, 1969; Trauma Counselor, 1982–2010; Technical Advisor, *China Beach*, 1988–91

"Sex, drugs, rock 'n' roll mixed with aerial combat, clandestine operations, (and) the plight of the Lao people make for an excellent story and maybe a lesson or two."—**Capt Tré Dahlander** (US Airways, ret.): RF-4 pilot, Ubon RTAFB, Thailand, 1971–72

"A wonderful experience of meaningful life ir **Kev Richardson**, author of *Pacific Paradox an*

"Counter cultures continually clash in Terence Harkin's novel, *In the Year of the Rabbit*...during the late stages of the Vietnam War. His insight into the contradictory values and desires of Easterners and Westerners teaches lessons in humanity to a depth beyond that normally found in books about that time and place. Harkin (also) covers a lot of ground about Spectre gunship action, of which I was a part, and gets it right."—**Henry Zeybel**, Lt. Col. USAF (ret.), author of *Gunship and Along for the Ride*; veteran of 158 combat missions over the Ho Chi Minh Trail

"Harkin's prose is muscular and immersive, detailing Leary's war experience with surprising imagery."—*Kirkus Reviews*

"The sequel to (the) critically acclaimed *The Big Buddha Bicycle Race*...*Rabbit* is a profound and compelling novel in its own right.... Much of the novel's interest comes from the unique relationship between Baker and Leary, which is at once loving and tense. The men view the world in ways that are fundamentally incompatible: Baker is, in his own words, "a gunner and a bomb loader" who likes combat and "that nasty feeling—those butterflies in my belly." Leary is an introspective pacifist. Yet the men bond through their shared experiences in the war.... At its heart, *In the Year of the Rabbit* is the story of a man's journey to find peace in a chaotic and violent world. The thoughtfulness and careful prose of *In the Year of the Rabbit* make Terry Harkin's second novel a thoroughly worthwhile read."—**Meg Bywater**, *The Veteran*

IN THE YEAR OF THE RABBIT

A Novel

TERENCE A. HARKIN

 Silkworm Books

When you come to a fork in the road, take it.

– Lawrence Peter "Yogi" Berra

ISBN 978-616-215-176-7
eISBN: 978-616-215-177-4
© 2021 by Terence A. Harkin
All rights reserved

First published in 2021 by
Silkworm Books
430/58 M. 7, T. Mae Hia, Chiang Mai 50100, Thailaand
info@silkwormbooks.com
www.silkwormbooks.com

Typeset in Minion Pro 11 pt. by Silk Type
Printed and bound in the United States by Lightning Source

Dedication

To Captain Kenneth Little, a pioneering African-American graduate of the U.S. Air Force Academy (Class of 1969). Like far too many veterans of Vietnam, Thailand, Laos, and Cambodia, he spent the rest of his life in self-imposed solitude, Missing in America;

To Private Craig Maratta, Private First Class Louis Brizzoli, Corporal Tom Shanks, and Colonel Robert Hagerman, friends and neighbors who died in Vietnam;

And to the people of Laos, who were caught in a crossfire of Western ideologies that proved that war didn't need to be nuclear to be catastrophic.

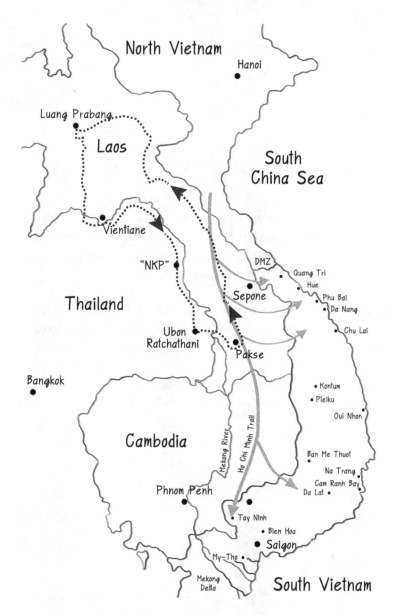

The Pilgrimage of Brendan Leary

Prologue

It was a bad sitting—
fly on my nose, butterflies
in my gut, sweat
forming on my forehead,
armpits, itching film
on my chest and arms and legs.
"Just observe," said Ajahn Po,
the venerable one, grandfather, uncle,
Master.

I fell out of my dream, out
of my book, into my movie
that was this lifetime and my past
life and the next, my comfort
torn away like a baby blanket
when the wind blew, the bough broke,
the cradle listing to starboard,
sinking fast,
my sails torn in the seas that wanted
to swallow me as much as Asia
when she parted her lips
and kissed me forever.

Swallowed forever into the pomegranate,
spit from the pages I had filled
with words written in my own hand.
Torn inside out to join the universal
consciousness? Or to die like an amoeba
in the primordial ooze, die before I ever
existed, die like a spent meteor reduced
to cosmic dust before its flames

can turn lush jungle into glass,
gone in the time a Bedouin blinks?

What is this life? What was this suffering?
What suffering did I inflict that earned
this fate? Why am I so certain I was once
an outlaw privateer, laughing lustily
at the plundering of burning ships
and the defilement of young virgins?
Why do I call myself an anthropologist,
an explorer, a linguist, a teacher
when I have lived in a cloud of purple haze,
failed as a soldier, failed as peacemaker,
failed as a lover, failed as a monk?
Why do I resist my destiny
as God's cannon fodder?

Why do I know my *kamma* sends me
to the Himalayas?
Why do I want to lead a Mongol horde
across the steppes of Asia?
What makes me want to sack Vienna?
How did Asia swallow me with a single kiss?

Valium

In blackness I begin to hear the sounds of an AC-130 gunship mission over the Ho Chi Minh Trail. "Thirty...thirty," from Colonel Strbik as the plane banks to the angle needed for the miniguns, the M-61 Vulcans, and the 40-mm Bofors.

"This is so cool!" I exclaim. "They told me you had been shipped to Nakhon Phanom, Colonel!"

The dream seems almost familiar, almost real, and like another bloated body rising to the surface of a murky lake, little pieces of the scene begin to break loose once again from my memory and float into my distorted vision: flairs going off below...the image of a truck appearing on the infrared sensor and then the NOD...Pigpen Sachs feeding 40-mm ammo into his gun.

"This is way cool! Sachs, I thought you were ambushed!"

Stepping up to my Nod-cam to start filming just as his gun gives off a deafening blast—

"Triple-A—accurate—break left!" shouts a garbled, scratchy intercom voice.

The plane lurches, tracers flashing through the cloud we just vacated, throwing faint red light on Lieutenant Liscomb who is looking confused trying to get his parachute snap to work, and I am hurled against the 20-mm gun mounts. The roar of the outboard engines dies and I feel my face contort. "Shit, we're gonna crash!"

My brain felt like a soggy dishrag, my skull a helmet of pain as I slowly opened my eyes at the base hospital Sunday morning, the day after the Big Buddha Bicycle Race ended in a river of blood. I wanted to check out. I wanted to go home to my bed at Bungalow Ruam Chon Sawng, but Dr. Lioci was calm and persuasive when he told me he wanted his team to keep me under observation. For one thing, he said, they had not yet determined the severity of my head trauma. I could barely follow. His voice sounded like it was coming through an echo chamber when he told me something about preliminary X-rays coming back negative but how he wasn't going to rule out a hairline fracture until he had seen some follow-up images after the swelling had gone down. There was *no* doubt, he said in his echoey voice, that

I was showing symptoms of a severe concussion—headaches, nausea, and blurred vision. I wanted to tell him he was full of shit, but I *was* experiencing headaches, nausea, and blurred vision. I wanted to tell him he was full of shit when he said I might still be in shock, but he got my attention when he said shock can be fatal, that it was something he needed the nurses and medics to keep an eye on. I surrendered.

No sooner had he left than Nurse Wozniak arrived with my medications, little pills that were being popped into my mouth every few hours to keep me pleasantly zonked. Given that she was the girlfriend of Major Horney, my favorite fire-control officer at the 16th Special Operations Squadron, I was confident she was taking good care of me. Sure enough, the drugs kicked in and, instead of feeling trapped in my hospital bed, I didn't want to leave at all. Alas, it was in the middle of that groggy high that First Sergeant Link decided to pay me a visit.

"The patient isn't to be disturbed," the duty nurse tried to tell him.

Link pushed by her. "Leary can rest later. We got an investigation going on."

"Dr. Lioci and Major Wozniak are going to hear about this," the nurse grumbled as she disappeared into the hallway.

Link didn't care. "I'm gonna ask you again, Leary—what do you know about Sergeant Prasert, the asshole who shot you?"

My lips felt rubbery and moved in slow motion. "You oughta get your facts straight, Sarge. He shot my *camera.*"

Link was fuming. "All right, the asshole who shot your camera—and almost took your fuckin' head off."

"Like I told you—he was a student who never talked politics. I used to see him around Ubon—sometimes with his druggie sister—but I hadn't seen either of them in a month. Thought they were long gone."

"Then why didn't you tell us you saw him near the governor's mansion the day of the assassination attempt?"

"Who fed you that line of shit?"

"Your buddy Wheeler. He slipped up when we questioned him alone."

"I wouldn't rely on Wheeler if I were you, Sarge. Wheeler's got a drug problem of his own. Like the bumper sticker says, he brakes for hallucinations."

"Listen, you punk, I was warned about you before you arrived at Norton Air Force Base. I don't know how the hell you hung on to your friggin' security clearance. As far as I'm concerned, your anti-war bullshit back at DODCOCS should have been enough to get it yanked before you left D.C. And then you had the nerve to pull that GIs for Peace shit out in California—under *my* watch."

"Sarge, get it straight. I never did anything but exercise my First Amendment rights."

"Forget all that 'rights' shit, Leary. This is wartime. A lot of blood was spilled yesterday. The Thai National Police, the Thai and U.S. Air Police, and the OSI are running a joint investigation, and you can bet your sweet ass they're going to get to the bottom of the security breaches that caused it. I don't know if you did it intentionally or you're just a fuck-up, but if we can prove you aided or abetted the Issan Liberation Front in any way, I promise you'll be doing some hard time. Now for the last time, why didn't you ID Sergeant Prasert?"

"I'll say it again—he was somebody I barely knew who turned up in my class unexpectedly. He never talked politics."

"This isn't the last you've seen of me, Leary." And with that, Link took his leave.

The young nurse we tried to interview at the first aid station during the bicycle race poked her head in, a little more sympathetic this time. "Sounds like he's blaming you for Intelligence screwing up."

I smiled wearily. "Sergeant Link blames me for a lot of things. Once in a while he's even right."

"Here," she said, giving me an extra pill. "This ought to help you sleep through the afternoon."

Before I could say thanks, I dozed off. I was talking to her again when I started waking up, telling her how she was *beautiful*, how she really should come out to L.A. after the war, but it was Jack Wu sitting across from me when I opened my eyes. "What the hell are *you* doing here?"

"I wanted to check up on you. And tell you that I feel responsible for the way things turned out. I've been around, I'm not a greenhorn like most of you guys. I did police work when I was in the Army. I shouldn't have let my guard down. But when I did ask around, all I kept hearing was that the Thai police and Thai intelligence insisted there was no problem. Now we know they've got a *big* problem—only they don't want to talk to Americans about it."

"What's *Link's* problem? He was grilling me before you stopped by. Aren't I supposed to be on bed rest?"

"Don't sweat Link," Wu responded. "Some serious stuff has come up. He doesn't know about it yet, and it doesn't involve you, but yesterday, right after the shootout, some Thai and American Air Police apprehended a motorbike taxi driver heading toward town along a dirt road that came from the ambush site. After a little questioning, he admitted driving your friend Tukada out there and took them back to where he dropped her off—at a stolen Air Force jeep parked just off the road. They found ammo and a field radio inside. The Thai National Police are still questioning him."

Link didn't come back that day, thank God. Instead, I had a more welcome group of visitors, even if it was all a little blurred from my tranquilizer high. Lutz, the sound man, was apparently on his way back to Tan Son Nhut when he stopped by with Wheeler and Zelinsky, my housemates at Bungalow Ruam Chon Sawng; Shahbazian, Detachment 3's iffy camera technician; and Moonbeam Liscomb, my hipster Deputy Chief of Combat Documentation. Zelinsky and Shahbazian looked a lot better now that the nicks on their faces had been patched up. The only thing that had hit them was safety glass from the shattered windshield on Shahbazian's Fiat Spyder convertible. We said a quick hello and then avoided each other's eyes in the awkward silence that followed. It was Liscomb who finally spoke, saying wistfully, "I guess we'll be putting that location shoot at Pattaya Beach on hold for a while, but we're going to get there."

"If they ever let me out of this dump," I replied.

All Shahbazian said when he looked at me was, "Damn."

Wheeler wasn't much better, muttering, "Man, what a bummer."

"We brought a little something for you," said Lutz, pulling out a cold bottle of San Miguel dark from one of the cargo pockets in his jungle fatigues. He had trouble popping the top off with the church key that hung around his neck, which got me thinking that he might have started his drinking a little early that day.

"Thanks," I said, taking a swig and immediately feeling my Valium haze intensify. "Just tell me this isn't the stuff you brought over for Lieutenant Hill from Tan Son Nhut."

Zelinsky had the old wicked gleam back in his eye. "He won't miss it. We only opened one case."

Lutz studied the bandages covering the right side of my face. "It's funny how we were half-expecting this back in San Bernardino on People's Independence Day."

"Yeah," I replied, "but back along the *real* Route 66 the bullet holes in the road signs gave you fair warning you were in redneck territory."

"*Nobody's* fighting fair over here," Liscomb said quietly. "We're guilty of overkill somehow, even though the Bad Guys keep sneaking around without showing their faces."

"Thank God Nixon's wrapping all this up with Chairman Mao," said Wheeler. Nobody replied. We didn't know what the hell Nixon was doing in China.

"I hope he hasn't been so busy wining and dining he's forgotten there's a goddamn war going on," said Liscomb.

"How are things for you back at the 601st?" I asked him. "Flying nothing but unarmed reconnaissance missions and being kept under house arrest—for leading one stinking peace march back in August? We both got reamed."

"That may be the only good thing to come out of the bicycle race fiasco," he answered. "After flying around on that Jolly Green rescue helicopter, taking hostile fire, and then helping to snuff it out, it looks like the brass is putting me on a slightly longer leash."

"Here's to longer leashes," I toasted, taking a swig of the San Miguel and passing it around. "To longer leashes," the guys repeated, and before I knew it the bottle was empty, I was alone, and Lutz was on a plane headed for Tan Son Nhut.

When I woke up Monday morning my head was throbbing, but I wanted to leave anyway. I couldn't stand being trapped in bed, hooked to a bunch of tubes and wires. When I asked about checking out, nobody seemed too happy about it, and before I knew it, Nurse Wozniak had shown up and was pretty much ordering me to wait till Dr. Lioci made his rounds.

When he arrived, he took a quick look at my chart and hung the clipboard back at the foot of my bed. "How are the headaches?" he asked.

"They come and go."

"And the nausea?"

"It comes and goes."

"How many fingers am I holding up?"

"Two—or three—or is it two?"

"How are you going to focus a camera?"

"I'm not," I confessed.

"We need to keep monitoring those symptoms, Sergeant Leary, and we're still waiting for the swelling and bruising on your face and head to go down so we can get some better X-rays. I also want the nurses to keep an eye on the stitches when they change your dressings. Do you understand there's a heightened risk of infection in the tropics?"

"I do. I give up. I'll stick around." I winced and settled in for what promised to be another week of hospital food, which I detested even when I could keep it down, and four doses a day of sedatives, painkillers, and Valium, which I grew rather fond of.

The drawback in the Valium department was that when I tried to write to my girlfriend Danielle and to my parents about the bicycle race, I had a hell of a time getting started, getting my thoughts organized, getting anything down on paper. Finally, I finished a pair of short notes saying that if they had seen anything in the papers or on TV about a terrorist attack in Ubon Province, not to worry—I was okay.

Only I was not okay. My physical wounds were healing, but deep inside, in my heart and soul, I ached. Prasert was dead. How was it possible that at the start of the year he had been a promising student and the caring brother of a woman I was beginning to love? How was it possible that, just days ago, I had held his sister Tukada in my arms, conjoined in blood but unable to keep her alive? The Thai fighter pilots were being cremated, and Murray, the pothead clerk-typist; Spitzer, my fellow cameraman; and Sachs, the door gunner, were being shipped home in body bags because of my misguided mixture of greed and good intentions. And there was no getting around it—I was responsible. The prescribed intake of sedatives soon stopped putting me to sleep. I tossed and turned in a cold sweat, and every time I closed my eyes I saw Tukada staring at me helplessly.

Mid-morning on Monday, Chaplain Kirkgartner stopped by. A tan, lean former college basketball player, he towered above my bed. "I'm sorry I can only stay a minute," he said. "Colonel Grimsley and the Thai base commander want an interfaith memorial service at noon."

"I understand," I replied. "Just do me a favor and save the theology and comforting words for the service. I'm not feeling very religious right now."

"Is there anything I *can* do for you?"

"There is. Can you make sure someone has notified Tukada's kin?"

"I'll get right on it."

"And please don't give up on tracking down her daughter and her slimeball husband."

"What would you do if we found them?"

"If he's in jail, I'll adopt Pranee myself."

Jamal Washington, my fellow cameraman, and Lonnie Price, one of the technicians at the photo lab, stopped by later that afternoon. They had just come from the memorial service for Sachs, Spitzer, Murray, three other GIs I didn't know, and the three Thai fighter pilots who had been riding the lead bicycles. Lonnie, whom I had first met back in the States working underground late at night editing the *sNorton Bird* for the Norton GIs for Peace, brought me a copper chain bracelet he had made at the base hobby shop, conferring me with "Honorary Brother" status. I felt a mixture of relief and regret to have missed the service. Just thinking about it was making me groggy. I wanted to go back to sleep, still hoping that when I woke up, the race and its aftermath would all turn out to have been a bad dream.

Link barged back in at the crack of dawn Tuesday. "Like I told you before, Leary, forget about your girlfriend's husband. He's already been discharged, shipped back to the States. I guarantee you Grimsley's gonna want to see your sorry ass over at the Little Pentagon when you're released from sick bay. He's especially gonna want to know what your girlfriend told you about her husband."

"Like I told *you* before, Sarge, she didn't even tell me she *had* a husband until a month ago."

"Maybe our Air Police captain can jog your memory, if you know what I mean." And he was gone.

I was sleeping restlessly when Nurse Wozniak knocked and Jack Wu and Major Horney reported in. Colonel Grimsley, the 8th Tactical Fighter Wing Commander, had confiscated all proceeds from the race since there had been no winner and there would be no rematch. "He's ordered Legal to distribute it to the families of the deceased," said Horney. "He also ordered Indian Joe and Sagittarius Smith to refund all the side bets."

"They weren't too cheerful about it," said Wu, "but I wouldn't worry about those two. They're the kind who always manage to land on their feet." I was sure Jack was right.

"Is Major Wozniak taking good care of you?" Horney asked.

"Excellent," I replied. "Is she still taking good care of *you*, Major?"

"She's putting in the paperwork to join me at Hurlburt Field in Florida when our tours are over." He winked and excused himself.

Wu stuck around. "There's an interesting development on the stolen jeep front. My friends at OSI tell me their investigation led them to Tukada's husband. It's possible he stole it and fenced it to finance a heroin deal. And now, thanks to his being discharged, their investigation's shot to hell. What makes this especially interesting is that our friend Indian Joe might have been the fence. Now they'll never know. Case closed."

"Have the papers said anything about the race?"

"That's maybe the strangest thing of all. The *New York Times*, the *Bangkok Post*, and the *Pacific Stars and Stripes* have been running front-page stories all week about Nixon in China. But the race? There's a single paragraph on page thirty-two of yesterday's *Times*. It did make page two of the *Bangkok Post*. But the *Stars and Stripes*? Nothing. A total blackout."

Over the next couple of days, Captain English, Lieutenant Hill, and Homer Harwell, my lead cameraman, popped in at various times to give me the same pep talk about how much they needed me back at the 601st. English told me he had put in the paperwork for a Purple Heart and a Bronze Star. The Valium must have been working because I had no idea what he was talking about but said thanks just the same. I had one welcome, unexpected visit when Harley Baker stopped by with Jim Scott, his Peace Corps buddy who also ran the American University Alumni Association's evening English-language school in Ubon. He cheered me up with the news he was personally covering the AUA class I'd been teaching. It was a bittersweet occasion, however, because Jim had just finished helping Harley move Sachs's personal effects back on base from their compound downtown so they could be shipped home.

Harley came back a day later with Sugie Bear and Ackerman, my former bandmates from the Band of Brothers, and a far more upbeat Woody Shahbazian, my Merle Haggard-loving friend and tormentor since our Norton Air Force Base days back in California, who led a chorus taken up by Harley and Sugie Bear about how we needed to get a new band together. It was a pleasant thought, but I noticed nobody was making any definite plans. Ackerman, the non-bullshitter, smiled his cool New Orleans smile and stayed in the background.

"Guys, I'm too drugged up right now to even get out of bed, but maybe you're on to something. Maybe it'll be a good idea to keep ourselves busy. That's what my mom told the wife of one of my dad's pilot friends after the unspeakable happened and he'd been killed in a plane crash. Only I can't imagine pasting on a stage smile and performing anytime soon. Maybe when my ears stop ringing and my head stops throbbing, we could ease back in by rehearsing quietly at the chapel annex."

Late in the week, I had a couple more surprise visitors, none of whom, thankfully, was First Sergeant Link. Liscomb came in a little before lunchtime with the first group: the Air Police captain and the pilot and door gunner from Liscomb's Jolly Green rescue bird. "We just had to get this off our chest, how sorry we are about your girlfriend," said the Air Police officer.

"We were in radio contact," said the pilot. "We were so damned proud of locating you and your friend with the handgun and figuring out you were friendlies and keeping you out of harm's way…"

"Except we had no idea that a non-combatant was mixed in with the guerrillas," said the door gunner. "If we'd known, maybe we could have held fire and given the police sharpshooters more time. But it was happening fast."

"We were taking bullet hit after bullet hit," said Liscomb.

"If they had hit us with one of their rocket-propelled grenades, we would have gone down with no time to autorotate," said the pilot.

"Thanks for doing the best you could," I told them. "We almost made it. We almost got her to triage." I didn't know what else to say. My mind flashed for a moment with the memory of Tukada dying in my arms. A sickening feeling of helplessness lingered. "Thanks for doing the best you could, and thanks for coming in," I said. And with that, I dropped back to sleep.

That afternoon, Chaplain Kirkgartner brought in two more guests. I thought they were children at first, dwarfed as they were by the chaplain, neither of them standing much over five feet tall, but they were too soft-spoken and polite to be kids. "Tukada's mother and father have come to see you," said Kirkgartner.

Her mother spoke in rapid Issan dialect and her father translated. "We want to thank you both for trying to help our daughter. She have problem with drug for many year."

The mother spoke again to her husband. "My wife talk to her on phone while she in rehab, and she sound very hopeful. None of us can know that her hus-band will take baby. None of us can know what that do to Tukada. So thank you for get her here for treatment. Even before, when she see me at Sattahip for American New Year, she tell me you both are trying to help. We will take her ashes home to Ban Ang Hin. And when we spread them on the River Mun, we will pray for her and remember your caring."

I thought I heard "Prasert" when Dah's mother spoke again to her husband. "My son have hard life," he said. "His mother die when he very young, and he go live with grandmother in Uttaradit. She will spread his ashes in the mountain there. As a child, always he sad. He very smart at school but no have frien', only like going off alone in the mountain. Later, when we send him to *wat* for Rain Retreat, we hope being novice monk make him happy, but he quit before he stay a week. Say he cannot be monk—he like to hunt too much. We worry about him a lot, but when he join Army, he seem happy for first time. When I talk to his comman-der, he say Prasert a good soldier. An' now dis. We don' understand what happen to him. I afraid maybe when young, he meet Thai Communi't insurgent in the mountain, train wit' them, not really hunt, before he join Thai Army. We can never know."

My head was spinning. "Prasert a trained insurgent infiltrating the Thai Army? I guess I don't understand either. I guess he had me completely fooled. I *liked* him, and I thought he liked me and my friends. I *admired* him for looking after Dah and her baby."

Dah's mother and father glanced at each other. "That what we come to ask about," said the father. His wife, a sad look in her eyes, spoke softly into her husband's ear. "When you two go back Sa-tates," he asked, "can you look for our granddaughter? We think she stay with father and grandmother in San Fran."

"I'll try," I said. "My old base is in Southern California, and I plan to stay in California when I leave the Air Force. I promise I'll look for her."

"In the meantime, I'll keep trying from here," said the chaplain.

Dah's parents seemed to have aged in the short time they stood there, and when they followed Kirkgartner out, they shuffled along like very old people.

I think I was glad to see all of my visitors, even Link, in the same way I was glad to see the nurses and medics—to confirm that I was still alive, that there was hope I might pull myself out of the bottomless pit I had fallen into. But I didn't have it in me to sweet-talk the nurses, not even the one from the first aid station who turned out in the end to be pretty nice. And I could barely remember how to small-talk with my friends. I seemed to be chopped in pieces. My heart felt happy when I had people around, but my eyes were tired, always on the verge of tears, and my mind was shot, zonked by drugs, a condition I might have fought had I been struggling for lucidity. I had been struggling long and hard for lucidity since conflicting reports about the Vietnam War started coming in while I was still in college. A lot of angry old patriots told me when I was a civilian and later, when I was still stationed Stateside, that you had to experience the war directly to understand it, that if you hadn't "been there," you had no right to talk about it. Well, now that I *had* "been there," now that I'd seen action and had a bitter taste of the death and destruction in the Thailand-Laos-Cambodia branch of the war, I knew I would never understand it. I needed to accept madness and confusion instead. Lucidity was no longer an option.

I was deep in another doctor-induced haze of sedatives and tranquilizers when Tom Wheeler and Mole, Dave Murray's old housemate, showed up late Saturday afternoon with a baggie holding the last of Murray's Laotian grass-opium blend, neatly rolled in Zig-Zag papers. "We think Dave would have liked you to have this," said Tom.

"Smoke it up for auld lang syne," waxed Mole.

I tucked the baggie under my pillow and looked skyward. "Thank you, Dave, wherever you are."

After a moment of respectful silence, Tom asked, "How you been doing?"

"I'm afraid I'm depressed as hell. At least my body's healing."

"I've been feeling pretty down, myself," Tom replied. "I may follow Dave's footsteps yet and go into drug rehab. Doing red rock heroin is starting to get to me. I don't get a rush, and I'm having to do more and more just to maintain."

"The same thing's happening to me with my sleeping pills."

"Man, the whole base seems down," said Mole. "Hell, the whole *town* has been gloomy. This has been *mai sanuk* big time. I think we would have taken it better if one of our planes had been shot down. We expect that. But a fuckin' bicycle race? Gimme a break."

Late that night I lit up, expecting orgasms in my lungs like the last time I had smoked Murray's personal stash. Instead, I slipped into a deep sleep that might have been a coma and got to live through the Big Buddha massacre one more time, distorted in new and fascinating ways.

Time becomes slippery, stretching like an unraveling Ace bandage. The world winds down, runs in slow motion like an old spring-driven alarm clock that gives off a few ponderous tock...tocks before expending itself completely. The finality of eternal silence is broken by the distant POP-POPs of AK-47 and M-16 gunfire, soon drowned out by the crunching gears of my Arri St. I pan left—Washington is down. Instinctively I pan right, going for the source, the heart of the action. A blur turns into one, two, four, eight frames, 1/3 of a second, enough time to register Prasert.

I charge, adrenaline high, fast as Lieutenant Asshole and his killer F-4. I'm small, a fast mover. Ain't no triple-A gonna take me down. Evasive action time, even looking through the eyepiece of my Arri.

Prasert fires. The lens shatters. The impact blinds me, sends me reeling backwards cursing Prasert and Ron Cooper, the conniving son of a bitch who got me into this mess, flipping camera circuits and brain circuits, snapping me into rage mode, autopilot. The barrel of Washington's M-16 burns my hand when I pick it up. He's still breathing... "Easy, Jamal. It'll all be over in a minute."

My right eye fills with fluid, milky, dim. Reptile mode. Prasert is the unchained tiger that charges me at the Bangkok Zoo. He's dog meat. He's history. He won't die. I shoot his face. Again. Again. Again. Pineapple that Lek won't need to slice. Scattered to oblivion. The torso stands a moment, a

steaming cloud of dust and blood vapor where a head should be, then falls. I
pull open his shirt: the SOB wears Pigpen Sachs's flak jacket...

I woke up disoriented in the dark room, thinking I was back at Ruam Chon Sawng, not understanding why tubes were poking into my arms. Even after I regained my orientation, I tossed and turned long into the night, shaken by the realization that I enjoyed shooting at Prasert, killing him ruthlessly. *Some pacifist*, I thought. And I wondered about a strange aftertaste, a bitter certainty that Indian Joe had sold Prasert the flak jacket. *It was only a dream*, I tried to tell myself, but the rage I felt for Ron Cooper—working on an air-conditioned sound stage back in San Bernardino—was real and deep.

Tom Wheeler and Harley Baker paid me a visit that morning on their way back from breakfast. "That grass you gave me yesterday turned out to be *nasty*," I told Tom. "I dreamed that I picked up an M-16 and smoked Prasert—big time, total overkill."

"Funny," Tom replied. "Mole and I smoked the same shit and it didn't affect us at all. Nada."

"Maybe you're a warrior after all," said Harley. "Revenge can be sweet."

"Except I think it was more than anger at Prasert. I think a lot of it was rage at myself. For cutting him slack, for letting my feelings for Tukada... Damn, I was crazy about her. I thought he and I were trying to get her straightened out. Who *was* he, anyway? And who the hell is the Issan Liberation Front? Things look pretty free around here to me, even with a war going on. What do they need to be liberated from?"

"I thought we learned to stay out of Thai politics," said Tom. "You know that nobody talks here. Nobody wants to show his hand."

"I already briefed you," Harley reminded me. "Stay here as long as you want, you'll never really know what side your best friend's on if he's Asian. He might be on both sides—covering his ass till it's over. It's enough to make you like the NVA for putting on uniforms and fighting fair and square, mano a mano."

Before Tom and Harley left I fell back into a fitful sleep, except now it was worse: my troubled mind began rerunning an old dream of my youngest sister. Wreaking revenge on Prasert made some kind of sense. Stabbing my sister, even in a dream, filled me with dread that deep inside I was a monster capable at any time of uncontrolled violence. I was damn glad when, an hour later, Moonbeam Liscomb stepped into the room. I told him about the dreams, and the lieutenant smiled compassionately. "We've all got that in us, brother. Why hate yourself for being human, why not accept it?"

"Obviously, you weren't raised Catholic."

"It doesn't matter what you were raised, everybody has violent thoughts and impulses some time or another. The question is: do we *act* on those impulses or learn to let go of them?"

"After having that dream, I'm afraid the feelings locked inside me are beyond my control. Not only can't I control them, I'm afraid they control *me*. How the hell do you just let go of violent impulses?"

"Meditation helps. But I also think you've stumbled onto what my Zen teacher back in L.A. called 'the interconnectedness of all things.' You're filled with rage at Prasert because he betrayed you, violating your trust in the worst possible way, taking the lives of people you knew and cared about—and loved. But at the same time, in some strange way, you also lost a brother."

"Damn," I said, letting it sink in a moment. "That's heavy, Rick—and sad. I'm afraid I only understood about half of what you just told me, but it's enough to get me wondering... Maybe I should try writing a new request for discharge—from a Buddhist perspective."

"I'm just learning this myself. You need to find a real teacher to help you."

"Prah Samrong out at Big Buddha speaks pretty good English. Maybe I should pay him a visit when Dr. Lioci finally gets around to signing me out."

Liscomb gave me another compassionate smile and squeezed my shoulder. "Now, there's an impulse you *should* act on."

Dr. Lioci told me I was a fast healer when he took out my stitches Monday and cleared me to check out of the hospital, but he did not clear me to fly. It was the same morning Tom Wheeler checked himself in for detox. Tom had told me before the bicycle race that he was thinking about it, and his eyes looked as sad as mine felt the day he visited me in the hospital and mentioned it again. Things had changed in the world of detox, however, since Dave Murray went in back in October. Now it pretty much meant an automatic medical discharge, which was not bad for Tom under the circumstances. He'd managed to stay in for two years—he'd still have his GI Bill if he wanted to go to school. And he'd been mailing grass home to his pre-Air Force business partners, so he had a little nest egg stashed away if they hadn't absconded with it.

Tom had prepped me, yet it was still a shock that morning to be walking down the main corridor toward the nurses' station and catch him out of the corner of my eye, propped up in a big hospital bed, all alone in a semi-private room. They'd put him on a sedative and started him flat out going cold turkey, which meant no visitors for the next forty-eight hours. When I came back to see him two days later, the old spark was starting to burn in his eye for the first time since the race. "This is moving fast," he told me. "They'll probably have me back in the States in a week to finish processing out."

It hit me that Tom might be the best friend I had in the world. I felt a ripple of fear at the thought of being left behind in Ubon without him. "Promise you'll stay in touch. Wappinger's Falls isn't far from Boston."

"I promise, man. I'm gonna try to send Lek a little money so she won't have to go back working the bars. It's just that I don't know what my cash flow's gonna be like. I'm hoping I'll be able to stay at my mom's for a while, but can you do me a favor?"

"Sure."

"Can you look after Lek? Do you think you can get her into your class at AUA? She's a smart girl."

"Tell me about it."

"Maybe she can land a straight job. Think you could help her with that?"

"I can sure try."

"But if you can't... If she can't handle school, or if she can't handle a regular job... I don't know quite how to say this, but if she ends up as your *tii-rahk*, that would be cool as far as I'm concerned."

I felt a catch in my throat. "I'm afraid it's a little too soon to start thinking about *tii-rahking* a friend's *tii-rahk*. My head's too full of thoughts about Dah. But getting Lek into an English class? That's something I think I can manage."

I forced myself back into my AUA classroom my first night out of the hospital—to preserve my sanity, to keep myself occupied, I heard my mother's voice reminding me. Miss Pawnsiri didn't wait for the end of class to talk to me, stopping at my desk while her classmates drifted in. "This is a good surprise to see you back so soon, Khun Bren-dan. My family worry about you too much."

Several other students expressed condolences about the bicycle race and my injuries, but no one mentioned Prasert, which left me wondering if Thai authorities had held back details of the attack or if my students were just being solicitous. It was daunting to think Prasert was gone, but another student filled his seat, and life went on. Getting back in the classroom was good for me, forcing me to focus on the here and now, doing the best I could to teach a new concept or two each night to mature, highly motivated students. Enough of them came to class prepared that we never got hopelessly bogged down, and if somebody did get lost, someone else would whisper a few words in Thai to clear things up—correctly, I hoped.

All in all, we continued making steady progress, but our after-class dinners became less frequent and I dreaded the nights I went directly home. Tom Wheeler had been right about being gone in a week, and Larry Zelinsky and his *tii-rahk* Peung had finally finished plowing through the paperwork required for them to get married and were out looking for a bigger place to live. Lek liked to eat early. By the time I came in, she had usually fallen asleep reading one of her Thai movie magazines or a "true romance" novel.

I wasn't even there the day Tom came to pack up his stuff. He wrote to Lek twice. Twice she found a translator to read it for her and write a response. And twice I helped her rewrite the translator's letter into readable English. In the first letter he reported that he had processed out at Travis Air Force Base, not too far from San Francisco, that there had been no hippie protestors in sight, and that he was hanging out with Sonny Stevens, the old *sNorton Bird* editor who was now not only out of the service but a full-fledged long-haired hippie himself. He also mentioned that there was money waiting for her at the Western Union office near the Noy Market. The next letter told how he and Sonny were going to ride the rails across the country when the weather got a little warmer. He wired her money one more time, and that was it—the Tom and Lek story ended with a quick fadeout.

I had been assigned a desk job in the orderly room, supposedly covering for Wheeler, until I was cleared to go back on flying status. The adrenaline rush I got facing my students at AUA had been enough to keep me alert teaching, but my first week back in the orderly room had been a struggle. My meds and the lingering effects of my concussion left me unable to work alone filing or typing for more than a few minutes at a time. Staring at Dave Murray's empty desk didn't help. Woody Shahbazian and Harley Baker stopped by late in the week just before closing time. "You're coming with us, bro," said Woody.

"We got a little surprise for you," Harley told me on the walk to the bus stop. Out at the main gate we caught a taxi and headed off for Harley's compound. Instead of his bungalow, however, they led me to the rice barn in back. Inside was immaculate. My drums were set up in the middle of the floor with two guitars perched in their stands nearby and a couple of mikes plugged into a pair of rehearsal amps. Harley and Woody broke into broad grins. I was stunned. "Jim and Pye moved into Sachs's old bungalow," Harley told me. "I couldn't let this go to waste." I was touched, glad to be included, even if I suspected that Harley was doing this largely for himself.

It felt strange at first, but as we got into a groove I found a soothing enjoyment playing with my friends in solitude, away from the base and away from the clubs. We started out jamming on a generic slow blues, but when Harley sang, "*My baby left me this morning, didn't even say goodbye,*" he turned it into "The Sun is Shining" and what became an Elmore James medley. His bottleneck guitar playing was powerful and the lyrics that he and Woody both seemed to know were filled with even more heartache on

"The Sky is Crying" and "Standing at the Crossroads." It was a surprisingly seamless transition to a couple of country ballads that Woody taught us. The first, "Streets of Laredo," I wasn't familiar with beyond hearing it on the juke box a few times down at basic training in San Antonio, but Harley had heard it plenty growing up in Stockton, California, and sung with Woody's clear tenor, the refrain *beat the drum slowly and play the fife lowly* was haunting. Guy Mitchell's "You Got Me Singing the Blues" had been a hit that even reached Boston and gave me a chance to lay down my sticks and do some jazz-style brush work, the softest, most soothing way I knew to play the drums.

Sam Cooke's "Bring It on Home to Me" segued nicely into "Time Is on My Side," and then, just as we were bringing that to an end, Harley decided to change things up and began playing a familiar guitar riff—the opening of "I Can't Get No Satisfaction." We played through the entire song one time and then took the volume down to a whisper for a few verses more before we brought it back up; Harley sang another verse and then started vamping on *I can't get me no!*—repeating it over and over before ending on a loud, drawn out *Satis-fac-shun.* Without missing a beat, I broke into the drum riff on Jefferson Airplane's "Somebody to Love," began singing the refrain a cappella, and once again, the three of us were off and running. That must have gotten us into San Francisco mode because, the next thing I knew, we were doing a blend of Janis Joplin's and Howard Tate's versions of "Get It While You Can," followed by Janis's arrangement of "To Love Somebody," which showed promise if we ever added more instruments.

I was fascinated by the way it only took a couple of drumbeats or a few notes from one of us for the others to knowingly ease into the next song. When Woody played rhythm guitar and sang the opening verse of Johnny Cash's "Ring of Fire," Harley responded with a bluesy bottleneck guitar riff that covered the horn lines on Cash's original. Somehow it seemed foreordained that we ended up jamming next on the Outlaws' acid-country arrangement of the 16th Special Operations Squadron theme song, "Ghost Riders in the Sky," the version Harley played for us months earlier at Ruam Chon Sawng the night his buddies on a Spectre gunship crashed and burned. I sensed a melancholy undertone of beauty and sadness and anger in "Ghost Riders" that continued as we slipped into "Gimme Shelter" and followed that with what would become our private theme song, "Sympathy for the Devil." On a superficial level, my mother's dictum of keeping busy seemed to be working, but I tired quickly that night and was exhausted at eight o'clock when we finished the last Stones number. Khun Jim, my boss at AUA, and his girlfriend Pye were sitting outside their bungalow on my way out. "Sounded good," said Jim.

"You did a great job fixing up that rice barn," I responded. "Got a feeling you'll be seeing a lot of Woody and me."

Maybe I enjoyed the music *too* much. Back at my bungalow, I sank into a depression that left me exhausted but unable to sleep. I was dozing off in the orderly room the next day when Liscomb stopped by to check up on me. "How you feeling?" he asked.

"I wish I could say okay," I replied.

"Let's take a walk," he said, leading me out the door and across the scraggly field behind the 601st compound to a grass-shack snack bar Zelinsky called "Howard Johnson's." After we'd taken a seat at the empty counter and ordered a couple of Cokes, Liscomb asked, "Are you still having those dreams?"

"It's gotten worse," I replied. "I'm scared something's seriously wrong. My sleep is disturbed, except it isn't by what you'd call dreams, and I'm having intrusive thoughts during the day, except they aren't really thoughts. It's just a bunch of flashes—gunfire, the thumping of chopper blades, Tukada's death rattle, Prasert's evil eye… I don't know how to turn it off, which makes me *really* want to go see Prah Samrong."

Liscomb gave me one of his warm smiles. "I think you definitely need a good teacher. You've experienced plenty of suffering—what Buddhists call *dukkha*. Now's a good time to start learning about the path that can release you from suffering." He pulled a box of incense out of the side pocket of his jungle fatigues. "My housegirl says for you to bring this along as an offering to the monks."

And so, the first Saturday after getting out of the hospital, I climbed on a local bus filled with villagers, a few chickens, and two gigantic tractor tires and headed out to the Big Buddha Forest Monastery, hoping Prah Samrong could cure the psychic gangrene that was eating away inside me. At the *wat* an old woman dressed in white, her head shaved, saw the box of incense in my hands and showed me where I could leave it with the other morning offerings at the base of Big Buddha. Somehow she knew I was there for Prah Samrong and had a novice take me to his *kuti*.

Like all the other *kutis*, Samrong's humble abode was largely unfurnished other than two small bookshelves, with only straw mats to sit and sleep on. Samrong was sitting in the shade of his porch reading when he heard us approach. When he saw who it was, his face lit up. "Welcome, Bren-dan! I've been worried about you since the bicycle race. What brings you here today?"

"A lot of reasons, actually. I was turned down once by the Air Force for discharge as a conscientious objector, but the bicycle race makes me think about applying again as a Buddhist. My friend Lieutenant Liscomb studied Zen Buddhism in the States, but he is only a novice. He thinks it might help me more to learn from you about Thai Buddhism, and I agree. But he also thinks I should talk to you about the disturbing dreams I've been having."

"That's a lot!" Samrong replied. "Let's start with your dreams. They can be tricky. Most people want to interpret them, but it is best if you don't try to understand. With unpleasant dreams, we want to stop them but we can't. We want pleasant dreams to never end, but they do—always. Pleasant or unpleasant, they are similar to what we call *nimittas*—what we see when meditating. With dreams and *nimittas* both—don't think, just observe."

For the rest of the day, we continued to talk. I started out by telling him how much I admired the simple, quiet life he and the other monks lived. "It's what we call the Holy Life," he replied, "following the Middle Way. It's something like the Golden Mean of the ancient Greeks—avoiding the extremes of overindulgence and self-mortification. In the Buddha's time, there were spiritual seekers who wandered the streets naked or who might sit in a cave without eating for weeks. In the cities, the rich and powerful could live in palaces, unaware of people outside their gates living in poverty and starving to death while they were dying from eating and drinking too much. The Buddha had experienced both extremes and realized that a roof over our head, clothes on our back, and one or two meals a day are all we really need."

As we continued talking, I learned that Samrong had grown up in a small village not far from Big Buddha. He had served in the Thai Army before becoming a monk, and we laughed about the similarities: the discipline, the uniform dress, the shaved heads. When I observed him chanting and meditating with the other monks, however, it was impossible to miss some profound differences between military and monastic life, the big one being that a Thai monk had entered monastic life of his own volition, giving up many worldly comforts and pleasures in the process, and stayed in robes even though he was free to leave any time he chose. As a result of living a life of restraint and reflection, a monk was a highly respected member of a Thai society that was, in so many ways, exuberant and sensual.

Another big difference Samrong explained to me was that a monk would not intentionally harm any living creature, not even a fly or mosquito, so strong was their prohibition against taking life—what he called *ahimsa*. I found the idea hard to grasp at first, but a couple of times later in the day when I was about to swat a mosquito landing on my neck, I discovered I could catch myself. Instead of trying to kill it, I could restrain the impulse and simply swish it away.

I stayed for the evening chanting and recognized it as what I'd been listening to with Tukada that evening long ago when an evening bicycle ride brought us to a village monastery. When Samrong invited me to come back the following weekend and try meditating with him, I was happy to accept. "In Thailand we call it *wipassana*," he explained. "In Pali and English you say wit' letter *v*, but we don't have that letter in Thai language. *Wipassana* mean Wisdom or Insight Meditation. Not too different from Zen Meditation in Japan and Wietnam."

Before I left he gave me some pamphlets, in English, to read. One was a translation of the *Anapanasati Sutta,* the Buddha's Discourse on Mindfulness of Breathing, with commentaries. The others were about basic meditation techniques. "Don't be scared. Meditation is difficult but simple. If you can watch your breath, you can begin meditating. It comes down to four words: *breathing in, breathing out.* And all Buddhist teaching, what we call the Dhamma, comes down to just five words, in English or Thai: *Do good. Cause no harm.*"

The following Saturday, I rode my bicycle out, knowing I could bring it back by local bus—provided they weren't carrying too many tractor tires. I needed to retrace the route of the bicycle race, to experience Route 66 as a quiet country road and not a scene of slaughter. Once again, I found myself as attracted to the quiet of monastic life as I had been only a month earlier to the ear-splitting noise of Ubon nightclubs. Sitting silently at what was formally known as Wat Pra Mongkol Ming Muang, it grew clearer to me that the time was coming, as I had recently mentioned to Rick Liscomb and as Greg Quam at the base print shop once said it would, to begin rewriting my application for discharge as a conscientious objector. At the same time, I knew I still had a lot to learn before I would be capable of expressing my beliefs clearly in Buddhist rather than humanist-existentialist terms, and I wondered if I could really grasp the counterintuitive ideas I was reading about and Samrong was trying to teach me.

In my need for purification, it crossed my mind that my ersatz Canadian passport—the forgery that Sommit down at Woodstock Music had helped me obtain months earlier when my first application was rejected—might turn out to be helpful after all if my new application failed and I decided to go AWOL. But I preferred to think I would succeed this time and told Samrong that if my request for discharge was approved, I was thinking of staying in Thailand. I asked him, "How hard would it be to become a monk here at Big Buddha?"

He paused a moment and then replied, "Wouldn't the monastery in Warin Chamrap be more accessible for you, Bren-dan, since there are already American monks living there?"

"Perhaps later," I told him. My powerful blood connection to *his* monastery made me want to come here first—to reflect on the impermanence of all things, especially the impermanence of human life. "I've read the booklets you gave me, but I'm not sure I understand. How do I begin doing meditation, and how do I know if I'm doing it right?"

He taught me that there were two components, concentration and wisdom. "For right now," he recommended, "work on concentration. Concentration will help you later to develop wisdom or insight."

He summarized the Discourse on Mindfulness of Breathing for me before we began our first sitting meditation. "You can go to the forest or the foot of a tree or any peaceful place like this *wat* and sit quietly in the lotus position with good posture, so you can sit straight without effort. For *farang*, sitting in the half lotus is good too. Simply breathe in and breathe out with awareness. Be aware of long breaths and short breaths. Be aware of your body feeling calm and at peace. When you sit for longer periods, be aware of pain and suffering that come up, but try to just observe. With practice you can experience all the Buddha's teachings through breath meditation. In time you will observe the mind inside your mind and feelings inside your feelings. For now, be aware that as you learn to concentrate your mind you will experience moments of liberation from desire and aversion—the source of all suffering. And as you experience pleasant, neutral, and unpleasant sensations, notice that they are all impermanent."

For that first sitting, Prah Samrong led me in a guided meditation that lasted for just fifteen minutes. Afterward, we talked about how that short period of time was enough to experience the coming and going of pleasant, neutral, and painful sensations, just as the *sutta* had described. Back in my room at Ruam Chon Sawng, I continued to practice late at night or early in the morning and found that over time I was able to sit for longer periods. Samrong had used the idea of all things being impermanent—even mountains and oceans—to teach me about meditation as a means of making peace with death. And the more I learned how the acceptance of death helped one develop a sense of liberation from the fear of death, the more appropriate it seemed that I should purify myself of the Big Buddha massacre right there at Big Buddha. It was a perfect metaphor for my entire war experience—in developing respect and compassion for warriors of both sides of the conflict, I had been surrounded by tragedy and grief. I had mourned but saw no end to my mourning. Now, in some mysterious way, Samrong's Buddhist perspective gave me a sense of acceptance, of inevitability, of deepening compassion. Two weekends at the monastery were enough to begin restoring a tiny spark of the spirituality that had somehow survived deep inside me, buried under layers of atheism, the ashes of a once-blinding faith that had transmuted into a dark certainty that the God I once thought I knew and loved was dead, that surely if there were a God, there could be no Ho Chi Minh Trail, that surely if there were a God, Tukada Maneewatana could not have been taken away from me and her daughter left an orphan.

Life without Tom, OR
Living with Lek

I had gotten Lek an application for AUA like I promised Tom. My values may have been on shaky ground, but I was a man of at least vestigial honor who liked to keep my commitments. Khun Jim was willing to do Lek a favor and let her start the semester late. He explained how she would begin with a basic-level class taught by one of his Peace Corps buddies where she could quickly bring her reading and writing of English up to her fairly advanced skills in listening and speaking. She never filled out the application. Instead, she asked me to tutor her at home, showing me a bunch of newsprint primers she had picked up at the market.

We did lessons one through three, and she showed promise, but within a few days I noticed the books sitting untouched. Next to them was a pile of Thai movie magazines and racy Thai romance novels that she read voraciously. One night we were sitting around reading quietly for several hours when she finally asked me to help her fill in the AUA application. She promised to take it directly to Khun Jim at the polytechnic high school the next day while I was at work. She went back to her primers and did lessons four to six on her own, which inspired me to start picking up work applications for her, starting at the U.S. Information Service in the middle of town on Route 66. I knew it would require extra red tape to find her a job on base, but I got her applications for the Chase Manhattan and Bank of America branches where several of my students worked and promised they would try to help. I got her applications for the Base Exchange—the "BX"— apparently a dream job for many Thais, with its possibilities of small-time black marketeering, and at the Green Monster, which meant steady work doing huge quantities of laundry for the six thousand GIs stationed in Ubon. I also went by the base theater and the bowling alley.

She set the applications in a neat stack next to her ABC books and didn't touch them for a week. When I pressed her on it, she curled up in my lap and ran her fingers through my hair and asked with a purr if it wouldn't be better to wait until she finished one of her classes at AUA. The applications were still lying there when Harley Baker stopped by on a lazy Sunday afternoon on his way home from the base.

We had just opened a couple of Singha beers, lit up a joint, and settled in on the porch when Lek called, "You dudes want some *sapparoht*?"

It was the beginning of hot season, and the thought of fresh, succulent pieces of fruit in my dry mouth seemed pleasant indeed. I had scarcely given her a hearty, "Yes, please!" than Lek had sculpted a pineapple into swirling patterns of tart sweetness and placed it on a silver platter. She set her creation on the bamboo table between me and Harley, handed us each an oversized toothpick, and disappeared.

Harley leaned back in his wicker chair and plunked his boots up on the porch railing. "You are a true fool," he said, picking up a slice of pineapple with his toothpick. "Why the hell aren't you *tii-rahking* her?"

"For lots of reasons," I responded. "I'm depressed as hell, in case you haven't noticed. It hasn't even been a month since Tukada was killed. And I'm also confused as hell. It's easy to forget around here, but there's a woman waiting for me back in the States who I met at a peace march in D.C. and moved all the way to California to live with me. I've been gone a year, but as far as I know, we're still engaged. And then there's the little matter of Tom Wheeler being my best friend. He hasn't even been gone two weeks. We New England Puritans have a funny superstition: you should let the husband's body cool before you make eyes at the widow-lady. You Californians would probably screw the widow and the cadaver."

Harley stared one of his shark stares. "Where'd you ever get that shit?"

"From every book and movie that's come out of California the last five years. Even an ignorant dirt farmer like you can't tell me you didn't have somebody read you the underlined parts of *Candy* or some of the other trash that Terry Southern writes."

"Maybe that's the way they do it in Frisco and L.A., asshole. In Stockton we're still into fucking chicks."

"Baby chickens or female human beings?"

"Foxes, birds, *ladies*—just like New England Puritans. What do you think they did all winter at Plymouth Rock in the days before television? They weren't reading their Bibles when the lights went out." Harley took a long tug on his beer.

"Getting back to your original question—I can't forget all the genuine affection I saw between Tom and Lek, and that in turn reminds me how exactly one year ago I had the same thing going with my fiancée in California.

Once I start sliding down that slippery slope into depression, there doesn't seem to be an end to it. It's not just Tukada—there's Dave Murray and Jeff Spitzer and Pigpen Sachs and the others I didn't know personally. Even Prasert, the little son of a bitch. You warned me with the story about your friend Vinh over at Bien Hoa. You liked Vinh. I liked Prasert, the little fucker. Meanwhile, I may never finish sorting out what Dah was all about, except that in some screwy way I loved her..."

"You do *way* too much thinking," growled Harley. "You're worse than a fool. You ain't ever goin' to understand love, and it don't matter if it's with some American broad or with a Thai chick. Plenty of smarter guys than you have tried, and nobody's done it yet."

"You're probably right," I replied. "I sure don't understand anything *here*."

Harley smiled another shark smile. "There's nothing to understand. Go downtown and have a good time. Like the song says, '*Get it while you can—we may not be here tomorrow.*' We're in a combat zone. Life is short, bro. I've been here six years, living with a Thai chick four of them, and I still don't have a clue what's going on in their clever little minds even when I'm conversing in deep, fluent Thai. All your damned struggling with morality—forget it. Every woman you see here in Ubon is a volunteer. Ain't no draft for bar girls."

"I'd just like to slow things down for a change. I'd like to try being Lek's friend. It might be nice to know a woman *without* getting involved with her."

"Wait too long and I'll take her myself."

"You already have a *tii-rahk*, remember? Your *neua kuu*—your soul mate, your true love, the love of your life."

"You're so naïve I could puke. Bigamy is the national pastime over here. It's the plot of every Thai soap opera—the major wife fighting off the minor wife. Or wives. You think anyone would care if I had two *girlfriends*?"

"Don't a lot of people die in those soap operas, fighting over the inheritance—or from plain old jealousy? From what I hear, girls around Ubon do their scariest knife-throwing when their old man 'butterflies.' Happened to Washington."

"That's just business."

"Well, lay off Lek. I can't tell you why exactly, but right now I'm feeling protective of her and want to give her a chance to make something of herself."

Harley polished off his Singha beer, burped, and glanced at the stack of ABC books and job applications lying on the plank floor. "I think you're wasting your time, Leary. 'Once a bar girl, always a bar girl.' Save your goddamned soul-searching. You're a man, right? Well, all men are the same. We point in the direction of money, booze, and pussy the way algae lusts after sunlight."

"I've been talking a lot to Moonbeam lately. And one of the monks out at Big Buddha. They kind of turn that idea upside down and say that when we're driven by our impulses, we're acting out of ignorance, that we still have 'dust in our eyes.' They say we can train our hearts to be cool and our minds to be wise and compassionate."

"Damn, you're irritating, Leary. Why are you always telling me shit like this and ruining a perfectly good buzz?" We drank our beers in silence.

Lek appeared and started clearing away what was left of the pineapple. "Why don't you sit down and join us?" I asked.

"Maybe in a little bit. After I *ap nam* and wash my hair."

She vanished. Harley lit up another doobie.

I tried to pick up where I left off. "Lieutenant Liscomb is into the Zen school of Buddhism, and Prah Samrong out at Big Buddha is from the older Theravada school. But both schools make you rethink Western ideas that we take for granted. Liscomb says that American materialism will never make us happy. All this chasing after possessions and wealth and sex and drugs— we're shadow boxing, chasing a mirage, an illusion. It's part of being raised on John Wayne rugged individualism. Buddhists say all things—living and non-living—are interconnected. And from that single insight, anyone following a more spiritual path through life can learn to act mindfully instead of being driven by greed and lust or fear and anger. A Zen master back in L.A. taught Liscomb that without mindfulness we're doomed to repeat a kind of chain reaction: ignorance will cause us to be driven by desire, and desire will cause us to be ruled by our egos, and our egos will cause each of us to think we alone are at the center of the universe. But that's just an illusion, which brings us right back to ignorance—and many rebirths till we get it right."

Harley exhaled a long stream of smoke. "Your philosophizing is giving me a fuckin' headache. I'm sticking with John Wayne and a life of mindless ignorance."

Lek came out of the *hong nam* wrapped in the beach towel decorated with the signs of the zodiac that Tom had left behind. "Har-ley, you stay for din-ner?"

He flicked away what was left of his joint and took his boots off the railing. "Thanks, but Mali's expecting me, and I'm already late." He stood up to leave. "Before I forget—I'm not scheduled to fly Tuesday night. Why don't you and Woody come over and jam?"

"Maybe, if I'm feeling up to it." We exchanged soul handshakes, and he clumped off down the wooden stairway. "Later, man," I called after him.

"Later," he replied.

"Bren-dan," called Lek, "I will take that beer now."

I pulled a couple of Singhas out of the refrigerator in the music room, where we had moved my somewhat less powerful stereo when Tom moved out. I brought the bottles back to Lek's room and handed one to her before stretching out on her bed, the only place to plant my body besides the chair she was sitting in while she put on her makeup.

"Are you really making dinner tonight?" I asked.

"Unless you want to take me out."

We were splitting the rent as long as Tom was sending her living expenses, but we hadn't nailed down our arrangement as far as food. When she was cooking for Tom, there was always enough for me to join them if I was around. "Great idea. How about the Ubon Hotel? Or should we try the Golden Palm?"

"Ubon Hotel is too expen-sive. The Golden Palm is good!" She stepped into her panties before dropping the towel at the foot of the bed. Her body was small but lovely, trim, and perfectly proportioned. Casually putting on her bra, she asked, "Can you help?"

I hooked it for her and watched as she picked out a dress to wear and slipped it on. Without having to be asked, I zipped it up for her, noticing that the brother-sister kind of platonic relationship was already down the tubes but that an old-married-couple sort of arrangement might work out. Excusing myself, I took a quick *ap nam* and changed into decent clothes before returning to her room. We drank the rest of our Singhas while she finished dressing, putting the final touches on her makeup, and we headed out. We took a *sahmlaw* to the Golden Palm, a comfortable indoor-outdoor restaurant located across the street from Maharaj Massage near the entrance to the base. The owners considered it a good omen that Lieutenant Glotfelty left their establishment standing the day he skidded his F-4 across Thanon Uparisawn into the Maharaj Massage parking lot. Given that it had been my virgin attempt at operating a movie camera from the back seat of a fighter-bomber, I shared their sentiment.

The night was balmy, perfect, as we sat out on the patio, eating several courses of hot and spicy soup, satay chicken, and *mii krawp*. I probably didn't need the pint of Mekhong whiskey, the bottle of soda water, and the bucket of ice we ordered, but I was beginning to feel slightly festive for the first time since the bicycle race. "What you an' Har-ley talk about, huh?"

"Nothing, really. Just guy stuff."

"What he say about have two *tii-rahk*?"

I laughed. "He said if I don't *tii-rahk* you soon, he'll take you, along *with* Mali."

"I sink Harley bet-ter be a gener-al before he do dat. A Thai girl can be very jea-lous, and when Thai girl jea-lous, she can be very expensive to make hap-py."

"Well, I don't think he was serious. What I think he *was* serious about is that I should ask you to be my *tii-rahk*."

"What did you tell him, Bren-dan?"

"What do you think I should have told him?"

She smiled. "You should tell him right now we need to be good frien.' Right now, you jus' want to help me to have better life."

"Were you listening to *everything* we said?"

"I don' *want* to lis-sen to every-sing. But you must remem-ber Ruam Chon Sawng have very thin wall!" She reached over to the side table and made us each a fresh drink. "Here's to jus' be good friend," she toasted.

I'd had a little too much to smoke that afternoon and way too much to drink that night. Mixing the beer and whiskey probably wasn't a great idea either, although Thai whiskey and Thai beer go together better than most countries' national beverages. And thanks to the *sahmlaw* drivers of Ubon, I didn't have to operate a motor vehicle. It seemed perfectly natural that Lek would lean her head against my chest on the way home. And it seemed perfectly natural that I would follow Lek into her room when we got back, and that I would help her undress the way I'd helped her put on her clothes before we went out, like a warm, affectionate couple who had been together for years.

What didn't seem like an old married couple, though, was when we began kissing each other hungrily and when she pushed me down on her bed and began undoing my pants. I helped her pull them the rest of the way off, and soon she was on top of me, moving her body with abandon, letting out some gentle moans that wouldn't carry too far into the other bungalows. And Harley was right, of course. A century of Father Boyle's catechism class wasn't going to keep me from going into autopilot. Lek began to moan louder, no longer giving a damn who in the Ghetto heard her. Of course, Harley was right. Give me a witches' brew of Laotian grass, Thai whiskey, Singha beer, and the Valium that I had momentarily forgotten about, mix in a little loneliness and a lot of sadness, and I was indeed a single-celled amoeba drawn inexorably toward Lek's powerful warmth.

We collapsed together, and when I rolled over on my back, she put her head softly on my chest. And just when I thought I could go to sleep with a pleasant smile on my face, it happened. The part where Harley was wrong. Harley was lucky because he was a frigging Neanderthal. He could fornicate with anyone, any time, out of some primordial instinct left over from a time when prehumans were weak and faced extinction on what was then a hostile, untamed planet.

No, the part that happened next didn't happen to the Harley Bakers of the world. I cried. I kept my eyes closed, but I couldn't hold back the tears. And as my chest started to heave, Lek lifted her head, asking, "Bren-dan, are you all right?"

"I'm sorry, Lek. I think you're great. I always thought you were great, from the first time you came over to visit Tom to that night you announced you were going to move in here and I wanted to jump on your bones while Tom was in the shower."

"I sink you very hand-some that night. When Tom was in show-er, I purposely tease you, move around to make you hot, because sitting there in same room wis you, alone, you were making *me* hot. Tom got fucked very good that night!"

As she often did, Lek made me laugh with her earthiness. I sighed deeply and continued, "I think you're beautiful. But I'm so damned mixed up. I still have a girlfriend in California who I'll be seeing in a couple of months. But it's not really her. It's getting so I can hardly remember her sometimes…"

"You still miss Tukada."

"How did you know?"

"Because I still miss Tom."

I pulled her tiny body back into my arms. She was sinewy and strong, but her skin was still young and soft. I kept holding her gently, feeling drained and sensing she was, too. "What can we do to make this heartache go away?" I asked.

"Nos-sing. No mat-ter how much we love them, we can never have them back, but we will al-ways have heart-ache. Tom may still be alive, but he might as well be in hea-ven wis Dah. They are both gone forev-er. The Buddha teaches to live right now, in the pre-sent mo-ment. Lek says, 'Just enjoy right now.' Stephen Stills sing—"

"*Love the one you're with, love the one you're with,*" we sang together.

I noticed Lek had tears on her cheeks, too, when she reached over to turn out the light. Tough little Lek. She put her head back on my chest, and we fell asleep.

"What You Need is Some Cheering Up!"

Monday night, Miss Pawnsiri stayed after class to talk to me. She hesitated a moment and then said, "My mother and grandmother want me to tell you they very sorry for you about bicycle race."

"Please thank them for their kind thoughts," I replied awkwardly.

"We would like you to come again, be our guest for lunch on Saturday."

"I would like that very much," I replied, accepting the invitation partly as a gesture of sympathy but more as a simple act of hospitality, the equivalent gesture Pawnsiri could make as a young, single female to what my male students could do informally after class any time they chose when they invited me out to dinner.

"It should be a little more fun for you this time, Khun Bren-dan," she said with a shy smile. "My English professor from Ubon Teachers College is coming, so you will have somebody else to talk to."

"It will be an honor to meet him," I replied, returning her smile. We nodded politely before she left to catch her bus. Gathering up my things, I seemed to move in slow motion, and once outside, I felt a strange reluctance to unlock the chain on my bicycle, knowing I'd be riding directly home without stopping for dinner with the guys from class. I hoped Lek might have some leftovers waiting when I got there, but the doors to the music room and her bedroom were both locked. Larry and Peung had only taken a week to move into a place of their own. I went back down to Mama-sahn's cafe and ate dinner alone, slowly, dreading the walk back to an empty bungalow.

Meditating that night was a mess, a taste of what Prah Samrong meant when he warned me it could be simple but challenging. For one thing, the bungalow was *too* quiet, so quiet that every sound in Ubon—motorbikes backfiring, *sahmlaw* drivers rolling dice and laughing, *jingjoks* clucking, even the faint roar of jet engines miles away at the base—took my attention away from my breath. I would bring it back, but instead of relaxing peacefully as I had with Samrong, my mind started racing through fleeting memories of Dah, Danielle, Tom, Lek, Link, my mother, my father, Nixon, Ho Chi Minh, helicopters, Prasert, and many thoughts that I forgot as soon as I had them, followed by a knotting in my stomach and then nothing at all.

The nothingness was not a peaceful nothingness. It was an *emptiness* that alternated with a kind of wakeful nodding off, a gap in my memory, a gap in concentration, something that might have been sloth or might have been forgetting. The process repeated itself, and then I did nod off, waking suddenly when my head seemed to be dropping deep into a well but had, in fact, dropped only a few inches toward my chest. I gave up and climbed into bed, where I tried meditating lying down—counting two breaths, losing count, getting to three breaths, losing count again, repeating the exercise in futility several more times, and finally falling asleep.

I didn't really feel up to jamming with Woody and Harley Tuesday night, filled as I was with a malaise that yearned for quiet solitude. The loneliness I felt at Ruam Chon Sawng was worse, however, propelling me to go ahead and join them. Changing out of my uniform into my street clothes, I reflected on our first rehearsal, acknowledging that in some instinctive way Harley, Woody, and I were grieving together that night, using music to say goodbye to Pigpen Sachs and the other friends we had lost, even if we couldn't put it into words and wouldn't have had a clue how to talk about it if we could. Thinking back, there seemed to be an undertone of grieving beneath everything we played. I sensed I *needed* to grieve, but as a beginning meditator, I didn't know if this was what Samrong would call Insight or if I was just back to overanalyzing. I made a mental note to ask him about it, along with asking him how to deal with a disturbed sitting like I had experienced the night before. There was one thing I was sure of, however. I didn't need help grieving for Tukada. Grieving for Dah left an undertone of sadness beneath every breath I took.

Riding my bicycle over to Harley's, I couldn't help wondering where grieving fit into Buddhist cosmology. On one hand, it was a form of interconnectedness—of the living with the dead. On the other hand, it was a form of attachment that brought suffering. I wondered if, over time, a deep understanding of the impermanence of all things could help reduce the power grief held over me.

The familiar experience of sitting down at my drums brought me a sense of comfort I had been unable to find meditating the previous night. The vibrations of the guitar strings and the thunk thunking of my tom-toms resonated deep inside me, reminding me of the times I *had* been soothed by Pali chanting at Buddhist monasteries. The three of us had just about finished warming up when I heard a cab pull up in the courtyard outside, and I could hear the vaguely familiar voice of Marcos, the brains behind Jay and the Ugly Americans. The trunk squeaked open, and after some banging around, it slammed shut. A moment later, Marcos pushed through the door carrying his portable Farfisa organ and an amplifier. "Hey, dudes, mind if I sit in?"

"How the hell did you find us here?" asked Woody.

"They told me down at Woodstock Music," Marcos smiled. "Word travels fast in Ubon."

"I thought your band went back to the Philippines," said Harley.

"Everybody except me and the Thai horn players. I talked the Siam Hotel into opening a piano bar, so I'm sticking around. Only I don't start for a couple of weeks, and I'm bored stiff, so here I am!"

While Marcos set up, Woody started us out quietly on "Streets of Laredo." Harley responded with his favorite Elmore James tune, Marcos now able to join in, both of them opening with long, improvised blues riffs before Harley began singing, *"The sky is crying—look at the tears roll down the street..."* Next, we went into "The House of the Rising Sun," which gave Marcos a chance to shine with some virtuoso keyboard work.

I was pleasantly surprised to discover that the heightened sense of awareness Prah Samrong was teaching me—working with my breath in meditation—could be carried over to the music. With just the slightest bit of intention, I could be more deeply mindful—of how I was affected by the very music I was playing, of how I didn't just hear it with my ears but felt it reverberating in my belly and heart, and of how in a nanosecond an intention to strike my drums could turn into a drumbeat that blended with the strumming of guitar strings and the pressing of organ keys to produce waves of vibrations powerful enough to relieve the tightness stored in my forehead, neck, back, and stomach. I pondered, too, how the extrasensory unity of the band seemed to validate Liscomb and Samrong's lessons on interconnectedness.

We repeated some of the songs from our last get-together, and when we got to ballads like "Bring It on Home to Me" and "Cry to Me," I noticed that while following Samrong's admonishment to "just observe," memories came up of soulful ballads like "That's How Strong My Love Is" and "A Change is Gonna Come" that I used to perform with the Band of Brothers and how performing them had filled me with a Holy Spirit that loved even atheists. I felt possessed in a less angelic way playing "Ghost Riders in the Sky" and "Sympathy for the Devil," but what all those tunes gave me was a sense of a force bigger than myself that connected musicians to their music and their fellow musicians and, when the time was right and miraculous, with their audiences.

"This stuff is too fuckin' morbid!" Marcos complained, popping me back to the present with a jolt. "You're in a depressing funk, and you need to snap out of it! If you're gonna do Stones, let's make it 'Brown Sugar' or 'Honky Tonk Women.'" Harley took his cue, and the rest of us joined him on the two Stones tunes, and then we played long and joyously on Marcos's old Ugly American arrangements—"Everyday People," "Gonna Take You Higher," and "Gimme Some Lovin.'"

I was drenched with sweat but feeling almost happy when we wrapped it up for the night, especially enjoying that I didn't have to pack up the drums. My mother's dictum of keeping busy seemed to be working well. It wasn't quite a second wind, but when Harley rounded up Mali and suggested that the rest of us join them for a bite to eat at the Thai-Chinese hole-in-the-wall around the corner, I decided to go with the flow. Khun Jim and Pye, who had been sitting out on their porch listening to the music, accepted our invitation to come along. As usual, I enjoyed chatting with Jim while the others bantered, relieved to know that Liscomb and I weren't alone in having concerns about the American military presence in Ubon. He surprised me with his skepticism about Nixon's motives visiting China, but I had to agree that nothing seemed to be changing as far as air operations out of Ubon went. And then he had a bigger surprise for me: "Why hasn't Lek enrolled at AUA?" he asked.

"What!" I gasped. "She told me she started!"

Lek was on her bed reading a movie magazine when I got home. "How is your English class?" I asked.

"Very good!" she replied, but her smile quickly started to fade.

"Why are you bullshitting me?"

"What you talking about, huh?" she scowled. "Who speak lie about me?"

"I don't think Khun Jim was lying. I think he's concerned about you."

"Goddamn! I a village girl! Only go to school six year! AUA student finish high school and col-lege! Some go to col-lege in U.S.!" She crawled off the bed and started pushing me out the door. "Why doesn't Jim make Pye go AUA? You know why? Because she village girl like me. If we go, they laugh at both of us! Now please go away!" she said, giving me a final shove. "Please leave me alone!"

Half an hour later, I was lying in bed trying to read myself to sleep when Lek knocked at my door. She came in and sat rather sweetly on the edge of my bed. "I don' have time for go school, Bren-dan. My father very sick. Money Tom send not enough."

I guessed what was coming. It struck me much the same as when Tom and Dah used to go on and off heroin—sad and disappointing and inevitable. I realized that our destinies were moving irretrievably in different directions and that the joyful days of our little tribe living together at Ruam Chon Sawng had passed. It also gave me a sinking feeling I was afraid to touch—that, in reality, I had absolutely no control over the mad world swirling around me and the motley crew of friends who occupied it. "So you're back working the bars?"

"Just tea dances in the afternoon," she lied, trying to make it sound respectable. "Bun-lii ask me to come with her. She don' like to go by herself."

"How does your father think you make the money you're sending home?"

"Goddamn, Bren-dan, you can be so stupid! He sink I'm waitress at Ubon Hotel."

When Woody and I showed up to jam on Thursday, Harley and Marcos were waiting for us with Sugie Bear, the bass player, and Ackerman, the sax man, from the Band of Brothers. My compadres had no sooner started tuning up than Angel and Kae, two of the Ugly Americans still living in Ubon, arrived with their trumpet and baritone sax. I looked at Harley and Marcos. "Okay, you two—what's up?"

"You guys need some cheering up," Marcos announced. "We're going to do some soul music and lift your spirits! In fact, we're going to lift your spirits so high that we're going to take a train trip to Bangkok and do a little concert Saturday night at Thammasat University."

"That's in two friggin' days!" said Woody.

"A *concert* with a band that's never played together? You've gotta be kidding me," I groaned. "I really don't think I'm up to it."

"Too late for that. The band's already been booked—as Domino Theory." Besides, most of you guys *have* played together, just not at the same time. This is for 'Thammasatstock II,' a big student music festival that's going on all weekend. But you've only got to do a forty-five-minute set, ten or twelve songs with an encore or two ready. We'll rehearse tonight, we'll rehearse on the night train to Bangkok Friday evening, and we'll rehearse in a dorm room Saturday afternoon. There are supposed to be some Thai record producers there. This could be very cool! This could be big!"

It was hard to avoid getting caught up in Marcos's mania. At the same time, I couldn't help wondering about the name Domino Theory and if it was a good idea to be joking about Thai-American foreign policy. Any chance to discuss it screeched to a halt, however, when a cab pulled up outside and who should get out but Annie Kim and the rest of the Chirping Sparrows, apparently taking a night off from the NCO Club. "What the hell are *they* doing here?" asked Shahbazian.

Marcos grinned. "I won them from Sagittarius Smith in a poker game. We get them tonight through Sunday, all expenses paid by the Big Man himself. We'll use them strictly as backup singers, and we'll keep it all simple. Mostly blues and the songs you've already got nailed down. Now let's get to work!"

And my motley mates indeed got to work, polishing up a rousing opening arrangement of "Everyday People." We worked on "Ghost Riders" next and were pleasantly surprised with the way Annie and the rest of the Sparrows came up with a haunting background chorus that made our spines tingle. We were just about to finish when Harley called for a segue into "Sympathy for the Devil," which worked beautifully. We liked the Sparrows' background singing even more, so much so that we decided to repeat "Sympathy for the Devil" at the end of the show and make it our calling card.

When Marcos said, "Let's try a few more medleys," we put together a few Stones tunes: "Gimme Shelter," "Honky Tonk Women," and "Brown Sugar." "How about 'Mr. Tambourine Man' and 'Eight Miles High'?" I asked, but Marcos overruled me in favor of two Van Morrison ditties, "Gloria" and "Brown Eyed Girl." It was fine with me, but after belting out those tunes,

Marcos worried about wearing out his voice and gave "Brown Eyed Girl" to Woody before moving on to "Sugar, Sugar" and "The Way You Do the Things You Do," where Sugie Bear had the leads.

Our ever-hustling leader warned the group that we'd be opening for an English band, Quantum Leap, who played mostly originals, so we worked on a country swing number Woody had written called "The Toast of the Town Just Got Burned." I had written some lyrics to a blues tune called "Horror Movie," and suddenly that was on our playlist. The Chirping Sparrows sounded great as backup singers, perhaps their true calling once they got back to Seoul or Memphis. Harley had an original tune of his own, "Hungry Sinner Blues," that sounded good backed with just guitar and bass. And then he astounded us—now that he had a full band and backup singers behind him—with a truly soulful rendition of "To Love Somebody." The horns, the singers, the lead guitar and keyboard, and the rhythm guitar, bass, and drums were all working as tight little sub-units within the overall band, which itself had fallen into a tight groove. All of us were exhausted, but we worked out rough arrangements of "Gimme Some Lovin'" and "You Can't Judge a Book by Looking at the Cover" for encores. The group was fired up, inspired, so busy rehearsing into the wee hours—with visions dancing in our heads of some kind of recording contract coming out of this—that none of us had time to worry about why a Thai record label would want to record a Filipino-Korean-American garage band.

My buzzed bandmates were finally wrapping things up at 4:00 a.m. when it occurred to me that I had to cancel my lunch plans with Miss Pawnsiri. Bleary-eyed from our late-night rehearsal, I stopped over on my bike late Friday afternoon, but she was still at the college. Luckily, her younger sister was there and seemed to understand. "Maybe you can do next week?" she suggested.

"Sounds good to me. Thanks! Tell everyone I'm sorry," I said before I hurried home to pack and take a cab over to Harley's to pick up my drums.

"*Thammasatstock!*"

It seemed a little strange that Harley wasn't home when I stopped by to pack up my kit, and it didn't help when Mali told me it was because he had gone to see Indian Joe on some "important business." "Don' worry," she said. "He tell me he be there in plenty of time for train."

"See you Sunday!" I called to her as I climbed back into the cab. I had given myself an extra hour in case there was any problem getting the drums on board. When I arrived at the station across the river in Warin, Marcos was already there and had arranged twelve second-class sleeping berths together in the same car, not far from the baggage car, so we could keep an eye on our equipment when we got to Bangkok. Woody showed up a few minutes later, followed by Sugie Bear and Ackerman, who had shared a cab from the base. Kae and Angel arrived on a baht-bus not much later, followed by the Chirping Sparrows, chauffeured by Sagittarius Smith himself.

"You coming with us?" I asked Smith.

He was not a happy man. "Got an NCO Club and an Airmen's Club to run. See you Sunday. Good luck."

"Where's Baker?" asked Sugie Bear.

"Had to stop off at Indian Joe's," I replied. "He should be blowing in any minute."

The day train that had left Bangkok early that morning arrived and a wide spectrum of Thai society began stepping off—businessmen and rice farmers, monks and soldiers, extended families and couples, young people and old, some traveling alone and many traveling with friends. A few of the people in third class had live chickens with them, and many of them carried home-cooked food and little pink, green, and white plastic bags of fresh fruit they had bought at stops along the way. A group of Thai men who were dressed casually and had apparently been on holiday together climbed down from the dining car with their eyes glazed and their laughter a bit loud from a little too much Mekhong whiskey. Amid the huffing and puffing of steam brakes and the rumble of diesel engines, a new locomotive inched back to the other end of the train and was hooked up for the return trip to Bangkok while crewmen at our end uncoupled the engine that had brought the train in. Still no Harley.

A few minutes later, a couple of the guys noticed that baggage was being loaded, so we found a cart and brought over our heaviest equipment, including my drums, which I didn't think would be welcome while the band rehearsed in the passenger compartment on our way to Bangkok. Still no Harley.

Marcos passed out tickets, and our little entourage began climbing on board. After doing a quick check that all twelve of us were going to be seated together as planned, he told the group to stay on the train while he and I went out to the front of the station to stand watch. The two of us waited impatiently, leaning against the wrought iron fence and staring off into the street, our eyes distracted by an occasional food vendor serving a new customer. "What's keeping him?" asked Marcos.

"When Indian Joe's involved, who knows," I replied. And still no Harley.

The stationmaster was starting to make final boarding calls in Thai and something like English. Sugie Bear tapped me on the shoulder, scaring the hell out of me. "Hey guys, we'll have to make do without him. That's the last call for the train."

I was disappointed at the thought of not having Harley's slide guitar licks, especially on the blues tunes. Sugie Bear was right, though, and the three of us headed back through the station to the platform. We were just settling into our seats when I saw a cab pull up outside in a cloud of dust.

I called over to Marcos. "Looks like he made it!"

Harley jumped out, handing his guitar case and a gym bag to Mali, who lugged them inside along with her small suitcase. He paid the driver, pulled his bulky amplifier-speaker out of the trunk, and raced into the station in time to put it with our heavy equipment in the baggage car. The train was just starting to move when they jumped on board.

"Where you been, man?" asked Marcos.

"They had me in jail. It's a long story. Break out the Mekhong and soda, and I'll tell you all about it."

As the train began to pick up speed, we settled in around several pairs of tables that faced each other across the narrow, Thai-sized aisle. Woody happened to have a liter of Mekhong with him, and the horn section had a few more pints in reserve. Two of the guys moseyed off to the dining car and managed to scrounge up some glasses, a couple bottles of soda and Coke, and a bucket of ice. The girls were hanging back, but the guys mixed up drinks for them, coaxed them to accept, and soon our whole group was unwinding.

When Mali went off to use the powder room, I turned to Harley and asked, "When did your old lady decide to come along?"

"She had a little too much time to think this afternoon. While she was waiting for me to get home, she decided she wanted to see our show in person, especially now that we've got female backup singers with us, if you know what I mean."

"Gotcha," I replied, and we clinked our glasses together in a little guy-toast. We polished off half our drinks, and by the time we finished freshening them up, Mali was back. After sliding over to make room for her, I asked Harley, "What's with this jail business?" I glanced at Mali. "Your girlfriend here said you were meeting Indian Joe."

"I *thought* I was meeting Indian Joe, but these Thai undercover cops had set me up. They were waiting for me—and there was no Indian Joe, just the truckload of Sansui stereos in the storeroom behind his gentlemen's club they showed me before they took me downtown."

"They were trying to blame *you* for a truckload of receivers?"

"Unfortunately, I had bought two of them with a couple of ration cards Joe had given me, but this was a roomful of Sansui 5000 amplifiers. Top-of-the-line shit."

"Damn!" Marcos exclaimed, leaning in a little closer.

"So I'm hauled off to the Ubon city jail, overlooking the soccer field, only the view wasn't too good from the wire cage they put me in. It could have been *worse*, though, because the Thai inmates were behind this wall of bars, being treated like livestock. They were wearing jail-issued sarongs, standing in a foot or two of sewage that made *klong* water look like a babbling brook in the Rockies."

The group was still drinking, but the laughter gradually died down as, one by one, they turned their attention to Harley's story.

Harley tossed back his Mekhong and soda and continued, "The Thais stood in this filth, just staring at me through the bars, while turds and all kinds of shit were floating around their ankles." Sugie Bear gulped. The Sparrows glanced at each other in disgust, but they kept listening. "And I look around and behind another wall of bars is contraband—tons of the stuff. Confiscated machine guns, a couple of M-16 and AK-47 assault rifles, a bunch of pistols and old rifles, and now they're carting in that big fuckin' stack of Sansui stereo amplifiers from Indian Joe's."

"You're shitting me!" I gasped.

"It was about then that the chief of the Ubon Police Department came in. He pointed to the stack of Sansui 5000s, and I got the distinct impression he was blaming me for procuring the whole lot of 'em. And then I knew I was in serious trouble because they brought me a nice, cold Coke and some *khaopaht* and offered me a Cyclone cigarette, something they do in tailor shops around here, not in a jail cell."

"Damn!" Marcos muttered.

"The chief of police says someone from the Judge Advocate's office will be in at five to ask me a few questions. It's only four o'clock, so I'm figuring I won't be taking a train ride to Bangkok this weekend with you guys.

"And right about then who walks in but Indian Joe—"

"About time!" laughed Ackerman.

"He spots the police chief," Harley continued, "and gives him a little nod of his head, and off they go to the chief's office. With that Sikh turban, he towers over the chief, and he's got those piercing blue eyes that look right through you, so Indian Joe is already a pretty imposing presence even before he opens his wallet. Next thing I know, they were unlocking the cage and carrying the Sansui 5000s out to *Indian Joe's* truck. While his driver was supervising the operation, Joe whispers to me that he paid fifteen hundred American dollars for me and his amplifiers." Harley's audience looked impressed, even the jaded Annie Kim. "Before you know it, the driver is honking the horn, the gate opens, Joe jumps in, and off they drove. Funny, though. As they turned the corner, Leary, I would have sworn I saw your prick first sergeant, Link, sitting up in the front seat with Joe. Except I could care less at that point because that's when the police chief turns to me and says, 'You're free to go.'"

"And on that cheerful note," announced Marcos, gathering up our bottles and empty glasses, "let's get to work."

My fellow musicians and singers made a game attempt at rehearsing acoustically for the next couple of hours, even though we couldn't hear anything but tapping sounds from Marcos's electric keyboard. Around nine o'clock, the passengers at the other end of the car started converting their seats and tables into upper and lower berths. The conductor turned the lights down, and we thought we might have to call it a night, but Angel remembered seeing a coffeemaker up in the dining car and asked the conductor if we might be able to plug in an amplifier. He didn't know, but Angel came back a few minutes later and said it was okay. The chef said we could run an extension cord, and the few people still up there were mostly drinking and quite open to some live entertainment.

We moved the operation forward and crowded into a couple of open booths. With Marcos's Farfisa powered up, even at its softest setting, we got a much better sense of how the numbers were pulling together. I was amazed. The music sounded terrific because Marcos was right—most of us had played together in some shape or form, and even if we hadn't, we had spent so many nights listening to each other that we quickly got on the same musical wavelength. Even the Sparrows, by frequenting the Soul Sister with Sagittarius, had a pretty good sense of our direction. It only took a few drinks for the straightlaced Annie Kim to relax, and the rest of the Sparrows, once they were a little tipsy, settled in like they had been with the band for years.

We called it quits around midnight, which still gave us six hours to sleep in our gently rocking berths. Mali had only bought a third-class ticket but, with a small gratuity to the conductor, was able to crawl up into Harley's bunk and keep him safely away from the temptations of our little flock of Korean backup singers.

The band was met at the station in Bangkok by a group of Thammasat University students, some with official-looking name tags and others in Thammasatstock T-shirts. They led us to a chartered bus that we loaded up for the trip to the college. With lots of help available when we got there, we had no trouble unloading the bus and carrying our equipment up to an old second-floor dorm room where we rehearsed after breakfast, next to a couple of other dorm rooms where we could nap and clean up. Even running short on sleep, we felt good, rehearsing non-stop until we took a late-morning siesta. After a quick lunch, we ran through the material several more times before we had our student roadies bring everything down to the stage, which was set up in front of what the students called "the Dome," the main administration building. It opened out onto a soccer field surrounded by a large expanse of lawn. In the distance, we could make out the green roof of a large auditorium and to the right, new classrooms that looked like something out of *Star Trek*. Marcos was right again—if these grounds were going to be filled with students in a few hours, it was indeed going to be big.

The only change we decided to make in the program was to have Marcos do an Otis Redding version of "Satisfaction" as a bridge from the Van Morrison medley to Sugie Bear's soul numbers. Harley's blues tune was more of a ballad, so we beefed up the bass and drums on my "Horror Movie Blues," still keeping it slow, and gave it a sort of Willie Dixon "I'm a Man" feel. Annie Kim talked us into adding a short two minutes of "Da Do Ron Ron" and a lush "Will You Still Love Me Tomorrow?" between the two blues numbers. They'd been on their good behavior musically and socially, so we dropped "Brown Sugar" to make room for them.

With a couple of hours left till showtime, the Sparrows went off to relax and rest their voices before dressing and putting on their makeup. The guys stayed down with the roadies to do a final sound check onstage and then make sure our equipment was stashed backstage where it could be moved into position quickly. The late afternoon was typical early hot season, which meant temperatures in the low nineties, but at least the humidity was low and a pleasant breeze was blowing. Once we were done, the horn players went up to practice a bit more. The rest of us stretched out in the room next door. It was easy to kick back. Two local bands were opening up, playing gentle, reggae-like rock designed to build up gradually to the evening performances.

At half past six, as the sun set and the lights came up, the guys drifted downstairs to stand by in the wings. The stakes were suddenly raised when, a little after seven, the easy listening was over. A heavy metal Thai band took the stage, led by a wiry dude with hair down his back named Kit Tii Kittikachawn, who played guitar like a right-handed Jimi Hendrix. We found it easy to believe it when a couple of the Thammasat stage hands told us Kit Tii's band was made up of bad-boy sons of wealthy Thai industrialists. Their massive Marshall speakers looked shiny and new like they were fresh off the showroom floor. Calling themselves the Kats, they were in the process of recording their second studio album. But they also knew how to turn their amps up to "10" and rock a live audience that already topped ten thousand and was growing fast.

By a fluke, the English band Quantum Leap was our lead-in, instead of the other way around. They were doing the early set because they had a month-long engagement at the palatial Erawan Hotel and still had to go back and do a full four hours of work that night. Watching the Kats' large Marshalls being replaced by Orange speakers the size of Druid monoliths left Harley and Woody staring with their mouths gaping. But looking hard at the back of the speakers from the rear of the stage and then walking up for a closer look, something was strange—I could only see cables connected to half of them. The changeover gave me a chance to chat with one of the musicians who was waiting in the wings.

"Hey there! I'm Brendan Leary, the drummer with Domino Theory."

"Bryce Bates, mate, the keyboard player. Good luck tonight! I'm afraid we won't be an easy act to follow."

"Maybe, but did you know the roadies only powered up half your speakers?"

He laughed. "It's all just for show right now. If they were all fired up, you wouldn't hear me bleeding Hammond organ! We're keeping the others in reserve for when we open for the Stones at Shea Stadium."

He wasn't kidding. Bryce, who was also their arranger-composer, explained that their Bangkok engagement was an out-of-town tune-up for some serious recording and concert dates back in England that summer. They had major backing, which paid for the Orange speakers and amps, the newest, biggest, baddest gear in the world. And sure enough, just as Marcos predicted, they were doing all original material written by Bryce and a couple of his bandmates. Quantum Leap was going to push us hard to outdo ourselves—and to freshen up our arrangements, given that so many of our numbers were covers of other people's hits. While they performed, we huddled far offstage, talking among ourselves about being ready to throw in some extra horn and guitar solos and changing up on some of the tempos to give our material its own Domino Theory sound. Marcos pepped us up, reminded us that we were doing three original numbers. Finally, he talked us through the entire set because sounding tight was now imperative and was not going to be easy for twelve musicians and singers performing together on stage for the first time.

Bryce had warned me, and sure enough, Quantum Leap was top drawer, finishing to a standing ovation. No sooner had the band trotted off the stage in triumph than roadies began lugging off their massive Orange speakers and amplifiers. They brought out our tawdry assortment of banged-up Ampegs and Fenders, which were dwarfed by comparison, even though ours had been plenty loud in Ubon night clubs. I barely noticed that they were miking up my drums. Woody lit up a joint and asked, "What is this, some kind of amplifier pissing contest?"

"Fuck 'em," said Harley. "We're Americans. We invented this music!"

I took a hit on the joint, passed it to the horn section, and peeked out at the audience. It wasn't Woodstock or Shea Stadium, but it was the biggest crowd I had ever faced, now easily topping fifteen thousand, big enough to fill the soccer field, the track, and the grounds surrounding it to overflow and forcing some of the students to watch from classroom windows.

"Damn!" said Sugie Bear. "I've never played anywhere bigger than a high school gym!"

"Get used to it," called Marcos, not bothered in the least when Quantum Leap's giant Hammond organ and Leslie speaker were rolled away and replaced by his cheesy Farfisa, sitting on spindly fold-out legs.

Ackerman was cool as usual. He'd played on the streets of New Orleans and at the Superdome. It didn't matter if he was busking for quarters or marching with a hundred-piece band. "Shee-it, Sugie. This ain't nothin' but another gig!"

Finally, the stage was set. The MC stepped up to the mike and tapped it a few times, calling for attention. "And now, ladies and gentlemen, making their Bangkok debut, a group of musicians who come from all over the world and who come to us tonight from Ubon Ratchathani, Thailand—let's hear a big hand for DOMINO THEORY!"

The crowd went wild, screaming, "Domino! Theory! Domino! Theory!" The MC tried to translate his intro into Thai over the crowd noise, realized he was wasting his breath, and waved us out.

Harley took a final hit on the joint, flicked it away, and with Marcos leading the way, my bandmates and I walked out on stage, trying our damnedest to turn stage fright into high-octane energy. "What's with this crowd reaction?" I called to Marcos as I climbed behind the drums. "Nobody gets that worked up over a board game."

"Maybe I should have told you," Marcos yelled to me. "Some of the students around here can get political."

"I thought nobody in Thailand talked politics," I replied, but he had already turned his attention to his keyboards. I did a few quick riffs on the drums and was blown away with what the miking had done. Suddenly I felt like Thor, the god of thunder. I was ready to rumble.

The band was dressed in jeans and dressy long-sleeved shirts with billowy sleeves and oversized collars. We might have felt intimidated by the rich Thai bad-boys and the touring Brits, with their fancy clothes and monolithic speakers, but we had a secret weapon—the Chirping Sparrows. When the Sparrows strutted out in black evening gowns, looking like fashion models walking a runway, the crowd was momentarily stunned, settling down and forgetting about politics as Marcos counted out "One, two, three, four!" and launched into "Everyday People."

Our whole ensemble sounded rich and full, and soon the audience was singing along and dancing. Our acid country rendition of "Ghost Riders in the Sky" might have stunned them a bit, but they kept dancing, and they danced with reckless abandon when we segued to "Sympathy for the Devil." His instincts good as usual, Marcos cut the Stones medley short and went straight to "Gloria." Once again, we put a Domino Theory stamp on the song, with the horns soaring in rich harmony with the Sparrows on the chorus, only to drop to an achingly long hush while Marcos continued alone on keyboard. He improvised a drawn-out rap about a midnight rendezvous, delayed by the heroine's insomniac daddy refusing to fall asleep in front of the TV, by her car not starting, and by locking her keys and her purse inside the car, which meant having to walk in her bathroom slippers until, finally, she "*knocked on my door*" and "*made me feel all-right!*" And then, "*GLORIA! G-L-O-R-I-A!*" so loud and full it scared me.

The song had barely finished when Marcos told us to go straight into "Satisfaction," which kept the audience on their feet and got them singing along with the chorus when he pointed the microphone in their direction. He moved up "Da Do Ron Ron," giving the guys in the audience a chance to fall in love with the Chirping Sparrows—especially Annie Kim, who could have blown Diana Ross off the stage that night. We moved right into Sugie Bear's numbers, "Sugar, Sugar" and "The Way You Do the Things You Do," and the audience stayed with us, buzzing with excitement between songs and eating up Marcos's jive patter. "When I heard Thammasatstock II was coming," he laughed, "I started rounding up the best musicians in Ubon

Province, musicians who came from Thailand, the Philippines, and the U.S.A.—a group of Issan All-Stars, really—and then added some beautiful singers from Korea, mixed them all together, and out came Domino Theory!"

"Domino!" Shouted one group of students.

Another answered back with "Theory!"

We quieted them down by accident, about our only miscue, by doing Woody's "Toast of the Town Just Got Burned." The band had welcomed it as a jazzy change of pace, a Willie Nelson-style county tune, but it was too full of puns for a Thai audience to follow, even this highly educated university crowd. A few of the coeds kept dancing gamely while the rest of the crowd looked confused.

Marcos cut it short, and suddenly the spotlight was on *me*, with my very limited singing voice, faking my way through "Horror Movie," the blues tune I had written with my weak voice in mind. I opened with the refrain, "*I had a dream—it was a nightmare*," to which the Sparrows admonished, "*Don't go out there!*" We repeated the first two lines, and the third time I sang straight through: "*I had a dream—it was a nightmare, but I had to go out anyway.*" The first verse went:

> *The night was black*
> *The fog was thick*
> *The princess cried out,*
> *"Daddy, come here quick!"*

The Sparrows came in with me for the refrain, and I went into the second verse:

> *I found the princess in the dungeon*
> *And unchained her from the wall.*
> *She knew a secret passage,*
> *But it meant we had to crawl.*

The Sparrows came in for another chorus, followed by a couple of nice solos by Harley with his bottleneck guitar and Ackerman on his tenor sax. We went through a couple more verses about being chased by a fire-breathing dragon before I finished with:

> *I tried to squeeze the trigger,*
> *But I couldn't fire the gun.*

I tried to move my legs,
But, Lord, I couldn't run!

And the Sparrows came in for a final chorus before we began repeating it and fading out, mixing our voices with Harley's guitar riffs and finally, on Marcos's command, bringing it to a crescendo finale.

I was relieved to have gotten through the song. Marcos, though, realized that by moving up the Sparrows number, we were going to be playing three slow ballads in a row, so he called for "Brown Eyed Girl" and gave Woody, with his big blue eyes, a chance to work the crowd of beautiful Thai coeds dancing at the foot of the stage. We ended the song on such a high note that a few normally well-behaved Thai college girls tried to crawl up on stage to get their hands on Woody, which woke up Security and left the audience buzzing.

Before we changed pace for our final couple of numbers, Marcos took a few minutes to introduce the band. They loved us all, but, not surprisingly, they loved the Sparrows most of all. Marcos, the consummate showman, picked up on the vibes and asked, "Would you like to hear one more by the Chirping Sparrows?"

The audience gave an enthusiastic "Yes!" and Marcos called out to the band for "Will You Still Love Me Tomorrow?" Annie stepped up to the mike, looking lovely but suddenly tiny and vulnerable as a soloist, filling me with an anxious need to protect her—until she launched into the song, starting out bravely on her own for the first few measures:

Tonight you're mine completely
You give your love so sweetly

On the next *"Tonight,"* the band and backup singers jumped in as if we had been playing together for years. Kae had done a great baritone sax solo on "Da Do Ron Ron." This time it was Ackerman's turn to wail out a New Orleans-flavored tenor solo, which inspired Angel to do the most extraordinary jazz-influenced trumpet lick I had ever heard out of him. Pounding away with heavy, dramatic kicks on the bass drum and equally dramatic tympani-style accents on the tom-toms, I couldn't help suspecting that part of the horn section's inspiration was the dream of sharing their bunks with the Sparrows on the train back to Ubon. The Thammasat audience loved the Sparrows, I thought, because compared to Thai female vocalists, who were almost always syrupy sweet, this was the first time they had seen Asian chicks with attitude, a tribute to the guidance of Sagittarius Smith. And I was getting the feeling that Thammasat was a place that especially liked women with attitude.

The moment the thunderous applause began to die down, Harley stepped forward and broke into a breathtaking opening blues improvisation that led us into a leisurely four-minute rendition of the tune he had written. His voice sounded aged and authentic, having acquired the sandpapery edge of an eighty-year-old Delta bluesman while he was still in his twenties. Drinking Jack Daniel's had helped. Harley finished with a rousing blues flourish on his guitar, and when the applause died down, the band went into its soft background riff while Harley began introducing "To Love Somebody."

"Thank you, *khob khun mahk*!" Harley called out, letting his guitar hang loose as he *waied* to an audience that spread out before us as far as we could see. He pulled out a bandana and wiped the perspiration from his forehead before he continued, alternating between English and Thai. "You're a great audience. That last song was a little number I wrote called 'Hungry Sinner Blues.' The band would like to dedicate our next number to Janis Joplin."

Some of the audience broke into respectful applause. Harley continued, "We feel very close to her, her band, which is an inspiration to our band, and to her music. Brendan, our drummer, had a band back in Boston called Stonehenge Circus, who opened for Janis when she performed there with Big Brother back in 1968.

"In my case, Janis and I go all the way back to 1963 when she first came out to San Francisco from Texas."

"San Fran!" shouted the audience. "Free speech!" They continued chanting, "San Fran! Free Speech!" a few more times.

Harley held up his hand, and when the audience quieted down, he cracked a smile. "Yeah, San Francisco was pretty freaky back in 1963. And Janis was another freaky young folk singer. But when my brother invited her to sit in with our band, suddenly, before our eyes, she became a *blues* singer. She never forgot that, and when she learned I was going into the U.S. Air Force, she promised me a job when I got out. I never really got out, though, and on the morning of October 5th, 1970, I got an emergency phone call from my brother back in the States. Janis Joplin was dead, down in Los Angeles, all alone in a hotel room."

The band began to bring up our volume, getting ready for Harley to jump in. He glanced off into the wings, making eye contact with Mali, and continued, "I'd also like to dedicate this to a beautiful woman who came with me all the way from Ubon—my lovely fiancée, Mali." After some polite applause, he continued, "I can't think of a better song to play in the memory of Janis Joplin than a tune written by a couple of Australians, recorded by Janis in America, and performed for you tonight by our very international band, Domino Theory…"

The audience applauded wildly once again at the name, a chorus of voices calling out "Domino! Theory!"

"…here in the beautiful, free country of Thailand!" shouted Harley.

"And about to get even freer!" a male voice proclaimed, the audience applauding energetically in response before quieting down when Harley leaned into the microphone and began singing "To Love Somebody."

I could have sworn I felt someone's warm breath on the back of my neck. It gave me a cold shiver and a powerful sense that Tukada's spirit was caressing me. Harley and the band finished the first verse and moved on to the refrain, with the Sparrows singing behind him in full, rich four-part gospel harmony, "*You don't know what it's like,*" singing it a second time, and then, perfectly, everybody stopped while Harley sang, "*To love somebody.*" The answer from the horns was divinely inspired, or at least cosmically inspired by Janis's blues band. They repeated the line and the response, and then Harley finished with, "*The way I love you.*" The audience sat in rapt silence as Harley sang the second verse.

I didn't dare close my eyes, but I felt Tukada anyway, warm, sitting behind me, pressing herself close, her hands on my chest, riding with me on my bicycle through the back streets of Ubon. And then I *saw* her, sitting three rows back in the audience, her navy work shirt tattered and bloodstained. Maybe it was the Valium or the joint we smoked before we went on. Maybe it was because I was tired and it was dark, but I missed a cue. My eyes had played tricks on me once again, the way they used to when Dah was still alive and disappeared for days at a time, and I would see her mirage at a crowded market or in a dark nightclub. I don't think the audience picked up on it, but I knew I'd screwed up, and I knew that Marcos knew.

It hadn't bothered Mali, who stood in the shadows at the side of the stage, tears trickling just enough on her cheeks to glisten from the spill of the lights that were illuminating the band. Watching Mali so fully present in our moment of glory made my heart ache even more for Tukada. Harley, the hardest of the hard, was allowing the fullest measure of his closely guarded tenderness to reveal itself before this throng of strangers that he wanted in some primal way to touch, to be his friends. Marcos, Angel, Kae, and I had grown bored with our own music, jaded by too many nights of smoky clubs and jabbering, inattentive audiences. Tonight though, Harley touched even us. Ackerman took an incredible staccato sax solo, his fingers flying over the keys before Harley brought us back to an improvised version of the first verse, and our ragtag band and elegant backup singers ended in a flourish that brought the audience to its feet.

We had run over our one-hour slot, so Marcos started us right into our reprise of the "Sympathy for the Devil" background riff while he introduced the band members one more time. And then, exactly as we had rehearsed it, the singers harmonized on a drawn-out *"Hope you guessed our na-yame."* Marcos cried happily, "Good night! Good night and thanks for coming out to hear Domino Theory! See you again next year!" And we ran offstage to the chanting of "Domino! Theory! Domino! Theory!" and the sweetest, loudest applause I had ever heard.

The student master of ceremonies came out, obviously having a good time himself, and asked in Thai if the crowd wanted to hear some more. We got an enthusiastic "Yes!" and out we came for my arrangement of "Gimme Some Lovin'," filled with jungle drums played by me and lots of other percussion—congas, bongós, maracas, clavés—played by Woody and the horn section. The Sparrows were spot on once again, backing Marcos on the refrain, *"Gimme, gimme some lovin' ev-er-y day!"* While the crowd sang along with them, dancing and flailing their arms ecstatically, I began to feel a rumble mixing with the music, growing stronger, bleeding through.

And suddenly it began happening. *I see Prasert pushing through the crowd, far back at first but advancing steadily toward the stage. Several of his compadres follow, and as they fire their AK-47s at random, the crowd reels in horror, splattered with droplets of blood, a cloud of scarlet vapor hanging in the air. Tukada pushes toward her brother but trips, pulls herself up, and then disappears under the crush of panicking students. A police helicopter appears above, firing at random into a crowd that quickly becomes a crimson sea of bodies. Prasert shoots back. He's hit by a stream of return rounds and bright tracers,* and then, just as suddenly, I snapped out of it.

It was a TV news helicopter flying overhead. I must have been playing drums on autopilot because the crowd was still dancing joyfully, reaching a frenzy by the time the song built to a final crescendo of pounding, primal percussion and hypnotic repetitions of *"Gimme, gimme some lovin'!"* They cried out for more, but I was wilting fast, dripping with sweat from the heat, from exertion, and from hallucination-induced anxiety. I saw Marcos hesitate a moment thinking about the Bo Diddley number we had in reserve and was relieved as hell when he answered, "We love you, Thammasat University! See you next year!"

We fled the stage for real this time. The rest of the band was exhilarated. I was stunned and wanted to curl up behind my drums, but they were already being moved offstage. Feeling vulnerable amid stacks of speakers and a jungle of scaffolding, with banks of Fresnel lights hanging precariously overhead, I chased after Harley and Mali.

Marcos had managed to get some business cards printed up that afternoon while the girls were primping and the rest of us were taking our siestas. We had seen him circulating backstage before we went on, passing a few out. The people at the dimmer board had scarcely brought up the house lights and the stagehands had barely finished clearing off our equipment to make room for the last band when we spotted Marcos, already off in the wings on the other side of the stage having a lively chat with a couple of producer types, one in a porkpie hat, the other wearing shades.

We started packing up our equipment, trying to keep it sorted from the other bands who were coming and going. "What the hell was in that ganja you were passing around?" I asked Woody.

"Who knows? It came from Papa-sahn."

"Well fuck him—it started making me hallucinate."

"I guess he mighta cut it with some opium."

"That's reassuring. And you're sure it wasn't LSD?"

"Did you ever think maybe you're just crazy, Leary?"

"All the time, Shahbazian. Except over here the line between insanity and reality is pretty blurred."

Marcos walked towards us with a big smile on his face. "Gather 'round, everybody!"

We huddled around our ever-hustling leader, and he announced, "It looks like Domino Theory has *two* producers interested. They want to come out to Ubon and hear us again and bring some executives from their companies. Not bad for a couple of days' rehearsal!"

We applauded Marcos and gave each other a bunch of hugs and soul handshakes. The Sparrows were jumping around like high school cheerleaders before they went back up to the dorm to change into their traveling clothes and the rest of us finished packing. I noticed a couple of older Thais who seemed a little out of place standing off in the corner of the backstage area, trying to look casual in Hawaiian shirts. Not paying much attention to them, I turned to Harley. "You told me about going to school with Carlos Santana in Stockton, but did you really hang out with Janis Joplin?"

"I may have embellished a few things, but she did sit in with my brother's band once. I know your band in Boston didn't open for her, but you did open for Hendrix and the Critters and the Yardbirds. Close enough. Nobody here's gonna be sendin' a private investigator to San Francisco to check out my bullshit."

"Then what are those two hard-looking dudes smoking cigarettes back in the corner up to?" I asked in jest.

He laughed. "They do remind me a little of the plainclothesmen who picked me up at Indian Joe's."

Baker and I and the rest of the guys packed up the last of the equipment and loaded it onto the bus that was going to take us back to Hualamphong Station. The girls were still upstairs changing, so we decided to duck into the downstairs men's room to wash up and put on our new Thammasatstock T-shirts for the train ride back to Ubon. Inside, we took off our sweaty dress shirts and splashed a little water under our arms and on our faces. "So this is the big time," I said.

"This is Thailand, man. Nothing is big time. I may love it here, but it ain't gonna be big time until some Vegas-Macao gangster types put in a couple of casinos and Frank Sinatra and Sammy Davis Jr. show up."

"Bob Hope doesn't count?"

"That whore? He'd play anywhere."

"If this isn't the big time, why are we making the evening news every night back in the World?"

"That's Vietnam, man. Nobody's ever heard of Thailand. Tricky Dick's a smart dude. He doesn't *want* anybody to hear about Thailand."

We had just finished buttoning up our shirts when we were interrupted by the sound of someone clearing his throat. Our two undercover types from back stage had decided to join us. They proved us to be smarter than we wanted to be, pulling out their badges in a way that also showed they were packing heat under their flowery shirts. The lead detective spoke impeccable English. "Very successful concert, boys."

We could barely say thanks before the pleasantries were over. "Why do you call this band of yours Domino Theory?"

"We don't have a clue. Our Filipino bandleader made it up," Harley answered, a little impatiently for someone who had just visited a Thai jail.

"Are you aware that Thammasat has many students who give the Thai government problems?"

"I'm afraid we're not very well informed about Thai students or their politics," I answered, creeped out by both my ignorance and by memories of Prasert and the Issan Liberation Front. "I think our leader was just trying to make fun of bigots in America and on our base who don't think people of different races can work together."

The other detective made a few notes. "Clever answer," said his boss. "Full of the idealism of youth. However, I wouldn't suggest you try to put a band together with a Thai, a Vietnamese, a Burmese, and a Chinaman." The partner asked him something in staccato Thai, the lieutenant answered, and they both had a little laugh.

"You'd have to call them Yellow Peril." Marcos had slipped in quietly and had been listening by the door. With an air of diplomatic immunity, he walked over to the sinks, turned his back on the proceedings, and began cleaning up.

The lead detective didn't seem to enjoy someone else making the jokes. "We understand that four of you are in the U.S. Air Force."

"That's affirmative," Harley responded.

"Are you aware that there are many students on this campus who want all American troops out of Thailand?"

I jumped in. "As I said, lieutenant, we're very poorly informed about Thammasat student politics, but they sure seem to like American *music*. And unlike the Issan, nobody was shooting at us."

Marcos, who was once a Navy brat, stage-whispered, "You only have to give them your name, rank, and serial num—"

"Surely the four of you serving in the United States Air Force realize that the Domino Theory is part of the foreign policy being carried out by the Thai and American governments since the Eisenhower administration. You wouldn't be mocking your own government and the Thai government that has been such a gracious host, would you?"

It was my turn to be impertinent. "Do you seriously believe the Thai government would collapse because of how our Filipino bandleader names a rock 'n' roll band?"

"Of course not. But important people may be displeased." He and his assistant both made a few notes.

"Next difficult question," purred Marcos, combing his thick black hair.

"Can you explain the meaning of your song about the prin-cess and the dragon?"

Harley answered. "It didn't mean a thing. Leary here was making fun of horror movies."

"Why was nobody laughing?"

"Too many words," answered Marcos with mock sincerity, smacking me on the back of my head. "I told you there were too many words in that tune."

"There are many students in Bangkok who have studied English since they were children. They are quite able to understand the words to your songs, perhaps *too* able. The Thai government is concerned there could be an encoded message in the lyrics. We have never heard of this song before. It sounds to us like a coded message from someone in the Issan to someone in the audience here."

"That would be impossible," I replied, "I wrote that song back in the States almost two years ago."

The lieutenant spoke again to the sergeant and made a few more notes. "Who is the Devil in the first song you played and then played again many times, your...how do you say?...theme song?"

"That was actually our third song," said Marcos, "but who's counting."

"The Devil means all of us," I interrupted. "Everybody's got a little good and a little bad in them, don't you think? It's what the Lebanese philosopher Khalil Gibran writes about."

"This is a Buddhist country. We don't give much thought to Lebanese philosophy. There are many people here who would not agree with this 'philosophy.' They would point to *arahants* living in our monasteries and to our beloved king. They believe that the king and our many monks are models of virtue. And you're saying they are partly evil, or that they are devils? We are a tolerant people, but you should think especially what effect your music has on our young people. Especially at a university where there has been so much trouble with students disrespecting authority. It's true, these young people get very excited about your rock music. But you wouldn't want them to misunderstand your songs, would you? You wouldn't want them to think you wanted them to revolt against the authority of the Thai government, would you?"

The sergeant muttered something softly to his boss, who turned back to his captive audience and smiled. "Did you notice how the mere mention of San Francisco was enough to incite these students? Are you aware that Rong Wongsawan, the writer who inspired the Free Speech Movement here at Thammasat has lived in self-imposed exile in San Francisco since 1962?"

Harley just about lost it. "Listen, Lieutenant, I don't know jack about Rong Wongsawan or any other Thai writers. The only thing I see people reading in Ubon are movie magazines. But I do know I've been putting my life on the line for years so your government doesn't get overrun by the North Vietnamese and their cohorts in Laos in Cambodia."

I cut in. "People like Sergeant Harley fly night after night on dangerous missions over Laos. We just play rock 'n' roll to relax. We never think about the words because they never make sense. Look at the Beatles: 'Lucy in the Sky with Diamonds,' 'I Am the Walrus,' 'Strawberry Fields Forever.' What do they mean? And the American song we played tonight, 'Da Do Ron Ron.' That doesn't mean anything at all. They're just good for dancing, that's all."

The lieutenant put away his notebook and his assistant followed suit. "I think that will be all for now, gentlemen. Thank you for chatting with us. I hope I made myself perfectly clear—about how you don't want to upset your Thai hosts while you are guests in our country." They started to leave. "Oh, I almost forget. May we see your work permits? We understand you may be coming back here to Bangkok to record an album."

Marcos reached into the valet pack he had hung on the mirror. He actually had his work permit with him and handed it over. "I wasn't aware American Air Force people needed work permits," he said.

"They do if they're working off their base." The detective turned to Harley and me. "May we see your military I.D. cards?"

They looked them over, chatting softly in rapid-fire Thai, after which the sergeant pulled out his notebook to make another entry. "Harley Baker? Didn't we read a report from Ubon about the arrest of a Harley Baker for black marketeering?"

"Did the report say he was released?" asked Harley.

"I don't recall," the Thai detective answered.

"It must have been the other Harley Baker. It's a very common name in America."

"You're a funny man, Sergeant Baker. Almost as funny as your Filipino friend. In fact, my partner and I enjoy your humor so much we're going to let the permit go this time. The concert is over. But no more performing in Thailand without proper papers. There are too many fine musicians here who are out of work. And they are musicians who know that Thai people want to hear love songs—sad love songs with words that make *lots* of sense."

We watched the two policemen turn and leave and waited a moment before saying anything. "Can you believe that?" grumbled Harley. "Who the hell ever tried to make sense out of rock 'n' roll lyrics?"

"Only people with way too much time on their hands," I sympathized.

We headed out to join the rest of the band for the ride to the station. "Nobody in their right mind tries to make sense out of rock 'n' roll lyrics," said Marcos cheerfully, confident that *he* at least was going to be recording in Bangkok in the not too distant future. "Next thing you know, that detective will be saying Black Sabbath is into devil worship," he said, slapping us on the back and climbing onto the bus.

"Where you been this time?" Mali asked Harley when he sat down next to her.

"You wouldn't believe it, but I'll try to explain anyway," said Baker as we drove off slowly into the snarled traffic of Bangkok.

When we finally pulled into Hualamphong Station, the night train to Ubon was a welcome sight. With no student roadies to help us, we pushed our equipment out to the baggage car on a trolley, loaded it up, and boarded the train. Shahbazian and Ackerman were so exhausted that they dozed off sitting upright before the train left the station. I wanted to join them, and as soon as the train was under way I asked the conductor to pull open the berths. Within the hour everybody was asleep, including me. Drained, the euphoria of the concert dissipated and the paranoia of my hallucinations still lingering, I fell quickly into a deep, dreamless sleep sweetened by gentle rocking along the endless miles of railroad track that took us back to Ubon.

As dawn broke, my traveling companions started waking up one by one and going off to the lavatories to get cleaned up. At the stops at Huay Thap Than and the bigger town of Si Saket, old women along the side of the tracks were selling fresh fruit and baked goods, food and money passing wildly through the open windows even before the train had come to a halt. We picked up bananas, mangoes, and pastries for breakfast, none of us spending much more than the Thai equivalent of a quarter, and washed it down with coffee that the porter wheeled through, his timing perfect. In Ubon we managed to fit all our equipment into three taxis for the ride back to Harley's bungalow. To the disappointment of the horn section, Sergeant Sagittarius was there right on time, waiting to drive home the new, improved Chirping Sparrows. Kae and Angel flagged down a baht-bus, returning home from our Bangkok triumph the same way they had come out to the station.

Marcos ran over to Sagittarius. "The band may have landed a record deal. Do you think you could set up a showcase for us?"

"*Pleeeease!*" begged Annie Kim and the rest of her Sparrows.

"How can I say no to that?" said the sergeant before he pulled away in his open jeep, looking more like a man heading for the beach than back to an Air Force base at war.

I dropped off my drums at Harley's and jumped back in the cab, eager to get home, eager to sleep in for the rest of the morning. I had no sooner stripped down to my undershorts and slid under the sheets than I heard my door creak open. "I miss you," said Lek, crawling in next to me.

"I wish you could have been there. I thought it would be a mess with too many musicians and too little rehearsal, but it turned out great. And guess what?"

"What?"

"Some Thai record producers are coming out to hear us in Ubon!"

"For sure, I not miss dat!"

I gave her a little kiss. "Mali came to Bangkok with Harley at the last minute. I should have asked you to come too."

"I couldn't, Bren-dan. I had to work, but still I miss you." She snuggled a little closer and put her hand on my chest.

"Why did you have to go back to work so soon? Couldn't you at least have waited until Tom's money ran out?"

"My father is sick, Bren-dan. Tom send enough to pay my rent, but he don' send enough for medicine."

"Why don't you study at AUA and get a job on the base?"

"You have a good heart, Bren-dan, but you make everything too difficult. For me to learn to read and write English and work on base, it take too long. War will be over." She got out of bed and re-wrapped her sarong. "Why can't you make me your *tii-rahk*? I can do dat right now, not have to go work bars. Don' worry, you can still marry your *farang* girlfrien' back in Sa-tates. I won' stop you." She gave me a teasing smile as she left the room. "Really, Brendan. I promise—*jing-jing*."

The moment she closed the door, something began going terribly wrong for the second time in as many days. The high of intense rehearsal, taking a road trip, performing for a big audience—it all came crashing down. Lying in bed alone I yearned for Danielle and ached for Tukada and almost called Lek back just to have somebody to hold and then hated myself for feeling those feelings and soon was depressed as hell. I thought about getting out of bed to meditate, but I was too depressed to even try. Instead, I lay there, wanting to sleep but kept awake by my racing mind. I started ruminating about Danielle, wondering where she was, what she was doing, wondering why she hadn't written for a couple of days and then realizing I hadn't been to the post office in days. When I finally got Danielle out of my mind, I started obsessing about the band and how it was all a pipe dream, how Ackerman was due to rotate out in a couple of weeks and how Sugie Bear, Woody, and I were getting short, which meant we would be getting orders of our own to return Stateside. A record contract was a pipe dream that Marcos might pull off someday—for him and the Chirping Sparrows—but most of us would be long gone, and like the police lieutenant said, there were plenty of good musicians back in Bangkok eager to take our place.

Security Clearances and Miss Pawnsiri

Monday turned out to be a busy day, full of surprises, most of them bad. I had barely sat down at my desk in the orderly room when the phone rang. It was Harley.

"Check this shit out," he said. "When I showed up for work this morning, there were a couple of OSI investigators waiting for me. I kinda hoped your friend Jack Wu might be with them, but no such luck. They started out debriefing me in Della Rippa's office, which gave Grouchy Bear a chance to tear me a new asshole for messing with the black market when I was already drawing staff sergeant pay, flight pay and hazardous-duty pay. He especially tore into me for selling electronic equipment.

"'Sir,' I told him, 'with all due respect, I thought Joe was using the stereo equipment for his new club. I had no way of knowing he'd told twenty other suckers the same story.'

"The OSI dudes took me over to their facility for further debriefing, and get this—in the process of answering what seemed like the same questions over and over, I learned bit by bit how a Special Forces B-Team stumbled across a cave up on the Bolaven Plateau where a Pathet Lao cadre was converting Sansui 5000s into field radios. The Green Berets did some interrogating and then transferred the prisoners to Ubon for an extended visit with the Wolf Pack's branch of the OSI. It's looking like every one of those Sansuis came from Ubon province."

All I could say was, "Damn!"

"And get *this*! Before they let me go, they informed me they were lifting my fucking security clearance and grounding me, at least until they do a little more investigating into my connection to Indian Joe."

"Link has tried to get mine lifted—but you? That's ridiculous!"

"But wait, it gets worse! They pulled my BX ration card. Try explaining *that* to Mali."

"At least they won't be able to blame you if any more black-market Sansuis turn up."

An hour later, it was my turn. Link sent me over to see Dr. Lioci. "Heard your band played at a concert in Bangkok last weekend. How'd it go?"

"Traveling by train was a little exhausting, but we did a one-hour set that went great."

"Glad to hear it." He put his stethoscope to my back and chest, asked me to breathe deeply a few times, then had me follow his finger left and right, up and down without moving my head. Satisfied, he made a note on his clipboard and smiled wryly. "If you're well enough to play drums in front of ten thousand college kids, you're well enough to resume flying. Good luck."

I no sooner got back to the orderly room than Link sent me to see Captain English. "Congratulations, Leary. Your year's almost up, which makes you a short-timer now. Advance orders just came in for your next assignment," he said, handing me a manila envelope.

I opened it up. Instead of Aerospace Audiovisual Service Headquarters back at Norton Air Force Base in California, it said: Weapons Development Test Center, Eglin Air Force Base, Florida. "What the hell?"

"Needs of the Air Force, Leary. Except there's been one other change. Your assignment has been pushed back two months. We can't let you go until we get at least one more cameraman in here to fill the slots left by Cooper, Guttchock, and Spitzer. More 'needs of the Air Force,' I'm afraid."

"Is there anything I can do to get this changed? My fiancée's in California."

"You can talk to Sturbutzel over at CBPO, but you know the answer. 'Needs of the Air Force come first.'"

Link was behind this, I was certain, but before I could finish closing the door to English's office, my nemesis glared up at me from his lair across the hall, looked me up and down, and spewed, "You can't imagine how much it pisses me off they're keeping you here an extra day."

Once again Link left my head spinning. Did he want me dead or just out of his sight? Maybe he was part of a cabal who added something to my records forbidding my return to AAVS headquarters. I wouldn't have put it past Colonel Sandstrom, the old B-52 bombardier, to send a known peacenik off to photograph the detonation of prototype bombs, bullets, and missiles right next door to Hurlburt Field, where Spectre's ghouls-in-training practiced killing trucks, not far from the huge Naval Air operation at Pensacola. Then again, there were so many commissioned and non-commissioned officers I had pissed off in my short career that it could have been anyone.

I didn't think it was possible, but my malaise took a nosedive. I'd had enough of the Vietnam War and all the other little wars we were fighting, but I couldn't stand the thought of going to Florida and helping to develop bigger and better bombs, either. I had to get to Norton, and so I took English's advice and headed over to CBPO.

"Nobody's got it in for you, Leary," Sturbutzel explained. "There's a slot open and the Air Force needs you to fill it. The only way you can get out of it is to extend here for a year. It's a crap shoot, but something might open up later for Norton."

I thought long and hard that afternoon about deserting and traveling to Bangkok on my Canadian passport, but I panicked that trying to get a work permit to teach English on a forged passport could land me in one of the Thai jails Harley had described all too vividly. When Liscomb stopped by later in the day, I told him about the choice of Eglin or extending. He asked me why I didn't reapply for discharge, but I was still far from being able to restate my beliefs in Buddhist terms. I wasn't flying till the following night and decided to go see Prah Samrong in the morning, hoping to sign up for some accelerated lessons in Buddhist studies.

After the hellacious day I had spent on base, it was a pleasant surprise to find Miss Pawnsiri waiting for me before class at AUA. "My sister give me your message. Can you come for lunch with my professor this Saturday?"

"I think I'd enjoy that very much."

"We hear about your band in Bangkok. My friends tell me you very good!"

"Word sure travels fast."

"Now that I know you are a musician, I especially hope you can hear me sing sometime."

"I'm not really a musician—I'm just a drummer. But I would like to hear you sing. And I hope you can hear my band the next time we play."

"I think that would be very exciting," she replied. Other students were drifting in and taking their places in the classroom, chatting softly among themselves. "I guess I better take my seat. Saturday about noon?"

"I promise. This time for sure!"

I went to see Prah Samrong early the next morning. When I asked him for help preparing my new application for discharge, he surprised me, asking me to give more thought to staying in Thailand. He knew of some airmen with Thai wives who had extended for years. It reminded me of Harley—except, unlike me, Harley thrived on combat. Samrong surprised me again, turning my thoughts on their head and helping me see that it could actually be an act of compassion for me to stay right where I was. I'd be sparing some other sucker from having to take my place, even if it was that slimeball Ron Cooper, whose late-onset fear of flying got me sent out as a combat cameraman and kept him on the sound stage back at Norton, but especially if it was someone Stateside with a wife and kids.

Before I left, I mentioned how thoughts of Tukada were still coming up, triggering feelings of guilt and sadness. He told me to keep working on learning how to "just observe," watching whether it was something coming from outside or from within that triggered the thoughts, watching if the thoughts were triggering feelings or sensations or deeper emotions, and watching how, no matter how long it took, it all eventually went away. "Learning to step outside yourself, to develop a witness consciousness, can be a powerful kind of mindfulness."

"What about when I'm not thinking about Tukada? There are times when every sound distracts me, breaks my concentration, makes me angry."

Samrong smiled. "Make the sound part of your meditation. When a noise distracts you, you can simply note to yourself: 'sound.' Observe if the sound brings up a feeling and notice how both the sound and feeling arise and disappear. Note how like all other phenomena, the sounds and feelings are pleasant, neutral, or unpleasant and note how we can lessen our suffering by neither grasping at the pleasant, which is like trying to grasp water, nor trying to avoid all unpleasant sounds, which is like trying to stay dry in a rain storm. And then bring your attention back to your breath. Or you can make sound the object of your meditation. Notice how—like thoughts, feelings, and other body sensations—sounds continue to arise and disappear, one after another like clouds passing in the sky. With practice, you can hear an ant's footsteps. By learning how rare it is to find complete silence, you can learn to accept all the sounds that fill our lives."

"What can I do other times when my mind still seems to be racing? I keep worrying about the future—how I'll pay for film school and if I'll find a job when I get out. And I keep worrying about the present—about flying combat again and having a first sergeant who has it in for me."

"*Oh-hoh*, Monkey Mind!" laughed Samrong. "The Buddha says that when we begin to awaken, we discover that the mind is full of drunken monkeys, dozens of monkeys jumping around, screeching, chattering, clamoring for attention. When we suffer in ignorance, we don't even know they are there. One of the great riddles of mindfulness, once we begin to become aware of our true nature, is that we must refrain from fighting these drunken monkeys or trying to banish them from our thoughts. That will only make them persist! Instead, we can use meditation to calm our mind and, over time, to tame the mind monkeys gently, like teaching a baby or training a puppy."

My trust in Samrong was continuing to grow. "How does someone who isn't born here become a Buddhist?"

"You've already begun by reading and by practicing meditation. But for a serious lay person, you can take the Five Precepts—to refrain from taking life, to refrain from stealing, to refrain from sexual misconduct, to refrain from unskillful speech, and to refrain from intoxicants."

"'Sexual misconduct'? I don't quite understand..."

"In Thai culture, in its crudest form, it means for a man not to have relation with a married woman. In its more refined form, it means to avoid promiscuity, to only be intimate with someone you love deeply. It also means, when a woman visiting monastery, to respect the monks' vow of celibacy and avoid all suggestive speech and behavior."

"And unskillful speech?"

"It is good to reflect deeply on all the precepts. Skillful speech at its simplest means not to gossip and tell lies. But it also means to refrain from speaking the truth if it is hurtful. This involves what some Western philosophers might call situational ethics. Like meditation, practicing just the five basic precepts takes practice."

"I'd like to try. How do I 'take' the Precepts?"

Samrong had me make the request by repeating it after him as best I could in Pali. And then he asked me to repeat the Five Precepts as he recited:

> *Panatipata veramani sikkhapadam samadiyami*
> *Adinnadana veramani sikkhapadam samadiyami*
> *Kamesu micchacara veramani sikkhapadam samadiyami*

Musavada veramani sikkhapadam samadiyami
Surameraya veramani sikkhapadam samadiyami

"For a soldier, these precepts can be difficult. For now, use them the way the captain of a ship navigates by the North Star. You don't have to reach the star for it to guide you on your journey." And then he had a final thought. "You know, Khun Bren-dan, because you weren't part of your friend Miss Tukada's family, you never got a chance to say goodbye. You did not go to her funeral. You never saw her body cremated and her ashes spread. In a few weeks, on the last day of our Songkran Festival celebrating the Thai New Year, some local villagers have asked me to lead a Bangsukun Atthi ceremony, a memorial service in sacred memory of the dead. Usually we do this to honor our ancestors, but if you can bring some relic belonging to Miss Tukada, it can be a way for you to pay your final respects to her as well."

The conversion of Spectre's AC-130s to "Cadillac" gunships was running behind schedule, with enough glitches in the video system for the 601st to still be sending out motion picture cameramen to photograph a lot of the action. Washington had been so overworked that Harwell had to be called back from a temporary duty assignment—TDY—at Danang to back him up. Needless to say, when Dr. Lioci cleared me to fly, it was going to be with Spectre whether I liked it or not. I didn't like it one bit.

Tuesday night I felt doomed. With Harley grounded, I was going to have to go out on a gunship operation for the first time without him along as my personal guardian angel. The weather was nasty, the moon hidden in a thick overcast, which could have made for a dull night, except word from In-tell had it that a lot of trucks were on the road. We kept looking and could only chase down a couple, traveling alone, until finally, late into the mission we found a convoy using one of the minor arteries. We encountered little resistance taking out fifteen trucks in the kind of fiery blaze that I once thought I had grown inured to. As the trucks tried to pull off into the jungle canopy, however, I was filled with dread that triple-A was going to open up on us any minute. And then my dread turned to nausea. From the garbled, confused chatter on the headsets, I realized we had inadvertently shot up four elephants.

"What's eating you?" one of the gunners asked me on the ride in from the flight line.

"The goddamn elephants. I like elephants. When I was a kid, I saw them with Ringling Brothers and they were *smiling*. They're smart. Their babies are smart."

The gunner gave me a hard stare. "They were under the goddamn trees, for Christ's sake. On the infrared sensors they looked like trucks. The IR operator made a positive ID."

"With all our fucking American know-how, you'd think we could tell an elephant from a supply truck."

"There's a war going on, Leary. The North Vietnamese would shoot us down without batting an eye if they had the chance. Their amateur cousins over here in Thailand just got done shooting up your bicycle race. Don't forget that."

Liscomb stopped by the ComDoc ready room the next day and asked me how it went with Samrong. "Intriguing," I replied. "He's got me thinking in a positive way about extending—thinking about how that might spare a married dude from laying his life on the line."

Liscomb was nonplussed at first, but after he thought about it a moment, his face lit up and he said, "You know, I may do the same thing. We're single guys. Our mothers would miss us if we got shot down, but we wouldn't leave a widow and orphans behind."

"Talking to Samrong at the monastery, my path seemed clear. That lasted until I flew my mission last night and we killed four elephants. It was an accident, but it bothered me more than when we kill people, and killing people bothers me plenty."

Liscomb understood. "You got a lot going on. Why don't you sleep on it tonight?"

I agreed, mulling it over the rest of the day and sleeping on it that night, and when I awoke Thursday morning, I had made my decision. I saw Captain English and saw Sturbutzel, the top sergeant at the assignment desk over at CBPO, and almost as quickly as Dave Murray had signed up for his re-enlistment bonus, I requested to extend my stay at Ubon for the full year left on my enlistment. I wrote to Danielle and hoped she'd understand, adding that I couldn't imagine her uprooting herself to join me at Eglin, where warplanes trained day and night using real bullets and bombs.

Friday, Lek and I went out to lunch together and she expressed new interest in starting school. It was partly that she didn't have her heart in working the bars anymore, staying at it only because she was trapped taking care of her baby and her father. Worse though, she'd had a couple of bad experiences with her clients while I was in Bangkok, one with a lifer who'd done way too much drinking and got rough, almost violent. The other was with a very straight airman who had come over to Ubon from Pleiku for a week of R&R, which Lek found a little bit strange to begin with. He was in his late twenties and claimed he was still a virgin, which she found to be stranger still. When she came out of the shower back at his hotel room, still wrapped in her towel, he started quoting from the Bible and calling her a Jezebel. She decided to pass on a paycheck and quickly called it a night, running out as soon as she could get her clothes halfway on and jumping into a taxi she couldn't afford.

When I got to work Friday afternoon, English called me into his office. "Your request to extend is going through."

"That was quick."

"We need you around, Leary. Good luck."

Over at Spectre ops, Harley was suiting up, his security clearance reinstated. "Back in the saddle again," he said as we rode the crew bus across the tarmac to the waiting plane. "They kept grilling me about how many stereos I bought. I kept telling them I'd bought two on ration cards provided by Indian Joe and they should either prosecute me or let me go back and fight the damned war. This went on for a couple of days. All of a sudden this morning they told me that because I had been so 'cooperative' with the investigation, I was cleared to fly."

"I'm glad you're back. I was afraid this might drag on awhile."

"I just thought they were running low on gunners. And then I ran into your friend Wu. He said he put in a good word for me with some of his contacts. Said you had extended, of all things, and he was afraid you might get hurt flying around in the dark all by yourself..."

Saturday morning it was hard to get out of bed, but thanks to a shot of black coffee at Mama-sahn's café I was in reasonably good shape by the time I got to Miss Pawnsiri's. Her family greeted me warmly once again, welcoming me with plenty of food and hospitality. It brought a smile to my face to see how pleased they were to have Pawnsiri's professor there as a second honored guest. Professor Natapong was pretty much what Pawnsiri promised—a personable, energetic gentleman in his forties who had grown up in a village near Mukdahan. While we ate and passed more food around, Professor Natapong chatted amiably with Pawnsiri's family, with Pawnsiri and the professor taking turns translating. He struck me as a symbol of the New Thailand my students liked to talk about when we got together after class. His family was already proud of him for being the first person in their village to ever leave the rice fields to attend college. Becoming a professor brought them even greater respect.

As lunch was drawing to a close, he turned his attention to me. "I understand you are a very good teacher, Khun Brendan."

"I think Miss Pawnsiri is being too kind, Ajahn."

"I've heard the same thing from Khun Jim."

"I'm flattered to hear that."

"Have you ever thought about staying in Thailand and teaching here?"

"That would be a great honor, professor, but right now I have plans to attend graduate school back in the United States."

"If your plans change, or if you ever want to come back to Thailand, please let me know. The way our college English department is growing, I should be able to help you."

"That would be excellent, Professor Natapong."

"And now, if you'll excuse me," he said, "I must be going. I have some things I must get done before I go to see Miss Pawnsiri sing tonight. Will you be going, Khun Brendan?"

"Miss Pawnsiri didn't tell me she was performing."

"I didn't want to ask you to do too much, Khun Bren-dan."

"Will you be performing in Det Udom?"

"No, tonight I will not be far from here. Maybe you and the professor can meet there."

"She's very good," he said. "You really should come if you can."

"May I bring some other friends?" I asked the professor.

"Of course," he answered warmly.

Pawnsiri smiled. "When we go out in the evening, we say the more people, the more *sanuk*."

"And the more food to pass around," added Professor Natapong.

Like the last time, Pawnsiri and her sister walked me and my bicycle out to Route 66. I stopped by Harley's to see if anyone there wanted to go out to a Thai nightclub on short notice and was pleasantly surprised that Harley, Mali, Jim, and Pye were all game. I stopped by Larry and Pueng's new place, but they weren't home. I managed to borrow a pencil at the noodle shop next door and wrote them a note. When I got home, Lek was hanging up some laundry to dry on the front porch. "Would you like to hear one of my students sing tonight at the Lotus Blossom restaurant?"

"I can go," she replied, "but I have to be at Sampan at midnight to meet that lifer from last week."

"You mean the one you thought was going to beat you up?"

"I see him last night at the club. He say he very sorry, he drink too much last time and he won' do again. But I wouldn't go home with him. So he ask me to meet him again tonight when he get off the swing shift. He promise to pay me double. I say okay, but only if he don' drink more than one drink and only if he treat me very, very nice."

"Can't you find someone else?"

"Of course! But maybe him *worse*. Bun-lii tol' me about big-shot contractor who used to come to Sampan. Always spend a lot of money, buy drinks for everybody, but when he took her home, he jus' want her to lie on floor naked so he can go pee-pee all over her."

"Okay, that's worse! But I still worry about you."

"Don' worry about Lek. I'm a big girl."

"You're only four foot ten! Why do you think your parents named you Lek?"

She tapped her head. "I'm a big girl in my brain. Have street smart. Maybe I bring him here, not go to his place. Maybe I keep the door unlocked. Maybe I'll call you if I have trouble."

"I guess I better be home at midnight."

She laughed her little throaty laugh and gave me a playful pat on the cheek. "Sank you!"

The Lotus Blossom, typical of Issan Thailand, was elegant in its simplicity, a garden restaurant that you entered by taking a wooden footbridge across a lotus pond. The stage was just big enough to hold a small house band, with a microphone and music stand set up for a singer. There would be four singers altogether who came up one at a time to sing an hour set. Pawnsiri would be the third, so she was able to sit with us awhile before she had to go onstage. Like the rest of the singers, she had a small portfolio of sheet music with her that she would pass out to the musicians before she performed.

Professor Natapong had brought his wife along and was sitting with a couple of Pawnsiri's classmates from the college. While we pushed a few more tables together, I introduced Harley, Mali, Pye, and Khun Jim. The professor already knew Jim, as did the students, so things were getting off to a fine start. The only negative energy I picked up on was when Pawnsiri came down to our end and I was about to introduce her to Lek. Pawnsiri had always dressed simply at school and when I had visited her family. She scarcely wore any makeup or jewelry, something that reminded me of the women in my own family back home, who were winsome enough without it. Tonight though, she was made up to go on stage, and she was smashing. She wore an evening gown made of Thai silk, a luminous mixture of golds, coppers, and oranges that covered one shoulder, demurely showing off the outline of her full breasts and voluptuous body that she usually kept hidden under loosely fitting blouses and skirts. Her long, silky hair, which had always hung simply down her back, was pulled up, held in place by a small tiara, with a few strands left in disarray, avoiding the mistake I felt many Thai women made of looking *too* perfect. She was wearing long, intricate gold earrings, a choker, and a matching bracelet, all in Laotian hill-tribe style.

"Oh, Khun Bren-dan, is this your *faen*?" she asked when I was about to introduce her and Lek. *Faen* was a funny, ambiguous new Thai word, a mixture of two English words—friend and fan, as in movie fan—that in translation could mean anything from admirer to betrothed to spouse to lover, but with an emphasis on lover. Pawnsiri and Lek *waied* and smiled at each other politely, at the same time flashing catlike glances that brought back bad memories of Lek and Tukada.

"It's hard to explain," I replied, caught off guard. "Her old American boyfriend just went back to the States. He was my best friend—*puan dii tii sut*. Lek and I are just friends—*puan taunon, mai faen*."

"I see," Pawnsiri said politely, her expression a little perplexed and a bit skeptical.

Lek looked pretty smashing herself that night, but she wore a wig to achieve an effect Pawnsiri attained naturally. She too was wearing a dress—with a high collar, puffed shoulders, and long sleeves—that was quite attractive, but it was cut to a near mini-skirt shortness, taking away a little of what might have been elegance. "We don' know yet," she blurted out. "Maybe we be *puan*, maybe we be *tii-rahk*."

"I see," said Pawnsiri, her eyes now twinkling. "Thank you for coming tonight."

Before she could head back to her seat, Larry and Peung arrived, smiling and *waiing* as they came over to our table. "This wouldn't be the Lotus Blossom restaurant by any chance?"

"It is," I replied, "and this would be my student, Miss Pawnsiri, who will be singing for us tonight."

Pawnsiri smiled and exchanged pleasantries before politely excusing herself. "I better get back to my friends so we can order."

As soon as she was gone, Lek and Peung started gossiping in Thai. The first singer was giving her sheet music to the band, which hadn't quite finished tuning up. Our appetizers started to arrive about the same time the band began playing its first tune of the night, warming up with an instrumental. When the saxophone player, who doubled as MC, introduced the young singer, the small but enthusiastic audience welcomed her on stage.

She did a couple of upbeat Thai pop songs, which brought back bittersweet memories of the New Year's Eve party just a few months earlier at Niko's, the massage emporium where I first met Tukada and where she showed up for an impromptu reunion with her former colleagues—back when I still thought I could save her. The audience loved the next couple of songs, popular tear-jerkers sung in a mixture of Thai and English, one about Bangkok and the other about a boyfriend with pretty blue eyes, the kind of songs the detective in Bangkok laughably suggested Domino Theory should start playing. Her voice was just a bit too soprano for my taste, which inspired me to give Pawnsiri a little thumbs-up.

The rest of the first set receded into the background as our main courses arrived and we began passing them around, soon passing them around again for seconds. Harley and I did some catching up with Larry in English while

Lek, Peung, and Mali chatted in Thai. Magically, two buckets of ice appeared, one for each end of the table, along with matching bottles of Mekhong, Coca Cola, and soda water. We just happened to have glasses at each of our places to pour these into, and before we had finished half our dinner, the party was beginning to laugh a little louder and enjoy itself, except Lek and Pawnsiri, who avoided making eye contact. I noticed that Pawnsiri was not putting any Mekhong in her glass of Coke, impressing me with her professionalism and self-discipline. The second singer, who was perfectly competent if a little repetitious in her selection of songs, passed pretty much unnoticed by our group. Professor Natapong went to the trouble of stopping by my end of the table to chat on his way back from the *hong nam*, smiling and asking me with a twinkle in his eye if I had reconsidered teaching at the college yet.

We had just finished dinner and had started to order some fruit and other desserts when the MC called Pawnsiri to the stage. Our group erupted in applause, and I gave her another, bigger, thumbs-up. The audience quieted and the dinner chatter stopped as the house lights dimmed. In the spotlight that fell on her, Pawnsiri, once the shyest of my AUA students, lit up the stage with her beauty, which came not simply from her appearance, but from the confident way she carried herself and from some intangible quality radiating from her heart.

I might have been biased, as were all of us, but she was good. She chose a variety of ballads and up-tempo numbers, and she chose a couple of obviously difficult songs to show off her range. Harley leaned over and said to me, "I guess those detectives back in Bangkok had a point. You can do a pretty decent show sticking with love songs—if you sing like Pawnsiri."

"She's excellent, isn't she!"

With about fifteen minutes left in the set, Lek got up. "I better get over to the Sampan," she told me. Before I could object to her leaving so early, she added, "This way I can talk to bartender, other girls, see if anybody know anything bad about my lifer."

By the time I stood up to walk her out, she had already reached the footbridge, heading for a couple of taxis waiting across the street. As she'd told me many times, Lek was a big girl who liked to take care of herself.

Sitting back down, something strange but familiar began happening to me. Maybe it had been a mistake making a third drink because I had no idea how many other times Larry and Harley had freshened it up without my noticing, a popular Thai custom that my GI friends had adopted. Maybe it was the empty seat that stared at me after Lek took off. Perhaps there was a change in the type of songs Pawnsiri was belting out, but I found myself understanding every word of the Thai lyrics, grasping every inflection. They were sad love songs indeed, eloquently written and impeccably performed, and they were making me miserable, every song reminding me of Tukada.

Fortunately, when her set was over, the houselights came up and chased away my melancholy. The last singer of the night began getting ready, handing her music to the keyboard player and adjusting the microphone before she took a seat near the stage, waiting for the rest of the band to return from a break. Pawnsiri sat down across from me in the space Lek had vacated. Her group from the teachers college beamed with approval and called out congratulations. "Didn't I tell you she was very good!" said Ajahn Natapong as he and his wife got up to leave.

Harley leaned across Peung and Larry and took Pawnsiri's hand, shaking it like a used-car salesman while Mali winced. He'd had too much to drink and was forgetting all the proper Thai manners Mali had taught him. "That was great!" he gushed. "Maybe we can figure out a way to use you on the album we've got coming up."

Once again, Harley was pushing it, turning what should have been a simple expression of appreciation into promises he had no way of keeping. I cut him off, saying, "I think we all enjoyed hearing Miss Pawnsiri sing, Harley, but isn't she a little too elegant for the kind of rowdy stuff we do?"

I turned back to Pawnsiri. "You really did sound great. There are supposed to be some record companies coming out from Bangkok to check out our band. Maybe we can have them come listen to you sing while they're here."

"You don't have to do that," she replied modestly. "But I would like to try Khun Har-ley's idea just a little bit. Can I come to one of your rehearsals?"

Before I could open my mouth, Harley answered, "Sure you can! You'll sound fantastic with the Chirping Sparrows backing you up!"

I wondered who would break the news to Annie Kim.

When I got back to Bungalow #4, I could hear Lek and her lifer back in her bedroom. Actually it was him I was hearing, making a snorting sound as he humped away, but at least I wasn't hearing anything out of the ordinary that meant Lek was in trouble. Worrying just the same, I kept the lights on, hoping enough light leaked through the gaps in our walls for her to know I was back here if she needed me. I picked up an old *Pacific Stars and Stripes* and managed, stopping and starting many times, to read a front-page article about a general at CINCPAC proudly declaring that a recent study showed there was absolutely no drug use among GIs in Southeast Asia. I was struggling to read the latest installment of *Beetle Bailey* when I fell asleep.

I woke up with Lek next to me in bed and the lights turned out. The luminous hands on my Baby Ben showed it was 3:00 a.m. "Bren-dan, you awake?" she whispered.

"I just woke up. What are you doing here?"

"I want you to fuck me. Fuck me hard like you did last time."

"Not while you're working the bars."

"You want me to *tii-rahk* you?"

"I thought Tom sent you enough money that we wouldn't have to think about that for a while. How much can I give you so you'll stay home?"

"I need fifty dollar more. Just this month, for medicine for my father."

"Okay, here's the deal. I can give you the fifty dollars if I skip a payment to my lawyer, but just for this month. And I want you studying English at AUA and applying for a real job."

"Goddamn," hissed Lek. "I not Tukada. Why you never send *her* to AUA? Why you never find *her* a job on base, huh?"

"Because I'm stupid," I replied. "I never thought of it." We lay there in silence until I fell back to sleep. When I woke up in the morning, I was alone.

27 March 1972
Dog Tags

I had been numb since the day Tukada died. In the hospital, teaching night school, back flying combat—all in a haze. Danielle became an ever more distant memory, but I was afraid to let go. Thammasatstock had distracted me for a few days, but even that was tainted by flashbacks, and once the high wore off, I realized I was still numb and content to stay that way. Thanks to Valium, it only took a single Mekhong and Coke or half a doobie to put me in a mindless buzz any time my jittery, jangly nerves started acting up.

AUA brought out the best in me. My mind remained hazy, but teaching forced me to stop ruminating and think outwardly, so I never succumbed to self-medicating before class or while I was prepping. Maybe I got it subconsciously from my dad and the FAA's eight-hour rule—no booze eight hours before a flight, which he followed religiously until they landed and the clock was reset. And even though Prah Samrong never preached it overtly, I figured out quickly enough that I also had to be clean and sober to meditate. Even with my mind lucid, however, practicing *vipassana* meditation wasn't easy for me, and I began to better understand Lek's complaint that learning to read and write English was taking too long. I sometimes feared I would never master meditation. For every sitting that brought me simple calm or blissful visions of pastel vapors, there would be others filled with physical pain or visions of apocalypse. Or I would sit for forty-five minutes paralyzed with anxiety because nothing was happening except feelings of anxiety. Yet somehow I maintained my abiding trust in Prah Samrong and kept at it.

I had friends who seemed to be looking after me—Khun Jim at AUA, Harley and Jamal at work, Marcos and Sommit in the music world, and Lek and B.J. back at the Ghetto—but I didn't know why. The only thing that had really kept me going, putting one foot in front of the other for the past year, was the expectation I'd be going back to the big audiovisual production center at Norton Air Force Base and Danielle's waiting arms. Now, instead, I was settling in to spend the last year of my enlistment alone at Ubon, faintly hoping that Danielle would still be there for me when I came home. As I depended less and less on my old fog of Mekhong whiskey, Valium, and Khon Kaen pot and managed to spend at least a few minutes every day clearing my mind through meditation, I felt a growing need to make a correction to my personnel records.

I marched into the CBPO as purposefully as I had done anything since the Air Force nabbed me. I paraded up to the desk of my old friend, Chief Master Sergeant Sturbutzel, and threw down my dog tags, which landed with a clink on the pea-green blotter. The first sergeant had been plowing his way through a foot-high pile of relocation orders. It was the hottest day yet of what promised to be a long, drought-producing hot season, and even a new ceiling fan was not strong enough to make the air-conditioning work in a corrugated steel structure that could scorch your hand on a day like this. I could imagine the sarge's mind drifting off to an equally hot day on the family farm in Mississippi, recollecting the long, neat rows he used to dig in the dark earth with a plow pulled by his favorite mule. I could imagine how on a day like this he tended to envy the mule. It took a moment for him to recognize me and for his mind to snap like a rubber band back to Southeast Asia. "Why if it ain't Brendan Leary, my favorite problem child. What in tarnation do you want *this* time, Sergeant?"

"I came to get my dog tags changed."

"And what the *hayell* is wrong with your dog tags?"

My innocent enthusiasm prevented me from being blown back a couple of paces by his searing breath. "They've got 'CATH' on them, and I'm not a Catholic anymore."

The first sergeant sat back in his oiled teak and elephant leather desk chair and lit up a cigar. The paperwork could wait. "So you've gotten to be as cynical as us crusty ole lifers, now that you've seen the world beyond the city limits of Keokuk. A lot of you boys think you're atheists when you're first sent over here, fresh out of tech school. Think you know it all. But then the base gets hit, or your plane gets knocked down, and y'all get religion real fast. Besides, son, there are plenty of Catholics who are secretly atheists."

"But I'm not a Catholic and I wouldn't want to be buried like one by mistake."

"Well then, why not make it NO REL PREF? That way, if you're wounded or feverish with malaria and decide to change your mind about this atheism business, you'll be free to choose a chaplain of *any* denomination. You'll have all your bases covered."

"But I do have a 'REL PREF.' I've become a Buddhist."

I could see his brain working up a sweat, thinking how I was a fruitcake that was going to be even harder to digest than the one his momma had sent for Christmas. The first sergeant swiveled around in his chair and leaned in close, stage-whispering, "Son, I think you been smokin' too much of that Laotian mari-ju-ana that's been goin' 'round. If you manage to get your ass shot over here, where the *hayell* do you think we'd manage to find you a goddamn Buddhist chaplain?"

I stayed firmly rooted in whatever newfound equanimity Prah Samrong had helped me develop. "Sarge, I don't need a chaplain. They've got Buddhist priests everywhere we do business over here. If I manage to get myself killed, all you've got to do is cremate me. Think how much easier a little jar of ashes will be to ship home than one of those big ugly body bags."

"The paperwork is all I care about, Leary. I don't care if they ship your damned ashes home in a thimble or a pine box—burying a Buddhist takes a Dipsy Dumpsterful of extra paperwork. And long after you're resting in peace, I'll be answering some congressman's staffer following up on your parents' irate letter. More paperwork." The sergeant stomped out his cigar and tossed the dog tags back to me. The meeting was apparently over.

Stuffing the tin chain into the back pocket of my baggy fatigue pants, I turned and walked away, deciding then and there that I'd be damned if I would die in Thailand. The curses of a thousand bar girls and a battalion of twin 37-mm anti-aircraft guns weren't going to be enough to bring me down. The double doors slammed shut behind me and the afternoon sun slapped my face as I stepped outside, which got me thinking how this might be a fine time to go downtown and find a gold chain for the little Buddha that Sommit and Vrisnei had given me when I first started flying. A little Buddha was going to do me a lot more good hanging around my neck than sitting in my sock drawer.

Flying Backwards

"Okay, boys, let's head for home. The swing shift is on its way."

Spectre 544 leveled off and began to lumber toward the Thai border, Tippy's Pizza, and some shut-eye. We had heard—late as usual—that Intell had been expecting a major offensive since January. Nothing seemed to change, though. The trucks kept coming and we kept blowing them up. "Another dollar, another day," said Harley, stepping back from the searing barrels of his twin 40-mm Bofors.

I rested my Arriflex in its open case and let my body collapse into the nest I had made for myself with my flak jacket, rucksack, helmet bag, and parachute. "Buy you a beer at the Patio when we get in?"

"You're on," he replied.

"Heads up, sir!" called the illumination operator, working as usual over the Trail as the rear spotter. "Something just flashed. They firing mortars at us, Major?"

The engines shrieked to full throttle. Major Mertons tried to get the big, clumsy bird to gain altitude, but smothering humidity clung to the gunship, making the propellers spin like jeep tires in mud.

"It's a fuckin' Strela! Fire decoy flares!"

The air outside glowed orange. *Maybe—*

"Still coming straight at us! Break and dive, sir!"

We started a hard turn so brutal I thought the plane would snap in half. Something solid emitting an eerie blue-white flame hit us from below and exploded in a short flash that melted the front two thirds of the left inboard engine, crumbling it up like one of Tom Wheeler's burning papers of red-rock residue, before it fell away into the night.

I pulled off my headset. "What the hell's a Strela?" I cried futilely to Harley over the garble of wailing turbojet engines, radio static, and rushing wind. *Who's the mouse now?* I thought, grabbing for my parachute. *Maybe they've been here all night waiting for us to let our guard down.*

"This might be the big one!" yelled Harley. As best I could make out in the darkness, he was competently tightening up his harness and clipping on his parachute. My chest pack seemed to be going on upside down and backwards. I didn't give a shit, clipping it to any metal harness ring my clumsy fingers could locate in the dark.

The gunship hung there, floating in the sky, three engines revving madly, seeming to settle down. Another explosion, muffled this time, and number one, the left outboard engine, began spitting fire. The engine exploded again and, like the tongue of a hungry dog, flames began lapping at the gash in the wing where number two used to be. The flames engulfed the entire left half of the overhead wing and spread outside along the full length of the fuselage. The fire must have damaged the rudder control because suddenly we skidded sideways like an airborne hockey puck. The burning wing dipped like a roller coaster from hell straight toward the ground, and Harley and I pitched head over heels, crashing over the 40-mm Bofors as we fell through the open side door, bounced off the molten tail, and dropped into the black night. Like a gray whale in the throes of death, the plane rolled belly up and went into a dive.

"Jesus, Mary, and Joseph!" I screamed. Both of us were bruised and burned, but our chutes were intact. They opened, and we swung beneath the canopies as if the hands of Jesus had reached down from heaven. Heaven must have been understaffed, though, because nothing was slowing down Spectre 544 as it plummeted to earth. Under the full moon, it appeared that Major Mertons and Captain Gunther might have gotten the aircraft turned right side up and leveled off, but they had lost too much altitude. Even depleted of fuel and ammo, the AC-130 scorched a thousand feet of thicket and bamboo as it pancaked into a narrow valley, its wings breaking off, trailing a river of fire behind it.

Harley and I knew we were in trouble long before we hit the ground. The fire and debris from the plane would attract local villagers or Pathet Lao or hard-core NVA regulars, and the choice would not be ours. We might have only minutes. At best we had a couple of hours. On the way down I could smell our burned uniforms and the stench of hair and flesh and blood mixed with burning jet fuel. I wasn't surprised when the ground knocked me on my ass, but I didn't seem much worse for wear than when I was first thrown out of the plane. Harley had spent years as an Air Commando in a real shooting war. When he planted his right ankle, the one he had broken a year earlier when Pigpen jumped him from the balcony at the Spectre Christmas party, it was deep in a mongoose hole. Spinning the wrong direction, Harley heard the now familiar pop. I got my parachute off as fast as I could and tried to make it inconspicuous, rolling it up and stuffing it under a shrub in the thick underbrush.

Harley's skin was white and clammy when I got over to him and helped him out of his harness. He was about to puke. Involuntarily, my own stomach churned. I needed a superhuman rush of energy. Instead, I was sinking into a bad dream. My brain was scuba diving—lucid, hyper-clear—and at the same time moving in slow motion at the bottom of a deep, dark Arctic sea. Harley was about to topple. I managed to grab him. "You wait here while I check the wreckage for any more survivors."

"We got to get the hell outa here, man," he scowled, trying to walk.

"Tomorrow, dude. I've got to get a splint on that leg, and then we've got to hide ourselves away so you can get some rest. We're in no shape right now to go on a night hike." I reached for his Bowie knife so I could start cutting up his parachute. "Where's your survival vest?"

"Never wear it. It's too damned hot when I'm humping ammo. Where's yours?"

"Never wear it. You weren't wearing yours and it was cramping my style trying to make movies. Besides, Captain Rush used to say wearing one was pessimistic."

I'd been carrying Grandpa Shepler's two-inch penknife with me for luck since I flew my first Spectre mission. Suddenly I didn't feel so bad that my little Buddha was still sitting chainless in my sock drawer. A little Buddha wasn't going to cut through nylon. Pulling out the penknife, I sliced Harley's parachute into three-foot strips and then worked a couple of sticks into his boot, laced it tight, and started binding up the calf and ankle. Right away I noticed that there was something wrong with my own left forearm and shoulder. I couldn't tell what was sprained, what was dislocated, and what was broken. What I knew for sure by the time I finished improvising a splint for Harley was that I had run out of soothing numbness. Harley felt around my left shoulder and told me to lie back. Wincing from his own injury, he managed to plant his left boot in my armpit and pulled at a forty-five-degree angle until something popped. I wanted to scream but kept it to a groan.

"Dislocated shoulder. Happened to me when I played quarterback," he said, using the last couple of cloth strips to bind up my arm, then signaled for us to head out.

Harley was a hardhead. He wanted to start walking, right now, fast. "This is the NVA up here," he snarled, "not those VC amateurs they got around Saigon. They're gonna hunt us down and blow our brains out like they did at Qu Son."

I hazily remembered something about Qu Son from the bleary day six months earlier when Harley started me on my on-the-job training. I hadn't been at Qu Son like Harley, but I remembered that it had been a mess and that a lot of people had died. Maybe this was his way of giving me a shot of *oliang,* that syrupy sweet French-Cambodian iced espresso concoction. I'm sure he was trying to heighten my awareness, not torture me. And I'm sure he meant to take more than two steps before he passed out, but pass out he did.

Sorry, I thought, concealing Harley in the shadows of a moonlit boulder. Going deeper into what still seemed like a bad dream, I knew I couldn't waste a second getting back to the wreckage, but my legs refused to obey me, only moving at half speed.

As I got closer, I choked on blasts of heat and smoke from still-burning patches of elephant grass that trailed the sheared-off wings. The tail and mid-section of fuselage I staggered through had been gutted by flash-fire with no sign of life remaining, only ugly heaps of ash and chunks of debris that I feared might have once been my fellow crewmen. What was left of the aft safety strap hung there limply, no longer attached to the rear spotter. Pushing on, approaching the stairs to what remained of the flight deck, I began feeling woozy like a kid getting high on model airplane glue and realized that any of the dried-out brush that hadn't burned yet was drenched with JP-4 jet fuel. I could smell even more fuel leaking through the fuselage walls and puddling on the floor of that forwardmost section—enough to blow what was left of the ammunition to kingdom come—and knew I only had seconds to get up to the cockpit.

Stumbling to the top of the steps, I froze. It was peaceful and quiet in a way that made my skin crawl. The tender trace of a breeze was wafting through what used to be the windshield and the steeply sloping nose of the AC-130. Major Mertons sat erect in the left seat. I began to pick him up and then stopped. Something was terribly wrong. With surgical precision, Mertons' throat had been slit by a sharp, fast-moving piece of debris. With equal precision, his face had disappeared. Captain Gunther had not maintained the same military bearing, slumping unceremoniously over the stump of the controls that had impaled him. My toes curled up and my body shivered, but I didn't have time to puke because the captain was still breathing.

With a burst of adrenalin, I threw him over my good shoulder and carried him down the wobbly stairway. I got Gunther out of the plane somehow and past the smoldering wreckage of the middle section, which was beginning to flare up again. Afraid to stop, unable to imagine what the remaining ammunition and jet fuel would do when they exploded, I walked for three-quarters of a mile until I heard Harley's commanding voice. "Forget it, man. He's dead."

And in that ink black and crimson nightmare my consciousness blurred. Pushing on through the underbrush, I spotted a small creek bed trickling towards a mountain stream. My heart pounded and my mind raced. *A way to the Mekong and home to Ubon!*

"Stay away from trails and streams," Harley mumbled.

My consciousness snapped back into focus. It was Harley's dead weight I was supporting and Gunther's body I had left behind at the rock. And Harley was right. We would be seriously deviating from standard operating procedure by trying to escape along a creek bed. Looking behind me, I could make out the irregular limestone cliffs of a karst formation only a couple hundred yards away and decided to reverse direction and head upstream. It was the limestone cliffs and the possibility of a cave that now stirred my interest.

"If there's water or easy mobility, that's where we'll find Bad Guys. You know that. Anywhere we can move, they can move twice as fast. This is their turf." Thanks to Ron Cooper and Moonbeam Liscomb, I was getting to do my jungle survival training on the job instead of at Fairchild, Washington, or in the Philippines, where Harley and the real soldiers got to go. If the son of a bitch had actually offered a plan, I would have taken it under advisement. But my gut told me the uneven cliff face was our best chance of finding a place to hide until Harley could move on his own. Then, if we didn't get ourselves shot or captured, we could let the stream lead us to the Mekong and the hallowed Thai border, provided we followed it from a discreet distance. Crawling on our bellies. Scraping off leeches with my little two-inch penknife or a stick of bamboo.

Halfway to the cliffs, we were working our way through a nasty bramble of wild tea roses at a bend in the streambed. I was soaked with sweat that felt like boric acid, searing me every time a thorn clawed at my flesh. As I lifted what looked like the last branch of the briar patch separating us from refuge, my heart began to sing. Even with Harley's dead weight dragging me down, spring returned to my stride, and I was once again the young Indian brave who ran cross-country for Newton High. I helped Harley up the embankment, threw his arm over my shoulder and spun around, ready for a final short sprint to safety. My heart stopped.

Gleaming softly under the full moon, the barrels of a couple of AK-47s were pointed directly at us. Somebody shouted staccato orders in Vietnamese, and soon we were blinded by high-intensity flashlights. A serious hard-core North Vietnamese unit—fully armed, trained, and uniformed, not a ragtag barefoot bunch of Pathet Lao volunteers—had headed for cover in the same karst formation three hours earlier when Spectre 544 began overflying the area. Now they were returning, eager to examine the wreckage and search for potential prisoners. What looked like a full platoon had us surrounded before either side had time to blink. Two young soldiers, in their teens, pointed the direction with their automatic weapons and marched us back to their artfully camouflaged shelter. An orange glow flared up in the distance followed by muffled explosions of fuel and ordnance. It didn't take the NVA search party long to figure out that Harley and I were the only survivors.

From the instant our parachutes opened, I could have kicked myself for believing Nixon's speeches about how the war was almost over. Plummeting through the night sky, I deeply regretted not paying more attention to Harley's horror tales about surviving survival school. With a fourteen-year-old pointing an AK-47 at my head, my lightweight mesh boots turned to lead. I wished I had taken notes instead of drinking Budweiser when Harley held court. At least I had *listened* to Sergeant Baker's war stories. At least I knew the score—this was a war of the psyche. Somebody in North Vietnam had read enough U.S. history to know that our greatest military success had been killing ourselves on our own soil during the Civil War. In the two great wars of the twentieth century, the U.S. had been glad to enter late. America had bled, but the rest of the world had hemorrhaged. The Vietnamese seemed to know instinctively that the American public had no taste for having its own boys killed in a protracted, far-off war. If ten Viet Cong had to die for every American they killed, General Giap had figured that into the equation.

The NVA operation in eastern Laos worked a little differently, however, thanks to the Ho Chi Minh Trail. There were few Americans operating on the ground here, and more than anyone the enlisted gunners, loadmasters, flight engineers, and cameramen flying with Spectre knew that Hanoi was playing a different game with American pilots. It was eerie how Hanoi seemed to know us better than we knew ourselves, how they knew the inflated value we placed on aviators, and how undervalued were the blue-collar grunts, whether flying or pounding the ground. Harley and I had decided long ago that if we were ever shot down and captured, our best chance of survival was impersonating an officer, Air Force regs be dammed. I wanted to live long enough to invade Bangkok one more time with Domino Theory, our work permits in order, filling up the National Soccer Stadium, shaking it to the ground. I wanted to earn a place in Thai history right up there with the Burmese sacking of Ayutthaya. There was plenty I wanted to do back in the World as well, and to do them I was prepared to play dirty and fight with the most potent psy-ops weapon I possessed—being a crazed rock 'n' roll drummer, a Ringo Starr wannabe, who never gave the press a straight answer. I hoped Harley would play along. And I wondered briefly how this was going to jibe with Prah Samrong's fourth precept—refraining from unskillful speech. I decided to worry about that later. The first precept—not taking life—was going to be a bigger challenge. Samrong had warned me that the precepts were tricky.

The convoy had stopped and Harley was barely conscious a couple hours later when a young North Vietnamese intelligence officer came over to question us. He was short and thin and nondescript other than his wire-rimmed glasses, which gave him the look of someone who had once been a serious scholar. We had already gotten a taste of Vietnamese-style psychological warfare. Unmoved by my screams, the young guards had stripped off our watches and bound our arms to bamboo poles that stretched across our backs. They were equally unmoved by Harley's splinted ankle, hobbling us with leg irons and keeping us on our feet for hours as the convoy made its way south. It was a small piece of luck, but Harley and I had been hurt badly enough that our captors hadn't thought it necessary to keep us incarcerated separately. The downside was that my jaw was swollen from the blow of a rifle butt I received when Harley and I tried to talk about Beatle press conferences in Pig Latin.

"My name is Lieutenant Duong, and I'll be walking with you for a while." A clicker signaled the column to move out. "You do not have any identification, and yet you carry printed pieces of silk saying you are *not* Americans. Do you care to enlighten us?"

"We're a couple of Czech tourists," snarled Harley, "who seem to have missed our bus back to the hotel."

Way to go, Harley! If you could lose the snarl, I thought, *giving a Beatle press conference might turn out to be amusing.*

"You speak English well for a Czechoslovakian."

"And you speak English very well for a Vietnamese," I replied. The lieutenant knitted his eyebrows. He didn't have any more of a sense of humor than our detective friends back in Bangkok. I gave him a twinkly smile anyway and pretended to cooperate. "That's Captain Baker. I think his broken ankle is bothering him."

"Like hell," said Harley, who wasn't playing along in the twinkly smile department. "We're twin brothers. Our mother was an American. She fell off a turnip truck while hitchhiking through Europe one summer and developed amnesia. When she came to, she was living in Prague with a band of gypsies."

The lieutenant nodded to our guard, who surprised Harley with a quick blow of the rifle butt. My game wasn't working. The press never treated the Beatles like this. The lieutenant looked at us hard while he lit up a cigarette. "I hate turnips," he said, taking a long pull, eyeing us carefully to see if either of us lusted for a smoke. "Are you sure it isn't *you* with the amnesia? Are you forgetting you are pilots? Have you confused your mother's 'turnip truck' with your burning gunship?"

I faked another smile. "I'm afraid you've outsmarted us, Admiral."

"You're too kind," said the young interrogator. "I'm just a lieutenant."

He flicked the almost unsmoked cigarette at my feet and took his time watching it burn before he crushed it out. He gave another nod to the guard, who raised his rifle to within a foot of my swollen jaw. "I want your name and rank—now."

I blinked. I didn't like it. I really didn't give a shit about this war. I had intended to be an innocent bystander, and now I could get myself killed by coming on too strong. Or too weak. "I'm Lieutenant Brendan Leary, Captain Baker's able-bodied sidekick. But our friends call us Batman and Robin."

Maybe it was the shattered ankle, but Harley refused to play along, snarling, "Nope. I must respectfully disagree. We're still just a couple of Czech tourists. Always were, always will be. You haven't spotted a big red Mercedes tour bus around here, have you?"

"We are prepared to treat you as prisoners of war under the terms of the Geneva Convention instead of war criminals. Even though you are out of uniform and carrying false ID."

"What do you mean 'out of uniform'?"

"We heard about the enlisted man who refused to salute your colonel—the one they call Grouchy Bear—"

"Because these were ruled 'party suits' by the Judge Advocate?" Harley stammered, glancing down at his tattered black flight suit.

"Exactly," Duong replied with a smile.

"How the hell do you know this stuff?"

"Because while you were playing at a bicycle race over at Ubon, we were fighting a war. The Thai government may be your ally, but much like Laos, Cambodia, and what you call South Vietnam, there are plenty of Thai insurgents eager to be trained and armed by the North Vietnamese Army. And they have planted spies everywhere, maybe working in your control tower, maybe doing *boom boom* with Colonel Grouchy Bear at Maharaj Massage." Lieutenant Duong savored Harley's glower before he continued. "We're quite capable of playing by the rule book, my friends, even though you seem to find this so difficult. But please. Under the terms of the Geneva Convention—your full name, rank, and serial number."

"Under the terms of the Geneva Convention," I replied, "aren't we entitled to medical care? And some sleep?"

"We are prepared to treat you as well as any of our own soldiers. My only fear is that you Americans may not be tough enough to live like a Vietnamese infantryman."

"We're plenty tough enough, Lieutenant. Or haven't you noticed we've been bombing the hell out of Vietnam?" Harley was in pain, feeling even gnarlier than when we took off under the full moon on what turned out to be a one-way hunting trip. "If you had the guts to send up your MiGs, we'd really kick your ass."

Lieutenant Duong smiled. "Why should we squander our air assets? We've already won the people's hearts and minds."

"The only battles you've won have been against the ARVN. My mother could whip the ARVN."

Duong smiled on. "And all *you've* done is bomb Indochina indiscriminately with your ships and airplanes and artillery. Your ground troops shoot wantonly. If you understood Vietnam at all, you would realize that every civilian you kill and every village you destroy drives the people further from Thieu and Ky and their ruling lackey clique. I am afraid you will discover too late that you are the new French. They were here for a hundred years and never understood our culture, and in the end they lost. They controlled our cities and made puppets of our decadent and corruptible mandarins. But the strength of Vietnam is in the countryside. The peasants could not care less who rules Saigon or Hué or Hanoi. They only cared that the French let a million of us starve to death in 1946, here in the most fertile rice-producing region in the world. Our granaries were overflowing with rice, but it was rotting, waiting in vain for French ships to take it to markets overseas. Was this the way France would liberate us from the Japanese, with whom they collaborated so willingly?

"To an Asian rice farmer, your French predecessors were complete barbarians, both rapists and whores. Now that you Americans have taken their place, I must congratulate you for one thing: it has taken you only ten years to make the kind of mess it took the French a century to create. The Vietnamese have been here for thousands of years, however. Our history will swallow you the way the steppes of Russia swallowed Napoleon and Hitler. And you, too, will retreat ignobly."

Harley was getting bored, a state in which he reached his peak of gnarliness. "Did you make this crap up yourself, or do they give you this spiel to memorize the way we train door-to-door encyclopedia salesmen?"

The interrogation officer had only the vaguest idea of what a door-to-door encyclopedia salesman was and so let the insult pass.

"How'd you learn to aggravate people so well in English, man?"

"I'm afraid we take our American enemies far more seriously than you take the Vietnamese. We study your American language and culture. We study your American history, except we study the true history, not the myth contained in your high school textbooks. You have forgotten that your Declaration of Independence was written by a slave owner. You have forgotten that your 'Land of Liberty' was stolen from Native Americans and Mexican settlers. And yet we could see the greater truth behind Jefferson's great truth—all men are truly created equal. Not just white men.

"When our time came to throw off the shackles of French tyranny, it was your Declaration of Independence that was our inspiration. You defeated a feudal king two hundred years ago to win your freedom. How sad it is today that you fight *for* the feudal class of Indochina, for the lapdogs of the French oppressors.

"You ask me why I speak English well. But shouldn't you be asking why you come to conquer Indochina without speaking Laotian or Vietnamese?

I had been lulled half to sleep, daydreaming I was back at a college teach-in. "Captain Baker speaks Thai so well that he is engaged to marry a Thai schoolteacher."

"Schoolteacher? Is that the new euphemism for prostitute?"

Oblivious to the chain on his shattered ankle and the bamboo that bound his arms, Harley tried to lunge at the lieutenant but barely flinched before he was jolted with pain. "Captain Baker is engaged to a woman of the highest character," I replied. "Her father is on the city council of Roi Et. Her mother has been an elementary school teacher there for many years. Captain Baker and I both love Southeast Asia and regret very much there's a war going on. Isn't that right?"

Harley couldn't help wincing. "Yeah, sure."

"We have plans to overrun Roi Et after Saigon falls," said Lieutenant Duong. "We'll be staging the assault out of Ubon." Duong was beginning to enjoy himself, enjoying a chance to use all his education and training to make a captive audience suffer as much as he and his men did in these tropical mountain forests. "We despise the Thais. More than the French. At least the French could sometimes fight bravely. They died well at Dien Bien Phu. All the Thais know is how to collaborate."

Harley took it personally, an insult to Mali. "The French were washed up. They'd already had their asses whipped by Germany. They couldn't even handle the fuckin' Arabs over in Algeria, for Chrissakes."

"The French were tougher than you think," said Duong, smiling smugly as we trudged behind him. "The Germans, the Vietnamese, and the Algerians—they all fought fiercely, each with different tactics, different technology, different traditions. You fought the Germans twice when they had already been depleted from years of warfare, when they fought on many fronts, their supply lines overextended. You boast of never losing a war, but you are no longer fighting Mexican missionaries or Indians armed with bows and arrows."

The Vietnamese lieutenant turned to me. "Are you sure your friend is an officer? I thought American Air Force officers were educated."

I pantomimed throwing a football as best I could with my hands tied to a bamboo stake. "Scholarship. Scholarship to play American football."

"I have heard of such things, but I found them hard to believe." And the lieutenant walked away, leaving us disoriented and exhausted.

At what I guessed to be three in the morning, the convoy pulled up for a few hours' sleep. The drivers settled down inside their cabs, and the rest of the porters and troops opened their bedrolls and slept out under the stars. Our guard pointed to the ground but made no effort to help us. The best Harley and I could manage was to slide our backs down the door panel of a nearby truck and push ourselves backwards to the truck's pair of oversized rear tires. Despite coughing up trail dust, we managed to fall asleep sitting up.

Before daybreak we were awakened roughly and shoved over the tailgate and into the back of a crude Russian truck, our leg shackles loosened slightly but our arms cinched tighter to the bamboo poles. The early morning was typical early hot season as the Vietnamese moved on down the trail—scorchingly hot and unbreathably humid by 0800, with little chance of the humidity turning into rain. An hour further down the trail we heard a sharp whistle, and the entire column melted into the triple-canopy jungle along the side of the road, within thirty seconds covered again with the camouflaged nets they were using when we were captured. Harley and I recognized the sound of an OV-10 observation plane passing overhead, oblivious to the convoy hiding under its nose. After a morning of suffocating and jostling under the canvas cover of the supply truck, we could finally begin to relax, certain now that our captors knew what they were doing, that we weren't going to be sighted by an American spotter plane and annihilated by a pack of F-4s. Miles of the trail were hidden by thick foliage, and when we came to exposed areas, we crossed quickly in small groups. At noon, when the heat and humidity had become oppressive even for the battle-hardened NVA, one of the guards took off our manacles, untied the bamboo poles, and pushed us out of the truck, jumping down after us.

I was just about to thank him when he poked his rifle barrel into my back and shoved me in the direction of a strange-looking group of bicycles, each with an elongated left handlebar, that had been loaded to capacity with supplies. I had no doubt Harley's ankle was broken and that he was still in agony. His face was gray, covered with large globules of perspiration from a nasty mixture of heat and nausea. The guard pushed him over to the supply bikes anyway. The two old men we replaced scuttled like spiders back to the truck we had been sitting in and skittered on board to ride and rest over the next leg of our trek, the most grueling of the day. The convoy moved out, Harley biting down hard on his lower lip, too stubborn to give our tormentors the satisfaction of a cry of pain as we wrangled the strange bicycles out onto the road. I felt lucky. The feeling had never returned to my left shoulder and forearm.

An hour down the trail, Lieutenant Duong joined us again. "Why are we headed south?" I asked, fearing that Harley wouldn't last another day in the mountainous highlands. "Captain Baker needs medical attention."

"Under the Geneva fuckin' Convention," Harley blurted.

"Seriously," I continued, "I thought you sent captured pilots to the Hanoi Hilton."

Duong's face brightened. "Perhaps. If you both admit you are pilots."

"Do you get a medal if we are?"

"Don't pay attention to Captain Baker, Lieutenant. He always gets like this when he goes hiking with a shattered ankle."

Duong did what we hated most, he remained silent. For minutes all we heard were the hard footsteps of our boots on the gravel road, the squeaking of our rusty bicycles, the muffled footsteps of enemy civilians in rubber sandals made from discarded tire treads, the lighter bootsteps of the pint-sized North Vietnamese soldiers, and the rumbling up ahead of the Russian-built trucks and their sputtering, smoke-belching engines.

I blinked first. "Seriously, Lieutenant, why are we headed south?"

"Don't worry. You will have the rest of the war to see Hanoi. But first, you get a very special privilege, a chance to help with a glorious offensive, a chance to shorten your own incarceration because this may be the great final victory we have struggled so long to attain. Today everybody heads south."

Harley had spent nearly a third of his life in Southeast Asia. He'd been through Tet, and it wasn't a good memory. He had trouble deciding whom he hated more—the American officers who skipped out to Bangkok, the South Vietnamese soldiers who were home on leave and didn't bother to come back, or the VC swarms who decided to commit suicide on what had started out to be the best Chinese New Year of the decade. "What the hell are you little farts up to this time?"

In Duong's extensive study of the English language, his instructors had neglected to teach him the informal term for expelling gasses of the digestive tract. It served his purposes best, both for saving face and irritating his weary captive, to once again give us the smug silent treatment before he climbed back into his truck.

For hours we pushed on. It became almost pleasant in the late afternoon after an unseasonable thunderhead built up over us in minutes and exploded. A little later, the trees thinned and we could feel a lukewarm breeze blowing in from the mountains to the north. We could catch glimpses of billowy clouds to the west that were turning into a handsome sunset. Even as the evening air cooled, however, Harley remained ashen and sweaty. I was afraid to say anything to the nervous young guard who followed us. The kid had his itchy finger on the trigger of an American-made M-16, and it wouldn't have surprised me to learn it was in AUTO, the 600-round-a-minute mode. I caught Harley glaring at it and suspected he was wondering how the hell it got into enemy hands. None of the possibilities were good.

Personally, I hated the things. High tech and flimsy. A plastic stock "to save weight." Prone to jamming. Making Colt a lot of money. The Czech rifles that American Special Forces carried weren't just for subterfuge. AK-47s were the weapons of choice among professional warriors. M-16s and A-15s, the harder-to-find Air Force model, were unpredictable, sometimes working too well, blasting off a full clip when one round would have sufficed. It wasn't like some old cowboy movie where a Zen-master Zane Grey gunslinger could shoot a pistol out of a bad guy's hand with a single shot. An M-16 with its high-velocity ammo could hit a hostile in the finger and take his whole arm off. Overkill. Or else they didn't work worth a damn, like the one Danielle's husband carried when he was fording a stream in the countryside outside of Huế. His didn't make a click as loud as a kid's cap pistol when it jammed.

It was strange, but we were almost happy when Duong looked in on us later when the trucks stopped to refuel. Sort of like seeing another American tourist when you're vacationing overseas—a welcome sight until they open their mouths. "Why such a big rush to get to the People's Great and Heroic Final Victory?" I asked.

"We have to get men and supplies to Qu Son by tomorrow night."

Harley was jolted out of his torpor. "Qu Son or Khe Sanh?"

"Qu Son. Does that name mean something to you?"

"Yeah, I've heard of it. Heard it's full of Montagnards with bows and arrows like Indians in a John Wayne movie."

"Very good, 'Captain.' Except it is now one of our favorite staging areas. We use the old American base there. Once it belonged to your Special Forces, your great Green Berets. If they only knew how much we despised those berets, how much they reminded us of the berets worn by France's Foreign Legion and the atrocities they committed. Perhaps that is why it was so easy for us to take Qu Son. Or perhaps it was because so many Montagnards, our ancient enemies, despised the Americans even more and were happy to betray them."

Harley's eyes burned with hatred.

"I'm curious," mused Duong. "Why would a pilot know about an insignificant Special Forces outpost?"

"My history might stink, but I'm a nut for geography. Never know where you might get shot down in this hellhole."

I decided it was time to change the subject. "Isn't that an M-16 your boy is guarding us with?"

Duong seemed to enjoy any direction the conversation took. "It is. Of course they're not very reliable for combat. I don't suppose I have to tell you something so obvious. Even 'pilots' must hear the horror stories. But we do like to shoot Americans with them whenever it is prudent. Very bad for American morale when your troops are found shot with their own ammunition."

A clicker signaled. Orders were given in Vietnamese, and the convoy began to move out. "I'm afraid the 'captain' will have to push on. Our old men need to rest. They will make this trip many more times. Whereas you will be relaxing in the honeymoon suite of the Hanoi Hilton in another week or two."

Duong walked back to his truck. Straining to balance the heavy load on the bicycles, we steered them back onto the dirt road. Everything around us was turning to silhouette and shadow. "I hate that son of a bitch," Harley muttered. "I hate every word out of his fuckin' mouth."

"He's a goddamn politician," I whispered. "When have you ever taken an *American* politician seriously?"

The boy guard poked me in the ribs with the gun barrel to shut me up. Body language at its finest, which got me thinking about the time out at the rifle range just before I shipped out when I accidentally slipped my M-16 into AUTO. Blew the paper target to dust. And I was what the Air Force called a marksman, I thought dejectedly.

By ten o'clock, the moon was high overhead, a near-perfect night for a forced march. The cumulus clouds from late afternoon had dissipated, and the moon was full, diffused only by the thin smoke that hung in the air, faintly stinging our eyes. The local hill tribes slashed and burned through the jungle to clear land for their mountain rice, the burning season coinciding with the killing season that would come to an end with the arrival of the monsoon rains. Harley was grunting under his breath with every step. Now that it was nighttime, I was thinking again about what to do if our column were attacked. It scared the hell out of me that we could be blown away by a ghost ship from our own unit. Harley would probably enjoy it, getting put out of his misery and taking Duong with him.

The young guard was growing as weary as we were and now walked with the gun slung over his shoulder. Watching his exhaustion gave me a fresh, wicked rush of energy. Once you got off the main trail at night, I figured Harley and I knew this area as well as the North Vietnamese did. Their advantage was in the village guides that were assigned to them. I'd seen the terrain plenty of times from the air and plenty more in the editing room. I knew a column this size would have big trouble finding cover if we got caught out in the open. They'd need every man, woman, boy, and grandfather they had to get their supplies hidden. Harley and I had a big advantage going for us if we timed our escape right. Our captors couldn't turn on their flashlights to look for us without giving away their position. The bad news was Harley. Could he give me one last quarterback scramble, far enough to get out of range of the AK-47s, before I had to start carrying him again? I might have just been dreaming on my feet, but I could have sworn I received a telegraphic communication from my redneck compadre: *Fuckin' A—do it!*

I started whistling. The sentry was too fatigued to care. Harley's half-closed eyes opened wide. I had once hated Spectre's pet song and could only say, "Sorry to hear that," when Harley told me he had written the new lyrics used by the 16th SOS. I was a blues-loving rocker from the northeast with a taste for jazz. I pretty much agreed with big band drummer Buddy Rich's assessment of country. I was allergic to the stuff. Tonight though, in the chilly mountains of Laos, the tune sounded magnificent. I led the way, to the beat of our heavy bootsteps, and Harley joined in, heartily whistling "Ghost Riders in the Sky."

That finally caught the guard's attention, but he didn't know what to do and called back for Duong. I was whistling so enthusiastically, knowing that Baker was with me, ready to give it one good shot, that I didn't notice Duong coming up from behind.

"I'm afraid we can't allow you make any noise whatsoever."

"Sorry to interrupt your truck ride, Lieutenant." We walked along for a minute in silence. "Where did you say you went to university?" I asked.

Duong was flattered in some minor way. "Patrice Lumumba University in Moscow—on an *academic* scholarship."

"Good English program?"

"Very good. Captain Baker might have enjoyed their remedial English conversation program. By the way, where did the captain go to school?"

"University of Southern fuckin' California," Harley blurted. "Put that in your Geneva Accords."

"I see your leg still bothers you."

"Got that right."

"And you, Lieutenant Leary, where did you study?"

"I started out at Holy Cross."

Duong's face showed a trace of surprise and warmth. "Really?"

"Really."

"My father went to Holy Cross. Good Catholic school. Not so intimidating as Notre Dame."

"Small fuckin' world," I said, feeling especially *un*-Catholic with sweat and dust caked on me from head to toe. I hated to see all this camaraderie go to waste, knowing that Duong would likely as not have me and Harley killed once we got to Khe Sanh or Qu Son or wherever it was they were taking us. Food rations would be precious on the trip north, and we would be getting deep into hot season. I didn't let myself wonder what I'd do if the roles were reversed.

"Sometimes, I think it's a very small world," said Duong as he slowed to wait for his vehicle to pick him up. "By the way, I'm afraid we received some bad news at our last truck stop. It seems there was no 'Captain Baker' or 'Lieutenant Leary' on any of last night's manifests. There were some sergeants by those names. If they turn out to be you two gentlemen, I'm afraid we cannot guarantee your safe passage to Hanoi. A class-conscious society like the United States of America does not value an enlisted man enough to make him a very good—what does Kissinger call it?—bargaining chip. We will have to evaluate your situation day by day. However, if you cooperate, I might be able to put in a good word for you."

Harley didn't want to cooperate; he wanted to fight. "How the hell did you get hold of our flight manifest?"

Duong climbed back into his Russian truck cab and pulled the door shut with a tinny clink. "Maybe you weren't listening. We have friends everywhere."

The lieutenant had almost earned my grudging respect, but now he was starting to get on *my* nerves. "How did you hear about this so friggin' fast?"

Duong looked down from the truck, giving me another one of his smug smiles. "Where do you think all those Sansui radios go that your friends sell so willingly on the black market? The electronics are excellent. Exactly the range we need for ground operations in Southeast Asia. I'm very proud of my father. After Holy Cross, he studied electrical engineering at MIT. Even though he is quite old now, he helped design modifications we can make in the field to turn a Sansui 5000 into a handheld radio transceiver."

"Jesus H. Christ," muttered Harley, looking sick watching Duong's truck drive further down the column. I, on the other hand, was happy as a Labrador retriever rolling in catfish to be able to cheer Baker up, whistling a few more bars of "Ghost Riders." The boy soldier pulled his rifle off his back and pointed it in my direction. Harley sensed the low hum at first, and then he heard it for sure. "You say your father was trained by those commie faggot professors at MIT?" he called to Duong, who was out of hearing range. "I guess you got that right about it being a small fucking world." He couldn't help grinning. "It's such a small goddamn world that not even your MIT-modified Sansui radios could tell you that our base at Ubon has sent the cavalry to the rescue even as you and I were wasting our breath trying to talk to each other."

Our guard was growing impatient. He was too proud to ask the interrogation officer to come back a second time. Instead, he shouted what I guessed was a Vietnamese version of "shut the fuck up!" and jammed the barrel hard into Baker's carotid artery for emphasis. Harley got the kid's drift and feigned a confident smile anyway. The kid got the last word in loud, staccato Vietnamese. But the AC-130 Hercules had banked and begun circling overhead in a pylon turn. Harley kept on smiling, which kept the young soldier steaming.

A flare exploded above us, the one Baker had been expecting. At the precise moment the young guard flinched, Harley rammed him with the bicycleload of supplies, knocking him off balance. Still smiling, Harley ripped the M-16 out of the kid's hands. The strap was wrapped around the boy's forearm, which caused the butt to cantilever across his face, breaking his nose and splitting open his forehead before Harley could pull the rifle away completely. Overhead, the gunship began firing, raining down droplets of molten lead and sending the column into disarray.

I charged full speed into the underbrush, shielding myself with my bicycle as I ran until it hung up between a rock and a hard shadow. I turned back and saw Harley fifteen paces behind me. He fired off a burst with the M-16, spraying a wide area and forcing Duong's truck to veer off to the left, but when Harley tried to spin around to join me, his heel caught in the uneven turf and he crumpled up in a heap. At the same time that Duong was jumping out of the cab of his truck, running around to the driver's side, and reaching in for an AK-47, I raced back to Harley, picked up the M-16, and shattered Duong's windshield with a well-placed shot. His driver ducked and Duong crouched out of sight, which bought me enough time to start dragging Harley back toward the undergrowth. Duong peered over the truck hood and started to take aim when a fresh burst from the Spectre minigun forced him to duck again. Harley and I disappeared from his view down a ravine and into the darkness of jungle canopy.

The air attack was vicious, an act of atonement for the sister ship that had gone down the night before. I could feel the burning anger that circled seventy-five hundred feet above us, anger that was being spewed with a vengeance at the NVA column. A second Spectre joined the attack, orbiting opposite the first gunship at the same altitude, and began lighting up the sky with its own tracers. It was a dangerous, almost reckless maneuver I had never before seen nor heard of, but the result was jaw-dropping. After blasting away an area the size of several football fields with their high-rpm miniguns, they sparkled the column with their 20-mm M-61s and used the 40-mm Bofors to ignite the lead truck's fuel tank. With a clear, bright target burning, the second AC-130 put several 40-mm rounds into the rear truck, waited for secondary explosions, and then broke off to the south.

In the midst of the chaos, Lieutenant Nguyen Hue Duong managed to drive his truck back to pick up the boy soldier with the broken nose, but the AC-130's guns smashed into the vehicle while Duong was lifting the unconscious farm boy into the back of the truck. A burst from the 40-mm Bofors tore across the hood, whose plating could not protect the engine inside, hitting the lieutenant with a piece of shrapnel and knocking off his glasses. Bleeding badly as he jumped behind the wheel, he tried the starter a couple of times, played the choke and gas pedal, turned over the ignition one more time, and gave up.

The lead Spectre commander continued to orbit while he guided in a flight of F-4 Phantoms on a run that turned much of the clearing into streaks of flaming jelly. A tanker and several trucks carrying ammunition began erupting in secondary explosions. Coolly and stoically, Duong slapped the boy back to consciousness and started pulling him to cover. That was when a straggling F-4 made its pass, and the pilot decided to jettison the last of his napalm. Duong and the boy never had time to catch their breath before they were burned beyond recognition.

Harley and I watched in shock and awe. The crew of Spectre 544 had clearly been reported KIA. This was a mission of revenge, an Armageddon as frightening as anything Father Boyle ever dreamed up for us in catechism class. Too late to save my soul, I was finally impressed with the fate awaiting non-believers—a napalm-and-rocket attack punctuated by the blasts of heavenly Gatling guns. As ear-splitting as a heavy metal rock concert. With searing colors splashing over rocks and trees, a psychedelic light show as blinding as anything flashing through the Fillmore, East or West. Holy Mother of all acid trips. Sound as piercing as the super-treble on Jimi Hendrix's upside-down guitar, screaming as mournful as Janis Joplin's whiskey-scarred death rattle.

When the F-4s made their second and third passes to mop up, you couldn't tell the percussion of incoming cluster bombs from the earth-shattering blast of an Iron Butterfly bass riff. The pounding secondary explosions from the burning ammunition trucks could not be distinguished from the adrenaline-charged thump-thumping of my own heart. And the young soldiers and grizzled porters of the 559th Transportation Group kept dying instead of going deaf at a free concert in Panhandle Park.

Baker and I watched as much as we could from the tree line to the west. When the lead gunship peeled off to look for more convoys, Harley and I set out—less than twenty-four hours after we went down on Spectre 544—careful this time to play the escape and evasion game by the book, working our way across paths and game trails and streams as quickly and unobtrusively as possible. "We've been damned lucky," Harley said in a hushed voice. "The convoy's annihilated. No Bad Guys will be looking for us. No Bad Guys know we exist."

"And neither does anyone in Ubon," I reminded him. "Too bad our radios burned up with our survival vests."

"You missed the asshole gook lieutenant, by the way."

"I was aiming for the windshield. I'm an Air Force marksman, remember? Nothing but bull's-eyes from Boy Scout camp through basic training."

"An Air Commando with a shattered ankle stuck in the jungle with a pacifist sharpshooter. Get me out of here before I puke."

We took advantage of the full moon to keep moving for several hours before we curled up in the brush under some low-hanging branches. At first light, we set out again, stiff from injury and a bad night's sleep. We wanted to head west-southwest, the shortest way possible back to Thailand, but after only a few miles of walking, we heard children laughing and saw smoke rising from the cooking fires of a nearby village. The smell of meat roasting and porridge simmering made my stomach roil with hunger. The North Vietnamese had fed us only a few handsful of rice and a tin cup of lukewarm piss they called soup during our brief captivity. We froze for a moment, staring longingly at those wisps of smoke, and then retreated stealthily back into a dark tropical forest of evergreen chestnut and oak. Without speaking, we hunkered down in the grass and ferns, listened for the sounds of human beings coming our way, and finally, knowing we hadn't been spotted, stretched out to rest until we could travel again under cover of darkness.

An hour after sunset, we resumed our trek, taking a long detour around the village, which was now quiet, with only a few fires burning faintly. An hour later, after traveling through endless stands of bamboo and elephant grass, we nearly stumbled into another sleeping village. We backtracked and slowly, gingerly made our way clear. We trekked on for hours without seeing any signs of human habitation, but now a thick canopy of limbs and leaves overhead obscured the moon, and we couldn't be certain we were fleeing in the right direction. It was cooler at night in the mountains, but I was covered with perspiration, partly from exertion, partly from the pain in my left arm, but mostly from stressing out that we might be trudging in a circle back to the burnt remains of Duong's convoy. Harley was worse off, traveling on his damaged ankle and using the M-16 as a walking stick. We came across a stream that was flowing fast enough to be potable and crawled down the bank to drink, hiding as best we could in the foliage. In silence, we forced ourselves to gulp down the water until our stomachs couldn't take another drop.

Before we got up, Harley tugged at my pant leg. This was hot season, when the creeks were low, and in the dim light I could make out several bloodsucking leeches attached to my calf. My stomach convulsed, and I remembered the leeches that infested Horseshoe Pond on Cape Cod when I was a kid. I remembered how disgusting it was, pulling them off our skinny limbs, but how in the bright summer sunlight, it was not disgusting enough to keep us out of the cool water. Now, scraping off leeches with the jagged end of a stick that was lying nearby, I chuckled at the smugness we felt a year ago back in San Bernardino, ensconced in the comfort of our air-conditioned editing rooms and sound stages. Careful to push out the leeches' tiny heads to prevent infection, I thought about how lucky I had been to have a mom who had been to nursing school and taught me well how to deal with bloodsuckers. Harley and I were about to tuck in our pant legs when I caught a glint of something reflecting in the moonlight on my partner's cheek. Grabbing his jaw with my damaged left hand, a jolt of pain shot the length of my arm. With my functioning right hand, I worked my thumbnail under the head of what looked like a giant tear and worked off one more leech—this time from Baker's cheekbone. "What the fuck!" he hissed.

I held the bloodsucker up for Baker to see. "Please don't tell me it's edible," I said, flicking it away.

Retying our boots and re-binding Harley's swollen ankle, I cringed at the thought that, concealed as we were in the shadows at the side of the stream, we had missed a leech or two. We were dazed, dinged up, and disoriented, but dreams of the Mekong River and Thailand danced in our heads, and we pushed on, sleeping fitfully and painfully breaking new trail.

I ended up carrying the M-16. Harley used a crutch I fashioned from the branch of a fallen tree. My left arm was pretty much useless, so I had to use my feet to hold the branch in place while I whittled away slowly with Grandpa Shepler's old two-inch penknife, which by a minor miracle the NVA had been too preoccupied to find tucked deep in the front pocket of my flight suit. We ate grass and leaves and any berries that didn't make us sick to our stomach, starting with a single berry and gradually increasing our dosage. Many evenings we watched deer grazing peacefully and wild boar rooting aggressively, but in neither case were we able to use the rifle without giving ourselves away. Instead, we patiently followed them to new clusters of edible grasses and berries. Once in a while, we got lucky and found some bananas or mangoes. Unripe, ripe, or rotting—we weren't picky. The good news, whether it was B-52 contrails at thirty thousand feet, fighter-bombers at ten thousand feet, or spotter planes just a thousand feet up, was that any of the aircraft we spotted occasionally crisscrossing the sky were American. The bad news was that nobody was looking for us and trying to wave an aircraft down was going to leave us exposed to Bad Guys on the ground.

We fell into a routine, hiking carefully through the thick forest during the day, staying off the trails, but discovering that even in early hot season, every leaf and every blade of grass we came across was covered with dust. The fine powder stuck to your throat, yet your mouth was too dry to spit it out, missing as we were such Boy Scout basics as a plastic canteen. Laos was filled with enticing creeks and streams, but late in the hottest, driest season of the year, the water level was at its lowest, increasing our chances of running into villagers any time we dared to stop to take a drink. So even though our throats were parched, we pushed on. Even though our feet were on fire, we didn't stop.

Staying off the trails meant hitting dead ends—thick stands of bamboo, streambeds too wide to cross without being exposed, limestone cliffs too sheer or bare to climb. The dead ends meant disappointment, forcing us to turn back and find an alternate route. We wished we still had our watches, but at least by tracking the sun carefully when we could see it through the thick foliage, we were able to cut down on the chance of going in circles, which was especially likely given Harley's uneven gait. Baker showed toughness beyond my imagination, ignoring his damaged ankle, but in this terrain and with Harley's bum leg, that only meant covering a few miles a day. Despite pushing on to the point of exhaustion, we had to keep our eyes and ears wide open. We were never sure what far-flung side branch of the Ho Chi Minh Trail we might still stumble across. At sunset, we looked for some kind of hole in the ground near a substantial formation of rocks or trees where we would neither be spotted by the enemy nor accidentally blown away by our own gunships. We slept from sunset at six till about midnight, when we set out again. We took some major gambles in the wee hours of the morning by occasionally using a game trail or a hiking trail that didn't look heavily traveled. Trails that gave the illusion of being almost level could turn your legs rubbery. Starting down the other side could be so steep your knees began to swell in pain. With the first hint of daylight, we cut back into the underbrush. The unspoken good news was that we seemed to be stumbling downhill more than we were climbing.

By midafternoon the sun would start hitting our eyes, but our fatigue caps were in our lockers back at Ubon. The days were merciless, a sauna that sucked the air out of our lungs, and the nearest snow to roll around in was somewhere north of Katmandu, which made it about twelve hundred miles from where Harley and I were sweating even in the morning shade. We couldn't believe our eyes one afternoon when we did see snow blowing up from a stream bed a short distance ahead. What we found when we inched closer was just as miraculous—thousands, maybe millions, of white butterflies rising in an undulating cloud and flitting off. Once again, the brutal sun slapped us back to reality. Often, even staying in the shade, the air was hot and stagnant and offered no relief. And yet when our bodies were about to give out, it was the sight of a level stretch up ahead that enticed us with the hope of a respite along the brutal trail. To our amazement, the mere sight of that level stretch was enough to give us our strength back, and we always seemed to be able to push ourselves just a bit further.

5 April 1972
Touch and Go

On the eighth night of our escape, clouds rolled in, and it began drizzling steadily high in the Annamites, where the weather, like the tides of war, could wash in from any direction. Thailand was hot and dry. In the U.S. it was springtime. High in the Annamites, however, the rain clouds were thick, and the soot from the end of the Laotian burning season turned the night indigo. A faint wisp of smoke wound its way through a stand of bamboo, a cluster of vegetation just dense enough to hide a thin gash in the hillside.

The trail of smoke came from the gash, the mouth of a limestone cave where I was coaxing a small fire into existence. Harley Baker, in a tattered, muddy flight suit that a week earlier had been starched and pressed and black as the eyes of the Grim Reaper, lay curled up on a pile of palm fronds resting uncomfortably. My bruised body ached as I squatted like an old washerwoman, blowing on the sparks of the smoldering kindling. Cold and wet, our lips swollen and cracked, we let minute after minute pass in silence.

Ever so slowly, soaking in the random photons of heat, we began to relax for the first time since the crash. Taking a look around, my peace was rudely interrupted. Now that my eyes had adjusted to the dark interior, I could make out a rock ledge behind us that served as some sort of an altar. Local villagers had filled it with dust-covered Buddhas, fertility goddesses, a crucifix, a plastic Santa, and an Easter Bunny, interspersed with the stubs of burned-out incense and candles. "You sure we should be lighting a fire?" I asked tersely.

"We're safe as in the arms of Jesus," Baker answered in a gravelly whisper. "The North Vietnamese won't be getting off the main trail tonight the way they're rushing to move south. And no hill-tribe Montagnard in his right mind goes out in the rain when he's got good toot and warm pussy in his grass castle, unless it's to plug some fresh thatch into his leaky roof."

I threw some more tinder on the fire, and Harley began to doze. I knew my partner needed rest, so I sat there with my back straight, doing my damnedest to stay alert. Except my mind wouldn't cooperate. I began having little flashes, mixed with sleep, a toxic mixture of dream and memory that rushed back at me from the belly of the airborne beast. *A fireball, the plane inverting, spinning jungle and moonlight, Merton's faceless face, the glint of rifle barrels—*

"Ahrrrgh! 'Twas the lucky ones what died!" growled Harley, staring belligerently at his leg—swollen and discolored a nasty mixture of green, gray, and purple—daring his wounds to suck him into the depths of shock.

A week that seemed like a year, and still I could not believe that twelve men from Spectre 544 were gone—"jus' like dat," as Lek and Peung would have said. I did not understand why God or fate or luck had spared me and Harley, only to turn right around and let us be captured by hard-core North Vietnamese regulars. How had we convinced our captors that we were officers worth sparing? Or had we? Why had they been marching south in such a hurry? How could the Communists be mounting a major offensive when In-tell had been promising for four years that Tet had finished the VC and that Spectre was kicking the butt of any convoy foolish enough to try an end run down the Ho Chi Highway? And then I answered my own question. Maybe the Viet Cong *were* finished. Maybe the hardcore North Vietnamese regular army was taking over the way the U.S. had taken over for the ARVN.

When would the carnival ride end? A direct hit from a Strela when it was supposed to be "home and mother." Captured when we should have been dead. How impossible had the odds been, I wondered, that those two Spectre birds would succeed so swiftly on their mission of revenge, lighting up the North Vietnamese with flares and tracers on only the second night of our captivity? I wondered what the odds had been that we would escape while our captors were mauled by airborne Gatling guns. "Thank you, God," I muttered softly, stifling for the moment my doubt in whom or what I was praying to. "Thanks for letting us sprint when we couldn't walk."

Harley crawled closer to the fire, acting on a perverse desire to hold his hand over the flame, barbecuing himself in a small, meaningful, perfectly controlled way. Holding it there way too long, he smiled when he pulled it away. "That's better," he said.

Now refusing to take his eyes off the corkscrew break in his ankle, the tough guy began to babble. "Guess this pretty well washes up my football scholarship to USC. Just when I've gotten tired of shooting people. Just when I'd rather be doing the hoochie-coochie with some big, blonde cheerleader from Orange County. Maybe one of Nixon's neighbor's daughters. Hell—

one of *his* daughters. Or maybe one of them naked hippie chicks we saw in *Woodstock*."

"You'da loved the hippie chick I hung out with the summer before I shipped over here," I replied. "Did I ever tell you about the big anti-war rally we organized back in San Bernardino? It was a hell of a fun way to spend Fourth of July. 'Peoples' Independence Day,' we called it."

"When did we stop shooting traitors like you, anyway? You're lucky I wasn't your commander, asshole. You'd still be pounding rocks at Leavenworth."

"If I were, you wouldn't get to hear the story of the beautiful chick who hung out with the outside agitators at the Movement House over near the University of Redlands. A young blonde, about twenty, firm, lithe, bra-less under her skimpy French T-shirt—"

"I can't stand it! A bra-less blonde!"

"Only you weren't supposed to notice, and you weren't supposed to call chicks 'chicks' at the Movement House."

"You're kidding!"

"Nope. We had to call chicks 'women.' Period. Except no matter how much she dressed herself up like some raggedy anarchist under layers of denim and khaki and olive drab, nothing ever hid the fact that she was fundamentally a stone fox."

"So your highly trained little outside agitator was inflaming something besides your revolutionary fervor."

"I'm afraid you've got the picture. People's Independence Day started off as a depressing, pissy little peace rally, but it snowballed on us. Not quite a March on Washington, but it filled a city park. Turned out to be the biggest political event to hit San Bernardino County since Grover Cleveland visited the Mission Inn. By the end of the day, we were euphoric and decided a celebration was in order. Heading up to the cabin Wheeler, Shahbazian, and I rented in Crestline, she just seemed to magically turn up next to me, crammed into my '64 V-Dub. But as I think about it, I spoke pretty eloquently that afternoon about how assholes like you shouldn't be off kicking the shit out of Cambodia until at least half of Congress could find it on the friggin' map."

"Damn, you're full of shit, Leary."

"Well, it sounded good to her. Because no sooner had we gotten to the cabin than she was in bed with me. I could hardly believe that a few hours earlier, I had been thinking some fire-breathing patriot was going to blow my brains out. And now, instead of Death, I was staring Love in the eyes. With a beautiful, sandy-haired hippie *woman* I had been admiring for weeks."

Harley was the best he had been since the crash, remembering now what it was he lived for and why he was hooked on that tumultuous sensation he felt in his gut every time he flew. He loved his life because at the end of every flight came the drinking and whoring, a nearly official part of the program. "Okay, you Commie faggot, so you're in bed with some bleached-blonde Joan Baez. You probably had so much to drink you couldn't get it up, right?"

"*Au contraire, mon frère*. Our clothes fell away like rose petals in autumn. We glided into bed like a pair of swooning swans locked in a love dance. This was heaven, no doubt about it, and I didn't care if I was dead, alive, or somewhere in between. My body felt possessed, tingling all over, floating weightless on the way to kingdom come. At the same time, back on earth, the king bee was going home for honey."

"If it was so damned great, why didn't you marry her, for Chrissakes?"

"Something happened that never happens to geese or king bees…"

Harley's grin was nearly ripping his face in half. "You son of a bitch! What did she do to you?"

"She wanted to know why I hadn't asked her about birth control."

"What!"

"That's what I thought. And then I told her I was sure that a thoughtful, intelligent *woman* like her would have taken proper precautions. She said I was right, she had, and we started in again with our frolicking, but our hot-air balloon of love had sprung a leak. It was a battle for time to make a safe landing before it crashed.

"And then, miraculously, it began to fill up again, and it rose a little higher, and higher yet, and the calm turned into a squall, and the squall turned into a raging tornado."

"All right!" Harley whispered with gusto. "And then?"

"And then, right as that ol' balloon was about to burst, she asked me if I'd blow up a B-52."

"What! Right in the middle of balling? What kind of chick would ask about—"

"Not even Joan Baez," I answered ruefully.

"Got that right. Joan Baez may be a worse stinkin' Commie than you, but she'd know how to behave herself in bed."

My rue had not abated. "So what had been building and building into an absolutely perfect day, just as we were about to put a cherry on top of the Hot Fudge Sundae of Life—wham! It was like some neighbor's kid had hit a baseball through the window."

"What did you do, for Chrissakes? You can't start humping and all of a sudden quit mid-stroke! Goddamn!"

"I did what I always try to do. I told her the truth. All the usual shit about how I had come to hate the damned war, clearly and unequivocally, probably as much as she did. I went on about how I hated the sight of a B-52. How every time I had to sit in the screening room watching dailies, seeing footage of that shark-nosed killing machine lifting off the ground made my blood boil. And how those suckers are so nasty-looking that even their own crews call them Big Ugly Fuckers. I told her how in the final analysis, however, I'm a pacifist, and there is only thing that truly makes a man a pacifist— his actions. How we're all quite capable of blowing up airplanes and killing people. That's easy. The hard thing is *not* acting like the violent animals we are."

"How'd you ever wake her up after that sermon?"

"It turns out Shahbazian and Frank Lutz, the sound guy from Tan Son Nhut, were outside my window gathering firewood, although what you need firewood for on the Fourth of July is beyond me. They could hear just enough of the conversation to really yuk it up."

"So what happened, for Chrissakes! Did the fireworks in your boudoir finally knock them on their asses?"

"No fireworks, I'm afraid. We just lay there next to each other for a moment. It was hot as hell that evening. Probably the hottest evening we had the whole time we lived up there. Now that I think about it, what the hell *were* those two SOBs doing out by the woodpile?"

"Probably gathering material for a new book on how *not* to make it with chicks."

"There was just a hint of a breeze blowing, and after a few minutes of lying there in silence, the perspiration on our bellies evaporated. The crowd was still dancing in the living room when we got up and dressed. Out in the kitchen I made a couple of gin-tonics, and we slipped out to drink them on the back porch that overlooks a dark pine forest. And then she left. Evaporated was more like it, like the heat of our passion. I don't know that we said two words. A week later I went by the Movement House and it was boarded up. I had dropped her off at home once—it wasn't far away—but I drove around for an hour and couldn't find the street. I didn't have her number. Figured I'd always see her at the Movement House. Now I can't even remember her name."

Harley was deeply offended. "You're either crazy or a true asshole. If she had asked me to blow up a goddamn B-52, I'd have volunteered to wipe out the entire Eighth Air Force. And I'd have thrown in my Air Medal, Silver Star, Purple Heart, and my Vietnam Cross of Gallantry for good measure."

"You're not kidding about your medals, are you?"

"My medals be damned. You *never* tell a woman the truth. Got that? I can't fuckin' believe my ears! Passing up a perfectly good piece of ass because you're a limp fuckin' pacifist."

"Funny…"

"What?"

"That's exactly what Lutz and Shahbazian told me."

"Next time, tell me a bedtime story with a happy ending, for Chrissakes."

"You okay?"

"I'm angry, asshole. You and your holier-than-thou integrity make me sick. I'd cut off my friggin' good ankle to be in bed with Joan Baez right now. Jesus, man, you never know when a piece of ass is going to be your last. You could be stuffed into a body bag tomorrow, and your poor imitation of monkhood ain't gonna do jack to stop it."

There was a moment of near silence when all that could be heard were the faint finger taps of the drizzle outside and the soft crackling from the hearth. My eyelids began to droop, and my head began to sink onto my chest.

"You know I fucked Lek."

A whip cracked in my head. I was sure that I had been dreaming, that I had not really heard what I thought I heard.

"All that teaching her to read and write and getting her a job at Chase Manhattan on the base? Forget it, man. She's a bar girl. Once she's got a number and a VD card, that's it. Once a bar girl, always a bar girl. She ain't ever gonna be a schoolmarm—or a BX cashier."

"You met Mali in a bar."

"She was an amateur. She was on spring break."

I stared, my eyes hard, deep, black. "Tom asked me to take care of Lek."

"He meant take her as your *tii-rahk*, so she wouldn't have to go back working the bars. How the hell could she work on the base? She hasn't been up before noon in the last five years. You were really pissing her off." Harley stared back at me—dully, coolly, the look of a shark going after its prey. "Besides, I figured you'd fucked Mali. Protective Reaction Strike. Nixon Doctrine. We're at war, man. Jungle Rules apply. Fuck or be fucked."

"Except I don't mess around with friends' wives and girlfriends, even when the friend turns out to be one notch lower than a rat turd."

"Then what about Dave Murray and Tukada?"

"We weren't *friend* friends. Besides, I knew her first."

"So it was Jungle Rules."

We glanced at each other and turned back to the flickering embers, staring at the orange glow, waiting for merciful blackness. "If we both make it back to California after this is over, stay the hell away from Danielle."

"Whatever happened to Free Love, Mr. Woodstock?"

I lay there in silence on the damp, rocky floor, listening drowsily to the crackling of the embers of our little fire. And when I finally fell asleep, I began to dream disconnectedly…

I'm walking over creaking floorboards through the musty, vaguely familiar rooms of what seems like my grandmother's childhood farmhouse, a house I've never seen. And then, in what might be a new dream, I'm walking down a long hallway suffused with bright sunshine, drawn along by the sound of angels reciting Gregorian chants. The hallway turns into a chapel that seems to be rotating around me, filled with tall, articulate American blondes in flowing, diaphanous gowns whose voices sound like mountain streams rushing through the Rockies. And as they coo the Gettysburg Address, one of the golden-haired angels steps out of the chorus and walks toward me, her womanly body undulating with each step, her angel gown slipping off one shoulder, her lustrous hair not quite long or thick enough to cover her pink breasts, strumming a guitar not quite large enough to cover her blonde and wholesome mysteries.

For a moment, I think I'm on the ninth floor of the Ubon Hotel, but no, it's Café Wha in the Village, and she sits onstage alone, the spotlight illuminating each of the tiny, almost imperceptible hairlets on her neck and arms and thighs. And in that glowing spotlight, she begins to sing a bittersweet folksong about how someday soon her cowboy lover will be riding in from California. And as my angel floats down from the stage and comes close enough to kiss, my heart swells with joy. I part her golden honey hair and gaze deep into her clear blue eyes and see that it's Danielle! Except I blink and now it's Tukada, her lips parted, her eyes half-closed, lying limp and heavy in my arms. My own eyes are seared by the bright glow of exploding phosphorous. Tukada and Danielle and the choir of angels incinerate in silence.

I bolted upright, disoriented at first. Inside our limestone cavern, the fire had burned itself down to a hot, red coal and a bone-white pile of ash. Exhausted, I stretched out and tried to force myself to sleep, but I kept thinking about those relics sitting on the rock altar at the back of the cave.

The Pope of Laos

The next morning, it had stopped raining when we stepped outside. A falcon was circling overhead, a hundred yards from the mouth of the cave, cawing for its mate through the swirling mist. We were in no condition to move, but we knew that sooner or later, hill-tribe villagers would be coming back to burn incense to Buddha or to whatever spirits they believed haunted that limestone cave, so we moved out anyway.

For two days and nights, we didn't say a word, just using hand signals to communicate. I had plenty of time to practice walking meditation, but I didn't feel like I was getting any closer to enlightenment than I was to the Thai border. Finally, while getting ready to set out again at midnight, Harley took advantage of the crickets and other insects chattering in the background to speak to me in a whisper. "You realize that nobody back at Seventh Air Force knows we're here?"

"That's a cheerful thought," I muttered. "We're hacking our way through the crotch of the world, and nobody cares. It's just our own personal bad dream."

"Well, screw 'em. Let's get the hell out of here anyway."

"You know, despite being about the sleaziest excuse of a human being I've ever come across, I can't help liking how you think sometimes."

"You'd better like it, smart guy. I'm gonna save your ass."

I was ready for a dramatic crossing of the Mekong, but the terrain seemed to be taking us back uphill.

On our third day after saying goodbye to the cave sanctuary, we spotted a helicopter that looked like Air America and began waving madly, but we couldn't get the pilot's attention. We pressed on in the direction he seemed to be heading and dropped to the ground when we came upon a listening post—an outpost protecting the perimeter of some kind of military operation. Over the next hour, we lay motionless and made out just three guards, paramilitary types in uniforms we didn't recognize. We continued waiting all day, hidden in shadow and thick underbrush, wanting to see another American helicopter landing before we identified ourselves. Late in the afternoon, we got our wish. A Sikorsky H-34 Choctaw, Air America's workhorse, flew directly overhead, and two of the guards came out to wave.

Harley called over to them in Issan-Lao and English, "*Baw ying! Baw ying! Pen puan!* Don't shoot! We're Americans!"

"*Kaluna maa yuunii saa saa,*" called the sentry who had stayed at his post. "Step out into the sunlight and stop."

We did as he instructed. "Please put gun on ground and put up hands."

The other two approached warily and patted us down, taking my little penknife and our M-16. Harley got to keep his crutch. We followed them for half a mile along a well-used trail into a Hmong settlement made up of ten or twelve thatch huts that appeared at first glance to have been abandoned by a clan moving off in search of more fertile farmland. Just after we entered the hamlet, the H-34 passed back overhead on its way home. Incredibly, at the far end of what I thought was an abandoned village sat an ornate Chinese temple with a six-foot-tall bell hanging out front in a little pavilion. The bell looked old and weathered, but for all I knew it attained that patina in a single decade. I only caught a glance, but it appeared to be inscribed in what looked like Chinese, Pali or Sanskrit or maybe Lao, and Romanized Vietnamese. We could hear what sounded like a handful of monks and village women chanting rapidly inside, chanting at almost twice the pace heard in a Thai temple, in what sounded like Chinese, accompanied by several exotic instruments, one of which I recognized as the wooden Chinese temple blocks we used to use in the percussion section of my high school orchestra.

Outside the village, the trail began winding downhill. We followed our escorts until we reached a pockmarked two-lane highway that led to what might have once been a trading post, except now it was surrounded by a no-man's land of barbed wire and barren fields and required us to pass two gated checkpoints to enter. Instead of being composed of huts built out of bamboo and thatch, most of the buildings were made of stucco in what seemed to be a mixture of Chinese, Vietnamese, and French-colonial styles. We wound up at a rustic villa made from a group of traditional thatch huts, some attached and others connected by shady verandas, all covered by a wide tin roof of more recent vintage. We were led up the front steps into a large room, much of whose back wall was taken up by a plastic-covered map of Laos that had been marked up in grease pencil. Along the adjacent wall, the bookshelves were lined with bottles holding what looked like some kind of lab specimens suspended in formaldehyde. An imposing hulk of a man dressed in jungle fatigues looked up from a small, cluttered desk. Our lead escort handed him our recaptured M-16 but apparently was keeping my old penknife as a souvenir.

"What brings you here?" the big man asked rather bluntly, as if we were crowding his space.

"Mighta been a SAM, but I think it was one of those new Strela missiles," Harley answered. "We're from the Spectre bird that got shot down a couple weeks back operating north-northeast of here."

"We had reports of possible survivors engaged in a firefight the following night, but the Spectre crew that spotted them was unable to make radio contact. Our patrols were alerted to be on the lookout."

"They can stop looking," I said. "We're the only ones who made it."

"Should we be saluting?" asked Harley.

"You can relax. My Marine Corps days are over. My code name is 'Confessor,' but for tonight, call me Tony. Tony Pope."

When we shook hands, I noticed a few fingers were missing or mangled, but the grip was still strong. "Sorry you missed our last flight out. You guys based down in Ubon?"

When we answered yes, he got on the horn and asked for a dust-off the next morning. "Both these guys are injured. Looks like maybe some broken bones that'll need to be reset." He signed off and turned back to us. "I'll have our medic check you over. He can at least put on some clean dressings."

"May I have my penknife back?" I asked. "It was my grandfather's."

Pope nodded to the lead guard. He handed it over to Pope, who took a cursory look and passed it on to me. "What the hell do you use *that* for?"

"Cut up some parachute for Baker's splint. Scraping off leeches—"

"And for committing Hari-Kari if he can't find his sword," said Harley.

"Very funny," said Pope, forgetting to smile. He turned to our escorts. "Please take these gentlemen to the guesthouse."

Following the guards out a side door, I noticed a wooden bucket of what looked like mushrooms hanging on the railing at the top of the stairs. "What's that?" I asked.

"Fresh ears," replied the lead guard.

Our escorts led us to a far corner of the compound where a tin-roofed bungalow with diagonally woven grass mats for walls awaited us. Inside our spartan guest quarters, two grass sleeping mats were rolled up and cots were set up in their place under the mosquito nets that hung overhead. I had the distinct impression that had we not been injured, we would have been sleeping on the mats. While the hill-tribe medic was patching us up, we were told there would be a *baisii* that night in honor of our escape and safe arrival. The Pope of Laos was kind enough to send over some old but serviceable jungle fatigues to wear while our black flight suits were taken out for washing and mending.

We hiked back up to the village that night and discovered it to be inhabited by Pope's militia and their families. Seated on the ground around a bonfire at a place of honor next to Pope and his Yao princess wife, we were served a small banquet of meats and vegetables, most of which we couldn't identify and probably wouldn't have wanted to if we could. We were just hungry enough to eat a little pig ear and chicken brain and not be too fussy about it. The leafy spinach tasted like grass, but at least it was cooked. Eating with our hands wasn't difficult once we learned to make a handful of sticky rice into a small, hollowed-out ball, the way I had seen Dah's hungry waifs do it months earlier, to dip into an assortment of spicy sauces and main dishes. The pork was almost pure gristle, but when the *lao lao* rice whiskey started flowing, it didn't seem to matter. It didn't even seem to matter that a scorpion was floating at the bottom of the bottle.

An after-dinner cordial was poured that looked and tasted an awful lot like blood. We washed it down with a few more rounds of *lao lao*, which seemed to bring out Pope's magnanimous side. Soon our host was telling us war stories of military glory—from World War II and the Hungarian Resistance down to the present non-war and teaching General Vang Pao how to call in close air support for a Hmong army that was still shooting bows and arrows when they ran out of bullets. After telling us his men had assassinated over a thousand Communist commissars and their lieutenants in the past five years and had the ears and skulls to prove it, we finally got a chance to ask him about the Chinese bell and the strange chanting inside the temple. He explained how during World War II, Vietnamese Communists and a detachment of Chiang Kai-shek's Fifth Chinese Regiment camped out here together, fighting a heroic but hopeless little war against the

Japanese. Out of a need to ease the sting of many defeats, and in keeping with a tradition that went back hundreds of years, some opium had changed hands, a practice that may or may not have continued. A small clan of the Chinese soldiers married local girls and decided to stay on after the war, especially when things started going badly for the Nationalists back home. "As a matter of fact, you've been invited to have your morning meal at the Ch'an temple," Pope informed us. "Ch'an is the Chinese precursor to Zen in Japan. The venerable abbot wants to say a few prayers to bless your journey home."

A couple of his half-Chinese warriors smiled at us proudly.

"We'd be honored, *wouldn't* we, Harley?"

"Whatever you say." I got the impression my partner had been planning to sleep in.

The high point of the evening, a story of incredible guile and courage, followed when Pope described how he plotted the Dalai Lama's escape from Tibet. He went on to describe training a cadre of young, fearless Tibetan refugees on a remote mountaintop in Colorado to be parachuted back into their homeland to disrupt the Chinese occupation. Tragically, there was no way for these brave young men to parachute out of Tibet when the operation turned sour.

He described some covert stuff he had done down in Indonesia when that government was getting cozy with the Communists, and he had plenty more stories left to tell, but Harley and I were exhausted and had to excuse ourselves for bed, our stomachs full for the first time in two weeks. After drinking a bottomless supply of *lao lao* while sitting cross-legged for three hours, our legs were so numb we could barely stand up. My efforts gave me a charley horse in my left hamstring, forcing me to roll over on my hands and knees and grab Harley's crutch. Once we were standing, we were embarrassed to discover that the altitude had affected our ability to hold our liquor, impairing our ability to walk to the point I thought we might have to crawl part of the way home.

Back in our guesthouse, Harley managed to get his boots and the rest of his uniform off by himself. I hung his clothes up for him on a couple of nails that Pope's interior decorator had been kind enough to pound into one of the exposed two-by-fours. Harley swung his newly bandaged and splinted leg up onto his cot and put his hands behind his head. I pulled down the mosquito nets, and as I bunked down for a good night's sleep, he said, "You know, I've been thinking about the way Spectre attacked that convoy. General LeMay's right. We should have done that to North Vietnam and eastern Laos a long time ago."

It must have been the *lao lao*. I really didn't feel like arguing. I wanted to sleep, but I couldn't help saying, "If we bomb them back into the Stone Age, what the hell does that make us?"

"I reckon that would make us the Head Cavemen, wouldn't it?"

"Seriously, how the hell is bombing North Vietnam and the mountains of Laos into the Stone Age going to help make South Vietnam democratic? And how the hell do you bomb rice farmers into the Stone Age? They're already living in the Bamboo Age."

"God, you can be an asshole sometimes. Correct that. Are you ever just a regular guy?"

"I'm starting to wonder."

The next day at dawn a messenger knocked on our thin door, carrying a note from Pope. We were socked in, high enough in the mountains for fog to turn into rain clouds. It looked like a twenty-four-hour delay on our helicopter. At eight in the morning, the Chinese soldiers who had toasted us the night before knocked on our door and asked if we were ready to go to the temple. With a fake show of enthusiasm, we went off with them through the morning mist and did the best we could to follow along with our hosts and their wives as they performed the ritual of offering the abbot and his two apprentices their morning meal. I had to sit painfully cross-legged. Harley at least got a chair. After the monks were served, we all joined in, passing around the food that was left. It was awful, a seemingly endless variation on the boiled grass we had eaten the night before, but somehow we got through it without anyone losing face. We were ready to go, but first we had to sit through a long invocation that was being said in our honor by the venerable head monk.

Finally, after some communal chanting in Pali and Lao, we were able to slip away. Back at our quarters, Harley stretched out on his cot, propping up his bad ankle and trying to get back to sleep. "Was that awful or what?" he asked drowsily. "Now I know why the Thais really fled southern China in the fourteenth century It wasn't invading Mongol hordes, it was that damned food."

"It's nice to agree with you for a change." I had some recuperating of my own to do and wanted to sleep, but I had a hard time finding a position that didn't aggravate my damaged shoulder or wrist or my bruised hip.

After tossing and turning for an hour, I got up and wandered around the compound, which was now empty. I had a sense that something big was going on all over Southeast Asia, something connected to Lieutenant Duong and his convoy's mad-dash attempt to push into South Vietnam. Pope and his band of brigands were out doing more than their fair share of fighting in this other half-forgotten Laotian part of the war, I suspected, with the drug business put on hold. Back at Pope's office, I took a closer look at the bucket of ears. They didn't look fresh, but they were ears, all right, along with a few fingers. The door was open, almost as if he had invited me in, so I did some more poking around. I couldn't make out the markings on the map for certain, but it looked like both sides were moving around a lot. We got to use helicopters. They got to hoof it. It also looked, as best as I could tell, like we were stretched pretty thin, helicopters or not. I checked out the pickle jars last. The contents looked an awful lot like those gag rubber shrunken heads we used to pick up at the five-and-dime around Halloween, except these weren't made out of rubber. Any of the jars that didn't contain a severed enemy head had what looked an awful lot like human brains floating around inside.

One jar in particular had a tape label on it that caught my eye—I would have sworn it read "JFK"—but I could hear the voices of the returning warriors in the distance and decided it might be a good time to rejoin Harley. When I stepped outside, though, I saw the weather had cleared and went looking for Pope instead. "Any chance of a late afternoon dust-off?" I asked him.

"Sorry. Air America's assets are tied up. There's another Hmong unit and an American advisor up north of here that's got itself in quite a fix."

The weather held, though, and at dark, Pope ordered an encore *baisii* in honor of our imminent departure. Tonight a couple of Pope's troops carried Harley up the hill to the bonfire. We did a lot better using balls of sticky rice as eating utensils, but getting back was still hell, with Harley's porters staggering all the way down the trail to our quarters.

I tried brushing my teeth in bed but was having a hard time finding my face. "For three years," I started blabbering, "everything was beautiful in America. We had a purpose, a vision. And it was all because we had a prince for president instead of a king. Ike wasn't a bad king, but Johnson and Nixon? Right out of Macbeth. When we had a Bonnie Prince, ah, that was a time. And an exquisite French Lady for his princess—Jacqueline and John. What magic—beauty, intelligence, and grace. What a waste—that a creep or two in Texas could take that away from us. And now we meet a son of a bitch who was in on it, and he's made himself a goddamned prince in the far corners of Laos where no American taxpayer will ever know he even exists."

Harley had been nodding, wasted on Laotian white lightning and bored to death with the drone of my voice. "You talkin' about Tony Pope—our host?"

"Damn right. You were totally zonked out, but I couldn't get back to sleep this morning. So I went over to his office to say hello and check on the status of our helicopter ride out of here. Nobody was there, so I had a look around. I started wondering how he had ended up as some kind of a CIA assassin in the boondocks of Laos outperforming the spooks working the Phoenix Program in Nam. And I took a look at the bottles on his bookshelf and discovered they're filled with a collection of shrunken heads and brains soaking in formaldehyde. So I started looking even more carefully at those jars and discovered one of them has a fuckin' brain floating inside it with a dirty piece of masking tape stuck to the glass, and you know what the tape had written on it?"

"Don't open till Christmas?"

"It says 'JFK,' for Christ's sake!"

Harley tried to play Dad. "It was a joke, asshole. Spooks and their gallows humor."

"You're right," I answered, stretching out on the cot. "I fell on my ass, I was laughing so hard. By the way, did you know Kennedy's brains disappeared after the autopsy?" I never heard Harley's answer. My aching eyes were closing of their own volition, the toothbrush I had been holding dropped to the floor, and I fell into a deep sleep. *And out of the dark void a dream bubbles up that I can fly—the same dream I had when I was a kid that I could glide out of my bunk bed and swoop like Superman over Boston Harbor, only now I glide*

out of my canvas cot and dissolve through the tin roof, soaring ten thousand
feet into the glistening, jewel-strewn heavens. The moon is full and bright.

"Thirty." We're banking. "Thirty." I can hear Major Mertons over the
headphones, but I'm having trouble seeing past the 40-mm Bofors. My camera
feels heavy, and when I get it to my shoulder, it seems to melt. Flares begin to
light up the trail below, but my feet are sinking into the quicksand aluminum
floor when I try to trudge to an open port. Like focusing through a fishing net,
through a shroud, my eyes have fogged over. All I can see are orange flashes.
Trying to look through gauze. Rocked by an explosion...

We were under attack. A mortar round hit close enough to knock me off
my canvas bed, dropping me to the floor with my arms and legs tangled in
my sheets. Harley had already limped outside. "Move it!" he screamed.

In the confusion, with my brain still damaged by Laotian rotgut, I forgot
for a moment which war we were in. When Harley waved with his crutch for
us to leave our trenches and attack the Kaiser's machine-gun nest, I charged
willingly.

Bursting through the screen door, I tripped on my untied shoelaces and
had to stop a moment to wrap the sheet around my waist like a sarong.
Suddenly totally, blindingly awake, I started wishing the sheet were a toga and
I could time-travel back to a college fraternity party. The German machine-
gun nest was in reality an H-34 Choctaw helicopter that disappeared over
a hilltop behind our hootch and beyond the barbed wire perimeter on the
opposite side of our little valley from the thatch village and Chinese temple.
Somehow we worked our way past a maze of concertina wire and found the
rocky trail that led to the landing zone where the H-34 had set down. "You
the guys from Ubon?" called the crew chief.

"That's affirmative," grunted Harley.

"Well, get the fuck on board and let's get out of here!"

Harley climbed on, losing his crutch in the process. I tossed it to him,
tightened up my bedsheet toga, and got one foot on the skid when a white
phosphorus grenade hit nearby, blinding me with a flash that scalded like
boiling water. "Damn!" I shouted as Harley pulled me in.

No sooner could I feel us lifting off than the crew chief grabbed his door
gun and began returning fire. At twenty feet above the ground, a burst of
AK-47 fire forced the pilot to swerve right, pivoting the tail rotor into the top
of a palm tree and spinning us back to the ground. Harley and I were thrown

on our backs, hard, barely able to catch our breath, alongside the crew chief and the other door gunner. "Double damn!" shouted Harley.

Scrambling out, I was tripped up by the bedsheet tangling with the skid but managed to stay on my feet. Harley winced as he climbed down and threw his arm over my shoulder. "Move it out!" he grunted, pointing into the tree line with his crutch. "Looks like we've been turned into a couple of Siamese twins, pilgrim. Good thing you ran track. Good thing I've got the eyes of a cougar. Good thing we love each other. We may make it back from purgatory yet."

"Fuck you, Baker."

We made it fifty feet beyond the tree line into the shadowy jungle, where we rendezvoused with the rest of the chopper crew. "Split up and meet back here in the morning if the coast is clear," said the pilot. "We called in a Mayday. Somebody should be out here looking for us."

Harley and I made our way another hundred yards deeper into the scrub, staying below the ridgeline, and hunkered down for the night. There was still plenty of fighting going on, mostly down below, but it never sounded like more than a handful of men engaging at a time. It seemed to go on for about an hour, and then, as Communist insurgents often did in Southeast Asia, they broke off and disappeared into the night.

"It's morning, blind man. We gotta move."

I had been certain I could stay awake all night in a state of high alert. I was wrong. "Shouldn't we just shoot ourselves?" I asked. Pushing myself up, I glanced around and was relieved to discover I could still see with my left eye.

"I'd rather watch you suffer."

As I guided Harley through the thorny underbrush using my one good eye, I had to hang on tight to my bedsheet with my one good hand. And my hatred for Ron Cooper—ensconced on an air-conditioned sound stage back at Norton—burned deep and pure and raw. "Were we really in a helicopter that crashed last night, or were we just sleepwalking?"

"We weren't sleepwalking."

Approaching the perimeter checkpoints, we could see that Pope's mercenaries were back in control. We exchanged a few terse "good mornings" and hobbled on in. Stopping by our guesthouse, I traded the tattered sheet for my flight suit and reported in to Pope. The crew from the H-34 had survived with only a few lacerations that had been patched up by Pope's medic and was already waiting there in Pope's command post for a second chopper that was due in soon to pick us up. "They'll drop these boys off at Nakhon Phanom," Pope told us, "and get you two down to Ubon where a couple of flight surgeons can check you over."

"What were you doing flying in here last night?" I asked the pilot. "Air Force helicopters don't usually fly at night."

"Well, Air America does. We had just finished an operation a little north of here and were heading for NKP, except the Bad Guys must have hit our fuel tank. The fuel gauge was going down way too fast, so we thought it might be prudent to spend the night with you guys, get the leak patched up and head back this morning."

"Woulda been a good idea," said the gunner, "if there hadn't been an ambush set up."

"Almost like they were expecting us," added the pilot.

"What happened to my M-16?" Harley asked Pope.

"I figure we can put it to better use out here in the boondocks than you can flying around in an airplane."

"You've got a point," said Harley, tossing Pope a little two-fingered salute.

"I think your ride's here," said the CIA man, cocking his ear slightly.

And sure enough, we heard the whirling blades of an Air America chopper a few minutes later as it came in from the west and dropped steeply into the landing zone. The helicopter crew headed out Pope's side door and hiked briskly up to the LZ. Harley and I straggled along and climbed in last. While we were settling in, one of Pope's ground crew showed up leading a pack mule and threw on a couple of gunnysacks labeled "RICE." We took off hot, heading due west for the Thai border at Nakhon Phanom, and as we leveled off, I made a mental note to be sure to send Ron Cooper a "wish you were here" card when we got back. By the time we were out of the mountains and over the Laotian flatlands with the Mekong coming into view, I was starting to get bored and a little inquisitive. "Why are they shipping rice *out* of Laos?" I shouted into Harley's ear over the rattling of the H-34's engine and whirling blades.

I opened my little penknife and poked the blade into one of the bags. Harley stuck one finger into the hole and pulled out what looked like a little chunk of red coal. He took my knife and scraped it, smelled the residue on the blade, and sprinkled some on my tongue. It tingled and then gave me a powerful rush. "Holy shit," I said.

Harley had no trouble reading my lips.

RTB'ing to Base

We made an unscheduled stop at the Royalist Army post just outside Tha Khaek, Laos, where the "RICE" bags were unloaded into a waiting jeep. Next came a quick hop across the Mekong to the Thai-American air base at NKP—military shorthand for Nakhon Phanom—where we dropped off the orphan chopper crew. Harley and I were happy to see an ambulance waiting when we got to Ubon and happier still to be whisked off to the base hospital, where they took X-rays, put Harley's ankle in a cast, put the broken wrist I didn't know I had in a cast, and gave me a sling to immobilize my aching shoulder. I wasn't going to be doing any photography for the next couple of weeks, especially when they finished taping a big patch of white gauze over my right eye. Dr. Lioci stopped by to check in on us and offered us a bed for the night, which we politely declined. We did accept a jeep ride to Spectre headquarters, however, when we saw a couple of medics come in drenching wet.

Songkran, the Thai New Year celebration, had started that morning and would go on for the next three days. It had begun quietly at the *wats* with ritual water-pouring—respectfully cleansing the hands of the monks—but when the ritual part was over, all hell broke loose. The holiday fell during the hottest weather of the year, and in the hottest province in Thailand, the local Thais celebrated by throwing buckets of water on each other, a tradition readily appropriated by the GIs on base. On our way to report in, the windshield of our jeep was hit repeatedly with bucketsful of water, but our new casts stayed dry. Before Baker and his crutches thumped two steps into the orderly room, the sergeant-in-charge looked up and hooted, "Whoo-*ee*, if it ain't Harley Baker! You better get your ass over to Roi Et. Della Rippa's up there with a bunch of the guys attending your funeral!"

"Well, I'll be damned," said Harley, leading me over to the locker room to switch into civvies and pick up our wallets and loose change.

"I'll report in to ComDoc later," I told him. We split the seam on Harley's jeans, pulled them on over his cast, and looking like a poor imitation of *The Spirit of '76,* headed off to find a cab. When we got to his bungalow, we weren't surprised to find the place empty. His *mama-sahn* caretaker told us that Mali, Khun Jim, and Pye had gone to a funeral in Roi Et. Harley toyed with her. "Funeral for who?"

His old *mama-sahn* enjoyed a good joke. "For *you*, Sergeant Hal-ley!"

We looked through our wallets and figured there was enough between us for two bus tickets to Roi Et. Harley cracked a smile. "Always wondered what it would be like to check out my own wake."

"As a ghost or while you're still alive?"

"Don't go fucking with my head. Let's get to the bus terminal."

"Don't you want to clean up?"

"And take a chance on missing my own funeral? Hell no!"

On the bus to Roi Et, for the first time in two weeks, we had a chance to let our guard down. "You still planning on staying in after the war?"

"I reckon so. You know any civilians hiring door gunners?"

"What if the next war's another mess like this one?"

"I'll just keep on doing what I'm told. It's not my job to decide where we fight or why. I'm a gunner and a bomb loader. I *like* combat. I *like* that nasty feeling—those butterflies in my belly. Maybe I'd get the same thrills touring with a rock band, but I'd be living out of a suitcase. This is steadier work. I can blow up some trucks and be home in bed with Mali the same night."

"I think you're jiving me. I can't believe you don't give a shit."

"Of course I give a shit. But *you* tell *me*—how long do you think I'd last if I start telling the Joint Chiefs and the President how to do their jobs. I'm a *lifer*, man. I'm one of the assholes you Fuckin' New Guys hate. Well, we hate you back because if we ever got into some real combat together, you'd probably get us all killed."

"We *were* in combat. We survived."

"That wasn't combat. That was dodging a bullet."

"What the hell are you talking about? We were in two firefights in Laos in the last two weeks. We've flown a hundred combat missions together. We were shot down, for Christ's sake! Are you crazy or just stupid?"

"Who's the one who turned in his gun card?"

"Where were you when Dave and Pigpen and Tukada were killed? Out driving around in a truck full of bicycle parts!"

"Who dreamt up the goddamn bicycle race in the first fuckin' place?"

He had me, and I hated it. "I did. And you're right; I got a bunch of people killed. But that's a low blow, man."

"Jungle rules—duck or bleed."

"Fuck off, Baker." I sat there in stony silence until I was overcome with a wave of exhaustion and started to nod off a few miles up the road. My eye patch seemed to play little tricks with my vision. At first, I saw a white pulsating light and then deep-blue ribbons and then blue-black and silver vapors. As the sun continued to alternate between beating down on the bus directly and filtering through the tall trees overhead, my little visions got prettier—blue marble, inside a waterfall, under a Sierra sky suddenly choked with vines and jungle canopy. The jungle canopy started growing thicker, the sky grew darker, and soon I was sound asleep.

Harley jabbed me in the ribs as we pulled into the central bus station in Roi Et, waking me with a start. Roi Et turned out to be a provincial capital similar in many ways to Ubon, but without the boomtown feeling of having a U.S. Air Force base nearby. We splurged on a cab to Mali's house, a trip we would have done by *sahmlaw* in more leisurely times. When we got there, neighbors directed us to a small, slightly run-down monastery nearby and told us the funeral had just started.

From the back of the little neighborhood *wat*, I could recognize Khun Jim and his hard-drinking girlfriend, Pye, who appeared to be a bit wobbly from tipping the bottle on the way up. I could also make out several of Harley's Spectre buddies, including Major Horney and Colonel Strbik, Captain Rush, and Captain Rooker, who were apparently allowed to come down from exile in NKP for Spectre funerals. Colonel Della Rippa was standing at the front of the hall, preparing to give Harley's eulogy. Off to his side, a line of nine monks sat cross-legged on a low riser. Behind him were several elaborate displays of flowers and wreaths next to a two-foot by three-foot black-and-white portrait of Harley, a bit fuzzy from being blown up from one of Mali's snapshots, but eerily impressive sitting on a large easel. Della Rippa, a little uncomfortable off an Air Force base wearing civvies, kept his eulogy brief, waxing poetic on Harley's courage in helping to keep Thailand free of Communism and safe for democracy. The Thais, not a people who talked much about their politics in public, stared at him blankly, even after Mali translated.

Marcos gave a second eulogy, praising Harley's musical gifts and calling him "the dude who brought bottleneck blues guitar to Thailand." Woody Shahbazian handed Marcos a guitar and stepped up to the microphone with his own Martin acoustic already slung over his shoulder. Marcos put his on, and they started strumming rhythmically. I missed hearing my percussion in the background, but I had to admit they sounded good on the opening to "Sympathy for the Devil."

Right on cue, Harley made his entrance, hobbling up on crutches to sing:

Pleased to meet you
Hope you guess my name

The mourners gasped and tittered in Thai as the song continued. I thought I heard the word *pii*—ghost—a couple of times. When Harley, Woody, and Marcos finished, the crowd applauded wildly and began to chatter. "Way to go, Baker!" shouted Rookie.

"Har-ley! Har-ley!" shouted the gunner contingent.

Mali ran up and threw her arms around him, tossing Thai etiquette to the wind and nearly knocking him off his crutches. "They tell me your plane shot down," she said through her tears.

He pointed over to me. "Well, a couple of us made it back." And then, looking at her seriously, he asked, "What do you say we turn this funeral into a wedding?"

Mali was laughing and crying at the same time. "Just a minute," she said and walked quickly to her mother and father. They talked among themselves a moment before consulting with the head monk.

"We almost went ahead with those Bangkok producers," Marcos said softly to Harley and me while we waited.

"Fortunately for you, the singers and your old bandmates were too shaken up," said Woody.

Marcos gave me a once-over from my bandaged eye down to my broken wrist. "I'll try to stall them off till you get rid of that cast."

We heard the mike crackle and turned our attention back to Mali and her father, who made an announcement in Thai that Mali translated for the English-speaking guests. "Given that April is propitious good-luck month and today is propitious first day of Songkran, the Thai New Year, please take your seats and stay a little longer for the wedding of Sergeant Harley Baker and me, Miss Mali Acharapong."

The congregants settled back onto the floor mats—or the chairs provided for the less limber Americans—while the nine monks adjusted their robes and returned to their places on the riser. Fortunately, I wound up next to Jim and Pye, who explained the goings on to me in a whisper. A sacred white string, the *sai sin*, was looped into two crowns called *mongkons* and placed on Harley's and Mali's heads by two of Mali's aunts. The crowns were connected by a single strand of sacred thread to symbolize the union of husband and wife. Harley had a little trouble getting down from his crutches to kneel next to Mali, but he persevered, and as they joined their palms in a *wai*, Mali's mother gave them each a burning stick of incense to hold. In the meantime, one of Mali's uncles had unwound the remainder of the spool of sacred yarn around the outside of the temple to keep out evil spirits. I was skeptical but decided to ask Harley to bring a spool along on our next plane ride anyway.

For the next half hour, the senior monk chanted, sometimes alone and sometimes with all the monks chanting together in the deep, rich tones of ancient Pali, resonating soothingly through my body, as powerfully and mysteriously uplifting as the Gregorian chants of my childhood. When they finished chanting, the senior monk sprinkled holy water over Harley and Mali, bringing back memories of the liturgy of my childhood in Boston, and apparently that brought the Buddhist part of the ceremony to a close.

I joined a procession that took us to Mali's family compound. Along the way, I learned from Mali's sister that for this propitious funeral that turned into a wedding, the usual Thai wedding ceremony, which can last two or three days upcountry, was being compressed into a single evening for Sergeant Harley. Again Harley and Mali knelt at the front of the assembly, still wearing their crowns of sacred white thread. This time there were plenty of chairs to sit in, now that the monks had left and we no longer had to worry about the Thai custom of keeping our heads respectfully low around Buddhist monastics.

The most senior guest, another of Mali's uncles, began the Brahmin part of the wedding—the *rot nam*, the pouring of lustral water—by anointing the couple's foreheads with three white dots from a powder made and blessed by the head monk before he left. Harley and Mali rested their forearms on a small ornate table with their hands hanging downward, palms joined. I noticed a procession was forming for the water-pouring itself, led by the older friends and members of Mali's family. I joined Marcos and Woody at the back of the line and watched as everyone filed past the kneeling couple, pouring the consecrated water from a conch shell over the hands of the bride and groom and wishing them lifelong joy and happiness. I noticed people glancing sympathetically at Harley's cast and sensed they were pouring the water a little quicker than usual. It was collected in ornate bowls filled with flower petals arranged in elaborate patterns, reminding me of how Lek could turn even a simple pineapple into a work of sculptured beauty. The flowers, I found out from Pye and Khun Jim, symbolized tranquility, longevity, and love.

A couple of guests behind me poured the last of the lustral water, bringing the formal ceremonies to an end. What began next as an informal reception quickly turned into a sumptuous Thai banquet. We were invited to seat ourselves on the floor on large woven mats, but those of us who couldn't, like Harley and Colonel Della Rippa, were politely offered chairs. When large bowls of steaming rice and a vast array of savory meats, vegetables, and condiments were brought to us from the kitchen, I surprised the guests sitting near me with my ability to form balls of sticky rice with one hand in the Lao-Issan style. I didn't bother to explain that I'd had plenty of practice the last couple of days eating with head- and ear-hunters in the Annamite Mountains of Laos.

Harley had been a real trouper going through the entire wedding ceremony kneeling on a broken ankle, but now he got to prop his leg on a little stool and get waited on like visiting royalty. The food kept coming for hours, along with Singha beer and Mekhong whiskey at a side table. Not long after the first drinks were poured, a local Thai band magically appeared in another part of the compound and began to play what sounded like folk songs at first before switching with growing frequency to lively Thai and Western pop numbers. The Thais and a few of the American guests were soon circling slowly and gracefully, dancing an elegant *ramwong*.

I bumped into Colonel Della Rippa at the bar and said, "I thought Pope, the CIA guy we were with in Laos, radioed us in."

"We got something, but I guess he didn't want to send your names out for security reasons, especially the way we've been getting intercepted lately with those damned Sansui field radios. And then the rescue helicopter was reported down. Your outpost was reported overrun. We figured whoever it was that survived Spectre 544 was shit out of luck."

Grouchy Bear and I toasted luck—Irish, dumb, and otherwise. By the time we got done toasting, Mali's sister was able to coax me into taking a stab at a *ramwong* or two. I swore I caught Harley wincing in pain from time to time, but he was enjoying holding court in his fairly fluent Thai, telling a very toned-down version of the story of our escape. It was after midnight when a fleet of taxis took us back to Ubon.

Dear John Bonfire

"Look what the cat dragged in," said Link with a glower. He pushed the roster across his desk and handed me a pen. "Sign in here, and I'll have Wu drive you over to Intelligence. They've got some questions for you and your friend Baker."

Harley and I ended up spending the entire morning being put through a detailed debriefing. Intelligence officers showed us aerial-reconnaissance photos of rest areas and fuel depots along the Trail in hopes we could identify them and put together our itinerary. They tried to overlay that information onto a detailed topographical map of the area and pumped us for information about the size and composition of the convoy. Just before we wrapped up, the subject of Sansui field radios came up, and they picked our brains clean. It seemed strange that Jack Wu had waited around for us, but I didn't give it any more thought once he dropped me off to see Captain English.

English took one look at my left arm and right eye and told me to take the rest of the day off. Stopping by the base post office, I found a few pieces of mail waiting for me that I decided to read while I relaxed at home. It was strange bicycling down Route 66 in the late afternoon, dodging occasional buckets of water with my left arm in a sling. With only one good eye and one hand brake at my disposal, I felt as helpless dodging Ubon traffic as I did flying with Spectre over the Trail. Pushing my bike through the gate to Ruam Chon Sawng also seemed strange, giving me an aching sense of being watched by the ghosts of Tom, Prasert, and Tukada. But it was good to see old Mama-sahn and Bun-lii, who appeared to have given up whoring and was waitressing at the little *rahn-ahahn*. B.J., sitting there with a couple of brothers I didn't know, beamed and called out, "Welcome back, bro!" and ran over to give me one of his elaborate hipster handshakes. "We heard you was shot down," he said, looking me over.

"Baker and I made it out," I replied. "Twelve others didn't." And that was all I could say.

"Lek's in Korat," added B.J. "She was real upset."

It was disappointing climbing the stairs knowing Lek's door would be locked. At least there were still a few Singhas left in the music room refrigerator, so I popped one open and stretched out on one of the rattan chairs out on the porch. Down below, the wiry Thai pugilist was working up a sweat shadowboxing while his soft-spoken *tii-rahk* was lighting their charcoal brazier, getting ready for dinner. I opened my bank statement and wondered how they would have sorted things out if I hadn't come back. Somehow my college had tracked me down and was asking for money. That was funny. Poser, Esquire, reminded me that I still owed his firm over $800, which was not funny, and Mom wrote to let me know how glad she was that the war was almost over and that I would be home soon. She didn't have a clue, and I couldn't say a word to straighten her out. She went on and on about how my hippie brother was giving his teachers fits again and how my baby sister had just turned thirteen. She wrote how Dad was telling all his friends how proud he was of me, underlining the word *proud*, and I could only cringe. *Proud of what?* I wondered and realized neither of them had the faintest idea what was really going on over here. Mom rambled on, describing the weather and the summer trips they were planning, and I felt like I was standing alone on a mountaintop listening to an ant-sized stranger blather from a distant valley. Realizing that I was hollow inside and couldn't make myself focus, no matter how hard I tried, I put the letter aside. I had saved dessert for last—a letter from Danielle:

Dear Brendan—

How are you? How's the war going? I hope better than things have been going back here. This is a terribly hard letter to write, for a couple of reasons. I was taking the Coast Highway up to Big Sur and your beloved Bug "shot a rod." That's what the mechanic told me when the tow-truck driver got to San Simeon. I'm really sorry. It's still there. Do you want them to repair the engine? If so, they'll need $500. Or should I have them junk it?

The other thing I'm feeling terrible about and don't know how to tell you, is that I've met somebody. In fact, we were headed to Big Sur when we shot the rod. I'm sorry it isn't going to work out for us. You were so good to me, especially when we first met and I was feeling so depressed about losing my husband in Vietnam. But now that the war is almost over, I know you'll be all right. Please don't be mad at me. I know that someday you'll meet a girl as sweet as you are.

Best wishes—
Danielle

I chuckled to myself—at myself—and felt a mask of numbness spread across my face. She hadn't even gotten the letter about extending that I had taken such care to write. I spotted Tom's old Ronson lighter lying on the windowsill and picked it up. Flicking it on, I set the letter on fire, letting it soar off the porch, but it blew out almost as soon as it left my hand. I followed it down as it floated toward the spirit house. Leclerc was checking me out, sipping on a Singha of his own next door at Bungalow #3. "Wazzup, Leary?"

"I'm trying to burn a Dear John letter, but it looks like she wrote it on asbestos."

"You just need kindling," boomed Leclerc, stepping into his room.

For a country without many telephones in 1972, news traveled fast. By the time I retrieved Danielle's letter, Leclerc had thoughtfully brought down his bucket-sized charcoal stove and was joined by B.J. and a steady trickle of other guys who brought over their own Dear Johns. One sucker had managed to accumulate three. "Try this," said Leclerc, setting down the brazier. "Your Dear John'll burn a lot better if we crumple up a few others and make a little pyramid."

To my amazement, a couple of the lifers joined the crowd. They had their own burnt offerings to make. I rolled one of the letters into a tube, lit it, and used that to get the others burning. The flames shot five feet into the air before they finally settled down. But the damnedest thing was happening. It seemed that everyone was coming home from work about the same time, and everyone had at least one Dear John letter to add to the pyre. Washington and Price just happened to drop by to see B.J. and Leclerc. They soaked in the proceedings for a moment, glanced at each other, and started crooning an old Temptations tune. When they got to the chorus, B.J. and Leclerc joined them, bursting into perfect four-part a cappella harmony, lushly singing, "*It was just my imagination—running away with me.*"

In the middle of the commotion, I noticed Harley and Woody making their way up the alley, Harley on crutches and Woody carrying their guitar cases. Without losing a beat, Woody took out their acoustic guitars, Harley propped himself up, and they segued in as the brothers faded out, singing a rousing country-folk-rock version of "It Ain't Me Babe." By the time they got to *"someone to die for you and more,"* every English-speaking denizen of the Ghetto joined in with a rousing *"It ain't me, babe. No, no, no, it ain't me, babe. It ain't me you're looking for, babe."* And then Woody, the born showman, sent one out to the redneck-lifer contingent: "Your Cheatin' Heart," the very song he had used to upstage me at the Ubon Hotel the night I unintentionally joined the Band of Brothers. Lonnie Price jumped in and did a verse Ray Charles-style, and damned if I didn't start liking the song. A second and third round of beers turned up by the time we sang the refrain for the last time, and in a way I never dreamed possible, the three castes of outcasts from Ubon Royal Thai Air Force Base had bonded.

I was safe in my own bed that night but had a hard time sleeping. My mind tumbled over and over like a clothes drier, full of thoughts and voices and visions of fire. Where I had once agonized over Tukada's death and been haunted in different ways by the violent ends met by Prasert, Murray, Sachs, Spitzer, and all the others from the bicycle race, I now felt tainted by the deaths of twelve crewmembers on Spectre 544. I felt as cursed as the Grim Reaper painted on the nose of every Spectre gunship to be a harvester of death, a Midas of mayhem.

In the middle of the night, I sat up with a start, remembering Prah Samrong's invitation to a Bangsukun Atthi ceremony. It was today, Saturday, the last day of Songkran, that he would be performing it. He had suggested it as a way of paying my final respects to Tukada, but when he told me the ritual was traditionally used by local villagers to honor their dead ancestors, it didn't really click for me. *Now,* all of a sudden, a ceremony in sacred memory of the dead found a place front and center in my thoughts. It wasn't something Lek could have helped me with, even if she were here. I had to process it on my own. I still couldn't sleep, but I felt relieved knowing I could say goodbye to the many ghosts that were haunting me. It didn't matter that they weren't my ancestors. Like most Americans, I didn't know who my ancestors were.

Samrong had explained to me that the villagers would be bringing ancestral relics to use in the ceremony. When I woke up at daybreak, I gathered up the only relics I had of Tukada—a ticket stub from *Tora! Tora! Tora!* and a snapshot Jack Wu had taken of her at Tadton Falls—along with a scrap of my old flight suit in honor of the crew of Spectre 544 and a program from the bicycle race in remembrance of the murdered cyclists and placed them in a lacquerware box I found in the music room.

Several young boys were already out in the alley, helping to bring the Songkran celebration to a rousing close by chasing each other with big bright plastic buckets filled to the brim with water. They laughed hard while they tried to escape each other, but they laughed even harder when they threw their water and were hit by a return barrage that drenched them from head to toe. The boys were kind enough to stop when they saw my banged-up body approaching and let me walk past them unscathed on my way to visit Prah Samrong at Wat Pah Mongkol Ming Muang.

I took a cab that morning instead of my usual *sahmlaw* and bus, reflecting along the way on the ritual Prah Samrong was going to be performing. It struck me as a lovely Thai-Chinese tradition, a way of giving merit and respect to their ancestors, unlike anything I could think of in the West other than celebrating the martyrdom of Catholic saints and honoring our war dead. Somehow that got me thinking about Tukada and bad *kamma* and how she had worried about the difficult rebirths and endless rounds of *samsara* she was responsible for by causing violent death and suffering. I refused to buy into her *kamma* gobbledygook, or at least I hoped it wasn't true because if it was, I was far guiltier than she.

Samrong did much of the service chanting in Pali, and from time to time, the villagers joined in. The effect was similar to the chanting I heard at Harley and Mali's wedding, transporting me to a place of soothing tranquility. At one point, we held up the relics we brought with us, and Samrong sprinkled lustral water on them with a bamboo whisk. A short time later, he wrapped each of us in white cloth, symbolic of the cloth that corpses are wrapped in before cremation, and then, after some more chanting, pulled the cloths away, a kind of baptism that purified us for a luckier, happier life. In a way that reminded me of the unknowable mysteries of the Catholic liturgy that I had once loved even as I warred with the Church's dogma, I found the chanting in an unknown language, the burning of incense and candles, and the sprinkling of holy water to be a great mystery that I couldn't understand but needed.

Afterward, a kindly old village woman, her eyes sparkling with a smile that covered her face with a net of fine wrinkles, took me over to the booths and tables that stood inside the gate along the driveway. "*Na,*" she said, pointing to a white dove in a little cage.

I bought it, as I was certain she wanted me to, and returned with her to the foot of Big Buddha, where we put several sticks of incense in a sand-filled urn, lit them, bowed three times, and knelt for a moment of meditation. As we stood back up, she gestured with her hands, flicking them away from her in a way that told me it was time to set the bird free. And as I did, I began to cry, saying a silent prayer to the departed spirits of the many people who had fallen around me in the past two months, seeing their faces and hearing their voices as they drifted off into the clouds above, almost as if they were being pulled along by that little dove.

We *waied* simply to each other, and the kind old woman wandered off into the crowd. As I started to make my way back out to the gate, I saw Prah Samrong walking in my direction. "How do you feel?" he asked, glancing at my bandaged face and the cast on my wrist.

"My body will heal, Prah Samrong, but today I feel a little sad."

He touched my shoulder gently. "You have looked two times into the eyes of Death. You have good reason to feel sad. We all experience suffering in this life, but you are maybe asking, 'Why so much? Why so soon? Why is it *I* who experiences this?'"

"I hadn't put it into words, but yes, that's exactly what I'm feeling."

"If you practice the Buddhadhamma, this suffering can bring you wisdom and compassion. Have you gone yet to Wat Pah Nirapai?"

"I've wanted to. There just didn't seem to be any time."

"Will you make time now?"

"I promise."

Wat Pah Nirapai

It was humbling to discover that the little hike Harley and I had taken out of Laos had earned the respect of the whole unit, almost a reverence. Captain English offered me some R&R in Bangkok, but I preferred to stay in Ubon, just resting and teaching my AUA classes on Monday and Wednesday before venturing out to visit Wat Pah Nirapai for a few days as I had promised Prah Samrong. I liked the name—"Forest Monastery without Fear." Khun Jim had found a replacement for me this time at AUA because even though we were listed as MIA, he could tell from the Spectre people who came to console Mali that there was little chance anyone survived. I deeply appreciated Khun Jim and my replacement for being gracious enough to let me finish up the term. Prepping and teaching my class was doing me a lot more good than hitting the bars or staying home in a dark funk.

Thursday morning, riding to the monastery in the back of a *sawngtao* jitney, two old women asked, "*Bai nai?* Where you go?"

"Wat Pah Nirapai," I replied, and they smiled.

"Ajahn Po very wise," they told me. Respectfully, they showed me how to open a rambutan to get at the sweet fruit and then insisted I take a bag of it to snack on along the way.

When I arrived at the monastery, a young Thai novice took one look at me and led me to the *kuti* of an American monk who was seated in the lotus position on his small front porch, deep in meditation. Slowly opening his eyes, he smiled, "You must be the American Prah Samrong told us about."

"That would be me."

"We've been expecting you," he said with an air that exuded strength and confidence. "My name is Anando. Samai will show you to the guesthouse. After you've settled in, come on back—in, say, half an hour."

The novice monk brought me to a large communal guest room over the kitchen and gave me a grass mat, a small pillow, and a mosquito net. He also gave me drawstring pants and a pullover shirt, both loosely fitting white cotton, to wear during my visit. It was a little tricky getting the shirt over the cast on my wrist, but it turned out that getting the shirt off and on actually helped stretch out my tight shoulder.

When I returned to Anando's *kuti*, he had been joined by Prah Suñño, a former Peace Corps volunteer in Udorn. He was of average height, and with his shaved head and olive complexion could have been mistaken for Thai from a distance. Even up close, his brown eyes looked Asian, but his nose and chin were pointed and definitely European. Prah Anando, it turned out, had been a FAC—a forward air controller—flying the kind of light observation aircraft that Liscomb flew around in. Except he operated in Laos around the Plain of Jars, what Spectre called "The Pan," while we mostly worked the panhandle to the south—the Ho Chi Minh Trail. He still had the piercing blue eyes of an aviator, eyes that reminded me of my father's, and when he stood up, he towered over us. Leading us to the abbot's quarters, however, he walked softly, and for the first time, I understood what Pawnsiri meant to "walk like a Thai."

"Samrong tells us you are a promising student," said Anando, walking on awhile before he continued. "He tells me that you, too, have powerfully experienced *anicca*—the impermanence of all things."

"I think Prah Samrong is correct about that. He told me I would find good teachers here. I assume he means the two of you."

"We're really still students here ourselves," Suñño answered. "We have at least two more Rains left until we have Ajahn Po's blessing to formally teach the Dhamma. But we'll be happy to translate for you when it's necessary, and we'll certainly pass down whatever we can of what we've learned."

The abbot's residence was larger than the other monks' quarters, but it was still modest, a single room built on stilts with the open ground floor screened in for informal meetings like this, my first interview. Stepping inside, we made three prostrations to the bronze Buddha sitting in back and three more to Ajahn Po before seating ourselves on the floor. The abbot was a tough yet warm-hearted Thai-Laotian in his early sixties whose body was still vigorous and whose eyes were perceptive and alert. Anando did the translating while I explained that this was my first visit, but that I had been studying *vipassana* meditation at Wat Ph'a Yai with Prah Samrong and that I was thinking about returning here to become a monk when I left the Air Force.

"Very good!" Ajahn Po replied, and then, with a gleam in his eye, he asked if I could get the pilots to fly a little more quietly when they flew over the monastery.

"I'll try," I answered, "but I'm afraid that cameramen don't have much influence over how pilots fly."

He smiled and then asked how many days I intended to stay. When I replied, "Three," he said, "*Dii mahk!*" and explained through Suñño that laypeople were welcome to stay for three days as a guest. If I stayed longer, I would have to shave my head, including eyebrows and mustache. In either case, I would be expected to observe eight precepts.

Suñño and Anando continued translating for Ajahn Po, asking me if I was familiar with the Five Precepts that devout laypeople followed in their daily lives. "I've taken the Five Precepts with Prah Samrong," I replied, "but he recommended giving them plenty of reflection. I wouldn't mind going over them again."

"The first, refraining from taking life, is actually pretty easy at a monastery," Anando explained wryly, "Even visiting murderers are on their best behavior."

"Perhaps not killing *people* here is easy," I replied, "but it takes a lot of practice to not swat a mosquito."

"It gets easier," Anando said with a tolerant smile.

"Number two, refraining from taking what is not given, might sound a lot like the Biblical commandment 'Thou shalt not steal,'" said Suñño, "but it has an interesting corollary—accepting graciously what is given freely, even if it's red ant curry from a villager in upcountry Thailand."

"That *is* food for thought," I replied. Ajahn Po enjoyed the joke, even in translation.

Anando continued, "The third, refraining from sexual misconduct, forbids relations between a man and a married woman but leaves issues like premarital sex up to the individual to work out."

"And that invites *plenty* of reflection," added Suñño. "There's a big difference between visiting a prostitute or barhopping and sleeping with your fiancée before you get married."

I was about to ask where *tii-rahks* fit in, but they were already elaborating on the fourth precept, refraining from unskillful speech. Much as Samrong had taught me earlier, Suñño explained that refraining from false or harmful speech involved more than just telling the truth. It meant refraining from blurting out a potentially harmful truth or a strong opinion without considering the consequences. "It also means developing mindfulness by refraining from gossip and idle chatter," Anando added.

The fifth precept struck me that day as perhaps the most intriguing—refraining from all intoxicants, a possibility that had never before occurred to me in my Irish-American lifetime. I had trouble imagining what Dad and his pilot friends would have made of the idea. *Who would laugh harder,* I wondered, *Dad or my fraternity brothers?*

"Are you with us, Brendan?" asked Anando.

"Yes," I replied, already uncertain if I was telling a white lie or practicing skillful speech. I had to shift a little to ease the pain that was developing in my right knee and lower back. I couldn't help noticing that Ajahn Po and his two disciples sat comfortably while remaining completely still.

Anando and Suñño continued translating Ajahn Po's instructions. "When a layperson stays at a monastery, they change the third precept—refraining from sexual misconduct—to refraining from *all* sexual activity while they are here. And they take on three new precepts: joining the monks and novices in refraining from eating solid food after midday; refraining from 'fun,' such as dancing, singing, music and entertainment, garlands, perfumes, cosmetics and adornments; and refraining from high and luxurious seats and beds." My three teachers went on to explain that if I eventually decided to become a novice, I would follow ten precepts. The main difference would be giving up the possession and handling of money.

I was fascinated at how similar the Buddhist precepts were to the Ten Commandments of the Judeo-Christian tradition and, at the same time, surprised at how an onerous moral weight seemed to have been lifted. Here, at last, was a middle ground between the Catholicism of my childhood and the existential atheism of my early adulthood. Instead of an omnipotent and frightening God making these demands on humanity, with a powerful subtext that the world was neatly divided into good and evil—"for me or against me" in Christian terms—here was a much more subtle belief system, an in-depth form of spiritual existentialism.

The precepts themselves were voluntarily undertaken by the individual and were open to endless reflection on how to apply them in the real world without creating unintended consequences. I especially liked that it was described as a path of moral purification that you traveled by degrees in order to reach spiritual enlightenment. I still had trouble buying into a belief in reincarnation There was too much Western science and skepticism that I carried with me, part of why I lost my faith in religious teachings in the first place. Nevertheless, I saw something comforting and compassionate in the belief that if you stumbled while attempting to walk the path in this lifetime, there would be many future opportunities to get it right. It wasn't simple, however. I found the connection between *kamma* and rebirth to be both comforting and challenging, something Tukada was struggling with when she took her last breath.

Tahn Anando walked with me after we left the abbot's quarters. "You're going to hear a lot of new concepts if you stay with this. Thais have heard these teachings since they were schoolkids. Just remember, much of it's interconnected. The lists are from a time when the Dhamma was handed down orally—and we're print-oriented. Don't let it throw you. If you and Samrong have talked about how suffering is innate in all of us, how everything we desire is impermanent, and how mindfulness and meditation can ease our pain, then you've been learning about the Four Noble Truths.

"And the precepts we take, whether it's five for laypeople or hundreds for an ordained monk, are guidelines to help us walk the Eightfold Path— Right Understanding, Right Thinking, Right Speech, Right Action, Right Livelihood, Right Effort, Right Mindfulness, and Right Concentration. Ajahn Po's Dhamma talks will help you with the first two—Right Understanding and Right Thinking. By staying here at the monastery, you will have lots of practice with the middle three—right speech, action, and livelihood. Practicing *vipassana* incorporates a balance of the last three—effort, mindfulness, and concentration."

By the time Anando left me at the guesthouse, I was looking forward to many uninterrupted hours of quiet reflection. The idea of quiet seemed quite appealing after months of screeching turboprops, squawking intercoms, howling wind, thundering guns, and grinding cameras, only to be replaced on the ground in Ubon by rumbling motorcycles, cacophonous street noise, raucous laughter, and rock music in clubs, on the radio, and blasting through our own speakers. One meal a day in the forest tradition would be challenging, but the idea of my bony body having to sleep on a straw mat on a wood floor gave me greater pause, reminding me too much of sleeping on the hard ground when Harley and I trekked out of the jungle.

As much as possible, I followed the schedule kept by the monks, which meant getting up at 3:00 a.m. and gathering for morning chanting and meditation from 3:30 to 5:15 in the Dhamma hall, the meditation hall where we also took our meals together. Compared even to the temples of an obscure provincial capital like Ubon, the hall was austere, hardly more than a large *sala* really, which kept with forest tradition.

I helped in the kitchen while the monks and novices went out on alms round, accepting daily offerings of food from supportive villagers. We ate our single meal of the day together around 8:30 a.m., after which we had time to bathe, meditate, study, and rest. The ringing of the temple bell later in the day meant mindfully hauling water from the well or doing other chores at 3:00 p.m. and coming to an evening cup of tea and Dhamma talk at Ajahn Po's *kuti* at 5:00 p.m. Sometimes, I was told, Ajahn Po's talks could continue long into the night, but while I was there, we met for an hour and then returned to the meditation hall between 7:00 and 9:30 p.m. for the evening chanting and group meditation. I was encouraged to either read books from the library, which unfortunately were mostly written in Thai and Pali script I couldn't decipher, or practice walking and sitting meditation, a more realistic proposition.

Meditating on my own, I sat for ten or fifteen minutes at first, gradually building up the time before my knees, especially, began to ache and resting or doing walking meditation in between. In the meditation hall at the beginning and end of the day, however, we sat for forty minutes to an hour at a time, and I soon understood why Tukada said that monastic life was difficult. The old pain in my knees and new pain in my neck and back eventually began to throb, as did my slowly healing wrist and shoulder. It was permitted to do standing meditation when we gathered in the meditation hall, and I would do so when pain completely obliterated my concentration. When I went back to sitting, without fail, I would begin comfortably, and then, inexorably, the pain would return, seemingly sooner than before, until—at last—it was time to return to the guesthouse. I was definitely going to be earning my three days of simplicity and tranquility by living a life of rigorous discipline and restraint punctuated with waves of psychic and physical pain and spiritual doubt, a challenging new direction for my life that I needed to explore.

With Ajahn Po's permission and Anando's encouragement, I began my second application for discharge as a conscientious objector, certain that I now satisfied the requirement that I submit a substantially different claim from the first. The simplicity of life in the monastery was reflected in my writing—thirty-five pages in the original application were reduced to three. I stated directly and simply that I wanted to ordain as soon as possible as a Buddhist monk and that monks in the Theravada tradition of Thailand didn't kill a mosquito, let alone another human being; as a Buddhist layperson, I now aspired to that same standard. With a few additional supporting letters, I felt confident that my application for discharge was going to be approved this time. My biggest concern was fearing how my father would take this. We hadn't spoken in several years, yet his presence continued to hang over me.

When I got back to Ruam Chon Sawng early Sunday evening, I wanted to continue meditating, I wanted to continue going deeper with my practice, but it wasn't to be. Lek had returned from Korat and was busy preparing a welcome-home dinner for me. It wasn't long before Larry and Peung, Harley and Mali, Woody, and Washington, the invited guests, began arriving. It was awkward at first around Harley and Lek, knowing they had slept together while Harley was living with Mali, a woman he intended to marry and did marry the very day we returned from Laos. Knowing they'd had sex behind my back while I was struggling to sort out exactly what my relationship with Lek was going to be. And then I remembered something Ajahn Po had said about attachment causing unhappiness. What claim did I have on Lek to deprive her of her livelihood? A shot of Mekhong with my Coke might have made it easier, but I refrained. It took some effort, but I decided instead to "just observe" as Ajahn Po had taught me, to experience my discomfort—sparks of anger and jealousy—and let them go.

Later, when Harley and Woody asked me when I could start rehearsing again, I was surprised to discover that I had lost my desire to play drums, my passion since the age of eight. The cast on my broken wrist gave me an honorable excuse to beg off.

Something strange was in the air when I reported for work Monday. Jack Wu was sitting at Link's desk in the First Sergeant's office when I stepped in. "What's going on?" I asked.

"Have a seat, Brendan." I did what I was told.

"I'm your acting first sergeant. Link's gone away—for a long time. A little black marketeering—cigarettes, booze—we can live with. But Link was involved with hijacking the jeep that the insurgents ended up using to ambush the bicycle race. Heroin might have been part of the deal. He was trafficking in porn that was produced or at least *re*produced at government expense with government equipment on government property in Europe and transported to Southeast Asia using Air Force aircraft. The last straw was moving large quantities of Sansui stereos on the black market. You know about *them*. Your debriefing helped wrap up the investigation."

"Holy shit." I didn't want to gloat, partly because I wouldn't have put it past Link to hunt me down someday back in the World and carry out his threat to kill me. I would have preferred to practice the compassion that Rick Liscomb, Prah Samrong, and Ajahn Po had been teaching me, but I wasn't there yet. Just the same, I was glad to be rid of the SOB. It wasn't a *happy* glad, however. I found it deeply disturbing to find myself hating Link and Nixon more than Prasert and the other Communist assholes who were actually shooting at us.

"What happened to him?" I asked. "And what about Indian Joe?"

"Link's headed for Leavenworth. General Gong didn't even want him in Long Binh Jail. Afraid he'd figure out a way to keep on operating there. I don't think Link's that clever, but who knows? As far as Indian Joe, I got a kick out of watching him at work when he hustled the Big Buddha Bicycle Race. But he owed the Thai government a pile of back taxes. And Thai Customs didn't like being screwed out of import duty, especially when he started getting stingy in the palm-greasing department. And then he crossed the line. A joint Thai-American team of investigators traced serial numbers on Pathet Lao and Thai Liberation Front field radios back to the Sansuis he had been moving. Under some intense questioning, his niece let it slip that he's back in Calcutta."

"So they were working for the enemy?"

"Not intentionally. I think they were just chasing the buck. But the result turned out to be pretty much the same."

Wu gave me a good looking over. "Captain English wants you to stick around the orderly room with me for a while, seeing as how your eye and wrist are pretty much useless for camera work."

I was given clerical duty, sitting now at Dave Murray's empty desk across from a New Guy who had replaced Tom Wheeler. When Captain English and Lieutenant Hill came in, I was up front with them about putting together another request for discharge, and they told me to go ahead and type it up if the office workload was slow. I wasn't much of a typist, but even with a banged-up left hand I got it done by noon, pecking away at it a little piece at a time. They were kind enough to let me make photocopies, and I started passing them out to select members of the Rat Pack and a very select few airmen of the 16th Special Operations Squadron in hopes of generating some new supporting letters. I had no doubt that letters from airmen who had served in-theater would carry extra weight, especially if they were career guys like Harley Baker.

A few days later, Harley dropped by the orderly room just as I was getting ready to leave and asked me to join him over at the patio. He was still on crutches and had also been stuck behind a desk, not the cup of tea of a man of action like Baker. By the time we reached the patio, the steamy afternoon had left us drenched with sweat. The rumble of trucks and jeeps and the roar of jet engines were in a way like the stench of the *klongs*—facts of life at the frontier of a war zone that I and every other *farang* soon learned to ignore. Today, however, the heat and humidity changed the equation, which meant that the fighters and gunships, loaded to their teeth with fuel and ammunition, needed the entire runway to get off the ground. I chose a picnic table in our favorite corner of the patio next to the airmen's swimming pool while Baker detoured to the juke box. "Damn, it's hot," he said, wiping the perspiration from his eyes.

I hadn't had a drink since Harley and Mali's wedding and was trying to abstain now that I was preparing myself for the monastery, but Baker was a hard man to say no to. He called for the young lady behind the cash register to bring us a six-pack of Budweiser while he dropped a bunch of quarters into the juke box, and before long the place was shaking with tunes by Santana, Hendrix, the Allman Brothers, and Jefferson Airplane. "I want the band to start doing these," he shouted over the music and the rumbling of jet engines.

I liked his selections and would have told him so if I could have gotten a word in. Instead, I watched his lips flap enthusiastically, his words drowned out in the sea of noise, and the next thing I knew empty beer cans began piling up in the middle of the table. "I don't know if I'll be going back to the band," I called to him during a lull between records.

"You'll be back. Once a drummer, always a drummer."

"I think you've got me confused with Buddy Rich."

The sun began setting, the halogen lights came on overhead, and the sky gradually turned purple, but the night remained hot and humid, the kind of weather I imagined when I first got orders for Southeast Asia. As the music faded out, I could finally speak in a normal voice. "I heard stories before I left San Bernardino about how the night air could be so thick on the Mekong Delta that a GI could cut it with a machete."

Harley dabbed his forehead and cheeks with the cold can of beer he had just opened. "You know the guys working the flight line hate the sight of you ComDoc cameramen. It means putting their olive-drab shirts back on even though they'll be soaked through with sweat in a matter of minutes."

"It's the same out in the field," I replied. "The grunts can't stand the sight of a DOD news crew. They're humping it out in the boonies and all of a sudden they have to get into full uniform so an information officer back at the air-conditioned Pentagon can pronounce another puff-piece news release suitable for the delicate eyes of Middle America."

Harley was deep into a second six-pack by the time I finished off my third Bud. Helped along by the Valium I had popped earlier in the day, I was already buzzed enough that my ears were losing their ability to discern discrete sounds. The whirring of the filter system at the enlisted men's swimming pool was as loud from a hundred feet away as the mosquito that was trying to decide whether to attack my ear or the back of my neck. Any sound that night could drown out my thoughts.

Harley crushed his empty beer can, which sounded to my ears like a firecracker going off, and added it to the pile before he lurched over to the perky, bright-eyed cashier, whispered something obscene enough in Thai to make her giggle, and brought back six more Buds. "I hope you got those to take home," I said to Harley.

"Whatever you can't handle, I can, you little pussy."

"Why do I get the feeling something's bothering you?"

"Maybe it's because something *is* bothering me. What the hell is a little snot like you doing over here, dampening my enthusiasm for this war?"

"Are you talking about my request for discharge?"

"Damn straight."

"Believe me, I would have rather stayed in California. But if I *weren't* here, wouldn't you still be rotting away somewhere in Laos? The way I see it, the NVA, the Viet Cong, the Pathet Lao, and the Khmer Rouge were raining on your parade long before I came on the scene."

"Why the hell didn't you just take a long vacation to Sweden and sit out the war?"

"Frankly, I was afraid I could never come back. Afraid I'd never get a shot at directing movies in Hollywood."

"So how does being an *egotistical* bastard make you a pacifist?"

"It doesn't. What makes me a full-blown pacifist is complicated. My Catholic childhood was a minefield of contradictions. My mom and her mother gushed over me, thought I walked on water. But all I heard from my father and *his* father was sarcasm or soul-crushing 'constructive criticism.' The old man would tell me he wanted me to go to college and then ride my ass for reading books and ruining my eyes—because he also wanted me to be a pilot. With the parish priest, it was hellfire and brimstone. Scary shit for just having an impure thought! With all three, it was blind patriotism. I hated it but didn't dare question them. Except the war in Vietnam dragged on for years, from middle school to high school to college. When the Tet Offensive came along, it stopped making any sense whatsoever. Like the stuff they were teaching us in high school about how our troops were going to be battle-hardened if we ever had to fight the Red Army."

"We will be."

"What's the point if the world becomes like *1984*—locked in perpetual war in Third World deserts and jungles for the young and poor to fight while the rich sit in their ivory towers at home? I started thinking a lot about passages from the New Testament about love and forgiveness and turning the other cheek and how that could be embodied by a gentle soul like Saint Francis of Assisi. I thought teaching would be a respectable way to stay out of the draft, even though my father said it was a job for losers."

"But you could have done your time and waited out the war."

"Except I was miserable. There was a lot more to teaching teenagers than standing in front of a classroom, and I was no Saint Francis. To work as a hospital orderly, I needed to convince my draft board that I was a conscientious objector."

"Why didn't you? Hadn't your fucking beliefs crystallized by then?"

"My thinking was way too muddled. The law said you have to be against all war, and I couldn't square that with defeating Hitler and ending slavery. I hoped I could hide out in the Air Force making training films."

"What was so bad about staying at the Pentagon?"

"It drove me crazy. If I was going to be in the Air Force, I wanted to be on a film unit, period. Except Nixon's campaign promises turned out to be a bunch of lies, and the war began to look once again like it was never going to end. I started bouncing between wanting out and wanting to be over here, to see it first-hand, to experience it. I actually gave credence to the assholes who said you don't know what you're talking about unless you've been here."

"I'm one of those assholes."

"I'm sure you are," I replied with a wry smile, but I was bluffing. *Where the hell is he leading me?* I wondered. "Well, I managed to get my ass thrown out of the Pentagon, and for once in my life, my timing was perfect. The Aerospace Audiovisual Service was shorthanded. Except there was a catch— my beliefs had started crystallizing for real because it was just about then that word got out about My Lai."

"And you're one of those bleeding hearts who think that Vietnamese women and kids and old people are innocent—that only young Vietnamese men are killing GIs."

This is going downhill fast, I thought. I tried to push on. "They crystallized a little more with the invasion of Cambodia and the shootings at Kent State, only now it was too late, I had orders for Southeast Asia.

"I hoped I could be an impartial observer, a fly on the wall. But you can't do a tour over here without getting blood on your hands. Even when I was 'just editing' bomb damage assessment footage for *Hits of the Week*—that stuff was going back to the Pentagon and the House and Senate Armed

Services committees to show how great the air war was going so they could justify dropping even more bombs. The titles we spliced in made it sound like we were bombing Hitler's factories in Hamburg, but it was rice farmers living in thatch huts. Anybody who fired back at us was annihilated."

"Jungle Rules, Leary. We're fighting a fuckin' jungle war."

"How can that be a winning strategy? We've been annihilating unarmed old men, women, and children who might have been on *our* side, for Christ's sake, or who simply wanted to sit out the damn war by taking *no side at all.* And all I could do was sit there at my editing bench doing my job, ruminating about napalm and so-called collateral damage, powerless to stop it or say a word. And now I'm up there with you—*thousands* of trucks destroyed and a second gunship down. It's madness without end."

"It'll end when we win."

"And if it doesn't? Even those innocuous Hometown News releases we put together back at Norton were a twisted part of the war effort. Guys like you serving overseas wouldn't know about it, but the Air Force and the Department of Defense sent out news clips that actually played on small-town TV stations. And when we ran out of good news to film, the DOD film crews started making it up—for years—until Senator Fulbright got wind we were staging those heart-warming scenes out in the boondocks of VC defecting and veterinarians inoculating water buffalo and dentists filling peasant children's teeth. Nobody saw the platoon of Marines with their M-16s locked and loaded just off-camera. And I was part of the program."

"So now that your worst fears have been confirmed, now that you've got dirt and blood under your manicured fingernails, you decide to turn down an assignment to Florida and extend over here at the shooting war. How do you explain *that* piece of ass-backward thinking?"

"I wanted to spare some other fool having to come over here."

"But now, even though you've admitted to me there are some wars you *could* go along with, your honor or conscience or whatever you call it, says, 'To hell with honesty. Get out at any cost and screw the technicalities.'"

"Fuck you," I blurted, hating it as usual when Harley was right. A little smile of begrudging admiration spread across my face. "Before the bicycle race, you might have been right. But *that* was senselessness beyond senselessness. In the hospital and my first week back at work, Liscomb encouraged me to visit Prah Samrong out at Big Buddha. And after spending a few days with him, a tectonic shift began to take place in my brain. It wasn't just what he said to me or the books he gave me. It was the simple life he lived. He and his fellow monks didn't need to overindulge in anything for their lives to be full and rich."

"From what I've seen, you enjoy overindulging as much as any of us."

"I think I've had enough. Following what Samrong calls the Eightfold Path—what you might call 'straightening up and flying right'—sounds pretty good to me. I need a break. Just the *idea* of sitting in silent meditation, developing concentration to the point we can watch our mind at work, watch how thoughts and feelings and emotions endlessly form and dissolve—it's something that had simply never occurred to me before."

Harley tossed his empty can onto the pile and snapped open another Budweiser. "You're making me thirsty."

"It's amazing to me how that mindfulness can then be carried over into real life. A monk won't step on an ant or kill a mosquito, even though a red ant can bite your butt so fiercely you can't sit down for a week and a malarial mosquito can flat-out kill you."

"Jungle Rules," said Baker. "Kill those little fuckers before they—"

"Whoever gave squishing a bug a thought back in the States?"

"God, you can be irritating, Leary."

"Whoever gave *violence* a thought, as long as it was Good Guy violence taking out Bad Guy violence? 'As American as cherry pie,' H. Rapp Brown called it."

"Maybe it's because the whole country has a deeply held belief in Jungle Rules, Leary, except you. They worked at high noon in Dodge City, and they still work for the L.A.P.D."

"Think about it: we were *entertained* by violence growing up—horror movies, cop shows, cowboy movies, Road Runner cartoons, even roach commercials! War movies had happy endings. Good Guys never died accidentally from 'friendly fire,' and villages full of innocent civilians were never napalmed and written off as 'collateral damage.' Our childhoods left us badly unprepared for real violence—King and the Kennedys, My Lai and the invasion of Cambodia."

"So now you're against cowboys, cops, and roadrunners?"

"When I got shipped over here, I hoped there might be a 'middle way' to look at war, to experience it without being corrupted by it, without becoming part of it. I expected it would take a heroic amount of willpower—fear and the instinct for self-preservation and the desire to avenge harm done to our brothers-in-arms are powerful emotions—but I thought I could handle it. Now, though, after two Spectre birds have gone down, after we've annihilated countless convoys and knocked out their bridges and they're still firing back and coming on down the Trail, after Thai insurgent suicide attacks on the base and against our fucking bicycle race, after the crew on Spectre 544 and the drivers and porters on Lieutenant Duong's convoy died horrible, violent deaths, after all that and more, I don't see how there can be a 'middle path' between war and peace."

"Well, you finally got something right, Leary—there isn't. There's only winning and losing. That's why God created Jungle Rules."

I tried to stay focused. "When a Buddhist monk enters the Eightfold Path, he abstains from intentionally harming any living thing. That's where I've gotten. I can't have anything more to do with the killing—on either side."

"That's one more thing you got right, Einstein. The sooner we get all you snivelers out of here, the sooner we can let the professional soldiers fight this damned war."

"You've only got one problem with that idea—"

"Yeah? What's that?" he asked.

"They're running out of professional soldiers to send over here. They know better than to force them to do more than a one-year tour of this fucked-up war. You're an exception. You volunteered to stick around. But for the run-of-the-mill lifer who's done his tour and moved on, the brass can't have *them* rebelling. That's why they were thrilled for me to extend, spotty record and all. They can't start the draft back up, and they can't start sending the National Guard or the Reserves because they're too full of double-dipping politicians and rich men's sons. Besides, they're needed at home now to keep college campuses and inner-city ghettoes under control. They do pretty well against unarmed civilians, but put those beer bellies over here, out in the bush or up with you flying night ops, and they wouldn't last a day—or a night."

Harley sucked his can of beer dry. "You're telling me they're gonna try to run this war with a handful of dumb, gung-ho suckers like me and a few planeloads of scruffy lottery-losers?"

I pinched his cheek and said, "You aren't dumb. In fact, for a gung-ho ex-jock, you're pretty smart." I started to get up.

"Before you go," said Harley, "I ought to tell you what it was I brought you over here for."

"Yes?"

"It sure as hell wasn't to hear you drone on and on about philosophy."

"Sorry if I got carried away. So what is it?"

"I'm not going to write one of those letters for you, you know, supporting your claim."

At first, I thought it was disappointment that was throwing me into a mental spiral, but why should I have expected anything more from Baker? I felt a flash of anger at myself for thinking I could persuade him to put himself in my shoes. Valium mixed with way too much beer was sending my head into a tailspin, but I took a stab at hiding my disappointment. "Thanks for at least considering—"

"Who said I did? I couldn't get beyond the first paragraph. I guess I know you too well. You needed to go all the way with your convictions. For me to buy that you've taken this high moral ground, you needed to walk the walk—no drugs, no booze, no pussy. Three days at a monastery doesn't undo a year of debauchery. Talk is cheap."

"Air Force Regulation 35-24 doesn't require sainthood or monkhood for me to be classified as a conscientious objector."

"In my book it does. The way I look at it, drugs, booze, and pussy are the rewards of being a warrior."

Fortunately, several of my colleagues who knew me longer and better than Harley Baker saw it differently. Late at night the following week, I sat cross-legged on the floor at Bungalow Ruam Chon Sawng using my bed for a desk while I sorted through two stacks of letters. It was hot and stuffy, but I couldn't turn on the ceiling fan without scattering the papers. I got up and opened the shutters. It helped—a little. The first stack was made up of letters supporting my original request for discharge, almost all from people back in the States. I could throw out any that were wishy-washy because the other stack was made up of letters from my compadres at Ubon and were far more compelling, coming as they did from fellow airmen in a combat zone.

The easiest to toss was Father Boyle's. As Tom Wheeler had coached me months earlier, the scuttlebutt from his contacts higher up the chain of command in administration was to keep the applications short and the supporting letters plentiful and strong, exactly opposite the fifty-page application I originally submitted. It had made Tom laugh, full as it was of poetry, quotes from existentialist writers, and excerpts from antiwar speeches I gave in California after the invasion of Cambodia, all guaranteed to piss off Air Force officers who would much rather be off fighting a war or enjoying a drink at the Officers' Club than sitting at a desk reading. Father Boyle's tepid attempt at supporting a lapsed-Catholic-turned-existentialist probably did me more harm than good.

I replaced it with one from Chaplain Kirkgartner, the hip young chaplain who, after the race riots at Korat and Takhli, came up with the House of Free Expression, a coffee house where black and white GIs could rap instead of beat the crap out of each other. Black dudes especially respected him because even in his thirties, he could hold his own with anyone on base one-on-one on the basketball court. I respected him because of all he had gone through to get Tukada into rehab and how he had found her parents and brought them to Ubon after the bicycle race. He concluded, "There is no doubt in my mind that the seeds for Sergeant Leary's present beliefs—embracing the non-violence taught and practiced in Buddhism—represent an evolution of his childhood church experience. Sergeant Leary has demonstrated a firm commitment to live out his pacifist convictions."

Even though Wheeler had stopped writing to Lek, he was one of the first people I heard from about my new application, sending me a notarized response almost immediately. "I have had a close relationship with Sergeant Leary for almost two years, starting with shared political interests at Norton Air Force Base in 1970, where he showed great courage in leading Norton GIs for Peace, relinquishing advancement in the Air Force and, for all we knew at the time, putting his life on the line by speaking out publicly against the invasion of Cambodia. He knew there was a possibility of being shot at in rural California, and that was a risk he was willing to take. I don't believe he told anyone but me, but when he was assigned to fly combat missions over the Ho Chi Minh Trail, he left his firearm in his locker, so unwilling was he to take human life, even in self-defense, had he been shot down. At Ubon, when he played as a white drummer in a formerly all-black soul band, he didn't need words to make a statement that racial peace and harmony is possible. Sergeant Leary was a major force behind the Big Buddha Bicycle Race, a project that brought Asians and Americans together in the spirit of friendly competition before it ended in tragedy. I fervently hope that his sincerity and integrity will be recognized."

Alas, although Tom's letter may have been strong, I feared it might be tainted behind the scenes by the fact he had been medically discharged after going through detox for his heroin problem. I thumbed further down the stack, and—aha!—there was no such problem with the letter from Frank Lutz, my munchkin sound-guy buddy from Norton and Tan Son Nhut. He wrote: "Brendan Leary was my sponsor when I arrived at Norton AFB, California, in April of 1970. The escalation of the war into Cambodia soon followed, and I could see that it troubled him deeply. He talked about his deep respect for the late Dr. Martin Luther King and his philosophy of non-violence, and in the years that followed, I never saw Sergeant Leary act or speak in any way contrary to those beliefs. I was on TDY at Ubon during the Big Buddha Bicycle Race and saw both his joy at bringing the Thai and American communities together and his deep sadness when the project ended in violence. I respectfully disagree with Sergeant Leary in several important ways. I believe that war can be morally just, especially when it is fought in defense of the United States or its allies. But at a time when we are engaged in a war filled with moral ambiguity, Brendan is trying to initiate a little peace in the world, something it sorely needs."

Spit-and-polish Jack Wu and laissez-faire Larry Zelinsky, two very different career NCOs I had known since my Norton days, also came through, supporting the moral claims of someone they philosophically disagreed with. Wu, the straight arrow who had just replaced Link as first sergeant, wrote: "I am a former Army veteran who served as a tank crewman and a signal corps photographer at home and overseas. My acquaintance with Sergeant Leary began in May of 1970 at Headquarters, Aerospace Audiovisual Service, Norton Air Force Base, CA, where I served as a motion picture lab supervisor. We have had many long conversations and I have had many opportunities to observe Sergeant Leary's conduct both on the job and while organizing the Big Buddha Bicycle Race. From the time I met him to the time of this writing, Sergeant Leary's opposition to war in general and the use of force has consistently deepened, even more so after he saw death first-hand in combat and in the terrorist attack on the bicycle race. As the acting First Sergeant of Detachment 3, 601st Photo Squadron, I unhesitatingly endorse Brendan Leary's application for discharge as a conscientious objector."

Zelinsky, the pudgy joker with the Cheshire-cat smile, summarized our contrasting beliefs and then wrote: "In the two years I have known and supervised Sergeant Leary, I have seen an unwavering deepening of his belief that this war and all wars are senseless and needless. Brendan Leary is, to my mind, a unique person, a person of remarkably strong convictions. Several of his friends have been killed during his tour at Ubon, but instead of seeking revenge, he has sought only to heal. He has quietly stood his ground against many career men who see the military and its might as the only way to settle the world's conflicts. He has been unduly harassed by the military, being passed over for at least a year for what is normally an automatic promotion from lowly airman first class to sergeant, all because of his convictions, even though he is a man with the intellect and education to have been a fine officer. I think it would be a grave injustice to keep a man such as Brendan Leary in the military for another day." I was glad to see no mention of the Blue Movie Syndicate's attempt at going into the porn business in either letter.

Baker might have been right when he said I had lost my moral compass, but he was the only one who seemed to have noticed in a town filled with lost souls. As I thumbed my way through the letters, trying to put them into some kind of order, I began to appreciate how many airmen I had met since coming to Ubon had come through, supporting my claim. I was especially struck with how diverse their perspectives were, from anti-war Greg Quam in the print shop, whose views were virtually identical to mine—only differing really in that he hadn't left the Catholic Church—to Homer Harwell, a career combat cameraman who took a gun-toting John Wayne approach to life and death.

Sugie Bear from the band wrote: "Sergeant Leary's deeply held beliefs on both war and race relations, from what I see and hear behind his back, have caused him to be strongly liked and disliked by many. But what impresses me about the man is that he does not hate anyone, friend or foe alike. He is a man who searches for the truth and is willing to act on it. It proved to be a blessing for my last band because he didn't let being white hold him back from playing with what had been an all-black group. The group we play in now is a regular UN of Asians performing alongside black and white Americans. Even though I am a Christian and Sergeant Leary says he is now a Buddhist, I can see that his Christian upbringing still lives with him in a powerful way: he will not break God's commandment against killing. In a way, he is too true to his Christian beliefs to remain in the military without always in some way contradicting himself. And therefore, in my mind, I believe he is justified in his application as a conscientious objector."

Among other things, Quam wrote: "I have known Sergeant Leary for over six months now. We have discussed a wide range of topics in that time, and Brendan has always, consistently showed a great awareness and concern for people." Later in the letter, he said: "His realization that he cannot in any way take part in a military organization will undoubtedly be a difficult one for the Air Force to understand and will continue to cause him much hardship, but it is one he has courageously taken. I urge the Air Force to honor this new request for discharge from a man who has demonstrated depth, sincerity, and forethought in all I have seen him say and do."

Jamal Washington introduced himself as a career man whose work as a ComDoc cameraman brought us together often during our tours in Ubon. He went on to write that although he was not in any way a pacifist, "the very fact that I serve my country to further the cause of democracy leads me to believe Sergeant Leary has every right to a fair examination of his convictions. I believe he is sincere in his belief in non-violent resistance to aggression, not wavering even when he flew in combat, not wavering when he was shot down and held captive, and not wavering when he met his ultimate test—the senseless slaughter of close friends by terrorists during the Big Buddha Bicycle Race. I know because I was with him that day." He noted that my off-duty involvement in both music and teaching continued to bring people together from diverse races and cultures. He concluded by saying: "If a man has tried to do his duty for as long as possible, but cannot in good conscience continue, then he has served to the best of his ability. To force him to continue would be a moral injustice to a highly creative individual and would weaken the very fabric of the democracy we are fighting to defend." I had to pause a moment. Damn if my old bunkmate hadn't brought a tear to my eye.

Probably no one surprised me more than that old warbird, Homer Harwell, my lead combat cameraman. The man with the perpetual five-o'clock shadow hardly ever spoke, but he wrote eloquently: "I am the lead combat documentation cameraman assigned to Detachment 3 of the 601st Photo Squadron. Sergeant Leary had a reputation before he arrived here for being disruptive and a troublemaker. In reality, he has proved to be a serious filmmaker who can both edit film and shoot it well. Sergeant Leary was put under my command after two of my men were shot down over Sepone, another went into alcohol rehab, and a fourth was held up back in the States for psych evaluation over late-onset fear of flying. I was briefed on his anti-war activities in Southern California, but he has not tried to force those views on anyone here. He has, however, earned respect in this unit for not backing down, either, when discussion has turned to tactics and strategies of the U.S. involvement in the Vietnam conflict.

"In this day and age, it is easy to remain silent, and to be silent in many circles is tantamount to agreement. It is especially difficult to speak up in a military environment that demands unswerving obedience to orders. As troubling as this can be for a career soldier, it is obvious that for Sergeant Leary, every order that involves killing would be morally illegal. Now that Leary has survived a plane crash and firefights that resulted in heavy loss of life, it is clear to me that even in serving as a cameraman, bearing witness to combat has brought Leary great moral anguish. It is clear to me that Sergeant Leary has tried his best to accommodate the demands of the Air Force, but for him, that is no longer possible. It is also clear to me that the very reason the United States fights wars to make the world safe for democracy and freedom is so that an individual like Brendan Leary is free to be Brendan Leary. I must therefore recommend that Sergeant Leary be expeditiously granted an Honorable Discharge."

Working my way down the stack, I came to one from Jim Scott, the Peace Corps volunteer who had given me my job teaching English at AUA when the Band of Brothers disbanded and who, paradoxically, was Baker's neighbor at their compound in town. While I wasn't surprised that Jim was willing to write a letter of support, the power and eloquence of his letter far exceeded my expectations. "In a world that seems intent upon its own destruction and yet where people seem unable to look beyond their own affairs, it is rare to find a person who believes in the welfare of his fellow man.

After observing his work with the American University Alumni Association language program that I supervise here in Ubon, I sincerely believe that Brendan Leary is this type of person. He has made that painful search of his soul and found to his dismay that he owes humanity more than he can ever give as part of a war machine. He realizes that destruction and death, which are the scourge of Southeast Asia today, can't be allowed to continue. He realizes, too, that war isn't inevitable and that if more people believed that peace was possible, then we could have it.

"This decision to thrust his beliefs to the fore and allow them to be tried and tested is surely a most difficult one. I sincerely hope that the U.S. Air Force will grant Sergeant Brendan Leary the C.O. status he requests."

It wasn't just my friends and fellow airmen who offered support for my claim. A diverse group of officers also went to bat for me, ranging from black radical Lieutenant Liscomb to hard-as-nails Colonel "Grouchy Bear" Della Rippa.

Liscomb wrote that he was a production officer who had known me since 1970 when I arrived at AAVS Headquarters and was assigned to edit several news releases he had directed. "Sergeant Leary clearly enjoyed his work and expressed a desire to make filmmaking a lifelong pursuit. Following the U.S. incursion into Cambodia, however, I noticed that a metamorphosis was taking place and was not surprised to learn that Leary was preparing to submit an application for discharge as a Conscientious Objector. I recall being concerned when he was given orders for Southeast Asia before his case had been decided and feared that his mental anguish might cause him to go AWOL.

"When I arrived at Ubon RTAFB, Thailand, in 1971, I was relieved to see Sergeant Leary making the best adjustment he could to a difficult situation. As one of the first black graduates of the Air Force Academy, I appreciate that Brendan is inspired by a man of peace like Dr. Martin Luther King and 'walks the walk' of racial tolerance. He was the driving force behind the Big Buddha Bicycle Race, but instead of hating the insurgents who attacked it, he grieved for all of those who died. He has endured months of night operations as a combat cameraman and survived the crash of Spectre 544 that took the lives of a dozen crewmen. Please honor Sergeant Brendan Leary's request for discharge expeditiously, as I have seen first-hand that his beliefs have grown ever deeper and more sincere and at the same time have grown ever more in conflict with his duties as a cameraman in the USAF."

Captain Alan Shelby, III, the lawyer in the Judge Advocate's office at Norton Air Force Base who helped me put together my original application for discharge, impressed me with his willingness to risk ruffling the feathers of senior officers in his chain of command. I had only written to him as a long shot, and he had every right to pass. Instead, he wrote: "I have read Sergeant Leary's most recent application for discharge and have no doubt now as I had no doubt then that he is sincere when he asserts his opposition to war in any form. His beliefs, which he originally claimed were philosophical, in fact always had a basis in the teachings and writings of such mainstream religious figures as Christ, Gandhi, and Dr. Martin Luther King. Now that Sergeant Leary has experienced war first-hand, his opposition to war has deepened and is further strengthened by the teachings and practices of Buddhism, a further development of his personal philosophy of life, which embodied kindness, love, respect for his fellow man, and non-violence. The average religious person probably thinks about God and his religion once a week. I feel that Sergeant Leary's religious, spiritual, and philosophical beliefs—which include opposition to all forms of war—are a daily touchstone in his personal life and his dealings with other people."

Even my former nemeses, Hill, English, and Della Rippa looked past their own strongly held beliefs and backed my claim. Hill wrote: "I have known Sergeant Leary since he arrived in Ubon in March of 1971, with advance warnings to expect trouble. Instead, I observed Leary to be respectful toward his officers and willing to follow Air Force regulations in redressing his concerns. He was a reluctant combat cameraman, but he carried out his duties diligently, exhibiting exceptional courage and fortitude when, after surviving the crash of Spectre 544, he helped a badly injured comrade-in-arms escape capture and return safely from enemy-held territory in Laos, for which he has been recommended for the Air Force Commendation Medal.

"As a potential career officer and lifelong conservative, I disagree with many of Sergeant Leary's beliefs, but in the year I have known him, I have never seen or heard Sergeant Leary deviate from his core convictions, only expressing them with more clarity and strength. Thus it is that I must support Brendan Leary's claim for conscientious objector status."

Captain English wrote simply and directly, concluding, "Although I do not agree with Sergeant Leary's beliefs, I do believe that he is sincere. He has clearly reached an impasse where he can no longer serve his conscience and serve in the United States Air Force."

Colonel Della Rippa wrote: "In addition to serving as commander of the 16th Special Operations Squadron, I presided over Sergeant Leary's original discharge hearing and recommended turning down his claim. I don't pretend to understand how or why, but over the subsequent six months, while he was flying with crews under my command, I believe Sergeant Leary's convictions grew deeper and I now consider him a most sincere conscientious objector. I recommend Sergeant Leary's separation from the U.S. Air Force for the good of the individual and the good of the Air Force."

The hardest to deal with was Dad. I was afraid to open the letter when it arrived, and then finally bit the bullet. Mom said in a short cover letter that she was turning this over to him, and it looked like he was trying the best he could to support me and understand the changes I had gone through. He was Old School, though—an old-school Catholic and an old-school World War II veteran who didn't question authority any more than he wanted his own authority questioned. "I can't honestly say why Brendan left the Catholic Church he was raised in, but I am certain he is sincere in his newfound beliefs." It was barely better than the one from Father Boyle that I had thrown out, but he was the only relative who had written at all. I put it aside and sorted once more through the stack of new letters.

The only person I was counting on, besides Harley, who failed to come through at all was Woody Shahbazian, my cabinmate back in California. He always promised, "Tomorrow," when I asked him how his letter was coming along, but in reality he was too busy with Papa-sahn across the river putting together a massive shipment of "Johnson's Baby Powder" that would pay his way through grad school when his GI Bill ran out. I continued to hope that Harley might reconsider, although I didn't know why. After waiting a few weeks, I decided to include Dad's letter with my supporting documents and decided that what I had was sufficient.

Apparently, the Air Force now followed Catch 22B to prove to Congress that it had put a fair and rational process in place for discharge petitions. Assuming that anyone wanting out had to be sane, they made me go through another psych evaluation to prove it, knowing that they had Catch

22A—"insufficient documentation"—in reserve to deny any claims they wanted to. To my amazement and amusement, I passed. Another interview followed with the head chaplain of the base, Colonel Daryl Pedigrew, an old-time Southern Baptist who nevertheless supported my claim. This time I took the advice of Edward Poser, Esquire, and waived a hearing. The supporting letters were strong enough.

On the first of May, ComDoc finally got the replacement we needed, but as always, there were complications. Cooper was officially gone. He had only recently been sent back to Norton to finish recovering from his malaria when his father, still in his forties, unexpectedly died of a heart attack. That meant a hardship discharge so he could go home and take care of his widowed mother and his kid brother, a development even I couldn't blame on a Ron Cooper scheme to avoid combat by using me as cannon fodder. The replacement who did come in was cross-training from the Air Police, which meant that he was completely green but a perfect student for me, his one-eyed, one-handed camera instructor. Between the two of us, we were able to film a few awards ceremonies and a base orientation film for new arrivals.

He was on his own the day that Harley and I were decorated in an embarrassingly ostentatious ceremony at the base theater for managing to make it back from Laos in one piece, more or less. Harley and I both received purple hearts, mostly for our poor parachuting. That made two for me earned completely by accident. Harley was deservedly awarded a Silver Star for disarming our guard, capturing his weapon, and making our escape possible, which meant that General Gong had to fly in for the presentation. I was given the Air Force Commendation Medal for tagging along. Before Harley and I left the stage, Colonel Grimsley announced that Baker was being promoted to tech sergeant, making him one of the youngest in the Air Force.

For someone who didn't want to be there in the first place and who hated awards ceremonies, and especially for someone with decidedly mixed feelings of admiration and consternation for Tech Sergeant Harley Baker, I noticed with a pinprick of irritation that I had ended up getting pretty well sucked in by the proceedings. "Keep this up," I said, "and before long they're gonna send you off to the Pentagon and make you Sergeant Major of the whole damned Air Force."

"For a fucking peacenik, you sure say the cruelest things sometimes. What the hell would my muddy boots and I do at the frigging Pentagon?"

Mr. Doumer's Bridge

While I was traipsing through the mountains of Laos, only Harwell and Washington had been available to cover the Spectre missions. They got by, it turned out, because the contractors had finally gotten back on schedule, ironing out the glitches in the video recording system and one by one putting "Cadillac" gunship conversions on line. Now the bomb damage assessment footage could be recorded directly off whatever sensor the pilot was using to site his target. All the fire-control officer had to do was remember to turn on the recorder.

My eye patch came off, and the eye seemed to be okay. When the cast came off my wrist, First Sergeant Wu sent me back to the ComDoc ready room, where I was assigned to work full-time with our Air Police cross-trainee. I had him practice loading magazines in a changing bag and threading up cameras blindfolded in case he ever had to fill in on a Spectre operation. We spent a day filming takeoffs and landings from different spots along the runway and watched dailies the next morning, discussing ways of smoothing out the camerawork. We were headed out the door to film some more when the phone rang. It was Wu. "Captain English needs to see you right away."

Climbing the stairway to the orderly room, my heart was racing and my boots felt heavy. When I stepped inside, Wu gave me a pained glance and picked up the intercom. "He's here."

I knocked on Captain English's door and reported in. He and Hill were waiting for me. "We need to send you out on a very important F-4 mission. Wing headquarters couldn't give many details, but they said it involves a new weapons system, and they couldn't risk sending out a trainee to document the bomb damage."

He seemed genuinely apologetic. "Hopefully, this will be your last combat mission."

"If it makes you feel any better," Hill added, "Lieutenant Liscomb will be flying along beside you in a sister ship."

Liscomb spotted me coming out of English's office and walked outside with me. "I think your discharge is going through this time."

"I hope so. I'm afraid I'm running on empty in the luck department."

"Let's hope you've got a little left in your tank. English thinks we're heading up through the Mu Gia Pass to Hanoi." My stomach lurched and left me feeling queasy. I noticed Liscomb was wearing a bracelet made of strands of sacred string tied around his wrist. He noticed that I noticed. "They let me go visit your friend, Prah Samrong, yesterday out at the Big Buddha. He gave me something to give to you."

Liscomb pulled out several more pieces of *sai sin* and tied them around my wrist. "Thanks," I said.

"We've got some time before the briefing. Come on over to my trailer."

It was dark inside, except for a stick of incense and a few candles burning at the little altar in the sitting room. I was surprised to see the silhouette of a girl meditating on the floor. "Who's that?" I whispered.

"Pook's been my housegirl. We're a gnat's eyelash from becoming *tii-rahks*, except she's scared shitless I'm not coming back from this mission."

"We may not be," I replied. "Thank God Prah Samrong and Ajahn Po have been teaching me how meditation can prepare you for death. They both say that by being prepared for death, you can be fearless in life."

Moonbeam smiled. "That has a nice Zen ring to it. Shall we join Pook and sit for a few minutes?" He lit a stick of incense and handed one to me. I lit mine, blew out the harsh flame, and fanned the tip until it glowed on its own. Rick did the same. We planted our sticks next to Pook's in a sand-filled ceramic bowl and settled back in a half lotus position on the grass floor mat. The smoke from the incense filled the room with the pleasant scent of fresh linen. When I'd meditated before, it had been by myself, with Prah Samrong, or in a hall filled with monks. This was the first time I'd sat with two other laypeople. The air-conditioning muted the sounds from the base outside. It was incredibly simple, and yet the effect of sitting together quietly with our eyes closed, just breathing, was powerful, filling my heart with serenity and warmth.

When we got to the briefing, Liscomb's wish that I hadn't run out of luck turned out to be well-founded. Colonel Grimsley informed us that our target would be a French bridge just outside Hanoi. "According to In-tell, Mr. Doumer thought he was working for the Roman Empire when he built this thing seventy years ago. Today we intend to prove him wrong."

The Doumer Bridge was four times the size of the ones the 8th Tactical Fighter Wing had taken down in Laos. It was a combination railroad-highway bridge that was funneling vast amounts of materiel from southern

China to the NVA offensive in South Vietnam. And it needed to be taken down ASAP, despite the fact the Seventh Air Force had been trying to do so since 1967.

From the back seat of my F-4, I could see Liscomb through my plexiglass canopy seated behind my pilot's wingman in the next aircraft. When the jets turned off the taxiway and formed up diagonally on the runway, Liscomb and I gave each other a thumbs-up, our pilots hit their throttles, and we headed north, small cogs in an aerial armada of more than fifty aircraft, made up mostly of F-4s out of Ubon. We were depending on lead flights of F105s and EB-66s out of Korat armed with newer, nimbler *laser*-guided missiles to take out *radar*-guided Russian-built SAM missile sites in the few seconds they had between the Russian radar being switched on and locking in on a target. We were just as dependent on two flights of F-4s that followed, running in a couple minutes ahead of us dispersing World War II-vintage chaff—Christmas tinsel!—to jam the NVA's radar. This was a daylight mission, however, and the triple-A was far nastier than anything I had witnessed on our worst nights over the Trail. Liscomb and I got to come in on two of the last F-4s, bouncing around in an ocean of man-made turbulence, watching SAM after SAM fired at our formation—at least 150 of the bastards—and scores of MiGs sent up, only to be driven away by our MiG-CAP escorts, flights of F-4 combat air patrols that specialized in shooting down MiGs. The bridge sustained hit after hit, but I saw only one span fall.

The next day the 8th Tactical Fighter Wing sent in a small flight of four F-4s to mop up. It could have been a disaster thanks to a scheduling screw-up. The chaff had been dropped early, and the MiG-CAP escorts thought the attack aircraft weren't coming and went home. But somehow this lulled the North Vietnamese defenses around Hanoi to sleep. With only two 3,000-pound dumb bombs and six 2,000-pound laser-guided smart bombs, the F-4s were able to drop three more spans and damage three others. And then the weather turned bad, which was fine with me. We hadn't lost a single plane on those two raids. There was no way that kind of good fortune could continue indefinitely, and even wearing a wristband of sacred string, I wasn't feeling like anybody's good luck charm.

Sunday, May 28, was Visakha Bucha, the biggest Buddhist holiday of the year. Buses everywhere were filled with people traveling home to be with their families, and bamboo rockets were being fired all over Issan Thailand, a pre-Buddhist custom that had been absorbed into Buddhist tradition. Called *bun bahng fai*, it was both a way of earning holiday merit for Buddhist laypeople and, according to Thai folklore, a way of bringing rain down from the heavens to this drought-prone part of the country.

Liscomb got permission for him and Pook to ride out with me and Lek to Big Buddha late that afternoon for an evening candlelight procession. Prah Samrong greeted our group and explained to me and Moonbeam how the procession was the highlight of Visakha Bucha, which marked the date of the Buddha's birth, enlightenment and *parinibbana*, or passing into Nirvana. "In different years," he told us with a little laugh.

"Kind of like Christmas, Easter, and the Assumption rolled into one big holiday," I whispered to Moonbeam.

"With a touch of the Fourth of July and Thanksgiving thrown in for good measure," he replied with his usual warm smile.

Shortly after sunset, while Prah Samrong remained inside chanting in Pali with the other monks, Pook and Lek lit our candles, and we joined the villagers circling three times around the Dhamma hall. Reflecting as we walked, I wondered if President Nixon had ever given a thought to the candles a thousand young Americans had carried around the White House on the eve of the Second Vietnam Moratorium a couple of years earlier.

On the cab ride back from Big Buddha, watching the *bahng fai* rockets fired from temples all around Ubon Province, I was reminded of countless SAMs that had been fired just a few hundred miles away, rockets that were not made out of bamboo, intended to bring down American aircraft instead of raindrops. Back at Ruam Chon Sawng after Lek turned in, I went down alone to the spirit house and lit some incense and said a little prayer to the Thai rain gods and war gods and any other gods, goddesses, devas or devils that happened to be listening that the air battle I witnessed over Hanoi would be my last. I prayed for everyone's sake that the madness would somehow end honorably for all sides.

On Wednesday, the last day of May, I couldn't help dancing a little jig in Wu's office when I opened a battered manila cover envelope and pulled out the message, one I had waited for over a year to read. My request for discharge had been approved this time, and the ever-heavier weight I had been carrying finally lifted.

Now that I was being relieved from duty, an honorable end of the war for me, anyway, it would next be a question of whether or not I had to return Stateside. I explained to English and Hill that my car was now a rusting, unsalvageable hulk along the Pacific Coast Highway and that I had arranged to enter a Buddhist monastery right here in Issan Thailand. I'd prefer to muster out in Ubon and save them the trouble of shipping me home. Captain English said he would see what he could do. I sent Mom a note saying I was being discharged early but that I might be staying on in Thailand. I don't know if my brain was off-kilter or on autopilot, but I started writing to Danielle when I caught myself and set down my pen.

The second Wednesday in June marked the end of the term at AUA. It had come up at one of the after-class dinners that I would be leaving the Air Force soon and entering a monastery. Several of my educated, middle-class students told me that they would like to do that too, for at least one Rains Retreat, the old custom in Thailand, but that they were too busy now that they worked in an office. "At Bank of America, Khun Brendan, it not like a rice farm," said one of my middle managers. "When it rain, we still come to work every day!"

That last night, at the end of class, my students presented me with gifts of candles and incense and material to make into a monk's robes, simple gestures that touched me deeply. Pawnsiri waited until the others had left, and I walked with her to the bus stop.

"If you are monk, how can we make music together with your band?"

"We might have to wait a little on that. A lot happened to me in the war, and I'm afraid I'll need all of the Rains Retreat to sort it out. Did they tell the class I was shot down over Laos?"

"Khun Jim didn't say Lao, but he say missing in action. We know where. Sergeant Anant explain."

"I don't understand why, exactly, but when I came back from Laos, I lost my desire to play drums. If I ever play drums again, though, I promise it'll be with you, Pawnsiri."

"When you finish being monk, will you stay here in Ubon? What do I tell my professor?"

"I think we have a lot to talk about. Let's go over to that *rahn-ahahn* and have a Coke."

She followed me back across the wide expanse of sidewalk to the old Chinese noodle shop where Khun Jim and Harley and I used to hang out, a tiny place with only three tables. I paid for the Cokes and joined her at the table in back. The cold condensation on the bottle felt soothing in my hand while I watched her put her straw to her lips and take a sip. "I thought you wanted to come to America to be a nurse?"

"I do only if you go back to America." She looked at me directly, no longer a demure schoolgirl.

I felt like a not-too-bright Saturday morning cartoon character, and a big light bulb had just gone off above my head. "Wow... I didn't get it. I'm so stupid sometimes. I guess I don't understand how any nice Thai girl like you would want to be with a GI. I thought only bar girls associated with American soldiers."

"To me, you're not GI. You're my teacher. My family like you. My professor think he can help you find a job. You can stay here. There is old Thai saying that a man is ripe for marriage when he's been a soldier and a monk."

"And you think *I'll* be ripe?"

"Yes," she replied, smiling shyly and finally turning away her eyes.

"You shouldn't wait for me, Pawnsiri. My heart's shattered. I don't know how much you know about the bicycle race, but a young Thai woman was killed whom I cared about very much. I still think about her. And I was engaged to a girl in the United States who only recently broke it off."

"Your story is very sad—like a Thai movie. But your heart will heal in time. I'm young. I can wait."

I was honored and overwhelmed. But even if we did want to pursue a relationship together, I was six or seven years older than Pawnsiri and afraid it was too much. And I had been so damn certain about going to film school. That was the carrot I had dangled in front of myself to keep going while I endured the Air Force and the war. Could I completely change course now? Did I want to? Even more confusing, I felt forever cursed to love the wrong woman. How could I know this was right? Could I master Thai and really raise a family in this culture, as much as I loved it from the outside looking in? What would happen when there was no more BX and Armed Forces Radio? Could I completely let myself go? Or would Mom and Dad find a way to pull at me from the other side of the world? Would I always regret not going to USC and taking a crack at Hollywood? What would happen if I brought Pawnsiri to America, even for a visit? I remembered the restaurant in Providence, a sophisticated college town, I thought, that gave us terrible service and dirty looks when Farida Shaikh and her brother from Princeton came in with a group of my friends for dinner—and they were Persian royalty who happened to have copper skin.

"This is such a change, Pawnsiri. You know I want to be a filmmaker someday. That's been my dream for years. I'm not sure I can give that up. Can we talk about this again in three months, after the Rains Retreat?"

"Yes," she said simply. I walked her back to the *sala* and waited with her for the bus. She looked so pure standing there. Somehow she had been protected from the war that was raging so near. Della Rippa was right. We were literally on a frontier where Communism and capitalism or democracy or whatever we were, stood eyeball to eyeball. Yet Pawnsiri seemed at peace. Was it possible she could grow up in Ubon and not know what went on night after night at the Corsair and the New Playboy? Many women in Thailand were more stunningly beautiful or glamorous than Pawnsiri. It was her clear eyes that drew me in. She wore little makeup, but her fine long black hair glistened and gave off just a hint of jasmine. She had an inner peace and strength that I admired. Somewhere in my Irish-American childhood, I remembered an aunt being called a "fine, handsome woman," a description that fit Pawnsiri well. She had the kind of inner strength and simple beauty that would last into her old age.

"I don't know how long I'll stay at Wat Pah Nirapai. Do you understand I may be a monk for a long time? Prah Samrong says that I have a lot of *kamma* to work out, and I think he may be right."

"I understand."

The bus pulled up and the door opened. We *waied* politely and smiled, and I said in my poor Thai, "*Pohp kan mai na khrab*—until I see you again."

"See you then," she answered sweetly, pleasantly.

Gift of an Alms Bowl

Pawnsiri's attention was flattering, but my old life was over. I was done with the war, with women, with rock 'n' roll and drugs, with hippies and squares, with politicians, businessmen, professors, and priests. I'd miss Mom's home cooking over the holidays and the sweet scent of her mother's macaroons and gingerbread cookies baking in the oven, but not enough to sit through a big turkey dinner worrying that Grandma Shepler or Grandpa Leary had found one of the liquor bottles we had hidden away. Or trying to tune out the Leary patriarchs complaining that Martin Luther King was moving way too fast with civil rights, or trying to explain after dinner why I couldn't sit with the men through endless hours of televised football. I wouldn't be able to tell them how—while they enjoyed the spectacle of giants crashing into each other with astounding speed and agility—I saw flashbacks of villages being lit up by napalm, convoys being chewed up truck by truck by Gatling guns, and sampans reduced to matchsticks by twin 40-mm Bofors.

I was done with America. I needed solitude, and there was only one place for me to find it—other than off in the jungle with the Aussie pilot who went mad after flying one close-air-support mission too many in his prop-driven Skyraider. I needed the tranquility I had found at Wat Pah Nirapai. It was still a gamble, though, because as much as I wanted to cut myself off from my former life, there was a part of me that didn't know if I could play by the demanding new rules, maintaining a vow of silence, giving up all worldly pleasure. There would be plenty of support from the brotherhood of monks, but how long could I live without the touch, fragrance, sight, or sound of a woman? Did I really want peace, or had I just been fighting authority? Had rock 'n' roll drumming been my essence, my passion, or just a manifestation of my anger? Was it a childish cry for attention, or was it something deeper—the heartbeat of the dance of life, music that was a universal call for love and compassion and joy? Was I a Druid? A pagan? Was *vipassana* meditation a form of spirituality that was an inevitable and logical progression from Catholicism and the emptiness I felt when I called myself an existentialist? I was going to find out—because permission to stay in Thailand had been granted.

Lek had decided to go home, once and for all, to Korat. Her father was truly sick and didn't need money for medicine. He needed *her*—to look after him and take care of her son. She wasn't leaving until I entered the monastery, however, and somehow she worked it out with Mama-sahn and Bun-lii and a bunch of the other old-time denizens of Ruam Chon Sawng so that pretty much the entire Ghetto would sponsor my ordination. The ritual for leaving the secular world and entering a monastery was typical of much of traditional Thai culture, a mixture of the *sanuk* and the sublime. It meant that the night before I walked through the gates of Wat Pah Nirapai, there would be a *pah-tii*. Late in the afternoon, Lek led me to the spirit house and gave me incense to light and a plate of food to set inside. "Pray," she said. "Pray to the *jao tii*, the spirits of Ruam Chon Sawng, to protect you on your journey."

I surrendered and prayed to spirits I didn't understand but whom I trusted because Lek trusted them. I followed her upstairs to our familiar porch balcony where she put me in one of the wicker chairs, wrapped a towel over my shoulders and proceeded to cut my hair short with a pair of scissors before carefully shaving my head, eyebrows, and mustache, a holy ritual rather different from that night in November when I shaved my mustache for a fleeting moment of pleasure with Tukada. Guests began to arrive in the alley below and in the open area underneath our bungalow where a little bar was set up. Lek pulled the towel off my shoulders, shook it out, and swept up the clippings of my hair that carpeted the wooden floorboards. Before she went downstairs, she presented me with a pair of white drawstring pants and a collarless white pullover shirt, much like what I wore on my first visit to the monastery, to wear until I presented myself to Ajahn Po in the morning.

Mama-sahn and her family, none of whom spoke much English, were among the first to make an appearance, bringing over a large table from her restaurant and laying it out buffet-style with an eye-popping selection of Issan-Thai delicacies. Bun-lii and a few of her girlfriends who had decided to take a night off from the bars were helping out. To send someone off to a monastery was an excellent way to earn merit for Buddhist laypeople, and for it to be a formerly decadent American airman I'm sure was earning them cosmic bonus points. The occasion was so auspicious, in fact, that Mama-sahn had put on what might have been her only blouse. The boxer and his beautiful girlfriend who spoke no English joined them a moment later, with Bun-lii hovering nearby to translate. Meanwhile, B.J. and Leclerc brought down a portable turntable and speakers from Bungalow #3 and, in an instant, had background music playing. In honor of the spiritual journey I was about to undertake, they abstained from ganja and red rock, staying with the Thai beer and whiskey that the other partygoers would be imbibing.

One or two at a time, the members of Domino Theory started drifting in for a low-key final appearance. Once the band tuned up, Woody, Marcos, Harley and Mali, Sugie Bear and Oi, Ackerman, Angel, and Kae all gathered near the bar. Harley had brought along the drums, but while I set up, I asked Marcos to perform as much music without me as he could. He said, "Okay," but I suspected he had other plans, especially when the Sparrows, led by Annie Kim, arrived with Sagittarius, creating a ripple of excitement among the gathering crowd and even more so with Woody and the horn section. "Ms. Kim keeps telling me she'll go out to dinner with me," Woody confided, "but there's a catch. First, I've got to interrupt my Sunday morning beauty sleep and go with her, hangover and all, to hear some Baptist missionary preach. Next thing you know, she'll want me to give up hedonism."

Lifers who had moved in recently and some of the brothers I never really got to know, other than burning Dear John letters together, began gathering at the bar, some of them with dates, and were soon spilling out into the alley. They were joined by Billy Hill and Colonel Della Rippa, both of whom shared a deeply held belief in never passing up free booze. Bun-lii and her friends called from across the alley, "Bren-dan—where your lip-stick?"

This was one Thai custom that I completely failed to grasp. For some reason, it was common to put makeup on a novice monk the night before he entered the *wat*. "*Khaw toht, Bun-lii. Mai dai!*" I answered, apologizing for not being able to indulge her.

Even though it was starting to get crowded, I was able to recognize Khun Jim and Pye coming up the alley, followed by Zelinsky and Peung. Jack Wu and his crew from the lab—Perez, Price, and Blackwell—drifted in a few minutes later. Perez had brought along a few of his favorite masseuses from Nikko's. In a brief flash of déjà vu from the People's Fourth of July Peace Rally two years earlier back in San Bernardino, I saw Lieutenant Rick "Moonbeam" Liscomb, dressed in elegant civvies, coming through the gate not far behind them, towering over his companions, Pook, Frank Lutz, fresh in from Than Son Nhut, and Lieutenant Glotfelty, my favorite fighter pilot.

Harley put his hand on my shoulder. "Stay tuned. I've got a few more of your old friends coming."

And sure enough, Sommit slid open the door to his old white Chevy delivery van and out stepped Vrisnei and Chai from Woodstock Music followed by Pawnsiri and Professor Natapong. I had almost forgotten that Pawnsiri was an old schoolmate of Chai's. "Treat Pawnsiri right," Harley said confidentially in my ear. "She really digs you."

Before I could answer, I heard "Brendan!" over the PA. "Come on up here, just for a few songs." It was Marcos, who had Domino Theory ready to go with "Everyday People." I grabbed a bottle of Coke and headed for the bandstand, unsure if playing drums was something I should really be doing on the night before my ordination but noting that with drumsticks in my hands, I wasn't going to get into trouble with any of my other vices. Sipping the Coke between numbers, I realized that I was so energized by the crowd and the good feeling it engendered that I didn't need Mekhong whiskey to quench my thirst that night. Before I knew it, an hour and a half had gone by, and we had run through our entire Thammasatstock repertoire, rousing everybody especially with "Sympathy for the Devil," which we repeated as an encore, the crowd singing along raucously on the chorus.

The revelers were having a fine time dancing, but I was drenched with sweat and ready to get up from my drums when Pawnsiri walked up to Harley and Marcos. After a quick conversation, the Chirping Sparrows stepped aside and Pawnsiri walked over to one of the mikes. It must have been planned because Harley and Marcos were able to break right into one of the songs the first singer had done the night we went to see Pawnsiri at the Lotus Blossom. The rest of the band joined in, so I figured I'd better not be a party pooper at my own party and joined in too on the sad but lovely ballad about the boyfriend of the village girl who went off to *"Bangkok, Bangkok."* It sounded wonderful, and then, before the applause died down, we went right into the song about a man with *"pretty blue eyes, pretty blue eyes."* Pawnsiri glanced at me warmly a few times, but since I had steel-gray eyes, I was certain she wasn't singing about me.

We finished, and the crowd was starting to break up when Lek stepped up to the mike. "Before everybody go, we have some-thing we want to give our old friend, Khun Bren-dan, before he leave tomorrow for Rain Retreat at Wat Pah Nirapai."

Mama-sahn took me by the hand and helped me out from behind the drums. Leading me up to the microphone, we met Lek and Bun-lii, who presented me with a traditional handcrafted stainless steel alms bowl in a saffron carrying bag. "Thank you," I said. "Thank all of you for making this such a wonderful night!"

When I stepped away from the mike, B.J. and Leclerc turned up the music on the stereo for people who were still in the mood to dance. I paused a moment, glancing at the alms bowl and then at Lek, who read my mind. "I will put in your room, Bren-dan."

I handed it to her and stepped back to the microphone. "Could I have your attention one last time? If they are still here, could Chai and Sommit come see me? The same goes for Ackerman and Sugie Bear. Thank you!"

Before any of them had a chance to come over, Rick Liscomb stepped up, followed by Pook, Lutz, and Glotfelty, and gave me a bone-crushing handshake. "You remember this guy?" he asked, pushing Lutz up to shake my hand as well. I noticed he had one of the Air Force's finest Nagra tape recorders hanging over his shoulder.

"Hey Frank, great to see you! What are you doing back in Thailand?"

"The lieutenant's talked Captain English into letting us do a boondoggle travelog down at Pattaya Beach." He handed me a reel of audio tape. "It also gave me a chance to record your farewell performance."

"Long live Bitchin' Guys Productions!" said Liscomb.

"Long live the Bitchin' Guys!" I echoed. "The bar's open and I'm buying!"

"Now that you mention it, I have worked up quite a thirst," Lutz replied before he headed off in search of refreshment.

Lieutenant Glotfelty had been hanging back, listening in. Without his helmet on, he looked even more like Charlie Brown than I remembered, albeit a tall, lanky version. "Do y'all think the monks would mind sprinklin' a little o' that holy water on my plane the way they do for the Thai pilots?"

Liscomb and I laughed. "If they've got a little left over, why not?" I replied.

"Over here, you can never have too much luck," added Liscomb.

"Well, good luck to you, Sergeant Leary," said Glotfelty, giving me a vigorous handshake before heading off to join Lutz at the bar.

Liscomb leaned in. "You're living an interesting life, Brendan Leary. Thanks for turning me on to Prah Samrong, by the way. He's showed me how, behind the outward ritual, this Thai *vipassana* stuff is not that different from the Zen I was studying back in California. I just can't seem to do it right now." He looked troubled, his eyes haunted.

"What's going on?" I asked.

"His work make him cra-zy," said Pook.

"She's right," Liscomb said. "I need to get out of here. That's why I dreamed up that project with Lutz and Washington down at Pattaya Beach. Luckily, Hill and English went for it."

"What's really going on?" I asked.

"That 70mm camera—it's so powerful that sometimes it records things I don't see in my viewfinder."

"What did you film?"

"A village in Laos. The village was leveled. Not a thing was standing."

"And?"

"When I put that big negative in the enlarger and printed it up, there was a beautiful little girl trapped under a collapsed roof. She looked like a sad, surprised angel, except there were no wings—and only a stump for a right arm. The village was supposed to be full of Pathet Lao rebels staging to move on Paksong."

"A little time at the monastery might do you some good."

"Except I don't seem to be able to sit still long enough to meditate anymore. And I'm not sleeping, so when I do sit still, I keep nodding off. I don't know if a monastery would help right now."

"If you change your mind, just tell a cab driver 'Wat Pah Nirapai.'"

"Thanks, brother. And good luck."

"Good luck to you, Lieutenant. I've got something here I want to give you," I said, taking off the little Buddha and gold chain that I was wearing around my neck. "Monks can't wear jewelry and you're still flying."

"Let me help," said Pook, putting the chain around Liscomb's neck and fastening the clasp.

"Thanks," he said with his Sam Cooke smile. I shook his hand and thanked him for coming and somehow knew I would never see him at the monastery, even with a Buddhist girlfriend pushing him to visit.

Following Moonbeam and Pook as they walked away arm in arm, I spotted Sugie Bear, Oi, and Ackerman walking toward me through the crowd, and my heart sank with the realization that this was probably the last time I would ever see most of these people. After exchanging pleasantries,

I asked Sugie Bear and Ackerman, "If your next drummer doesn't need my set of drums, can you give them to Chaplain Kirkgartner? He'll figure out something to do with them. The same with any of my clothes that are still here tomorrow."

"No problem," they said. Sugie Bear glanced at the tape reel in my hand. "Whatcha gonna do with that?" he asked.

"Let me see if Sommit can make copies for you down at Woodstock Music," I told them.

"Good idea," said Ackerman, giving me a strong soul handshake goodbye.

"Good luck, bro," said Sugie Bear.

"Thanks for your letter," I said.

"I just wrote the truth," he replied, giving me a soul handshake of his own. Sommit and Chai were standing with Vrisnei and Pawnsiri halfway down the alley, waiting for the crowd to thin out. I walked over to them. "Can you come upstairs a minute? There are some things I need to talk to you about."

The four of them followed me up to my room. "First of all, Chai, may I give you my bicycle?"

He laughed. "If you insist, Khun Bren-dan. We can come back for it tomorrow."

I held up the tape Lutz had recorded. "And perhaps you and Sommit can make copies of this for the people in my band—and for Miss Pawnsiri."

Pawnsiri glanced at me and smiled.

"As long as there is no rush, we would be happy to," said Chai, taking the reel.

I gazed at all four of them a moment and then addressed Sommit. "All I'm taking with me are a few odds and ends from this room and my shower shoes from the *hong nam*." I handed him a leather satchel. "In case it doesn't work out for me at the monastery, can you keep this with you? It has some of my papers, some clothes and a pair of shoes in it. I think it might be hard to find my size in Ubon if I discover I'm not suited for monastic life."

"We will be happy to hold this for you, Khun Bren-dan," said Sommit, putting the strap of my old leather travel bag over his shoulder. And then, leaning in, he intoned softly, "Do you still have 'special' passport Chinese *papa-sahn* make for you? Just in case?"

I smiled. "It's in the bag, Sommit. Just in case."

Vrisnei gave me a sympathetic look. "If you cannot stay, Khun Brendan, do not feel bad. Many Thai people cannot stay either. They say they are too busy with their job or their family, but for many Thai men, it just too difficult."

"Thanks for your concern, Vrisnei. But even if I only stay for the Rains Retreat, there are two other things I need help with. Can you hold my money for me? I can't bring it to Wat Pah Nirapai."

"No problem," said Sommit. "We will open an account for you."

"Thank you so much," I said, handing him an envelope filled with six hundred dollars in baht, the sum total of my savings and separation pay. "And can one of you mail this for me?" I asked, picking up a thinner envelope. "It's a letter to my family letting them know where I'll be for the next three months."

Vrisnei took it and smiled. "I go to the post office every day."

"Thank all of you."

"*Mai pen rai*," they replied.

"We are happy to help," said Chai.

"Don't worry," Vrisnei added, "there will always be somebody from our family here in Ubon."

We *waied* and they started out, but as she used to do back at AUA, Pawnsiri stayed behind. "I'm so happy Khun Harley ask me to come sing with your band tonight."

"Me, too. If I never play drums again, I'll always have that wonderful memory—playing drums while my favorite student sings."

"We must play together again in October when Rains Retreat is over."

"That would be nice."

"And I will come to see you at the monastery before then, if that does not disturb your meditation."

"If Ajahn Po allows us to have visitors, it would be good to see you."

"Vrisnei is being kind when she say Rains Retreat too difficult for many Thai people. But I know this is important for you. You can do this if you remember to be kind to yourself. Be patient. If you can be soldier for three year, you can be monk for three month. Meditation can make some people go crazy, but your mind is strong. For all people, there is pain in body, but again be kind and be patient and it will get better. Remember you can always bring your attention back to your breath.

"And if you take vows to ordain as monk, there will be many rules to learn and obey. But don't worry, it all come back to what Hindu people call *ahimsa*—'Do no harm, revere all living things.'"

We could hear Sommit, Chai, and Vrisnei talking with Professor Natapong at the bottom of the stairs. "I better go. My friends are waiting to take me home."

Walking with her out onto the porch, I wanted to touch her hand, but I didn't know when and where that was possible in proper Thai society. Instead, we *waied* and I smiled politely. "*Pohp kan mai na khrab.*"

"*Pohp kan mai na kha,*" she replied with a warm Thai smile before she started down the stairs.

From the alleyway below, Professor Natapong called up to me, "Going to monastery very good! After Rains Retreat, you speak Thai *geng mahk.*"

"I hope you're right, professor."

Pawnsiri joined her group, and I watched them walk away. I took a long breath and went over to the music room to pack up the stereo system into the shipping boxes we held on to so carefully back in the days when we had calculated the only way to make up for our horrible GI salaries was to clean out the BX and ship our discounted booty home. Jamal Washington, my old camera compadre, was asleep on the bamboo daybed, so I tried to work quietly. I heard footsteps behind me and turned to see Lek. "Are you really going back to Korat?" I asked her softly.

"I have to, Bren-dan."

"Can you take this with you?" I asked, looking around the room at the half-packed cartons.

Her face lit up, and she kneeled down beside me, throwing her arms around my neck and giving me a big kiss on my cheek. "You a good man, Bren-dan. My father will like very much."

Washington stirred, mumbled something, and turned over on his side. I put my finger to Lek's lips and made a shishing sound before we finished packing up. Even though there wasn't all that much left to do, it involved enough squatting for my back and knees to start aching by the time we were done. I pulled Lek up, turned out the light, and quietly slipped out without disturbing Washington. "Let me help you pack," she said, following me back to my room.

I opened the saffron carrying bag and carefully fit in the incense, candles, and cloth that my students had given me. I put in my passport and Grandpa Shepler's penknife, figuring I would put in my toiletries in the morning. "Here," she said, handing me a mosquito net that I was able to squeeze in. "That was from Bun-lii and her girlfriends. And this is something from me," she said, handing me a small sewing kit. And that was it—all that I would need, all that I was permitted.

Finished, we sat down together on the side of my bed. I was still wearing my white pants and shirt and was too tired to take them off, falling back with my head on my pillow. Lek lit the mosquito coil, put the ceiling fan on low, turned out the light, and lay down beside me, still in her dress. I stretched out my arm to give her a place to rest her head, and she snuggled in close to me.

"You know I'm very fond of you, Lek."

"I very fond of you too, Bren-dan."

There was a long pause. The ceiling fan made a soothing hum while I collected my thoughts. "I just don't know if it would work out in America."

"No, you're right. You're completely right. I can't leave father and baby."

"But will you ever think about me?"

"I will sink about you a lot, Bren-dan. My *tahaan akaat*—my air force soldier—who become a monk."

"I'll think about you, too, Lek."

"And you know what I will wonder sometime?"

"What?" I asked.

"If *this* is true love. Jus' Lek lying next to Bren-dan, listening to the ceiling fan."

We woke up snuggled next to each other, still dressed from the night before. Lek got up and changed. I took a shower, shook the wrinkles out of my clothes as best I could, and packed up my toothbrush and safety razor. We woke up Washington in the music room next door and started down the stairs together for the last time. B.J. called down from next door. "Hold up! I'm coming with you!"

He was still buttoning his shirt when he caught up with us. Just before we reached Mama-sahn's little café, Lek woke up a cab driver and told him we had a fare for him as soon as we finished breakfast, and put my bag in the back seat. We had some duck soup with noodles, not my favorite way to start the day, but I savored it anyway because, to the best of my understanding, the single meal served each day at the monastery would be vegetarian. After a cup of sweet Thai coffee, we headed for the cab. Lek climbed into the front seat, the rest of us got in back, and off we went. I was thankful for the company.

Crossing the Warin Bridge, Lek's face brightened. "In some villages, boys ride elephant to the monastery."

"I guess that makes *two* Thai customs I won't be following—riding elephants and putting on girl's makeup."

B.J. flashed one of his toothy grins. "I got to get me a picture of that— Leary riding an elephant in drag!" We all laughed and then rode a few minutes in silence.

"On a serious note," said Jamal, "we're going to miss you at the 601st."

"And I'm never going to forget what you and I have been through together. Promise me, bro, that you'll make it out of here in one piece."

"Promise. I'm on my final thirty days. And a week of that's gonna be with Liscomb and Lutz down at Pattaya Beach."

As we turned off the highway onto the dusty road that led to the *wat*, B.J. scribbled out his home address. "In case you ever want to meet up out in Colorado for that ski trip."

Before the cab stopped, Jamal wrote his down, too. And then Lek handed me a slip of paper with her address in Thai. "For taxi driver, in case you ever come to Korat."

"Wait," I said, handing the addresses back to Lek. "Can you ask Sommit and Vrisnei to put these in the travel bag I gave them last night?"

"No prob-lem," she replied.

I climbed out, shut the door, and slung my saffron bag over my shoulder, lingering to watch the driver turn the cab around. Before B.J., Jamal, and Lek pulled away, we gave each other a final *wai*. And as my friends drove off down the unpaved lane and back onto the highway to Ubon, I felt a twinge of fear and loneliness. I turned slowly and walked through the front gate of Wat Pah Nirapai, dressed in white, carrying only my alms bowl and the few requisites I was allowed to bring with me.

Walking down the wooded lane towards a monastery that was surrounded with acres of forest, my ears were filled with the gentle sounds of birds singing, leaves rustling in the breeze, and my own footsteps, and I was filled with a growing sense of joy, a sense that I had found my true home. Anando and Suñño greeted me and showed me to a *kuti* this time, not the guesthouse, where I left the bowl, the mosquito netting, and a sleeping mat from the storeroom They were out of pillows. I brought the candles and incense to the Dhamma hall and placed them before the large bronze statue of the sitting Buddha at the front of the hall where other offerings had been left that morning. Next, I was taken to see Ajahn Po, who explained with Anando and Suñño's help that I would initially take eight precepts and spend two weeks as an *anigarika*, wearing white robes. I concurred.

If I found that I was able to endure the discipline of monastic life and wanted to stay on, I would receive ordination as a novice, which meant following ten precepts and seventy-five training rules and dyeing my robes saffron. At the end of the Rains Retreat, if I decided to remain at the monastery, I could ordain as a monk and take up the full Patimokkha—all 227 rules of discipline. They warned me that I would see young Thai men take full ordination immediately after they arrived, but that was permitted because they had already spent time as novices in their teens and had grown up with Buddhist monasticism as an integral part of their culture. It all seemed reasonable, if challenging.

The same as I had done recently as a guest, I arose with the rest of the monks when the temple bell rang at 3:00 a.m. to begin our day. The once-mysterious Pali chanting, like many things Buddhist, proved elegantly simple as I learned to understand it. We began every morning by chanting and repeating three times, "*Buddham saranam gacchami,*" which translated, "I take refuge in the Buddha." We continued with "*Dhammam saranam gacchami*" and "*Sangham saranam gacchami,*" also repeated three times, which meant, "I take refuge in the Dhamma (the reflective teachings of Buddhism)" and "I take refuge in the Sangha (the fellowship of Buddhist monks and committed laypeople)."

My change to *anigarika* meant that I would no longer stay to help in the kitchen, instead going out with the monks and novices on *pindabaht*, carrying the alms bowl that Lek had presented to me. Wearing sandals was permitted the rest of the day, but for this oldest of Buddhist rituals, we went barefoot. We stayed off paved highways, and the dirt roads and paddy dikes felt good to my feet, helping me feel connected to the warm earth. Walking past rice fields and through neighboring villages at 6:00 a.m., I realized that the whole community moved to the rhythms of the temple bells. We would see husbands and wives along the way, walking their water buffalo to their fields or already at work plowing. Others, village women and children and a few men who weren't plowing that day, would stay behind to prepare a morning offering. Kneeling respectfully at the side of the road, also with bare feet, they offered the food they had made to the passing monks, who depended on the generosity of the villagers for their survival.

By 8:00 a.m. we were back at the Dhamma hall. Now that I walked with the monks and novices, I was able to observe how Suñño, Anando, and several other junior monks still under Ajahn Po's protection took turns washing and drying the feet of Luang Paaw, our Venerable Father, before we entered. Once we were seated, additional food was offered, some of it prepared in the kitchen by local villagers and some brought to the *wat* by Ubon townspeople. The food was presented first to Ajahn Po, handed to him by a male supporter since it was forbidden for a monk and a woman to touch. The abbot accepted it, dished some out, and then passed it along in order of descending seniority to the other monks. They added it to what was already in their alms bowls before it eventually reached newcomers like myself. Any food remaining was shared with our lay visitors. None of it was allowed to be stored overnight. Monastic rules required that we go out into the community every day to earn our sustenance.

After all the food was offered, Ajahn Po led the monks in chanting a kind of blessing, what might look and sound to a Christian like an invocation, celebrating the merit and good *kamma* being shared and encouraging supporters to continue to do so. After contemplating the food before us, Ajahn Po rang a small bell and we ate, mindfully acknowledging the many hands it took to produce this meal—easy to imagine in rural Thailand—and then eating in silence. While we ate, we observed our thoughts and feelings when we took a spoonful of food, placed it in our mouths, chewed carefully, and then swallowed, one bite at a time. From my place at the back of the hall, I was struck with how the large Buddha image in front sat deep in meditation but seemed to be watching over us, and how Ajahn Po mirrored the Buddha and how the other monks mirrored Ajahn Po.

After sweeping out the meditation hall—mindful to brush insects back outside without harming them—and then rolling up the mats that we and our guests had been sitting on and cleaning our alms bowls, we had time to bathe and wash our robes before beginning a period of self-guided meditation back at our *kutis*. Anando recommended starting out with a walking meditation after breakfast, pointing out a thirty-foot path not far from my front porch that was laid out just for that purpose. "It will help you digest that large morning meal," he said, "and by preventing drowsiness, you'll be able to do sitting meditation later with clarity and alertness." Prah Suñño, standing nearby, agreed.

After spending most of the next six hours doing walking and sitting meditation, taking an occasional break to read about Dhamma or study Thai from books in the *wat* library, afternoon work time turned out to be a reinvigorating change, giving my body a chance to get the kinks out and my mind a chance to rest. We were encouraged to treat our chores as another form of meditation, engaging in simple activities like raking leaves, sweeping the paths, and hauling water from the well in a mindful way, again not harming any living creature while at the same time observing thoughts, feelings, and sensations as much as possible the way we observed our breath when sitting absolutely still. Like sitting meditation, work meditation would sometimes clear and calm my mind and other times reveal just how cluttered and unfocused it could be.

Following work, we gathered at Ajahn Po's *kuti* for tea, accompanied by a Dhamma talk.

I appreciated the talks more and more as my understanding of basic Thai improved and especially as Suñño and Anando helped me understand the earthy Lao-Issan dialect Luang Paaw Po was fond of using. The abbot was full of instructive ironies, often doing the unexpected in order to break through the villagers' slavish following of empty ritual and superstitious fear of *pii*, or ghosts. The most notable example was how he built the monastery itself over an old burning ground where bodies had been cremated in a swampy forest rumored to be so infested with evil spirits that the villagers had been deathly afraid to come here. On the other hand, he *emphasized* ritual with his American students, a subtle way of teaching us the humility he saw us lacking, by giving us frequent opportunities to prostrate our tall, proud bodies before him and other senior *bhikkhus*. At the same time, if he saw us getting too comfortable in our daily routine, he wasn't averse to switching things around. And so it was, just as I was beginning to look forward to our afternoon tea, that he would cancel it and instead deliver his talk after the evening chanting, often discoursing long into the night, knowing we would be hearing the temple bell in a few short hours announcing the new day. And somehow, because it was Luang Paaw Po, being tested and pushed by him made us love and respect him even more.

I still wondered about rebirth and its connection to *kamma*, but my trust for Ajahn Po continued to deepen because, with a little reflection, so much of what he taught us rang true. It was that profound truth in his teaching that helped me push on when I struggled with physical pain during my sitting meditations and with my wandering, cluttered mind during any form of meditation—walking, sitting, or standing. Fortunately, it was easy for me to embrace Ajahn Po's teachings on the importance of moral purity when embarking on a spiritual journey, his discourses on the inevitability of suffering and death in the human realm and the added suffering created by consciously or unconsciously avoiding pain and attaching to pleasure, his homilies on how little we really needed and the suffering created by trying to build a cocoon of comfort that never turned out to be enough, and his thoughts about the need to balance wisdom and concentration in meditation practice. Over time I discovered I could trust and accept pretty much everything Ajahn Po taught us that I was able to understand, and I grew confident that I would someday understand what I didn't understand today. And then all that trust and confidence was abruptly shattered one evening when Ajahn Po dropped what was for me the spiritual H-bomb of all Buddhism: *anatta* or no-self.

"For laypeople," Luang Paaw explained, "belief in *kamma* and rebirth and the practice of making merit—what Thais call *bai wat tahm bun*—is enough to make them good Buddhists. These are things that all laypeople are able to understand.

"But for those of you staying here for Rains Retreat, we can go deeper, we can contemplate *anatta* and how like Nibbana it cannot be explained, it can only be realized."

Dukkha and *anicca*—suffering and impermanence—I could understand. But *anatta*, the third pillar of Right Understanding? The mere thought of letting go of my selfhood was sheer terror. How could I give up my ego, my essence, give up being *me*? I felt like I'd been blown off a cliff at Acapulco, driven by gales of contradictory thoughts and conflicting emotions, trying to reach out for some kind of lifebuoy in the storming sea that was drowning me. Was I a coward, or did I have guts and integrity? Was I a leader, a spokesman for the downtrodden of the world, or was I a spoiled, whining college boy? What was I doing in this strangest of all places in an already strange land sitting among fifty Thai and American monks and novices, their heads freshly shaven, their bodies wrapped in yards of coarsely woven ochre? Struggling to understand fully the Thais' strange, musical language. Able to ask where the bathroom was, but stumbling over questions about the path to enlightenment. Sitting after a few hours and sometimes only minutes with my knees and back screaming in agony, feeling like I was wearing a straightjacket that would never come off. Feeling like my jaw and cheeks and forehead were being twisted by a corkscrew when what I wanted was simply to wear a Buddha-smile like the one Tom Wheeler had been born with. The pain eventually receded, but the fear returned—*anatta*.

How could this fear stand out when I've lived a life of fear? I wondered. *Anatta*—"no-self"—an idea that seized me with the same panic I felt skiing the black diamond runs at Stowe when I had barely learned to keep my skis together. I thought I had detached myself from America, but its history and culture lay hidden inside me. *How can I give up my identity? How can I give up being* me?

I liked the idea of being interconnected with the cosmos, but I didn't want to be just a grain of sand in the desert, a drop of water in the ocean. And then one morning I remembered a relaxation exercise from Theatre 101, where if you acknowledged the tension in a specific part of your body and didn't fight it, didn't try to make it go away, that tenseness would more often than not go away by itself. That morning it took what felt like several hours and what in reality might have only been a few minutes, but the tension in my face and gut finally melted. As I scanned my body, I felt the same sensation I had when I first began to let go and glide down those powdery Vermont hillsides making my first S-shaped parallel turns. It was a feeling of exhilaration, joy, of just feeling without thinking. Intoxication without being intoxicated. It was all of that, except I was not the skier, I was the ski slope and the wind and sun and the feeling of skiing.

Somehow this strange new experience gave me a sense of hope that I was making spiritual progress, a sense that turned to confusion a few days later when no matter where in the monastery I sat in meditation, I cried for hours at a time, swept over with waves of sadness and joy. I felt myself disappear. And then, at last, my mind was blasted with the realization that by giving up our small, limited, tortured illusions of individuality and ego and selfness, we became forests that soared to meet the sun, constellations that spread myriad light rays to the farthest reaches of the cosmos. I couldn't totally give myself up to this infinite possibility, but the potential alone was thrilling in a calm and soothing way.

Over the coming weeks, I stopped judging whether I was brave or cowardly, wise or foolish, selfish or generous. I came to see that qualities which I had once been taught to believe were conflicting were, in fact, parts of the same whole. I stopped worrying if I was or was not mad and if the world was or was not mad. Because the world was already *anicca*, a living organism that was itself in constant flux and change. Navigating the world was best done with what Thais called a *jai yen*—a cool heart and mind—that accepted the final unchangeable truths: impermanence and death.

"I've noticed you've been struggling since Luang Paaw's talk on *anatta*," Anando said to me one day. "Reflect on it, but don't obsess. Some well-respected teachers in Thailand believe *anatta* should only be taught to senior bhikkhus. And other *ajahns* debate if *anatta* has perhaps been mistranslated. Does it mean no-self or non-self or not-self? Some forest monks, after long retreats in caves or deep in the jungle, believe *anatta* has been revealed to them as true self."

With Anando's help, I began to feel at peace and began to understand that if the path I took through life was difficult and different from anyone I grew up with, it didn't matter, it didn't need to be defended. I still grieved for Tukada and felt a sickness in the bottom of my heart that I had failed to save her in so many ways. I grieved for countless others killed in the war, friend and foe alike, and felt a pang of humbling guilt for surviving while they were cut down in their prime. I still ached over Danielle. But slowly, I began to accept Ajahn Po's lessons on how pain and loss and suffering were inevitable parts of the human condition. Somehow, in learning to fully accept the inevitability of old age and sickness and death in my own life, the fear of death and disease continued to loosen its grip on me. At the same time, Luang Paaw taught us how understanding the Buddha's teachings allowed us to develop great compassion for those who suffered and died in ignorance.

Ajahn Po told us one night that people's lives are like candles. Some burn slowly and some burn fast, but fast or slow, everything is impermanent. From acceptance of that eternal law comes fearlessness and peace, he said. And so it did. Whatever goodness I was born with, I felt, was being unshackled. And from my inner darkness, innate and from the many mistakes I'd made in life, I also felt unshackled, the black cloud transforming into a blue-and-lilac silken ball that carried off my fears and dreams, pains and pleasures, hates and loves, my armor of feelings and avoidance of feeling.

Here at Wat Pah Nirapai, for a dope-smoking, whore-loving, draft-dodging hippie, the possibility of being decent no longer seemed repulsive and square. Here I experienced a shocking new possibility that something like peace, happiness, and tranquility might exist on earth for those who could learn to observe the world and their emotional response to it with mindfulness and equanimity. It was easy. Just turn yourself inside out, cover up your neurotic defenses with pure and total vulnerability, suck in the cosmos, and breathe it out. All one. Japanese Zen masters believed that some people could do it in a flash. The Buddha took five years. But I still had two-thirds of a human lifetime left to live. There was hope, however remote, of doing my own brain and heart and soul surgery and surviving.

One morning when I asked Anando if all monasteries were this demanding, he laughed. "No," he said, "in Bangkok when I first ordained, I stayed at monasteries where we ate two meals a day, got up much later, and were free to watch television in our spare time. New monks were encouraged to spend the entire day studying Pali scriptures instead of practicing meditation. On the other hand, as a Westerner, I could say I was *too busy* meditating and get myself out of doing chores. In reality, I wanted discipline, and when by chance Ajahn Po's only English-speaking monk passed through, he told me he had exactly what I was looking for out in Ubon. I think of Luang Paaw Po as the General Patton of abbots, and he's never disappointed me."

"I'm beginning to understand why Prah Samrong at Big Buddha sent me here. I don't think it was only to hear Dhamma from you and Suñño in English."

"I suspect you're right," he answered.

I mentioned to Tahn Anando the comparison that Prah Samrong had made of life in a monastery to life in the military. The ex-pilot smiled and said, "One does seem to prepare you for the other. In fact, a lot of the support for Wat Pah Nirapai comes from Thai soldiers stationed in the province, from the regional commander and his staff down to the lowliest foot soldier. There is one big difference, however."

I waited for him to continue, but he delayed a moment.

"You came to us at the beginning of Phansa, the Buddhist Lent and Rains Retreat, when many men ordain temporarily, and so you haven't seen it yet, but it is far easier to leave monastic life than the military. Once the retreat is over, a monk is free to remain or to disrobe and return to his household."

Even though the daily routine varied little from the three days I first stayed there as a guest, it took me most of the Rains Retreat to fully acclimate to my new life. Time blurred and it took me weeks to send off a note to my family about how my friends in Ubon had given me a rousing send-off but how I now suspected that was because they knew my life would soon be so demanding, the opposite of anything I had ever experienced in the United States or Thailand.

I agreed when Ajahn Po told us one evening, "Monastic life is a paradox, both simple and difficult." Another Buddhist riddle for me to contemplate and experience. With each passing day, it seemed that life at Wat Pah Nirapai did grow a bit more challenging, and yet I felt a growing sense of not wanting to disrobe when rainy season was over.

One of the first contradictions we faced was that just because it was called the Rains Retreat and this was supposed to be rainy season didn't mean that monsoon rains fell in the Issan, the most drought-prone region of Thailand. There were hot, sticky days when I felt tortured, when the only thing that came up in hours of meditation was an insistent craving for chocolate ice cream. And even when the rains finally came, now that I no longer lived and worked in the comfort of air-conditioning and ceiling fans, I learned that the monsoon rains were warm rains and the days were full of humidity and the nights filled with mosquitos and the possibility of malaria.

It so happened that the year I chose to go forth on my spiritual journey, drought had come to the Northeast. Rice paddies that had been mirrors of rainwater the year before turned into rock-hard clay that broke into a grid of jagged cracks under the unrelenting sun. The dust and dung on the road and fields crept between our toes and under our nails and dug into the creases in the dry skin of our feet and ankles. Our nostrils stung and our throats felt scratchy and swollen in the thick air. At night the air was death itself—hot breath devoid of oxygen that smothered us in perfect stillness. My brain reeled, its juices baked out, my thoughts gasping, suffocating, forgetting themselves before they were fully realized. The porch of my *kuti*, the meditation hall, the shaded pathways in the forest itself—none offered relief. A splash of cold water on my face, a half-hour of walking, not even a nap seemed to offer any comfort. And yet sometimes I went deep...

Sitting. Sitting. Wondering where it was this dream began. All sensation is extinguished. Pain that spread like cancer through my knees and feet and thighs and crawled along my spine, a vise that crushed me in its vicious grasp now turns to ether. Gnarled legs that feel arthritic, useless as an ancient beggar's, so stiff after sitting, sitting long into the evening on the nights that the four phases of the moon ordain to be Wan Prah, the holy day, legs that turned to twisted scrap iron now float like toy zeppelins past my ears. From the shallow basin where the villagers wash their feet before treading the tiled floor of the Dhamma hall, I can be mistaken for a marble sculpture of the Buddha, cool and immobile to sight and touch.

A flash of insight that a monk dies a thousand painful deaths every time he lights a stick of incense and closes his eyes to the mundane world, and I pity the novice testing the chilled waters for the first times, barely penetrating the surface of his own mystery. Superficial minutes, hours, days spent in tedium and doubt, exploring an inconsequential inner world that in an unexpected flash turns eternal nothingness inside out, transforming wrecking yards of pain and suffering and disease into hummingbirds and distant dying suns, a flash within a flash that becomes the cosmos. And I wonder what dream brought me to this dream.

As they are lowered into a vat of consecrated acid, the knots in my sciatic nerve dissolve, the hammering in my brain turns to helium that fills my chest, pulling me upward. The breathing slows. There is so little of me left that thimblesful of oxygen are all that is needed to sustain me. And in a distant galaxy I hear gunfire. A few sporadic rounds. A rumble in a different neighborhood, somebody else's turf. Somebody else's movie. More staccato than the stiletto utterings of the North Vietnamese lieutenant. Ten thousand tiny footsteps gently shake the dark dirt highway and turn into the rumbling of a distant train the Indian scout can only hear with his ear pressed hard to the searing steel track.

One steamy afternoon as the humidity built but the skies refused to open, I tossed on my straw mat, glued to it by perspiration, stuck there, unable to turn over, unable to move, feeling like a fly trapped in a fresh web. I went to the Dhamma hall—the open-air meditation hall—in the hope that the height of its ceiling would cause the air to circulate. And as I sat there, wavering, nodding, barely able to maintain the slightest semblance of mindfulness, the image of a huge snowflake began dancing in my mind's eye. *It whirls and becomes a blue flame cloud and then blue vapor that transforms into crystal dust. Vermont in February—snow falling in blinding waves, pine boughs catching it in great white puffs, rocks and stumps and stream beds and foothills blanketed.*

I contemplated my giant ice crystal, my head still bobbing with fatigue, until a chill swept over my body, and I could feel an Arctic breeze blow through the *wat*. I contemplated the snowflake in all its countless variations, in-depth, in awe of possible manifestations, and without understanding why at first, I began to laugh to myself. No self was easy—that day. *No self / snowflake. The illusion of uniqueness. One ice crystal among millions, no two alike. Knowing all will melt in their time and return to the river, the sea, the sky, my mind seems to blaze with the cold light of an Arctic dawn.*

And with this taste of what Thais called a cool heart and mind, my thoughts became calm and cool, and the calmness and coolness spread through my entire being. I napped peacefully for an hour until the bell rang and it was time for the afternoon chores.

Much of the time after the rains finally came, it was a relief to turn life into a ritual and turn myriad daily decisions over to tradition and the wisdom of Luang Paaw Po, but there were days when sitting after sitting I wanted to jump out of my own skin. Other days I was surprised by how much my sittings varied, one being calming, another deep, the next full of aching and itching, still another where nothing happened at all, just a spiritual dead end, and another yet where with my eyes closed my vision was filled with luminous vapors, usually cool blues and violets. There were days that I imagined that I was part of an army of the serene; on those days walking meditation, fifteen paces back and forth, became guard duty of tranquility. Occasionally, I laughed to myself, especially doing walking meditation, thinking how mad this would look to almost any of my Western friends and family. Those days, I thought of Wat Pah Nirapai as a wonderful insane asylum where the patients were taught how to be their own therapist.

But even as my days were often tranquil, my nighttime dreams were full of shocking imagery, either violent or carnal. Scenes of picnics that seemed like Impressionist paintings could turn into bloodbaths or orgies. More disturbing were the many dreams and nightmares that I forgot the moment I awoke but which had seemed important, perhaps transformational, and were now forever lost. The recurring dreams I did remember seemed equally disturbing because they contained no meaning, only fear and anxiety. I dreamed of shrouds in their many forms, transforming from cables supporting the rocking mast of a sailboat at anchor to the thin lines that attached me to a parachute. The parachute lines I held in my hands could dissolve, and it would be a movie camera I was looking through, except I couldn't get the camera into focus, as though I were trying to film through a silk parachute canopy.

One dream I had only once but did not forget: I feared I was inside my own coffin, although I couldn't see it, only sense a horrible claustrophobia. A parachute was floating down softly above me, covering me, and I couldn't make out any of the weeping faces that gazed down, except Father Boyle, from his lilting Irish tenor pronouncing my Last Rites.

My understanding of Thai and Pali developed slowly but steadily, and as it did, I was often pleasantly surprised how often Ajahn Po's evening Dhamma talks connected to something that had come up in that day's meditation. Tahn Anando and Tahn Suñño continued to mentor me, showing me how much of what I was going through fell into the same Five Hindrances that Buddhist meditators had been struggling with for the last twenty-five hundred years: anger and aversion; greed and lust; sloth, torpor and sleepiness; restlessness and agitation; and doubt. They explained how Ajahn Po often taught in opposites, training his students to use thoughts of love and acceptance to deal with anger and hate; generosity to deal with greed; death and decay to cool off feelings of lust; humility to balance too much ambition; trust and faith to allay doubt; and non-attachment to offset an excess of striving. And yet all this had to be done with mindfulness, because without some degree of striving or intention, undertaking the practice of meditation itself could end up misleading us into a state of slothfulness and lethargy.

Anando and Suñño continued to remind me to bring my awareness gently back to my breath every time it ran away—which was often—in order to continue developing my concentration. When I could sustain deeper levels of concentration, my mentors reminded me of the old challenge: whether I experienced something beautiful or pleasant, something repulsive that I did not want to accept I was capable of thinking, or simply experiencing something neutral, I was not to analyze it the way teachers had taught me for years but instead to continue developing my witness consciousness and "just observe."

For three months I struggled, painfully adapting my large Western body to the customs of Thailand and monastic life. There were no chairs around, and a Thai would never put his bottom on a pillow. That was where he placed his head, the most sacred part of his body, to sleep. In the meditation hall the only thing we were permitted to sit on was a thin cloth. My injured knees, shoulder, and even my wrist often rebelled, something I was taught to deal with by ignoring, by concentrating on, or by noting with *metta* or loving-kindness. I tried to meditate in my *kuti* for sittings that lasted forty minutes, about how long it takes a stick of incense to burn. With time I was able to sit in a half and then a full lotus position for an hour. I continued developing my *vipassana* practice, working with my breath as Prah Samrong had first taught me at Big Buddha. Sitting for longer periods magnified the challenge of training the mind, however, because my mind now had more time to drift every which way but where I tried to concentrate.

In the quiet and stillness of the forest, sounds of nature that once welcomed me—*jingjoks* clucking, cicadas buzzing, leaves rustling in the breeze—became distractions. The singing of birds turned into screeching. Worse, I was jarred by jets from the base taking off or landing, depending on which way the wind was blowing, and trucks that sounded like something American politicians might use on the stump but here were blasting out loud advertisements about movies playing nearby in Ubon for the benefit of villagers without newspapers or television. On a rainy day when everything seemed to be at peace, the Bangkok train would pass, blasting its horn as it approached Warin. Sometimes that single train whistle was enough to destroy my concentration for hours. Anando suggested doing a Noting Meditation. "It can be done by noting thoughts or by noting sensations arising in different parts of your body, but in your case, try noting to yourself each time you hear a new *sound* how it arises and falls away."

"Pardon the pun, but that has a familiar ring to it. Prah Samrong at Wat Ph'a Yai helped me with this when I first started. There were a lot of distractions back in Ubon."

Prah Suñño, the wiry ex-Peace Corps volunteer, smiled. "You're also dealing with what Buddhist teachers have called 'Monkey Mind' for the last two thousand five hundred years."

"Ah, yes! Something else Prah Samrong tried to teach me about. We finally figure out our mind is filled with drunken monkeys and still they go racing around the moment you let your guard down!"

"Keep practicing. If the breath doesn't work as an object of meditation, try noting as Prah Anando suggests, or just focus on your sense of touch—your body seated on the floor, the cloth on your back, the air on your shaved head."

Remembering a little story, he continued. "When I accompanied Ajahn Po to Bangkok last year for a conference on international Buddhism, the air-conditioning was broken in the hall where he was supposed to speak. Across the street was a new disco, blasting away. The Brits who were putting on the conference kept scurrying between opening the windows to relieve the suffocating heat and closing them up to keep out the ruckus. Throughout the evening, Luang Paaw sat serenely with a smile on his face, at one point leading a guided meditation and, when he was asked, giving a Dhamma talk—on patience."

Patience helped me get through days of relentless pain and suffering that were interspersed with days of peace and tranquility. But in my seated meditations and when trying to lie down with awareness just before I went to sleep, time and again I saw the Ho Chi Minh Trail passing slowly beneath me in black-and-white and heard the kill sequence beginning on the intercom: "*Thirty...thirty.*" Almost as often, it was a mental movie in living color of cluster bombs falling on Vietnamese jungles and villages and sampans. I could still see clouds of napalm rising so high that the wingman was flying through the flames. It was puzzling to me but equally vivid when doing walking meditation on the path outside my *kuti* how the speed at which I walked, ever so mindfully, and the scale of the clay earth and grass beneath my feet could transform themselves into the speed of an AC-130 flying over the Trail, and the tufts of grass would dissolve magically, instantaneously into elephant grass and patches of bamboo-filled forest. "I wish I could turn it off," I told Tahn Anando.

"Perhaps you've got a lot of *kamma* to work out. You were surrounded by war."

"When I visited Prah Samrong at Wat Ph'a Yai before he sent me here, he told me the same thing."

Meditating that day, as I relived the war, the question arose: *why did you survive and so many others die?* And Tukada's face floated up from the void, as beautiful as a marble Aphrodite, a sleeping baby, a rotting corpse whose warm and silky flesh now fell away.

Ajahn Po talked a few nights later about how meditating on the bones and ashes and even the corpses of the dead was an ancient practice that went back to the time of the Buddha himself and had been passed along for centuries by forest monasteries like Wat Pah Nirapai. He described the horror on the villagers' faces when he chose to build his monastery here, on an old burning ground. They were filled with superstitious fears of ghosts haunting this spot and the woods around it. But it was precisely this superstition that made Luang Paaw Po choose the spot in the first place—a chance to teach by example. With what felt like a burst of insight, the thought popped into my head that I needed to return to the crash site of Spectre 544, if I ever could, and meditate on the bones of my doomed fellow crewmen. And a more painful insight hatched from within that insight—I needed to mix my tears with the red clay of the hills along Route 66 where the Big Buddha Bicycle Race ended in sun-curdled puddles of blood. Much as Ajahn Po was teaching the villagers to confront their fears, I needed to confront the *pii tai hong* that were haunting me. I needed to walk Route 66 and the bomb-pocked trails of Laos to somehow tame and finally escape the restless, unhappy ghosts that followed me.

On a Sunday morning a month into the retreat, Pawnsiri came to visit, accompanied by her mother and sister and by Professor Natapong and his wife, bringing food for the monks' morning meal. After we ate together with the monks and the other guests in the Dhamma hall, we found a quiet spot with some log benches where we could chat. Pawnsiri disappeared a moment to Natapong's van and returned with a small pillow, covered in fine white cotton and decorated with white embroidery, which she gave to the professor to present to me. I had been getting by without a pillow, using my carrying bag filled with my extra robes to rest my head on at night. "Thank you so much, Khun Pawnsiri. Did you decorate this yourself?"

When she blushed and lowered her eyes, her sister answered for her. "She work every night for a week, Tahn Bren-dan."

The monastery was crowded with guests on Sunday mornings, most of them families of monks on retreat. When the others began to drift away, my friends kept their visit brief and left with them. "Thank you for coming," I said.

"I think you will sleep better now," said Pawnsiri with a demure smile.

"I'm sure I will. These floors are hard and the mats are thin."

Sitting up all night on the full moon of the second month, Ajahn Po gave an earthy talk filled with Lao-Issan peasant humor. On the subject of hindrances and the value of monastic life, he told us, "Sometimes people can be like oxen. You have to tie them down by all four feet before you can give them their medicine." And when a novice asked if it were necessary to sit for long periods of time to attain wisdom, he answered, "Chickens can sit for long periods. Monastery cats sit all day. Do they acquire wisdom? You must also work on the quality of your practice. But that is something you can do any time—sweeping leaves, hauling water, going to the bathroom, eating. Everything we do can teach us wisdom."

A young monk who was planning to return to his government job after the Rains raised his hand. "Back in Ubon, life is so hectic. Many of my friends say they want to meditate but they are too busy with work and with their families. How will I find time to meditate?"

"If you think you are too busy, just ask yourself, 'Am I too busy to breathe?' Emptying an ashtray can be a form of meditation if you do it mindfully."

Sitting up a week later on the night of the last quarter moon, Ajahn Po talked especially to the new monks and novices about "if only" meditations. "If only this pain in my knee would go away. If only that old song would stop playing in my head. If only I could stay awake. But instead of worrying about 'if only,' like we say so often around here, just observe. You don't need to judge. This isn't a race, it's a path you're on."

And on that night of the last quarter moon, the pain in my knee grew stronger and stronger, and as the other monks and some of the villagers continued to sit up with their backs straight, I grew ever sleepier. Several times, my head dropped suddenly and jerked back up. A brief fear of falling turned to embarrassment. I switched to the standing posture, which brought me back to a state of wakefulness. I sat again, and sure enough, the thoughts came up: *If only my knee were healthy, if only I were more disciplined and could force myself to stay awake.* But I discovered I could catch those thoughts and let them go, or just watch them come up, hang around for a bit and then disappear, and I could bring my awareness gently and simply back to my breath: short, long, deep, shallow. More "if only's" came and went over the next two months: *If only I could speak better Thai and Lao, if only I* could understand every word spoken by Ajahn Po, that *would get me on the direct path to Enlightenment*. And later: *If only I could learn these Pali chants and take my full ordination*, that *would surely take me further down the path*.

My gangly, banged-up American body continued to struggle with sitting for hours at a time in the meditation hall. Early in the second month, I discovered a little trick. By being one of the last to enter the hall, I could sit near a pillar in the back and, without being noticed, occasionally rest my aching sacroiliac. Several days later, Luang Paaw gave a talk on healthy people who think they have to walk with crutches.

To my amazement, as much as sitting in complete stillness could be physically painful, it never grew boring. Instead, it held endless possibilities to observe a continuous stream of thoughts and feelings that go unnoticed in everyday life. I had been intrigued with an idea I had picked up somewhere back in California that instant enlightenment was possible in Zen. Real sitting brought me to the humbling realization that Thai-style *vipassana* or insight meditation was probably *not* going to be a method for me to attain instant and eternal bliss.

There were many "if only" days to come that were disconcerting although strangely entertaining, lessons in how filled up our minds are with both the sacred and the profane, the profound and the mindless. There were entire days when I heard "Who's Making Love to Your Old Lady" from the first opening of my eyes before dawn to long into the night, lying on my mat trying in vain to fall asleep, knowing that in five hours it would all begin again. One night, I pleasantly remembered the "Dear John" bonfire and, in a small way, missed the lost souls of the Ghetto. "It Ain't Me, Babe," "Just My Imagination," and "Your Cheatin' Heart" floated up from I don't know where and popped up again from time to time in the days that followed. On a particularly hot and humid day, my mind tormented me with the same thought over and over: *If only I could have a dish piled high with chocolate ice cream, surely that would put me on the road to Nibbana.*

On the first quarter moon of the third month, I managed to sit up all night. The accomplishment was tempered, however. A skeleton that Ajahn Po kept off to the side of the large bronze Buddha at the front of the meditation hall danced before me in the dim light for hours on end. A few nights later, Winston Churchill, Franklin Roosevelt, Abraham Lincoln, and almost every other great man I had ever studied or read about appeared in that same dim light, taking the place of the dancing skeleton. Toward the end of the third month, however, I sensed that I was beginning to go fairly deep almost every day, possessing now a sense of a Witness Self watching over this fellow that I once lived inside of, a body that went by the name of Brendan Leary. On one of those days, after looking forward to going into a state of especially deep concentration in the meditation hall after the Dhamma talk, Mickey Mouse, Donald Duck, and Goofy, followed by Bullwinkle and Rocky, Boris and Natasha, Bugs Bunny and Elmer Fudd, the Roadrunner and Wile E. Coyote, and almost every cartoon character I had ever watched began parading before my eyes, taunting me and my attempt at a spiritual journey. When I asked Tahn Suñño about it, he looked a bit worried for a moment, then said simply, "You've got some strange *kamma*."

The single object of meditation that came up that I never mentioned to my teachers was probably the one I *most* needed to talk about, to get guidance in how to handle. In this perfect environment where I had given up drugs and alcohol without a second thought, with no regrets and no craving, where I had given up my high, soft bed and got by fine with a single meal each day— in this environment of men at their best—I was tortured at least once a week with female imagery, sometimes pure, sometimes erotic, sometimes vulgar and pornographic. It was upsetting at first, disturbing. I tried to apply Ajahn Po's dictum to "just observe," and over time, I seemed to make peace with it. If even highly developed monks could have violent, angry thoughts, as they sometimes admitted, then something similar surely could happen with lust.

Sexuality, we were taught, wasn't evil. It was a worldly pleasure that a monk voluntarily gave up. But it was also a powerful force that devout laypeople needed to treat with great mindfulness. I worked with that imagery when it came up, and by "just observing," it began to loosen its hold on me. When I tried my hardest to push those thoughts away, however, they seemed to regain their power, causing me great restlessness. I realized that similar to thinking about killing as opposed to actually doing it, a good man or woman could have sexual thoughts without being controlled by them and engaging in sexual misconduct. It was reassuring to note that by the third month, even though sexual thoughts and feelings hadn't disappeared, they recurred less frequently and had lost their ability to shock me.

Perhaps because we were getting near the end of the Rains Retreat and the married village men were likely to have begun to think about returning to their wives, Ajahn Po gave another of his salty Issan-Lao Dhamma talks where he revealed his own struggles with lust as a young monk. One day, while walking with his teacher, they came across a turd in the road. "Where did that come from?" he was asked.

"From a dog?" Ajahn Po replied.

"It might have come from the most beautiful maiden in the village."

Luang Paaw went a little further, describing a time when he went on a month-long retreat, deep in the jungle, determined to purge himself of all thoughts and feelings of lust. And after the month was over, he returned to his monastery confident that he had triumphed completely in purifying himself. The next morning, a young lady came to make an offering of food for the monks. One glance at the lovely village girl and Ajahn Po's heart was racing, a month of hard inner work thrown out the window. "And just in the nick of time," said Ajahn Po, "I remembered the turd in the road."

When the Rains Retreat came to an end a few weeks later, while most of the men were returning home to their villages and the waiting arms of their wives, I requested and received permission to take full ordination. I had already given up my worldly possessions. And like a recruit who enters basic training, I had already given up a substantial part of my identity when my head was shaved and I put on the white robes that were dyed saffron a few weeks later when I became a novice. Now I was to take a step deeper into what Ajahn Po, like Prah Samrong, called the Holy Life. Once again, Tahn Anando brought me to the *bot*, the chapel where Ajahn Po would perform my ordination. In becoming a monk, I would enter a five-year apprenticeship or *nissaya*, which would mean an even deeper experience in humility. It was the same apprenticeship that Suñño and Anando were in the process of completing.

Following an ancient tradition, we had agreed beforehand that Ajahn Po would be my preceptor, or mentor, as he had been for Suñño and Anando. It meant that for as long as I lived at Wat Pah Nirapai, Ajahn Po would look after me like a father, teaching me how to follow the 227 rules of discipline and helping me reach a thorough knowledge and understanding of Buddhist teachings or Dhamma. In return, I, along with a few other junior monks under Ajahn Po's dependence, would be responsible for caring for him, attending to many of his personal needs such as washing and folding his robes, cleaning his living space, helping him prepare for the alms round in the morning and helping to bathe his feet when we returned. I was expected to show loyalty and respect for my preceptor and help to care for him if he fell ill. It was also expected for me to find a suitable teacher in Ajahn Po's place if I were ever to spend more than a week at another monastery, where the same sort of mentor relationship would be established.

So it was that at a propitious moment in my ordination interview, after making sure my upper robe was arranged properly over my left shoulder and my right shoulder left humbly exposed, I bowed deeply to Ajahn Po and asked three times, "*Upajjhāyo me bhante hohi*," which meant "Venerable sir, please be my preceptor."

Ajahn Po responded, "*Sāhu*" or "very well." He asked me if I was at least twenty years old, if I was in good health, free of debt and government and military obligations, and if I had the consent of my family. I had written Mom a few weeks earlier, telling her I was thinking seriously about taking full ordination and staying on at Wat Pah Nirapai. I hadn't heard back. Taking my family's silence as approval, I answered yes. He checked that I had begun to master Pali chanting and that I had reached a basic understanding of the Buddhist precepts. When I had answered satisfactorily, he brought the ordination to an end by announcing that going forth, I would now be known as Santisekkho—"seeker of peace"—thereby giving up the family name passed down by my Irish ancestors for a thousand years and the names my parents had chosen for me at birth.

And for days, I meditated in peace, walked in tranquility, slept without fear or guilt. I practiced taming my vestigial lust and anger with *metta*, teaching myself to accept emotions I was afraid of or ashamed of, much as I had been liberated in a more mundane way by learning to love and accept the pain that arose in my stiff, awkward, broken body. But the tranquility did not go uninterrupted. *A headless cyclist races across my field of vision. A blind nun appears, followed by a beauty queen with a malignancy growing out of her neck. Churchill dances again on the bones of the skeleton that hangs in the glass cabinet next to the altar. Einstein. George Bernard Shaw. Saroyan? I'm not certain. Is that Dylan Thomas? Garcia Lorca? For sure, that's Wilfred Owen. Bobby Dylan and Joan Baez sing mutely.*

I just observed, a pilgrim content to take a journey without answers. *How does the blind nun do walking meditation? Why does the headless bicycler keep flying through my vision? If it is sometimes okay to cry when deep in meditation, is it okay to break out laughing in the meditation hall? The blind nun holds her water cup with such delicacy that she can tell by sound and weight when the cup is full from the rainwater cistern.*

On the twelfth day, the headless bicycler revealed himself to me: *"When you think you have let go of all pain, the true pain will begin."*

My knees ached in my sleep and when I walked, when I brushed my teeth and when I sat listening to Ajahn Po's discourses, when I rode into town on the hard bench of a *sawngtao* and when I walked with my alms bowl on our morning *pindabaht*, when I sat with my legs folded for our morning meal and when I squatted to move my bowels. On the good days and the good nights, my knees ached. On the bad days and nights, my feet, ankles, legs, buttocks, lower back, upper back, shoulders, elbows, neck, and knees ached in a Hallelujah Chorus of pain.

It was around that time that Ajahn Po had us spend an entire week working with *metta*, directing loving-kindness toward the bits and pieces of ourselves that needed it. By employing *metta* mindfully, I discovered I could patiently accept the pain in my knees, feet, back, and neck, sometimes letting it go completely. Working with *metta*, I discovered I could sit from ten to twenty minutes longer than before, sitting for longer periods of reflection now instead of just toughing it out enduring pain. Later that week, Luang Paaw asked us to contemplate desire from the perspective of loving-kindness. That opened my eyes to the subtle degrees of desire we have for so many things—food, sleep, fun, power, intoxicants, sex, freedom from pain—and to forgive myself for craving those many forms of comfort and pleasure. By the end of the week, I began to smile at how many things *metta* could be applied to, especially Ajahn Po himself and the bowl-shaped bell that we sometimes grew desperate for him to strike at the end of an especially long sitting period. The last of these exercises answered an old Christian riddle: How does one turn the other cheek when revenge seems to be so instinctual? In a guided meditation, we alternated offering *metta* to ourselves and to those we loved, after which we alternated offering *metta* to ourselves and to entire cities and regions and countries and the entire planet. And then the great insight: as he guided us back to earth and close to home, we alternated offering loving kindness to ourselves and to everyone who had ever harmed or hurt us.

One surprise was how many fellow soldiers (Link, Toliver, Cooper, Tukada's husband, my devilish guardian angel, Baker), fellow Americans like the last two presidents, and fellow Learys like my father and grandfather came up in this concluding part of the exercise in comparison to Lieutenant Duong and the faceless enemy we had been battling so brutally. Reflecting on the unease I felt at the beginning of the meditation, I realized how simplistic Father Boyle's injunctions against selfishness had been, especially as I reflected deeper and realized that without feeling *metta* for ourselves, it would be impossible for us to have much to give to anyone else in the world.

Not long after I ordained, a new American monk came to stay at Wat Pah Nirapai after living in Sri Lanka for several years. His back had gone out even though he was a young man, and so he meditated sitting in a chair that had to be brought in for him from the library. A couple of weeks after he arrived, he asked me to shave his head, and while I did, he told me about his fiancée back in Boston, whom he had given up but whom he still thought about from time to time and fantasized about while masturbating.

"*Boston,*" I said. "I hear it's a great city."

"I guess it's got a lot of history for an American city. Where are you from?"

"Boston."

We had a little laugh, but it bothered me that he was using a chair to meditate, and I could hear echoes of my father's voice saying, "*You're dogging it.*" It bothered me more that he admitted breaking an important rule of conduct, even though he told me he was keeping a journal and making a serious attempt at doing better. It also bothered me that he had resented it in Sri Lanka when the old women who brought him his food each day asked him to give them Dhamma talks. I would have understood if he said he was only a novice and not yet qualified to teach, but this was simply a case of not wanting to be bothered. The American monk was a strong, pleasant, handsome fellow whom I avoided when I could. His ordination papers were in order, but I sensed he was a fraud. Worse, I feared he would read my mind and know that on the full moon I would see Tukada's face in the silver clouds or Pawnsiri's or the Malaysian princess's or Danielle's or even the Perfect Lady's, and the clouds would transform into the bodies of young and perfect women and into their thighs and flat bellies and the mysteries that were deeper and more profound than anything they taught us in Catechism class, and I too would violate my sacred oath. Except I did not keep a diary and did not record my progress in learning to control a drive that came from a dark, secret place so deep inside me it didn't seem like a part of me at all.

I had reached a point where I was certain my *kamma* would uncover me, betray me too as a fraud, a point where I felt my unworthiness in every way— stealing Ajahn Po's time, stealing the respect of villagers from monks who truly but unremarkably deserved their respect. And it was at precisely that point that much of my troubling mix of lust and pain evaporated. The vise-grips on my throbbing kneecaps and tailbone loosened. The straightjacket, strapped on so tight it nearly stopped my heart from beating, turned to gossamer and floated away. I sat for a full afternoon while my fingers, resting on my knees, turned into grapevines that tapped into the ground beneath me and seemed to lovingly hug me as they wrapped themselves around my torso. Out of the compost heap, I had arisen, purer, even if I would never be truly, completely pure. And it was about then that Ajahn Po warned us in a talk about Letting Go of Defilements: "When you think you've got no more lust or anger to let go of, BEWARE! They'll arise in big ways and in ways so subtle you never knew the flavor existed."

And sure enough, there came a night when I sat up from my dreams, my hands flailing at cymbals and drums that had long ago been packed away, startled to see a clapboard wall instead of ten thousand teenage girls reaching for the stage and crying at the beauty of my superband's music. I ached in a new way and yearned for a hilltop monastery in Laos, where there would be no more danger of Americans coming to distract or discredit me. The mercenaries flying with Air America might be from the States, but they didn't need monasteries. They ruled their own heavens. I feared aloneness yet needed solitude. I was drawn to Laos, yet didn't know how I could break the commitment I had made to stay with Ajahn Po, my mentor, for five rains.

The next day, following afternoon tea, I was able to catch Suñño, Anando, and Ajahn Po talking together quietly. Luang Paaw smiled. "It looks like you have a question, Santisekkho."

"The new American monk has me wondering. If he can come here to Wat Pah Nirapai all the way from Sri Lanka as a junior monk, would it be possible for me to travel too? Perhaps go *tudong* to Laos, for instance?"

Anando and the abbot conferred. "Customarily, Ajahn Po wants a young monk to honor his commitment and stay here under his tutelage. But Prah Samrong has told us how you've seen combat and how your plane was shot down. In a way, trekking out of the mountain jungles means you have already been *tudong*. You understand the difficulties and isolation you will face. We often meditate and sleep in burning grounds where cremations take place. But you've survived a plane crash. We don't think you'll fear a charnel ground or the ghosts that local people think haunt the forests you'll pass through."

Ajahn Po said something to Suñño. "Luang Paaw says that in your case, if you insist, you may go. But first, you must make your *glot*—"

"*Glot?*"

"Something you must take with you on *tudong*. It's a large handmade umbrella with a cylinder of netting hanging from it. You suspend it between two trees to provide shelter on nights you don't stay at a monastery."

"There are parts of Laos that are not Buddhist, where people still worship spirits, and you will be completely on your own," Anando interjected.

Suñño concluded, "If you promise to stay away from places like Sepone where the war is still raging and promise to be back here for the next Rains Retreat, Ajahn Po will simplify the preparations for you. We can find an old *glot* in the storage room for you to mend. To make a *glot* completely from scratch can take months for a new monk."

I bowed and *waied* respectfully and took my leave, prepared to face the challenges that lay ahead.

It was the American monk from Boston who first told me about using our *chakras* as objects of meditation, something he had learned about in Sri Lanka, he said. I really didn't know what a *chakra* was other than being an Indian term, but I was skeptical of the American monk and suspected at the time he was getting his Hindu and Yoga and *vipassana* teachings muddled up. I also suspected that he brought it up after one of our evening Dhamma talks to test Ajahn Po in some strange way.

To my mild surprise, Luang Paaw Po smiled and replied, "Very good question! On the simplest level, we can let go of areas of pain or tightness by imagining we have an extra set of nostrils and breathing through the pain—in our neck or our knee, for example. In your case, breathing through your knees and back can help you heal and sit again cross-legged with the rest of us.

"But pain and tension in our forehead can get even more interesting. Using our extra nostrils to breathe through our third eye, sometimes this can help us go very deep. Also, the crown of our head, or maybe the most powerful of all meditations, breathing through our heart. Sometimes it helps to visualize a ball of light first and then bring it inside your head or chest before you start breathing there. Try it. See what works for you."

And as I worked with it that night, breathing through my heart actually frightened me with the intense emotion it released, especially when it took me back before the war to flashes of wars that raged within my family: "*You're dogging it!*" "*Screw you!*" "*Show some respect!*" "*Why should I?*" "*Get a haircut!*" "*Get off my back!*" But by opening myself up to those tiny slivers of memory, I saw that I could finally heal. I could reflect on their absurdity, how I could never remember how the fights began, only that they flared up fast, only that it felt good—cathartic—in the heat of battle, and that it felt like hell afterward. How like all wars, there were no winners in the end. And how by not forgiving my father and grandfather and by not forgiving myself, the embers of those battles still burned.

A few days after talking to Ajahn Po about going on *tudong*, Samai, the young novice, came to my *kuti* and told me that several guests had come to see me. I expected it to be Pawnsiri and her family or Professor Natapong or maybe Lek visiting from Korat. Instead, I was surprised to see Harley, Mali, and a ghost I only faintly remembered from my past—Captain Lisa Sherry. Mali *waied* politely, her face expressionless. Harley and Captain Sherry emulated the gesture, a little awkwardly, but I was struck with the distraught look on their faces and felt my newfound serenity begin to crumble. "It's good to see old friends," I said, "but it doesn't look like you're bringing me good news."

"It's about Rick Liscomb," said Captain Sherry, her eyes tired and red. "Our old friend Moonbeam volunteered to go on temporary duty up to NKP so Sergeant Washington wouldn't have to cancel his R&R."

"I thought Washington was back in the States," I said.

"He extended," said Harley.

Lisa continued, "Rick checked in with me by radiophone over at Danang before he left and told me he was looking forward to flying with your old friends, Colonel Strbik and Captain Rooker."

"And Captain Rush," said Mali.

Harley cracked a weary smile. "Yeah, the NOD-man was with them too. They'd become a regular hard crew, and being from Spectre, they were the best damned crew up there."

Captain Sherry picked up the story. "The brass said they were just going to be doing some mopping up around An Loc, but things are still pretty hot over there. In fact, the fighting never really let up during rainy season this year. Spectre birds from Ubon and Stinger AC-119s from NKP kept getting pulled off night work on the Ho Chi Minh Trail to bail out ARVN infantry units under heavy attack."

"Radio Control Invert at NKP had cleared their operating altitude," said Harley, "but somehow, even though the roads were muddy as hell, the NVA got 37-mm anti-aircraft guns up into the hills above them and chewed them up pretty good. There was no way they were going to make it over the mountains to Ubon, let alone NKP, so Colonel Strbik and Captain Rooker headed for the South China Sea. The crew was all set to bail out when they reached the coast, and Jolly Greens were standing by. I mean, they knew the starboard wing and the tail section attached to it were in bad shape, but things were looking good for a slow descent. And then out of the blue, it all came off, and they cartwheeled into the jungle."

Lisa stepped in for the hard part. "There were no survivors."

"He had been keeping quiet about it," Harley said, "but Liscomb was pretty much *tii-rahking* his housegirl, Pook. She locked herself in his trailer, and nobody could get her out for three days until finally her father came from Korat and took her home."

"Needless to say," said Captain Sherry, "that was the last Stinger out of NKP to fly a daytime mission in Vietnam." Her eyes were red, but the daughters of French farm girls and American fighter pilots who had lived through World War II didn't cry.

My desire to go on a pilgrimage grew stronger in the days after my visit from Harley, Mali, and Captain Sherry when I dreamed each night of missions over the Ho Chi Minh Trail and relived distorted funhouse images of dread and disaster. From somewhere inside me came the message that going on *tudong* would expiate the sin of survival. I saw again the peasant-boy soldier with the broken nose and Lieutenant Duong torn apart by miniguns that crashed down from a heavenly hell before they were incinerated in a wave of liquid fire. My desire to escape from Thailand grew overwhelming on the nights I held the living ghost of Tukada in arms of mine that were drained of strength and devoid of feeling. Murray and Spitzer and Sachs were sprawled just out of reach, their blood cooking in the brutal sun, fading away to blackness with the ringing of the temple bell that awakened the monastery at 3:00 a.m.

Suñño and Anando picked out an old *glot* for me in the back of the supply room behind the meditation hall. I noticed that they passed over several that were in better condition. The ever-perceptive Anando caught my look and said, "We don't want you leaving us too soon, Santisekkho."

And so, little by little, I sat out on my porch with the sewing kit Lek had given me, carefully patching the mosquito netting to protect me from those potentially deadly insects that I had vowed not to harm and repairing the top to keep out both insects and rain. I put off dealing with one of the arms of the umbrella, hoping that it was only bent, but when I tried to straighten it out, the arm broke. I sat there puzzling over how to replace it when good fortune came my way in the form of one of the village elders who often helped out at the monastery. "*Na,*" he said, and I followed him off into the forest behind my *kuti* to a copse of bamboo.

He found a stalk that had recently fallen and, with his machete, skillfully stripped away a piece that was exactly what I needed to repair the *glot*. Back on my porch, I used Grandpa Shepler's old penknife to adjust the length and bore holes at each end to attach to the umbrella. The next day I busied myself sewing in the new arm and testing it out, making a few adjustments so that I could open and close it easily. I spent a few days after that trying it out, running a line between two trees and making sure I would be able to set up my portable shelter even if I might be working in the dark or in the rain. I smiled to myself, thinking back to the days when Jamal Washington had me loading a film magazine and threading an Arriflex movie camera with my eyes closed.

The Mad Monk

In the midst of dreams within dreams and memories within memories, the Mad Monk awakens one night, afraid that he is Brendan Leary, a wounded soldier lost behind enemy lines, awakening in a grog to the smell of smoke coming...from where? His closet? How did he get a closet behind enemy lines? He awakens from his dreams, high on cough medicine, which makes him wonder if he isn't only dreaming he's awake. Is it his waking mind or sleeping mind that is playing tricks on him? Isn't he a monk? It's confusing because monks don't have closets. It's just a memory, he figures in his sleep that might be wakefulness. And the intense memory that seems too real to be a dream becomes even realer when he opens the armoire door and can see through the wall into the next room where he sees the ashes of Tom's joint that has started the bed on fire with leaping tongues of flame that are licking the wooden roof beams. Except Tom and Dave have been gone for months, gone their separate ways to oblivion, and Larry has married Peung and moved away. Or has he dreamed that too? The Mad Monk runs to Tom's door in disarray, knocking loudly, waking the neighboring brothers. "Tom! Larry! Dave!"

Before the brothers reach the stairs, the Mad Monk pulls, and effortlessly the door rips to pieces in his hand. Rushing inside, he sees that for sure his friends are gone and that indeed they left a burning roach on the wooden bed frame. Rick Liscomb and Jamal Washington burst in behind the Mad Monk with buckets of water, which they throw at the burning walls and bamboo curtains. The Mad Monk throws himself over Tom's stereo, which is covered with dust and cobwebs, gathering it up and carrying it outside. A human chain begins passing buckets of water up the stairs, leaving Bungalow #4 smoky and wet. When the human chain sees that the fire is out, the assembled brothers, hipsters, lifers, and their tii-rahks begin laughing and dancing and hugging each other like fools. That is when the roof explodes, shooting flames next door and onto the thatched roofs of the stilt houses outside the compound. The Mad Monk knows he should return to the monastery and report for duty. Instead, he runs back to his room that is Brendan Leary's room to start salvaging his clothes and his own stereo now that Tom's is safe, but the roof has already collapsed. The fire resurrects itself with a vengeance, leaping from bungalow to bungalow.

Bamboo shacks in the fields outside are surrounded by the conflagration. From rooftop to rooftop, the flames spread into town. At the moment Bungalow #4 begins collapsing completely, crashing down from its eight-foot pillars, the Mad Monk runs back into his secret room, the one that appears only in his dreams, leaving the screams of the brothers behind him. In a curtain of smoke and flame, he drops from the back of the building, deciding it is time to disappear, and blindly follows the wall to the tiny door behind the spirit house where he makes his escape.

The fire spreads wildly, leaping from the porches and rooftops at Bungalow Ruam Chon Sawng until the entire neighborhood around the Ghetto is swallowed up in flames. It is hot season in the Mad Monk's dream, and the sun has turned shops and apartments and schools and even clusters of palm trees into kindling that explodes whenever the flames touch it, igniting new neighborhoods ever closer to downtown. The Corsair and the Soul Sister— gone. Niko's bathhouse, the USIS office and library—smoldering piles of ashes.

The next morning when I mentioned my dream to Anando while we cleaned up after breakfast, he told me yes, there had been a fire in Ubon the night before, a rather large one according to the villagers who had come to the monastery that morning to cook and bring offerings. It was about then that Ajahn Po announced that there would be a conference of abbots from the outlying *wats* coming up that afternoon and that the monks and novices had extra work details immediately after breakfast, primping our patch of jungle oasis for the visiting *ajahns*. Even in the simplicity of monastic life, this was not going to be a routine day of sitting and reflecting, and thoughts of going *tudong* were put on hold. It wasn't until noon that we got a chance to bathe and tidy up our *kutis*. The sun and humidity continued to sauté us even while we threw bowls of tepid water from the large earthen *klong* jars over our grimy flesh. My favorite hours for sitting were long past, yet the air was too thick under the tin roof of my room to even take a nap. I dragged my rattan sleeping mat out on the porch, but the burning sun turned the insides of my eyelids into bright orange globes. The air was so heavy and stale that I felt like I was still inside, sealed in a cramped closet. I left the mat on the porch and went back in, lying down on the blanket I had smuggled out of the storeroom and folded up for an extra quarter inch of padding on the plank floor. Today, though, it felt as hard as the floorboards themselves as I tossed and turned. The blanket stuck to my clammy skin, unfolding every time I moved until it seemed to be everywhere in the room except under my bony body.

My nap was exhausting me. Better to take Tahn Anando's advice and walk off my grogginess. Like a caged animal, I paced back and forth over the shady path outside my *kuti*. I had some brief flashbacks of flying over the Ho Chi Minh Trail, but they faded away, and ever so slowly, my face began to relax. The muscles in my back and legs and arms began to feel warm and supple, the soreness melted away. After half an hour of walking, I felt refreshed and alert. It was time to try sitting meditation.

I lit a stick of incense and placed it in the sand inside a glass jar on the porch railing. Mosquitos were thick in late rainy season. I lit a mosquito coil and decided to try out hanging my *glot* from beneath the porch roof, carefully tucking the edges of the mosquito net under the borders of my grass mat to prevent squadrons of insects from invading through the open floorboards.

I settled into the lotus position, and when I closed my eyes and scanned my body, I found surprisingly few areas of tightness or pain. But it was taking a while for my mind to settle down, a process that was delayed by echoes of the Temptations singing "Ain't Too Proud to Beg." *And then the visions begin. At first it seems like a mural or a bas-relief of old European buildings with a saffron background. I wonder a moment if the saffron is woven from silk. The background is moving, however, and I realize the sky has turned to flame. My mind's eye watches building after building explode into conflagration as Bombay and Moscow, Athens and Rome, Berlin and London, New York and Tokyo burn in succession. Dresden, Paris, San Francisco, Singapore, all being devoured by fire. No meaning. Just observing. Wondering if these firestorms are images of wars past or thermonuclear war to come. The sky continues to swirl and roar, belching shades of ochre and crimson. Venice and Budapest and Constantinople all crumble before my eyes. Am I having a premonition of the fall of Saigon and Phnom Penh and Vientiane and Bangkok? Am I losing my mind at last? How do I know if I am?*

The Temptations faded back in. "*It was just my 'magination—running away with me…*" A temple bell rang in the distance. It was time for a couple of more hours of raking leaves and sweeping cobwebs from the shutters of the Dhamma hall before the dignitaries began arriving.

For the next two days, I tried to sit in meditation and only experienced agitation, a feeling of wanting to leap from the monastery rooftop, of once again wanting to jump out of my skin. On the third day, I went to Ajahn Po to request permission to leave Wat Pah Nirapai for a pilgrimage to Laos. More strongly than ever, I felt the need to meditate on the bones of my fallen comrades.

"Have you finished your *glot*?" Luang Paaw asked me in Thai.

"I would be honored if you would inspect it, Ajahn."

He walked with me to my *kuti*, where the *glot* was still hanging from the roof beam of the porch. He looked it over carefully, opening and closing it a couple of times and finally smiling. "Very good! Now I know that if the netting rips while you are on your journey, you can mend it and not die of malaria from a lone mosquito who gets inside. Come," he said, and I followed him back to the screened reception area beneath the living quarters of his *kuti*.

Luang Paaw took his place in a carved teakwood seat of authority. I bowed three times and sat humbly before him. "I have warned you, Santisekkho, *tudong* better for a more experienced monk." He paused. "On the other hand, you have much *kamma* to work out in Prathet Lao. Maybe this will help. We want you to return here for the next Rains, but if you keep pushing ahead and reach Luang Prabang, their holy city, ask for Wat Pah Pohn Pao. Ajahn Saisamut is very wise teacher. Please, Tahn Santisekkho—be careful. Stay in the valley along the Mekong. War still very bad in the Lao mountain. In Cambodia, many American journalist disappear."

And with that, I had Luang Paaw Po's permission, if not his blessing, to take my leave of Thailand.

The Long Road Home to Luang Prabang

That night, out of the pleasing drone of Ajahn Po's evening Dhamma talk, a simple prayer emerged: "*Hatred never ceases by hatred but by love alone is healed. This is the ancient and eternal law.*" The Mad Monk began to repeat it, over and over, a chant, a mantra. "*Hatred never ceases by hatred but by love alone is healed. This is the ancient and eternal law.*" The Mad Monk needed to repeat his mantra even though he understood it completely. *Why was so much of the world still lost in ignorance?* he wondered. *How had so much of Asia forgotten teachings that had been passed down for centuries?*

The following day he continued chanting his mantra silently on *pindabaht* and while he ate his morning meal, and he repeated it to himself while he cleaned his alms bowl and put it back into its saffron cover. Back at his *kuti*, he continued chanting softly. He packed a canvas carrying bag, also dyed saffron, with the simple requisites he was permitted, not much more than a ground sheet (a sturdy sitting cloth that would serve as his bedding), his toiletries, two other sets of robes, his passport, a roll of twine, his sewing kit, his grandfather's penknife, and a few "luxuries"—packets of instant coffee and tea, a small teapot and metal cup, and a box of matches. Placing the alms bowl and a water bottle in last, he slung the strap of the bag over his shoulder and squeezed his way through the narrow door. Out on the porch, he picked up the *glot* and rested it on his other shoulder. Struggling at first to balance the load, he made his way down the steps and began to walk ever more steadily toward the gate. His pilgrimage to Laos had begun.

The first day would take him back through Ubon and on north along Route 66. In a day or two, he would turn east and make his way to the north bank of the River Mun, which would lead him to the Mekong River and Pakse, Laos. Crossing the Warin Bridge, he could see fire damage just off to his right in the direction of the Noy Market, the place Larry Zelinsky had taken him on his first expedition into Ubon, the day he had seen Tukada for the first time.

At the traffic circle on the north side of the bridge, he looked to his left and saw the Chalerm Seen Theatre—where he and Dah had seen *Tora! Tora! Tora!*—still standing but its walls and billboards charred. Turning right along Prommathep Road, he walked directly past the riverfront market and saw up close that it was in ruins. A dark pall of ash spread across both sides of the street as he continued along the left bank. Buildings were blackened, restaurants and shops gutted, hotels dark. He followed the street where it curved to the left toward the post-telegraph office. When he reached the once-familiar corner only a block and a half from Yoon-on Store and Woodstock Music, he stopped—

The Apocalypse had come to Prommaraj Road. A carpet bomb attack gone awry? A mad bomber or a Pentecostal F-4 pilot on a secret mission to destroy Gomorrah? Or was it Communist agents from the Vietnamese ghetto? Was this a shocking new phase of the Easter Offensive that had been dragging on all year? Had rainy season been just a lull? Had General Giap dreamed up a massive expansion of the war? Was this preparation for a pincer movement that would advance from Phnom Penh and Angkor Wat in the south and Luang Prabang and Vientiane in the north? Would the North Vietnamese Army push on into hot season and celebrate the Lunar New Year by marching down the streets of Bangkok before the next monsoon?

It was too much to think about—so vast, so grand that it caused his mind to spin. But what he saw when he got to Woodstock Music and Yoon On Store, just a single family's business, was worse: the building was reduced to bulldozed piles of rubble. He looked for the ghosts of Vrisnei, her brothers Sommit and Chai, and her mother and father, the soft-spoken Chinese merchants. All he found was soot and dust. His dizziness grew deeper. "Hatred never ceases by hatred," he chanted softly, "but by love alone is healed. This is the ancient and eternal law."

Walking north, away from the river, and turning back along Kaenthani Road toward Route 66, he passed the Ubon Hotel. It had survived the fire, but the top floors were boarded up and sandbags lined the corners of the parking lot. A flash of Tukada popped into his mind, and for just a moment, he saw her walking ahead of him in a candlelight procession at Big Buddha celebrating Visakha Bucha. With the blink of his eye, the procession expanded into the vast multitude that crossed Memorial Bridge from Arlington Cemetery toward the White House, and then it was Danielle walking close beside him. The honking of a baht-bus brought him back, but the sounds of motor scooters and trucks disoriented him further.

The Mad Monk crossed Route 66 and sought out quiet side streets to take him to Bungalow Ruam Chon Sawng. Destroyed in his dream of conflagration, it was vibrant and untouched when he got there. Bun-lii and Mama-sahn sat inside the *rahn-ahahn*, peeling vegetables. Stepping inside the gate, he could see a Thai family living at Bungalow #4 and another Thai family next door where B.J. and Leclerc used to live. He had been taught about *anicca*—the impermanence of all things—and had meditated on it often, but there was a threshold he had crossed into too much change. In a trance, he walked to the spirit house at the end of the alley, lit a stick of incense, and said a silent incantation to the *jao tii* who lived there, asking for protection on the long walk ahead of him and praying for clarity to return to his mind. As he passed the restaurant on the way out, he heard Bun-lii's voice, now only partly familiar, saying, "*Sawatdii*, Tahn Bren-dan."

Looking back, he saw her and Mama-sahn *wai* respectfully. The Mad Monk smiled with more serenity and wisdom than he really possessed and walked on, staying on unpaved back streets as he continued north, closer to the base, to bid his farewell to Harley and Mali. When he got to their compound, Mali answered the door. "Harley not here," she said. "He do too much amphetamine, OD, go by medevac to Philippines."

The Mad Monk's mind reeled again. "Have you heard how he's doing?"

"Maybe him die. I don' care. For me war is finish. I'm going back to Ubon Teachers' Col-lege. One more year, then I go home to Roi Et. With Har-ley, always I worry too much." She *waied* and stepped inside.

The Mad Monk felt lost and alone and wondered if he had made a mistake leaving Wat Pah Nirapai. He pushed on, still confused but determined to not turn back. He had two more calls to make before his *tudong* began in earnest. Walking to the northern end of town and crossing back over Route 66 where it headed off toward the Big Buddha, he proceeded up the narrow lane to Miss Pawnsiri's family house. Ringing the bell at the front gate, he hoped she would be home, but it was her younger sister who came out. Feeling an ache of disappointment, he tried to speak to her in Thai, afraid his thick American accent was filled with too much inflection and too many wrong tones for her to understand that he was going *tudong* through Laos and that he thought his pilgrimage would take about a year. He tried repeating the message a little slower, still not sure how much had gotten through.

"Just a minute," she said and disappeared into the house. She returned with a sooty envelope, "For Brendan Leary" written on the front. The Mad Monk opened it and found his forged Canadian passport inside.

"Khun Sommit and Khun Chai come here after fire. They say maybe my sister can bring to you at Wat Pah Nirapai. Afraid maybe fire started by Communi't, maybe not safe for American in Ubon Province."

"Thank you, little sister. I will keep it—'just in case,' like Sommit used to say."

"*Chohk dii*, Than Bren-dan. Good luck to you."

Now that he had said his goodbyes to the living, the Mad Monk had one stop left, something he feared even though he knew there was nothing there to fear. A little further north on the other side of Route 66 was Tukada's old villa. The gate was locked, the lawn was overgrown, and vines hung from the veranda. Dah's violent death had cursed the place, leaving it empty and abandoned. The Mad Monk sighed and moved on, deciding to take advantage of the mildness of this cool season afternoon and continue walking north under the midday sun along the shoulder of what Ubon GIs laughingly called Route 66 and which he saw now, from signs along the road, was in reality Thailand Route 212.

Just past the village of Ban Hua Reua, he recognized the hills at the site of the ambush where snipers had once lurked, triangulating on the cyclists racing below. "*Hatred never ceases by hatred but by love alone is healed*," he chanted softly to himself.

The Mad Monk climbed to the ridgetop where Prasert and Tukada had died, but his mind, which so often danced with images lately, went strangely quiet. He persevered, spreading his sitting cloth and saying a simple prayer: "May I be well, if not today then somewhere down the long path I'm treading. And may Prasert and Tukada be well in whatever form they are reborn, and may they someday work through their *kamma* and find peace."

Cutting a length of twine with his grandfather's penknife, the Mad Monk hung his *glot* between two shady trees, arranging the mosquito net carefully after he crawled inside. He sat there the rest of the afternoon and into the night, closing his eyes and willing a vision of Tukada to appear, but the Mad Monk saw nothing but blackness. He grew tired and wanted to sleep but pushed himself instead to continue meditating. *What seems like hours pass when suddenly, out of the blackness, his mind's eye is blinded by exploding trucks and fiery rivers of napalm. Shadowy drivers and the soldiers riding with them jump from the trucks and flee in vain. Sporadically the Mad Monk hears a scratchy voice crackling over an intercom—he can't tell if it's a fighter pilot or a Spectre fire-control officer—sounding like Mission Control on a moon landing except it's describing an earthly moonscape in the making. "Looks like we got us some Crispy Critters," the Mad Monk hears as North Vietnamese trucks and their crews are immolated by molten jelly.*

It wasn't until deep into the night that the Mad Monk finally fell asleep, only to be awakened a few hours later by the harsh rays of the morning sun. And like a moth drawn to a flame, the Mad Monk was called even more powerfully back to the hills of Laos and the narrow dirt roads that ran through them. Once again, he chanted, *"Hatred never ceases by hatred but by love alone is healed. This is the ancient and eternal law."*

After taking out his alms bowl, the Mad Monk put his sandals into his cloth bag and doubled back barefoot to Ban Hua Reua, hoping to find a few generous villagers who could provide his morning meal. Other monks had passed through before him, which meant that offerings were sparse until he came to a noodle shop whose proprietress ladled out several dishes she had just started preparing for lunch. He found a fallen tree trunk in a patch of shade where he could rest his back while he ate his breakfast before heading east on unpaved side roads toward the village of Tam Sum. There on the banks of the River Mun, he intended to spend the second night of his journey. In the late afternoon, he found a small, run-down monastery in the middle of the hamlet. He was shown to a vacant *kuti*, filled with spider webs he was too tired to sweep out, just having time to hang his mosquito net and unroll the grass mat he had been given before the bell rang announcing the evening assembly of the monks. Although he sat with ten other *bhikkhus* that night, he felt achingly alone.

Taking leave after the morning chanting, he removed his sandals, again placing them in his bag, and walked barefoot through town with his alms bowl, partly filling it, but continuing on for an hour toward Phibun Mangsahan and the Kaeng Sapeu Rapids before he found a quiet spot under a shady tree not too far off the road for his solitary breakfast. When he finished eating, he put his sandals back on and continued down the dusty highway, remembering moments from his first visit to the rapids with Dah, Prasert, and his friends from Ruam Chon Sawng. Traveling on foot, however, he couldn't recognize a single landmark from the day they were whisked out there by taxi.

He was permitted to have a second meal before noon, a concession Ajahn Po made to the energy a monk expended traveling on foot, but the sun had already passed overhead when he came to the next village, which meant he would go a little hungry, with only a cup of evening tea to tide him over. A few hours later, he reached the immigration checkpoints at Chong Mek, Thailand, and Vang Tao, Laos, one of the few places where the Mekong did not delineate the Thai-Laotian border, flowing further east instead. Leaving his U.S. passport in the bottom of his bag, he silently thanked Sommit and Indian Joe and the old Chinese *papa-sahn* that his forged Canadian passport was in order and he was permitted to push on. He intended to spend the night in a monastery near Phonthong, Laos, halfway between the Chong Mek checkpoint and the Mekong ferry crossing to Pakse. The Mad Monk was wearing flimsy shower sandals, however. His progress was slow, and it grew dark, with no village in sight. Even though he hung his *glot* under a tree not far from the highway, there was no traffic that night, and he ached with an unnamable fear until he finally fell asleep.

In the morning, the Mad Monk awakened to the sound of a temple bell ringing in the distance. No sooner had he started walking east toward Pakse than he spotted the earthen dike that led to a small monastery. The dike crossed golden fields of rice where villagers were already at work swinging their sickles. Pushing on to Phonthong proper, he was able to find women and children and old people at the side of the road who were happy to fill his alms bowl with rice and heaps of savory curries. Several miles out of town, he found a quiet place under a tree to eat his morning meal and then set out once more for the ferry that would take him across the Mekong to Pakse. By the time the weather-beaten ferry was halfway across the river, he was feeling disoriented once again. This time, however, it was largely from the motion of the old wooden boat, which had to point forty-five degrees upstream to counteract the current, and from the black fumes belching from its engine. He found himself wondering why the French had never built a bridge here, and then wondered why he wondered. The French had built no bridges crossing the Mekong anywhere that would have connected Laos to Thailand.

By the time he reached the center of Pakse, the capital of Champasak Province, the late morning sun was beating down on his shaved head and even in the so-called cool season was harsh enough to lull him into a trance in which he barely recognized the French colonial architecture of the town he was walking through. Leaving the central market, he passed a large building that looked like a palace, and he remembered rumors he had heard as an airman in Ubon that a decadent Royalist prince was building a monument to himself with American aid money.

Behind him, he could hear the drone of World War II-vintage propeller-driven aircraft taking off and wondered if they belonged to Air America or the Royal Lao Air Force or if he had come unglued in time and slipped back to an earlier war. The streets were bustling with bicycles, pedicabs, oxcarts, and a few trucks. But they were also busy with Lao soldiers in jeeps and troop transports and with foreigners who looked to be American soldiers wearing civilian clothes in a poor attempt to disguise their identity. The Mad Monk had come to Laos to visit the ashes and spirits of dead airmen, and so he was confused and surprised by a compelling need to get through the town and away from these living soldiers. He was glad provincial capitals were small in Laos and was soon relieved to be back in the country. It took him almost two hours to reach Ban Huaxe, where Route 23 branched off to the east from the main highway that followed the Mekong south toward Cambodia. The poorly paved Route 23 soon turned to ruddy laterite and clay as it began heading uphill toward the Bolaven Plateau and the town of Paksong.

Even as he slowly gained altitude, the tropical sun continued to beat down harshly on his shaved head, almost harshly enough to switch off the part of his brain that had sworn to follow the monastic rules taught to him by Ajahn Po and the monks Anando and Suñño. He felt a push and a pull, a *push* to continue his pilgrimage to the end of Route 23 at Muang Phin where he has sure he could find the downed aircraft he was searching for, and a *pull* to return to Ubon Ratchathani, renounce his vows, and check into whatever room was left with working air-conditioning at the Ubon Hotel. He thought about what he could be ordering from room service—Singha beer and *mii krawp* and satay chicken skewered on a stick and a heaping dish of chocolate ice cream for dessert—and then he snapped out of it. He was back on the poorly paved road, learning to ignore the burning of his sandaled feet. He thought about how he had once camped out in the woods of Massachusetts with the Boy Scouts and, more recently, on the beaches of Mexico. How much worse could this be? He would at least be on roads, no matter how poorly paved they might be, or, at worst, dirt trails. Hadn't he trekked out of steeper mountains than these with Harley across leech-infested riverbanks and miles of jagged undergrowth?

He would have stayed true to his simple vows—traveling on foot, sleeping under a tree protected only by his *glot*, eating only food that was offered to him before noon—except that he saw the bicycle, just lying there next to a large needlewood tree where a side road turned off to the north outside Ban Huayhe. On the other side of the tree sat the still form of a man in the baggy hat and the rumpled, faded olive drab of what looked like a Pathet Lao uniform. "*Sabai dii ruu, khrab?*" the Mad Monk asked in a gentle voice. There was no answer.

Dead? he wondered as he walked closer and stopped. Lifting the brim of the cap, the monk saw that a single bullet had entered the soldier's temple, leaving the back of his head shattered. Next to him lay the rusted three-speed bicycle, deemed not worth plundering by his executioner. The Mad Monk asked the dead soldier for permission before he took his bicycle, permission that was not denied. He pushed it to the road, fitted his carrying bag into the basket in front, and lashed his *glot* to the cargo rack behind his seat. Climbing aboard, the Mad Monk again felt dizzy and disoriented even though the late afternoon sun was behind him. He pushed off just the same, and with each thrust of his foot into the pedal of the old English-style bicycle, Brendan Leary, Prah Santisekkho, the Mad Monk, repeated the phrase, "*Hatred never ceases by hatred but by love alone is healed. This is the ancient and eternal law.*"

It was dark when he pedaled laboriously through Ban Ito, three thousand feet up in the Annamite foothills. He camped outside the village in a grove of mountain oak and yellow pine where he could keep the bike hidden in the morning when he walked back with his alms bowl in hopes of being offered breakfast. Sleeping alone that night, even with the war rumbling in the distance, was not as terrifying with the bicycle lying nearby. Returning to Ban Ito at dawn, he sensed that generosity might not be practiced as fervently by animist, non-Buddhist hill tribes as in the lowlands because the offerings—rice, curry made with rotting river fish, leaves of something like wild spinach—were scant. Pushing on in the morning light, however, he saw enough of the bomb craters that had torn up the highway and the fields around it, burned-out jeeps and trucks pushed off into the ditches and *klongs*, and trees and fields burned black by napalm and artillery to realize that food was scarce for everyone on the Bolaven Plateau.

When he reached Paksong, once a bustling market town for the French coffee plantations that surrounded it, he found a ghost town, the French planters gone, the coffee beans unharvested. It was before noon, though, and when he saw that people were approaching in the opposite direction, he quickly parked his bike, stepped out of his sandals, and took up his alms bowl. He gladly accepted token offerings of sticky rice from several small families of peasants, just a husband and wife and child or two, walking past him through the ruined town.

After Paksong, he continued climbing into the Bolaven Plateau, pedaling steadily along the dusty road toward Sekong. "*Hatred never ceases by hatred but by love alone is healed. This is the ancient and eternal law.*" He needed to find the lost plane. He needed to make peace with himself for surviving, to grieve, to pray to the unknowable heavens for the release of the restless ghosts—the *pii tai hong*, the villagers called them—of the downed airmen into a better realm. Roaming from village to village, through intermittent patches of war-scorched forest and freshly slashed-and-burned upland rice fields, he drove himself on through Ban Thongset, Muang Tha Teng, Ban Dakbon, and nameless hamlets in between. The roads looked vaguely familiar, especially when he saw hulks of destroyed trucks pushed off along the side, but his memory was of the nighttime, lit palely by the moon or too brightly by flares and white-phosphorus rockets or washed out in grainy grays and milky greens and whites on night-vision monitors.

When the sun set and the Mad Monk finally stopped for the night, he marveled at the beauty of the stars strewn across the clear, black sky. But higher now in the mountains of Laos in cool season, even after crawling into his *glot*, he needed to bundle himself in his second set of robes, leaving only his third set of robes and his canvas carrying bag for a pillow. At dawn on the outskirts of Sekong, people stared at him, but he had passed another monk on a bicycle going in the opposite direction, hadn't he? Or had he seen himself riding back to the safety of Thailand? Was it a dream, a memory, or a mirage from the day before? Or were they staring at his *farang* skin, alternately pale and burned, or the way he towered over them?

He walked his bicycle through the streets of Sekong, and people put offerings of rice, fish soup, and wild greens into his bowl, even though it sat in the basket that hung from his handlebars. The rules were surely different in the mountains of Laos. Or were the people so war-weary they had stopped caring about rules and regulations? So tired of being puppets dangling from strings and dying for powerful outside forces that a foreigner dressed as a harmless if deranged monk was a pleasant diversion from the last ten years?

He saw the road bending north and remembered that this was the direction Spectre 544 had turned that night. He pedaled on through Ban Songkhon and past several burned, abandoned villages before bearing off to the west toward Ban Nongbua and on to Salavan. He could remember Spectre hunting here but wasn't sure which night. A few miles north of Salavan, back on Route 23, Thai mercenaries in Royal Lao uniforms trudged past. He knew they were Thai because they weren't using rapid Lao-Issan dialect, instead speaking in the leisurely, measured cadence of the Lanna region of Northern Thailand that allowed him to understand every word. It must have been an artillery unit because the jeeps plodding along behind the troops towed howitzers whose barrels seemed even longer than the barrels of the 105s carried on Spectre gunships.

Up ahead, in the direction the artillery unit had come from, was a strange black cloud on a day too clear for a black cloud. Riding a mile closer, the Mad Monk realized it was a thick flock of buzzards, some with wingspans of more than five feet, circling over *what*? The Mad Monk smelled something like pork cooked with gasoline. Advancing on foot, he saw that charred bits of what had once been Pathet Lao and NVA soldiers hung from the branches of leafless trees. The stench of death overpowered him. Feeling nauseous, he climbed back on his bicycle and continued pedaling north along the dusty road. His mind felt spongy, as if it had been cut adrift and floated aimlessly inside his skull, overwhelmed by fear and sadness. *"Hatred never ceases by hatred but by love alone is healed. This is the ancient and eternal law."*

He pushed on for several more days, sleeping under the trees with only his *glot* to protect him. Usually he managed to find a few rice farmers willing to feed him before noon, but several mornings he went hungry, getting by with a cup of coffee to start the day and tea or water to sustain him later. At night he slept far enough off the road to see occasional convoys of North

Vietnamese trucks pass by without being seen himself on these westernmost arteries of the Ho Chi Minh Trail. The mountain air remained cool, or he might have had to stop in the noontime sun to sleep. Instead, he pedaled on—always uphill, it seemed—and remembered the power of the Lao *sahmlaw* drivers in Ubon. Past Tumlan and Ban Thongkatua he pressed on, fording the Huay Phim River where the good French bridge had been destroyed and then realized he had made a wrong turn and was heading due west into the flatlands. He doubled back to Ban Nongko and found a Hmong walking path heading north, at least the way north *should* be, according to the sun, if the sun was where it was supposed to be as best he could guess without a watch.

The path led to a stream that he forded carefully, awkwardly navigating his bicycle down and back up the slippery banks. On the other side, a little further up the dirt trail, the Mad Monk spotted what he hoped was the road he had missed. At Ban Tat Hai, he knew he was close because there below him was the other French bridge he had seen the Wolf Pack take down, sending in Phantom after Phantom until the steel spans had melted from rockets and napalm and 3000-pound bombs. He knew this part of the Trail, knew he was back on Route 23 heading north, and now he pushed himself hard, certain that Muang Phin and Route 9 were dead ahead. Route 9, where Nevers and Spinelli had gone down with Larry Burrows when South Vietnam's finest rangers had been cut to ribbons trying to invade from the east.

Finally, the Mad Monk came to a primitive trading village where his trail intersected a badly damaged, pothole-filled road running east and west. An old man approached, accompanied by a young boy on crutches who was missing most of his right leg. The old man offered the Mad Monk sticky rice he carried in a hollow bamboo tube and a few dried-out leaves of wild spinach. His limbs were thin as grapevines, his face leathery and lined with wrinkles, but his hunched body still seemed strong and his eyes were focused and alert. Checking his bearings, the Mad Monk asked, "Is this Highway Nine—*anii route kao, baw*?"

"*Maen*," the old man answered, using the Lao word for yes. "*Poen pai sai, kap*? Where do you go?"

"Sepone," the monk answered. Speaking slowly in English and Thai and using hand gestures to point east, he asked, "Uncle, is that the way?"

"There is no more Sepone," the old man answered in dialect that was close enough to Issan Thai for the pilgrim to understand. "Two year ago when South Wietnamese come in American helicopter, Pathet Lao and North Wietnamese soldier drive them away, kill many. After that, only American plane come. Sometime bomb fall down jus' like rain, from plane so high they fly above the cloud. And now every building destroyed. Only a few wall still stand up." He paused and asked, with an almost imperceptible squint in his eyes, "Where you come from?"

"Thailand," the monk answered, not wanting to talk about the country of his birth.

"Be careful," the old man warned. "Even for monk, Laos dangerous. Too many bomb drop everywhere. Some bomb don' go off, but still can explode if you step on them."

The Mad Monk glanced at the boy, who hid behind the old man. "Thank you, Uncle. I'll be careful."

"Are you American?" asked the boy, peeking from behind the old man's leg.

At first, the Mad Monk felt trapped. "*Baw*," he lied, "I am Canadian." The old man smiled, and the monk wondered if Ajahn Po would let him count this as skillful speech. "*Sabaidii*," said the monk, pushing off in the direction of what was once Sepone.

"*Sohk dii*," the old man answered, wishing the *bhikkhu* luck. The boy just watched.

The pilgrim continued several miles in that easterly direction before he slowed down and circled back a few hundred yards, overtaken with a powerful sense of knowing where the Strela missile came from, a sense that it had been fired from right about here. Looking around carefully, he noticed some burned treetops on the north side of the pockmarked highway. Leaving the bike and his baggage hidden in the shrubs at the side of the road and taking only his sitting cloth, he hiked in along a footpath that soon narrowed into little more than a game trail. It was slow going for over an hour. He was afraid he hadn't gone much over a mile and had now become disoriented yet again, losing the sun in the mixture of tall bamboo and fifty-foot pine and broadleaf trees. Thorns ripped at his robes and tore at his skin, sweat burning the lacerations on his legs and arms. It was time to turn back. Taking a last look into the trees, he saw what he was looking for: the camouflaged tail of Spectre 544 hidden in a thick cluster of leaves and branches.

The bamboo rising from the charred ground was so thick he couldn't approach the plane directly. Backtracking, he found another trail, well worn, that took him to the wreckage. He could still make out the swath of broken, scorched tree trunks that the plane cleared away when it bellied in, a controlled disaster that showed great airmanship by Mertons and Gunther to the bitter end. Most of the wreckage was badly burned, and many smaller pieces had been carried away for scrap. Enough remained of the fuselage, however, for the Mad Monk to hear the angry ghosts of his crewmates calling over invisible headsets as he stepped inside. Walking slowly through the burned-out shell, he flashed back to Tukada's bleeding body and her dying words and shuddered, believing now without a doubt that those who died a violent death had been cursed to linger long in the spirit world and face a difficult rebirth.

The Mad Monk kneeled and spread his sitting cloth, crossed his legs into the lotus position, and went into a deep meditation, almost a trance, where he seemed to fold up into himself like a cheap plastic raincoat and disappear. He hadn't quite disappeared, however, because tears began to flow, and he could finally reflect on how he'd never had time to cry and wouldn't have allowed himself even if he did. He cried now for the many faces that floated up from remembrances of the crash and from remembrances of the bicycle race, remembrances that had eluded him when he sat up all night on the hill overlooking Route 66. Major Mertons and Captain Gunther, the pilots on Spectre 544; Major Hart, the navigator; and the other officers, Barclay, Richards, Del Rio, and Howard; Master Sergeant Penner, the flight engineer; Sergeant Vodvarka, the spotter; and the gunners, Edwards, Dixon, and the foolish Thommasi, whose bags were packed to go home and who had volunteered for one last mission to make his separation pay tax-free. Pigpen Sachs didn't even get to die with his boots on. Did that make him KWBR— killed while bicycle racing? The faces of Dave Murray, Jeff Spitzer, Prasert, and Tukada floated before him, filling him with emptiness, but he ached more when they disappeared and he saw nothing but blackness in their wake. He especially wanted to hold onto Tukada, to pull her back and seat her on his right, to feel her warmth, but she was the very first to disappear. And when he thought he was finally finished, his memories purged, Liscomb, Strbik, Rooker, and Rush appeared, dancing and laughing, which made him miss them all the more when they evaporated into the dark night. He especially wanted to shake Moonbeam's hand, to thank him for saving him the day the bicycle race ended in disaster, but it was too late for thanks and too late for farewells, and the Mad Monk kept crying long after he ran out of tears. It was nighttime when the pilgrim left the crash site, once again repeating the same phrase over and over, a mantra to his madness, a mantra to his redemption: "Hatred never ceases by hatred but by love alone is healed. This is the ancient and eternal law."

The night sky was sprinkled with stars, and a pale sliver of moon peered from behind the drifting clouds, but the Mad Monk was barefoot now, his sandals lost in the bramble. Bleeding from rocks and thorns, he stumbled into pitch-black triple-canopy jungle, losing his bearings and struggling for hours to find his way back to Highway 9. When he got there, his bicycle was gone, reclaimed, the Mad Monk was certain, by the vengeful ghost of the Pathet Lao soldier who once rode it. He searched up and down the road nevertheless, wanting to make sure he had returned to the right trailhead. It was not till an hour later when he had given up and started walking west on the main highway toward Savannakhet that he found his canvas carrying bag and equally precious *glot* sitting neatly next to a pile of rocks at the side of the road. He picked them up and continued walking until he heard a twin-engine Stinger gunship that was circling several miles away in the mountains behind him begin exchanging fire with 37-mm guns on the ground. Not wanting to think any more about Liscomb, Strbik, Rooker, and Rush, he turned north along a lightly traveled trail, settled down under a giant ficus, opened his *glot*, and prepared for a fitful night of sleep. He yearned for peace but was surrounded by war. How would Laos put itself back together? How would the Mad Monk heal himself? "Hatred never ceases by hatred but by love alone is healed. This is the ancient and eternal law."

He thought of Luang Prabang, the town mentioned to him by Ajahn Po, and remembered how several old Thai-Laotian monks had described the ancient capital nostalgically. It was the oldest town in Laos, for centuries the home of the Supreme Patriarch of Lao Buddhism. They recollected arriving there as young novices and living in awe among the city's many *wats*, which were filled with bronze and golden Buddhas and holy relics. *Luang Prabang*—the words themselves were soothing to the Mad Monk's ear and called out to him. He pictured a Shangri-la perched above the clouds in a dreamy mountain valley and remembered his promise to Ajahn Po. He vowed to end his *tudong* at Wat Pah Pohn Pao. Before the next Rains Retreat, he would ask Ajahn Saisamut to be his teacher.

For forty days and forty nights that might have been one hundred and forty days and nights, the Mad Monk wandered through a manmade wasteland. On the sixth day, he came across the skeletal wreckage of an Air America helicopter and, in the valley below, the village where Tony Pope once encamped with his small mercenary army. The Mad Monk was bewildered because he was sure it had been south of Route 9, somewhere in the hills around Salavan. Had he and Harley actually hiked in a circle that passed near the wreckage of Spectre 544, somehow crossing Route 9, perhaps in a stream bed at night where a bridge had been destroyed? Or was he wandering in circles *now*? It didn't matter. Pope's village was leveled, a shallow pile of rubble. The huge temple bell survived, turned on its side, covered in dust amid the ruins. The thatch huts had been reduced to ash, but when the Mad Monk made his way to the north end of the hamlet, he could still recognize the distorted, half-melted tin roof of Pope's headquarters. A charred wooden bucket lay on the ground next to what remained of the veranda, the enemy ears and fingers it once held now looking like overcooked bacon. Inside, the jars displaying Pope's strange collection of shrunken heads and brain tissue were all smashed, the contents moldy and unrecognizable. The Mad Monk hurried from the village, nausea clawing at his stomach, and continued his trek through the never-ending wasteland.

And when he escaped the wasteland, he wandered in the Laotian wilderness, painstakingly making his way north, climbing the steep, lonely trails of the Annamite Mountains that formed the long frontier with Vietnam. His feet bled, and no god spoke to him. He was only visited again and again by his inner and outer demons—the ghosts of his lost compadres and the ghosts of the dead enemies he had been powerless to spare.

There were days that he saw no one and could not eat, sworn as he was to only eat food that had been offered by laypeople. There were days that he went hungry and craved a teaspoonful of chocolate ice cream with every step and every breath he took. In hill-tribe villages that were not Buddhist, he was sometimes ignored completely. Other tribal peoples, the children naked and the women bare-breasted, only stared, having never seen a *farang* before. Still other villages, Buddhist and animist alike, shared what they had, but nowhere in the hills of Laos was that much. Once, when he had gone two days without food, he came to an abandoned hill-tribe village built in a circle around a mango tree. The ground was covered with fruit in all stages of ripeness. The sun was only halfway to its zenith, but no one was there to offer him food. Praying to the spirits that haunted the roof beams of the huts, the Mad Monk was told by an invisible voice that the freshest of the fruit had been left for him that morning. He gorged himself and then left a mango offering on the porch to the *pii* that had spoken to him.

By the time he found the faded French sign that identified Route 7, the road west through the Plain of Jars toward Luang Prabang, the villagers in that remote province had abandoned their huts and were living in caves. There were nights that the dark, distant horizon lit up—the same way Sepone had once been set ablaze—as bombs rained down like seeds of death sewn by a profligate Grim Reaper. The Mad Monk himself began sleeping in small cutouts in the hills, seeking safety from the falling shells. He came upon village after village that had been burned to the ground and tanks, trucks, and artillery pieces with the markings of opposing North Vietnamese and Royal Lao armies that now sat useless and destroyed. He passed villages and trading towns where every monastery, school, and hospital had been leveled, and all that remained untouched were mysterious clusters of ancient stone jars, some as much as ten feet tall, sitting alone on small plateaus and reminding him of miniature Stonehenges. Forced north along the highway by a karst formation he couldn't climb, he came to what must have once been a provincial capital—a thousand buildings laid waste, only dust and ash left to blow in the wind. On the edge of the destruction, a single sign survived, the French lettering faded but readable, pointing the way to Luang Prabang.

He stayed off the old highway, traveling instead on steep and treacherous hill-tribe footpaths, trying as best he could to avoid the war that had raged there in the Northeast more intensely than anywhere in Laos. One afternoon he realized the world had turned silent and wondered how many minutes or hours or days the fighting had stopped before he had noticed. For the next week, he did not hear an airplane, a cannon, a gunshot, when abruptly the earth opened up a mile in front of him in a wall of black mushroom clouds that thundered so loudly it pounded his chest and shook the ground beneath his scarred feet and almost as abruptly dissolved into the sound of a gentle breeze. And when the silence was filled after a few days with the sound of two doves calling and he noticed throaty gurglings of frogs in the early evening and the sawing of cicadas and crickets in the afternoon, it was then that the Mad Monk began to remember that he had once been ordained as Prah Santisekkho, "seeker of peace," and that in a former life he had been a combat cameraman named Brendan Leary who once lived a life before that as a pilot's son in a quiet suburb of Boston.

Stepping through the Gate

In the northwest corner of Laos around the holy city of Luang Prabang, the weather was getting hotter. Today, the sky was deep blue with billowing clouds riding the winds above, a respite before the overcast skies, merciless humidity, and steady rain that monsoon season would be bringing soon enough. The countryside that surrounded the ancient capital was hilly but not as severe as the mountains along the border with Vietnam, and the valleys were growing wider, planted with wet rice in paddies like those in northern Thailand. Perhaps because the town was still revered by the Neutralists, the Royalists, and the Communists alike, the area surrounding it had been spared from the war that had raged in so much of the rest of the country. Walking along a winding country road was pleasant.

It was about that time, as I neared Luang Prabang in search of Wat Pah Pohn Pao, that my madness slowly left me. It might have begun simply a few weeks earlier when a homeless villager offered me a sturdy pair of sandals and, although they were several sizes too small, my feet began to heal. Now, after months of sleeping alone outdoors with only my *glot* for shelter or in caves hiding from American bombs and North Vietnamese artillery, I began to accept the hospitality offered by the rice farmers I passed and found that even on a thin grass mat on the wood floor of a peasant's rebuilt hut or the hard ground of a cave filled with refugees, I slept deeply for the first time since I left Wat Pah Nirapai.

One day I came across a remote village that, though poor, had somehow been spared from the war. I slept several nights there at a modest monastery built entirely of hand-hewed wood and celebrated my first Laotian New Year, very similar to Songkran in Thailand but here called Bun Pii Mai. Following Theravada tradition, the villagers poured holy water over my hands and the hands of the other monks to begin and end the holiday. I felt mysteriously purified deep inside as well, humbled before people whose lives had scarcely advanced beyond the stone-age tribes who lived in the hills above them without even the benefit of the wheel. Here in the valleys, the rice farmers had progressed to large wheels of solid wood on carts that were pulled by a team of oxen. In the midst of what seemed to be an enduring cease-fire, I was able to relax and appreciate in the lowland Laotians much of the simple elegance I had admired in their Issan Thai cousins on the other side of the Mekong. I noticed for the first time how all the females, from youngest to oldest, whether rice farmer or storekeeper, wore ankle-length sarong-like *sinhs* made of hand-spun silk. The silk was handwoven on simple looms that sat under almost every thatch hut in the village but was fit for Thai royalty—or nightclub singers at the Lotus Blossom. Thanks to the cease-fire, while the mothers worked their looms, I was able to enjoy all three days of Bun Pii Mai listening to the laughter of their children playfully throwing water on each other on these hottest days of hot season.

The mountain air could be troubling, sometimes giving me strength but often burning my lungs and eyes with smoke from the slash-and-burn farming of the hill tribes nearby, smoke that still held the scent of the lingering wars. But regaining my sanity meant once again cleaning and folding my robes correctly. Bathing in the cool mountain streams had reawakened me, and it was time to press on.

It was just outside Luang Prabang, on the north side of the River Khan, that I finally found Wat Pah Pohn Pao. Walking through the gates, my heart swelled with the feeling that I had found my truest of true homes. The monastery sat on a wooded hilltop, spartan and serene in the same forest tradition as Wat Pah Nirapai, except for a remarkable golden temple that greeted my eyes from the very top of the hill. As I walked up the red clay lane toward the temple, the sun was beating down hard, and there was not a soul in sight. Entering the *viharn*, I found several young novices sweeping up the hall who were happy to put down their brooms and lead me to their abbot, Ajahn Saisamut. He seemed satisfied that Ajahn Po had trained me correctly in both my bearing and my ability to chant in Pali, and he seemed pleased that I spoke a passable smattering of Issan Thai.

A few days after I arrived, Ajahn Saisamut gave an evening Dhamma talk on what remained for me the great spiritual riddle of Buddhism: no-self. As Anando had told me months earlier, the abbot explained that there was intense debate among Buddhist teachers in Thailand and Laos whether the concept of *anatta* should even be taught to laypeople. When we were dismissed for the night, I approached him, saying, "I've had difficulty with *anatta* even as a monk. While I was on *tudong*, there were times I thought that I had gone mad. After a few days, I would feel lucid again and would sit under a tree, always in broad daylight, reflecting on the experience. It had seemed as though I had disappeared and that it had only been the empty shell of a body that had walked on. Was that an experience of *anatta* I was having?"

"Perhaps you've had a taste of understanding," he answered. "When you have reflected on it deeply and absorbed it, you will develop great compassion for those who still stumble blindly in the sensory or material world." I turned to leave, but Ajahn Saisamut called me back. "Tahn Santisekkho, something came for you today."

He handed me a tattered blue aerogramme from Thailand, but the light was too dim in the hall to make out the pale handwriting on the envelope. I thanked him and returned to my *kuti* where, sitting on the floor and lighting a candle, I saw that it had originally been addressed to me at Wat Pah Nirapai and forwarded by way of an undependable Laotian postal service to my current residence in the uncertain hope that sooner or later I would make it here. Holding the letter close to the candle, I began to read:

November 22, 1972
Dear Tahn Santisekkho,

My sister tell me you come today and say you go to Prathet Lao. I am very sad when you come here and I not here to speak with you. Now I cannot say "Sawatdii" and wish you "Chohk dii" when you go tudong. Sir, please be careful—you know the war is dangerous too well. I worry for you too much.

Sir, do you know that I am very sad? Do you know that I want to cry but I can do nothing? I don't understand my feelings. Why do I think like that? You explain you have much kamma from the people who die in the bicycle race and you have more kamma from people dying when you fly to Prathet Lao in the American War. Sir, I understand you must go to Rains Retreat. But how long must you stay a monk? Why do you have to be a monk in Prathet Lao? Sir, it is too dangerous for American. Too dangerous for everybody. I don't understand, but if you are happy, I am happy for you. But in my own mind, my heart is very much broke. Sir, when the November days slip away, all I can think is that my love is gone from me. Why cannot you stay in Thailand?

Tahn Santisekkho, I think of you very much. Can you remember in the past when we sit together in my house? Sir, when I get up in the morning, I have to look at your sitting-place. I don't have anything of yours to hold on to except that memory and one small photograph that my sister took of us. Tonight the moon is shining, sir. I look at it to look for your eyes. I see your eyes, sir, and I afraid you fault me for not let you be a monk in peace. Never mind. You don't worry about me. I know you have much kamma. I know you must find peace before you can love somebody else who has love to give for you.

Will you think of Thailand? How long much time that I cannot see you again? Will you be a monk until you die? Sir, do you realize? Never, never more for us. Sir, if you give up your robes someday, will you have somebody to take care of your heart? I can see if you are sad. If you feel sad, I do too. If you give up being the monk, please think of me for the first.

I'm so confusion when I think of you. I feel like everything in Thailand going backwards in time, before the American War. Because American people don't care about what they did here, and so many thing very bad. Thai people no more trust American government, because so many people in Vietnam and Kampuchea and Prathet Lao who trusted American government now suffer and die. I am so glad you not same as other American. Sir, I think you belong to live here in Thailand.

Oh, very sad for me, sir. Future isn't sure. Maybe when there is peace I can come to Prathet Lao, but isn't possible at this time. I think in the future better when I finished my study. Please write to me, sir. Let's me write again. Every night I have to watch your picture and kiss it before I go to bed. I wish you to be happy and prosperous. Please don't worry about me. Please take care your heart and body for your long life. Please don't forget write to me.

> *Love and sincerely*
> *Yours student and friend,*
> *Miss Pawnsiri Leemingsawat*

I stared at the aerogramme for a long time and then read it again before I folded up the tissue-thin paper and put it next to my toiletries in the small bookshelf on the floor near my sleeping mat. I was stunned at the intensity of Pawnsiri's feelings and had no idea how to respond to so much innocent passion. I had worked hard to develop a cool heart, and in the depth of my madness, it was the memory of a *jai yen* that gave me a direction to crawl when I pushed myself with great resolve to climb out of the abysmal darkness into which I had fallen. I could function now, go through the motions of being a monk, but I realized that something inside me was still damaged, and it frightened me to realize that I had no idea how long it would take me to truly heal. Instead of trying to respond immediately to such unintentionally jarring emotion, I would guard the letter carefully until a day came when I could reply. I couldn't help noticing that I had difficulty believing that a decent human being could love a wretch like me at all, let alone deeply. At the same time, I wondered if I should even be asking these questions, if I hadn't drifted off onto a dangerous spiritual detour. If no-self were the deepest eternal truth, how was it possible for love like this to even exist? Wasn't *metta*—compassion—the only true love possible in the end?

I couldn't answer Pawnsiri, but her letter reminded me that I needed to check in with my family, if only to let them know that I was still alive. I explained that they hadn't heard from me in months because I had gone on a pilgrimage through long stretches of Laos that hadn't had mail service in years, if ever, leaving out my bout with insanity and mention of the war that until recently had still been raging. A package arrived a few weeks later, also forwarded to me from Wat Pah Nirapai. It turned out to be a tin of my grandmother's Christmas cookies, which was troubling in that they were *cookies*, that they were for *Christmas*, a Christian holiday, and that they hadn't arrived till May. Ajahn Saisamut saw no such problems, ringing the temple bell and announcing that a special treat had arrived in honor of a special holiday, Buddha-Christmas! I smiled later that night when I wrote Mom a thank-you note telling her how she and Grandma Shepler had created a new Lao holiday.

As I meditated in my *kuti* in the days that followed Pawnsiri's letter, I found that the struggles I had gone through at Wat Pah Nirapai were not over. Sitting with my eyes closed, staring at blackness, feeling nothing, stuck in a spiritual and emotional logjam, I took a slightly deeper breath, giving myself a little push and suddenly felt, instead of being blown away in a raging storm, as if I had intentionally taken an uncontrolled hundred-foot dive off that cliff at Acapulco, leaping far into the void of *anatta*, letting the universe turn me inside out.

I sat through the experience without flinching, trying to just observe this inner drama. I reflected further, wondering how a concept could be so jarring. Was it only a Westerner who experienced this? Were Americans particularly vulnerable? I began to understand that even though I had only taken a baby step toward letting go of my ego, it was the core of my Western identity. Even the *anti*-cowboy defined himself by this psychic inner core. *Maybe Freud was right and the Buddha wrong*, I wished for a moment before surrendering to the realization that a lot of Freud's ideas had been attacked by his own followers. Was this perhaps Buddhist symbolism, a Buddhist analogy? I would come back to this again and again before surrendering with humility to an unanswerable riddle: even if I could embrace *anatta* with my mind, how would I incorporate it into my heart? Like the thrilling nightmare roller coaster rides we took at Revere Beach when we stood up, defying gravity, and hurtled down the rickety tracks with our hands flung out into the night sky, I had been flung out over the dark void. Except that instead of being a nightmare that ended with my awakening in the nick of time, this seemed to be an awakening that I could only escape for a few hours at night in the deep, soothing forgetfulness of sleep.

At the end of the second month, Ajahn Saisamut asked if I would like to visit Wat Tham Xien Maen, an abandoned cave monastery across the Mekong from Luang Prabang, where Ajahn Piyadhammo, his vice abbot, was on retreat. He mentioned that halfway between the boat landing and the cave, I would come to Wat Chom Phet, a tranquil hilltop monastery built by the Thai army in the 1800s. "Where are you planning to spend the Rains Retreat this year?" he asked.

"I would like to stay with you, Ajahn."

"In that case, you are welcome to stay awhile at Wat Chom Phet or at the cave with Ajahn Piyadhammo, or you may come back here any time before the start of the Rains," said the abbot.

Our morning *pindabaht* had been limited to the hamlets that surrounded Wat Pah Pohn Pao. The Lao peasants could never offer us as much rice and curries as at Wat Pah Nirapai, but it was enough. Now I crossed the

Nam Khan, a tributary of the Mekong, on a French-built steel bridge and entered Luang Prabang proper for the first time. Turning right, as I had been instructed, I headed west toward Phu Si, a sacred hill that rose three hundred feet over the center of the small but revered city-town. The hill was dotted with abandoned monasteries and shrines and crowned by a seventy-five-foot tall *chedi* that held ancient Buddhist relics and could be seen from almost anywhere in the town. Making my way around Phu Si to the ferryboat pier, I was enchanted with the discovery that Luang Prabang—ancient capital of Laotian monarchs and home for centuries of the Sangharaj, the Supreme Patriarch of Lao Buddhism—was in fact a tiny jewel tucked away in the mountains of what seemed indeed like Shangri-la.

It was late in hot season and the Mekong was at its lowest. After taking a longboat ferry across the slow-moving river to the village of Ban Xien Maen, I headed northeast on a dirt trail that ran parallel to the Mekong toward the cave monastery that gave the village its name. After passing the old Thai hilltop monastery halfway to my destination, I began looking for Ajahn Piyadhammo. A young Laotian novice, who couldn't help gawking at the gangly Westerner in monk's robes walking towards him, sent me further up the mountain to the limestone caverns where Piyadhammo was doing his intensive self-retreat. The *ajahn* was sitting on the front porch of a small hut that he shared with a hiveful of bees. Lean and tough, ruggedly handsome, but with the trace of a warm smile on his lips, he reminded me of a young Ajahn Po and a monastic version of Sergeant Jack Wu. He sat as immobile as a marble statue, seemingly immune to the cotillion of bees dancing over his nose and brow and lips and eyes. When a mosquito landed on my own nose, it took all the mindfulness I could muster to prevent my hand from lashing out instinctively. Sensing my presence, Piyadhammo slowly opened his eyes. "Welcome! You must be the American monk that Ajahn Saisamut wrote about."

"I'm traveling on a Canadian passport, actually. But I did serve in the American Air Force."

"You might want to be careful who you tell about your service with the Americans."

"Practicing Noble Silence should help," I replied.

June 1973–August 1975
Fly on My Nose,
Leak in the Universe

It was during the second week of my retreat with Ajahn Piyadhammo that I, a monk who had not too long ago walked in a raging storm of madness, started to taste expanding periods of tranquility. It might have been what the Pali scriptures referred to as *samadhi*. There was no monkey mind, only stillness, the riddle being that if the mind is *completely* still, how can the mind know this? It might have been where Ajahn Po was guiding us the time he asked, "What mind is watching when your mind is finally still as the forest pool?" Was there a Witness Mind that watched as the brain itself ran like a telephone switchboard?

We slept at night in Piyadhammo's *kuti* and spent the day, after *pindabaht* and our morning meal, in a nearby cavern meditating. In the uninterrupted silence deep within that cave, I began to hear what Ajahn Po had once referred to as the Sound of Silence. It was vaguely similar to monastic chanting in that it was made up of strands of two or three notes. Where Pali chanting coursed through your body, however, the Sound of Silence lodged in your brain, drilling forever at your skull. It was a powerful silver sound beam—high, electric, piercing, a test pattern. When you heard it, your mind was tuned in. Your outer mind could watch your inner mind at rest.

Tahn Anando had once told me there was no mention of anything like the Sound of Silence in the Pali texts, and Ajahn Piyadhammo concurred. In the days that followed, sitting in the cave monastery with hours to contemplate without interruption, I began to wonder if the Sound of Silence might be a recent development in the human brain brought on by the Electronic Age. I reflected further, wondering if this sound, what Anando had called a possible exception to the law of impermanence—this sound that always seemed to be there when your concentration was developed enough to tune in to it—was the result of recently unleashed electromagnetic radio energy transmitted wildly through the earth's atmosphere or if it were a ringing like the ringing of cymbals in my ears that used to linger for days after my band performed, the modern world's residual sound from a lifetime of PA speakers, televisions, telephones, and stereos, an aftereffect of no-dead-air-time radio. Was the brain evolving or mutating, part of a New/Old Radio

Network, the Armed Forces Radio of holy men and mad monks? Reflecting a little further, I, the Mad Monk Santisekkho, reached a small insight: even the Sound of Silence was subject to the law of *anicca* after all. A little like the birth of a mountain or a glacier, it may have developed very slowly. Possibly it didn't start until sometime after we were born, unless like our ability to speak, our ability to hear the Sound of Silence was intrinsic and just needed to be nurtured. Perhaps it started with consciousness, perhaps not until adolescence or even later. But wherever it came from and however it developed, it was most assuredly switched off by Death.

I continued to work with the Sound of Silence in the coming weeks, both as an object of meditation and a subject of reflection. In the late afternoon I gave my mind a rest, joining Ajahn Piyadhammo at the mouth of our cave monastery. As we sat deep in concentration with our eyes closed, we could hear the senior *bhikkhus* and their novices chanting in Pali from the nearby hilltop meditation hall that the Thai soldiers had built at Wat Chom Phet. Even though they used only three notes in a minor key, the deep resonance of their voices filled my body with warm waves of energy. Wave after wave of that vibratory energy coursed over me, letting me fall back again into the arms of the Jesus of my childhood, the Buddha of my present and future, wrapping me in contentment, baptizing me in a newfound faith, and as I submerged into the font, closing my eyes, the Blue Light appeared. At times it was a pin prick or at most a tennis ball; other times it was the Big Bang, the cosmos—gaseous, expansive galaxies swirling on the tip of my nose, swirling to the ends of the universe.

We left the cave monastery in July as planned, in time for the Rains Retreat, rejoining Ajahn Saisamut at Wat Pah Pohn Pao, "Peacefulness Temple." In the mountains of Laos, especially compared to my first Rains at Wat Pah Nirapai, the next three months passed quietly, the daily routine demanding but comforting. My body had for the most part healed from the crash of Spectre 544, although pain from the old wounds could pay a surprise visit any time I sat in meditation. Fortunately, my body was young and steadily grew more flexible.

I had time to write to my parents, and thinking how Mom and Dad, not to mention Grandma Shepler and Grandpa Leary, might be worried about my soul now that I had excommunicated myself from the Church, I tried to write something comforting about the similarities between a Buddhist *wat* and a Catholic monastery, how there was much here that reminded me of our Catholic heritage, from something as vast as going on a pilgrimage to simple rituals like lighting candles, burning incense, and being blessed with holy water. I thought how Pali chanting had been such a soothing part of Buddhist ritual for me from my first visit to a *wat* with Tukada to Harley and Mali's wedding to the evening chanting I listened to across the river on retreat with Ajahn Piyadhammo. The same as at Wat Pah Nirapai and every other monastery I had stayed at, I chanted with my fellow monks at Wat Pah Pohn Pao every morning and evening and on many other occasions. I was happy to explain how similar Pali chanting was to the Gregorian chants we grew up with. Pali was an ancient Indian language, a partner to Sanskrit the way Latin was to Greek. In both cases the tones resonated through our bodies, possessing an intrinsic power and beauty whether or not we understood every word. I left out visions of the Blue Light and giant snowflakes, *nimittas* of dancing Churchills, bouts of madness, and any mention whatsoever of no-self.

It was shortly after Wan Ok Phansa, the full-moon day in October that marked the end of the Rains Retreat, that Ajahn Piyadhammo told me there had been big changes in Bangkok a few weeks earlier. A large student protest at Thammasat University had erupted into violence resulting in more than seventy student deaths and almost a thousand injured. American-made helicopters were reported to have been involved, a detail that especially troubled me. But the next day the ruling junta—Thanom Kittikachawn, Praphat Charusatien, and Thanom's son, Narong, who was married to Praphat's daughter—had gone into exile. "These connections of powerful families not so different from Russia, Germany, and England before the First World War," Piyadhammo smiled. "And not so different from Laos today. The leaders of the Pathet Lao, the Neutralists, and the Royalists are all cousins."

I wondered if Kit Tii Kittikachawn, the crazed guitar player at Thammasatstock, came from the same military family. And I wondered if the days of weekend-long festivals of music and love had come to an end at Thammasat University.

It was also shortly after the Rains Retreat that Ajahn Saisamut, the abbot, suggested that Ajahn Piyadhammo continue as my teacher. We agreed, and over the next two years, with Ajahn Piyadhammo as my guide, my meditation practice developed. Here, too, at Wat Pah Pohn Pao, we sat up all night four times a month on Wan Prah, the Sabbath day on the lunar calendar. Those sittings gave me an abundance of opportunity to practice working with pain—pain that lingered in my knees and back, in the wounds to my head and eyes, and in my dislocated shoulder and broken wrist—with *metta*.

On nights I felt especially brave I started to let *metta* open up and heal my wounded heart, and other nights I went further and imagined that the Roman breastplate that covered my ribs dissolved and that I could breathe joyously, directly through my heart into my lungs. As I worked with it those nights, breathing through my heart continued to frighten me with the powerful emotion it released, with the way it opened me up to pain I had been unconsciously holding onto for years and at the same time to let out feelings of love and compassion that I had kept equally bottled up. One night my heart and mind tumbled back again to years long before the war when the battles I fought were with my father and my father's father...

"*You're dogging it—get to work!*"

"*I'm your son, not your slave!*"

"*Show some respect!*"

"*Why don't you earn some instead of demanding it?*"

"*Quit being a prima donna! You're not a Beatle—get a damned haircut!*"

"*I'm a musician, and all my friends are musicians. Why don't you get that?*"

"*When we were your age, we had real jobs!*"

"*You were never my age. You two were born old!*"

And somehow, even though the tormented flashes grew longer, by allowing those painful memories to see the light of day, I allowed myself to heal, allowed myself to see the possibility of forgiving the wounds my father and grandfather had inflicted on me and of forgiving myself for falling into the trap of defensiveness, lashing viciously back at them. And then, just once, I experienced a powerful yet frightening sensation of opening up completely. For a brief moment, I allowed the love I still held for them to fly as freely as the dove I released at Wat Ph'a Yai.

More often than not, however, that sense of liberation was so intense that I pulled back and simply followed my breath or scanned my body as new sensations came and went. I wanted to write to my father, wanted to reach out, but couldn't find the words, afraid I would only rekindle his anger, however good my intentions might have been.

My mom and grandmother kept the new tradition of Buddha-Christmas alive, and this time with a proper address, the package containing a tin of homemade Christmas cookies arrived from the United States in December. I noticed it was also a crafty way of inducing me to stay in touch, even if it wasn't much more than saying how much the Lao novices and monks here at Wat Pah Pohn Pao enjoyed exotic confections from America. At night, though, and while meditating, thoughts, feelings, memories long buried clawed their way back from my mind's graveyard: *I'm small, frightened, looking up at Mrs. Santa Claus—my grandmother—snapping, going into a rage, eyes like a mad dog, trying to push her daughter—my mother—down a flight of stairs...and another time my sister and I are being rushed across the street and upstairs to a neighbor's attic bedroom, tucked into bed, but peering through the window, we see Mrs. Santa Claus gone mad again, raving in the back seat of Grandpa Shepler's Hudson as he drives away...to where? How can he drive to Pittsburgh from Boston when its midnight?*

It was amazing how much writing a simple thank-you note home conjured up. Not only did it induce memories of childhood trauma, it also triggered a powerful memory of the letter Pawnsiri had written one year earlier, a memory of being overwhelmed by the emotions that exploded off the page and an unease that I could not reply. Now that I could sit in tranquility for hours at Wat Pah Pohn Pao in the meditation hall or in my *kuti* or across the river deep in a cave, now that I had attained some level of hard-earned serenity, it was possible for me to reach a little further out into the world. And so it was that in some mysterious way a few days after writing that simple thank-you note, in a state of tranquility after half an hour of walking meditation, I returned to my *kuti* and found Pawnsiri's letter tucked away on my bookshelf. Carefully picking it up, I reread it and tried as best I could to respond:

December 12, 1973

Dear Pawnsiri,

I am sorry it has been so hard for me to answer your letter, that it has taken so long. You deserve better than that, but I must confess I was overcome by the passion you expressed. In the past, when we talked in person, I always thought of you as shy. No more!

I am afraid that I was damaged badly by the war, something you said you understood and could help me heal from. But now that I have had time to reflect, I see that I was damaged before I came to Thailand, going far back into my childhood. To the world, we looked like the perfect family. But that made it worse because inside was hell. I felt so alone, and there was no one I could tell any of this to.

So as a child I became emotionally detached, already numb inside. And the war has made me more so because I never know when my friends will be taken away from me. Whether they die in combat or are sent back to America, I miss them the same. And in some sad way, it makes me afraid of the love you offer me, afraid that too will be taken away. Instead, I loved a woman at Ubon who was unattainable, who in the United States and France we call a "femme fatale" and who in Thailand you call a "pu-ying jai dam."

If she had lived, especially if we married and went back to the United States, there is a good chance she would have ruined my life—from her heroin addiction that she could not control, however much she tried and I tried to help her, or from being unfaithful to me and going with other men. That would have broken my heart. And I knew all this in my mind. I knew there was a chance she would get me hooked on heroin, too. I knew she could never stay faithful to one man—that men for her were another form of heroin—but I loved her anyway.

What is wrong with my heart and mind that I would love someone like her and be so broken and shut off that I am afraid of the love and commitment you offer me? I am trying to find the answer. Or learn to just accept that about myself—to see that all that was in the past and to see that in the present and in the future we can be there for each other completely. Loving each other deeply, but more than that, taking good care of our hearts and minds so that we love and care for each other for the rest of our lives, no matter how difficult it might be raising children or adapting to each other's culture, whether we end up in the U.S. or stay in Thailand.

I'm afraid that communicating—really communicating—will be difficult, especially raising bicultural children. Our two languages couldn't be more different—the alphabets, the tones, so little shared vocabulary, the different thought process behind the way we put words together. I think we can overcome that—you by continuing to study English and me by committing myself to mastering the Thai language. But a bigger concern is that I will always be too much a child, incapable of giving back as much as you give me.

And still, I think we should try. Can you wait another year for me? I think that's how long it will take me to feel ready to return to Ubon. I want to be strong, Pawnsiri, I want to be really strong in my body, heart, and mind.

> *Caring about you deeply,*
> *Tahn Santisekkho*

Inside the golden temple, the centerpiece of Wat Pah Pohn Pao, the walls were lined with remarkable murals of hellfire and brimstone and other forms of torture that Father Boyle would have embraced. Depicting Buddhist cosmology—hungry ghosts with mouths so small they cannot eat, hellfires, and demons torturing humans still filled with worldly desires and fears— they gave me plenty to contemplate besides my breath. Sitting in front of those walls, meditating with my eyes half-closed, thoughts arose that I observed, examined, and let pass by like clouds blowing in a gentle breeze. *Did I lose my faith in God when I lost my blind faith in my father? What poison was lodged inside me that kept me from admitting to Dad that I loved Jack Kennedy as much as he did, instead pointing out his failure to support the civil rights movement and his failure to call off the Bay of Pigs? Oh yeah, because Dad was a saint to my cousins and everyone he worked with—and I was the one who saw him storming out of the house, leaving Mom in tears. But why did she allow me to get sucked into their battles, comforting her, only to turn on me when Dad unleashed his anger and sarcasm back in my direction?*

Why doesn't my sister remember the lamps that flew and the raging voices? The time he stormed away and was gone for a week, only to return red-eyed on

NoDoz after driving twenty-four straight hours back from Florida? What old flame from his flight-instructor days had he looked up in Arcadia? Why didn't Dad and Mom divorce? How did they end up more in love after putting each other through hell? Why did Mom and Grandma Shepler gush over me while Dad and Grandpa Leary did nothing but ride me? Why couldn't they find a Middle Way? Why did Mom tell me how Dad bragged to his friends about me without opening up real communication at home once I was no longer a child? Why did they never figure how much I craved that?

Why did I barely know my dad's mom? Why did she move to Florida, and why was Mom so tense on the rare occasions when she did visit? How did Dad manage to stay so close to Grandpa Leary yet dutifully call his mom every week without fail after his parents separated?

Are genetics and heredity and environment the new kamma *in the age of science, a hidden ingredient?*

Grandpa Shepler—why couldn't they all be like him? Teaching me how to fish on lakes and on the deep sea, reading comic strips to me out of the newspaper while I sat in his lap, showing me how to use his drafting instruments? How did my mom's father and mother stay married after her binges and violent outbursts and after she had been hospitalized in a psychiatric ward? What was it like sleeping in separate bedrooms? Why did I still ache for him?

They were actions from the past that couldn't be changed, questions that couldn't be answered. And so I let them go, came back to the present moment, breathing in, breathing out. Just breathing.

Piyadhammo and I remained steadfast in maintaining our vow of Noble Silence, so that when we did talk, it was rare that it was not focused on Dhamma, the Buddha's teachings. Inasmuch as a great deal of the Buddha's teachings dealt with accepting the impermanence of all things, with letting go of attachments to pleasure and aversion to pain, and with preparing to face death with equanimity, talk came up from time to time of what in Laos was called the American War. I learned that Ajahn Piyadhammo had once been an officer in the Neutralist army made up largely of paratroopers commanded by the brilliant Captain Kong Le and had been with Le in 1960 when the captain backed Souvanah Pouma in a successful coup. Piyadhammo had admired Souvanah Pouma's attempt at pursuing a

Buddhist Middle Path in Laotian politics. Alas, he grew disillusioned when he saw American aid diverted to Royalist generals who talked tough about defeating the Communist Pathet Lao but who never fought. He believed reports that much of the money was being funneled to bank accounts in Switzerland and villas in France.

In the course of several of these quiet discussions, as I began to grasp the complexity of the wars that were raging around us, I was humbled with the realization that I would never really understand how world politics and a small civil war could erupt into the total devastation of so much of this little, insignificant, incredibly beautiful country. "Does a country have its own *kamma*?" we wondered.

Why was Laos suffering now, and what would the *kamma* be for the United States of America in the years to come? Would the American War in Laos ever really end? Was the cease-fire holding, or were both armies secretly maneuvering to gain some unknown advantage? Returning one day from a week in the cave, as our riverboat neared Luang Prabang, I finally got it…sort of. There were at least *three* wars going on: the Vietnamese civil war, the one I got to see up close, that had spilled into Laos along the Trail and on the Bolaven Plateau; the Laotian civil war in the Plain of Jars and the caves that ran north from Ban Ban to Sam Neua, the one we heard about from the Air America crews passing through Ubon when it wasn't safe to land in Pakse or when they needed to use our BX; and the final mess in the Golden Triangle, a drug war that mixed remnants of Chinese Nationalists trying to turn the clock back to 1949 with Laotian and Burmese warlords of every possible political stripe. That seemed to have been where the lean, eagle-eyed CIA agent was working who brought Zelinsky footage of his private thousand-man army to cut together in exchange for a flintlock musket. Then again, there were private armies all over Laos.

Deep in meditation one afternoon, I heard the voices of Harley Baker and Brendan Leary percolate up from deep in a cave of their own. "*Maybe the problem is that everybody's right," says Brendan. "The Viet Cong and the Viet Minh and the NVA and the Pathet Lao and the Pathet Thai and the Khmer Rouge are all absolutely correct in wanting to clean up their corrupt governments, do away with feudalism and get all the farang out of Southeast Asia. And the U.S. is absolutely correct in not wanting some new mutation of Hitler or Stalin to take over half the world while we do nothing.*"

"Maybe the real problem is that everybody thinks *they're right,"* Harley answers.

It was only a few weeks later that I mentioned to Ajahn Saisamut and Ajahn Piyadhammo that I was still troubled seeing night operations over the Ho Chi Minh Trail whenever I did walking meditation. They conferred briefly and suggested a little mantra to repeat while I walked: "*Buddho*, present moment; *Buddho*, only moment."

The next morning, when my walking meditation was once again interrupted by visions of the war, I evoked my new mantra, and the Ho Chi Minh Trail transformed before my eyes into a simple dirt pathway that I was walking over slowly, mindfully. The Trail came back again from time to time, a little less often as time went on, but the mantra never failed to bring me back to the present moment, just walking.

In March, at the beginning of hot season, Ajahn Piyadhammo and I went back to the cave at Wat Tham Xien Maen for another month-long retreat. Somehow his presence helped me go into a deep meditation for many hours, day after day, only coming down each morning to accept a single meal brought by three old women from the village nearby. During an all-night sitting on the twenty-ninth day, I heard the beating of a bass drum… faintly…in the distance at first…but eventually rattling the cave as jarringly as a Surin elephant or a North Vietnamese tank rumbling through. I reflected upon what *kamma* I had accumulated in my brief career as a rock drummer touring the bars and hotel rooms of New England college towns. The pounding continued all night and into the morning of the thirtieth day, until I, Prah Santisekkho, the Mad Monk, stumbled outside for my morning meal and realized the beating was not a bass drum after all. It was my heart.

When Ajahn Piyadhammo and I returned to Wat Pah Pohn Pao that morning, I was feeling especially enthusiastic, having had a taste of going deeper than deep in my meditation that last night in the cave and wanting to go deeper yet. And the next morning, as I sat on the porch of my *kuti* with my eyes closed and my legs crossed in a full lotus, I was tortured for the next hour by a fly traipsing over the tip of my nose. Not allowed to swat at it, let alone kill it, undertaking the monk's discipline meant continuing to keep my eyes closed and my body still, just observing. During that hour that seemed like a week, I became excruciatingly agitated, not knowing if the fly was still there or if it was my imagination creating a sensation that was realer than real. I came to the wry realization that it didn't matter because both the reality and the *nimitta* affected me just as strongly, left me just as uncomfortable. Both were the tiniest, mildest forms of *dukkha*, and yet those sensations of discomfort could grow within that single hour of sitting to feel utterly unbearable—and in an instant turn into no feeling at all. Out of this came another small insight. The Little Bang theory, I called it: if we are capable of bringing on even a small part of our own suffering with imaginary slights or ills, then aren't we also capable of letting go of that small part of life's pain?

When I told Ajahn Saisamut about my experiences of the past few days, his face lit up. "Very good!" he said. "Keep practicing! When you can see how everyone has a fly on their nose, you will develop great compassion—and a warm smile!"

I was healing in Luang Prabang. My first impression hadn't changed. I had found what still felt in my heart like my truest of true homes. On retreat in the cave across the river, it felt as if I had crawled back inside my mother's womb and was beginning to put myself back together piece by piece. What I couldn't answer was how long this gestation would take, only that unlike a baby it was going to take longer than nine months.

My father's silence spooked me. On the other hand, I was relieved that he wasn't begging or insisting that I come home. His presence continued to pop up in brief flashes, like the night on my third cave retreat when I heard a stentorian voice echo from deep within, "*God cannot be dead. Your Father is still alive!*" And for a brief moment I felt my kid brother, the hippy, sitting next to me, poking me in the rib and saying, "*Forget it, man. In a family of pilots and businessmen, we're junkyard dogs.*"

It was no longer often, but I continued to be haunted by ugly memories: *only a two-year-old, I watch giant adults, parents I love who feed and clothe me, throwing lamps. I feel small and afraid, and when I try to beg them to stop, when I want to bellow at the top of my lungs, my lips move, but I am mute...* Other times it was flashes of Dad leaving Mom in tears: "*You idiot, you imbecile—how can you be so immature!*" Just echoes, turds floating in a

Thai jail... No context. A mystery how the battles began, how they ended, what made them feel fleetingly cathartic... Still a void. Like Creation itself, unanswerable, unknowable. Instead, I forced myself to do what I knew I needed to do—to let it all go, to live in the present moment.

And so I continued on with Ajahn Piyadhammo as my mentor, building a serene sense of well-being, one breath at a time. Until everything changed.

In the Year of the Rabbit

The night before the Communists came to Luang Prabang, I dreamed about the dusty road near Wat Pah Nirapai, six hundred kilometers south-southeast in a part of Thailand where Laotian and Kampuchean were as likely to be spoken as Bangkok Thai. It was the middle of monsoon season, and I think it was the silence of the rains stopping that night that woke me up. All I heard was the sound of lingering drops of water sliding off the pitched rooftops, splattering in the puddles below, and what might have been bootsteps and the gruff barking of commands in the distance. I lay in my *kuti* on a grass mat that scarcely cushioned me from the teakwood floor, the thick night air closing in on me, and finally, I fell back inside myself and into the night's embrace.

"*I'm wet,*" I heard in the darkness—Miss Pawnsiri's voice, the musical ripples of a mountain brook.

And as I fall ever deeper, sunlight begins to break across the ruler-straight horizon, slashing at my pale farang eyes. The cobalt dawn turns crimson, streaking across once-fecund clay, sucking the last drops of moisture out of the cracked earth. Dry as the tit of an old hag, the land no longer nourishes the seedlings of rice that have been planted with tenderness and backbreaking labor. For the second rainy season in a row, there has been no rain. In my dream that is too real to be a dream, I know that another drought has come to the Issan and that the poorest people in Thailand are about to grow poorer and hungrier yet.

I walk at the front of a line of monks, our heads freshly shaven, our ochre robes folded perfectly and wrapped around our bodies impeccably, the way that Ajahn Po has trained us in the austere forest discipline. Blinded by an acidic brew of grit and sun and perspiration, I lead the junior monks and novices toward the village of Ban Lok. Our alms bowls will not be overflowing this morning. A bit of frog and some stir-fried cricket will be all that some can offer. Rice will be doled out by the spoonful.

Counting steps as I walk, hypnotized by the rhythm of our calloused feet beating down on the silt-covered road, I move calmly, my mind switched off, empty of all memories of the past, dreams of the future. The copper sun has just cleared the rooftops of the village when I spot a whirling cloud in the distance that hugs close to the ground as it blows in our direction, finally transforming into a phalanx of cyclists racing towards us. As the bicycles draw near, I stop my procession and watch. And my dream becomes a dream within a dream, a slow-motion movie with a soundtrack so beautiful I begin to cry, the sound of angels singing full, rich chords that swell my heart, a sound so beautiful I can't remember ever hearing anything lovelier. The whistling of a primitive wooden flute intrudes for a moment before it resolves into otherworldly music filled with the echoes of Issan temples, Tibetan monasteries, and Gothic cathedrals.

The race spreads out for miles, so vast that I have to step out of myself and soar above my dream to take it in. Mixed in with hundreds of other cyclists are Sachs, the gunner, and Spitzer, Spinelli, and Nevers, the cameramen. Sachs and Spitzer wear bicycle shorts and singlets that are torn and caked with blood. Spinelli and Nevers don't seem to mind their sweaty flight suits. The Thai fighter pilots pass in a precision formation, matching each other stride for stride, poetry in motion at 128 frames per second. Lieutenant Barry Romo glides past, still wearing his bloodstained jungle fatigues, at the head of the platoon he led into the Ashau Valley and which to a man was either killed or wounded. My heart swells in happiness at the sight of Moonbeam Liscomb and Pook, followed by Colonel Strbik, Captain Rush, and Captain Rooker. It takes me a moment to realize that the Thai beauty queen riding with them is Rooker's cross-dressing boyfriend.

Led by Major Mertons and Captain Gunther, the crew of Spectre 544 rides by together, their disfigured bodies restored. Toward the end of the peloton, the Pathet Lao soldier from Paksong approaches on the old English three-speed I once stole, riding next to Lieutenant Duong and the young guard with the broken nose. Prasert follows just a few feet back. Taking up the rear are Tom Wheeler, with Lek sitting behind him, laughing, holding on to his shoulders, and Dave Murray. They ride leisurely, their eyes half-closed, passing a doobie between them, even though Dave, astride his vintage penny-farthing, towers over Tom. And from inside and outside my dream I am surrounded with the voices of a thousand angels woven through with the sound of the wooden flute, and I see myself ride by, my legs strong and sinewy like a Laotian sahmlaw driver's, and seated behind me—her face as sad and perfect and faintly smiling as a Da Vinci masterpiece—is Tukada, lovely even with her silken hair caked in blood and clay.

I watch myself and the other cyclists disappear in a cloud of fine Issan dust before I turn and walk again across the thirsty landscape at the head of the line of monks toward Ban Lok. Listening again to the rhythm of our footsteps, I scarcely notice that a sahmlaw *passes us, its passenger hidden in the shadows of the canopied cab. The driver, silhouetted by the hard morning light, strains his muscular legs against the pedals as he climbs the gentle grade. I hear a faint voice calling, like a memory, a butterfly from my childhood. "Khun Bren-dan."*

I haven't heard my Christian name in three years. Rubbing my eyes, I squint at the rickshaw that is turning back towards us, dust-softened light streaming into the carriage. It's Miss Pawnsiri, the respectable Thai schoolgirl who, Harley used to tease, was in love with me. The one who I insisted was a platonic friend and student and nothing more. The one who wrote me a love letter so passionate and sincere that it took me a year to reply.

"I have come looking for you," she says. "Khun Jim go back United States. No more Peace Corps. We need English teacher at my school." She hands me the white pants and shirt I once wore from Ruam Chon Sawng to the monastery on my ordination day. Neatly folded, emitting the pleasant scent of laundry soap, they are wrapped in a clear membranous plastic sack. "Come, I will take you to where you hide your bicycle."

I smile, a bit puzzled. "I think the dead Laotian soldier stole it back..." And as the monks walk off without me along the shoulder of the red clay road, I climb into the sahmlaw, certain that the time is now propitious to leave the monastery. Pawnsiri looks lovely, her eyes radiant, her hair suffused with the perfume of fresh-cut jasmine. I wonder why she is wearing a long, loose-fitting cotton dress instead of the smartly tailored uniform of a Thai schoolteacher until I notice she is great with child. "Who is the father of your baby?"

"You are, Khun Bren-dan."

"How is that possible?"

"It is a mira-cle."

I awoke ten seconds before the temple bells rang at 4:00 a.m. There was a sound of footsteps in the forest leaves. Ajahn Piyadhammo climbed the wooden steps to my *kuti* and whispered my name. "Tahn Santisekkho, the Communi't come today to Luang Prabang. It is not good for a Canadian to stay here. Even a German can be mistaken for an American these day. And the Communi't will maybe shoot American. Even Thailand people maybe not safe."

The war had been over since April in Vietnam and Cambodia. This was just mopping up. The fragile cease-fire had finally broken in Laos, and the last piece of French Indochina had fallen under Communist control. I quickly grabbed my carrying bag and filled it with my alms bowl, toiletries, my grandfather's penknife, a sitting cloth, a change of robes, and finally, my passports and Pawnsiri's letter. One of the villagers had an oxcart waiting for us behind the main meditation hall. As we climbed aboard, Ajahn Saisamut came out to see us off. "Remember, Tahn Santisekkho, that if you return to Canada, you will only find true happiness when you no longer attach to happiness."

I bowed respectfully. "Thank you, Ajahn, for helping me find peace."

We joined a stream of refugees flowing south toward Vientiane, the capital, where the Mekong River ran west to east and formed a porous border with Thailand. The procession inched along in silence, the night sky lightening at dawn and turning a dismal gray. For hours, the only sounds we heard were footsteps and the pounding hooves of water buffalo mixed with the groaning of wooden wagon wheels and the soft clanging of the cowbells that hung on the oxen that pulled us along. It wasn't until late in the day that I finally spoke. "When we cross the river into Thailand, Ajahn Piyadhammo, I think the time will come for me to give up my robes and go back into the world."

His smooth, imperturbable face looked concerned. "Are you sure?"

"I had a dream last night. A young Issan schoolteacher came to me and asked me to be a teacher at her school."

"A monk can be teacher. Should you trust a dream for such an important decision?"

"I think she wants to marry me. She used to be my student, and we used to walk together to the bus stop after class. She once invited me to her home to meet her family and another time to meet her professor, and I thought she was simply being kind. I think she was eighteen, but she seemed younger, and I always thought of her as a student. It was one case where I felt virtuous, having a young, attractive female friend who remained just a friend because there were too many other times when I behaved badly. My friend Harley climbed off the bus coming from the base one day and saw us waiting together for her bus at the little *sala*, talking softly, and the next time he saw me, he told me authoritatively as the husband of a Thai wife that Pawnsiri was in love with me.

"I was flattered, but I didn't know how to talk to her about it. So we mostly talked about her plans to teach biology in the district school but how her older sister was a nurse in Bangkok and how she herself still dreamed of being a nurse in America someday. I didn't understand it was so she could be with me, but I promised I would ask my mother, who was a nurse before she became an airline stewardess, if she had any friends from nursing school who could help.

"And she listened to all this, smiling pleasantly, obediently, not hearing what she wanted to hear. Now she is a woman, though, and fate has kept me in Asia far longer than I ever imagined. She is of good character from a good family. I think she will be a good wife who will raise good Buddhist children."

"Did you hear about the Pathet Lao in Vientiane?" Piyadhammo asked. "Last week, the day after the full moon, fifty girl Pathet Lao soldiers marched into town, and that's it. There was no one to resist them. The Neutralist and Royal Lao soldiers all ran away, disgraced. But perhaps, at last, there will be no more bloodshed."

In the mountains to the north and east, Hmong hill tribes who had sided with the CIA had been decimated, but the kind of panic that swept South Vietnam had not spread to the lowlands of Laos. Along the Mekong basin, it had been a smaller, more dignified war, Piyadhammo had taught me, where the Neutralist faction—those seeking the elusive Golden Mean of the Greeks and the Middle Way of the Buddha—shared in power and had once had a chance of winning. The Communist, Neutralist, and Royalist factions were led by princes who happened to be cousins who got along pretty well together when they didn't discuss politics. The Communists' propaganda had been highly effective, however, attacking things like government corruption, drug trafficking, and prostitution, which the Americans seemed to condone through ignorance, neglect, or active participation. The fighting in the mountains had been fierce, and yet the stakes were never as high as in Vietnam, partly because there had never been enough U.S. money and matériel in-country to mutate into the vast web of graft, corruption, black marketeering, and general depravity that spread out of Saigon and entangled the whole country.

Laos had been impoverished when the first French colonial troops ran aground along the banks of the Mekong in the nineteenth century, and it had stayed that way. The massacres of civilians on the roads out of An Loc and Quang Tri and Danang were impossible to duplicate in Laos because there weren't enough soldiers and rice farmers to clog the highways the way Highway 1 had been turned into a trail of blood and tears. There was no airport as large as Danang, where thousands of refugees could keep a DC-10 on the ground and hundreds of deserting government troops would walk over the backs of their own mothers to escape. It was fortunate that the secret wars in Laos ended in a whimper, with the Pathet Lao in control, because there would never have been enough Neutralist and Royalist soldiers in a country of three million—even if they had decided to stand and fight—to resist the victorious army of Vietnam, a country with ten times its population, if it had decided to push on to the Mekong and the Thai border after traveling freely in the Laotian half of the Annamite Mountains for the past twenty years. And so a bloodbath was avoided.

Just the same, our caravan of pedestrians, bicycles, water buffalo, and oxcarts pushed inexorably south along the muddy, half-paved roads, stopping only for mothers to nurse their babies and for old people to rest. Two times a day, when the skies cleared, a group of women boiled rice, and with luck, there might be a bit of Mekong River fish to throw in or some greens they found growing wild along the road. Occasionally an armed personnel carrier would scramble north to make a last, brave, hopeless stand against a Pathet Lao army that was allied to a Vietnamese army that was now the fourth biggest in the world, thanks to the spoils of their unexpectedly quick and decisive victory over the Saigon regime. In a way, we were lucky in Laos because there were many places along a five-hundred-mile stretch of the Mekong River to escape into Thailand. For the South Vietnamese and the Khmers, retreating into their capitals had been a trap when their armies collapsed, leaving pro-American factions surrounded by tough, determined enemies.

It was the middle of rainy season, and the river was flowing with muddy water that had come all the way from the Tibetan highlands. Avoiding Vientiane, we crossed into Thailand a few miles to the west at a wide, desolate stretch where the water was barely ankle-deep in hot season but now required us to climb aboard a bamboo raft that floated high atop what looked a lot like C-130 aircraft tires. For over a week, I hadn't left the oxcart except to tend to life's most basic necessities, hiding under a canvas tarp when it rained or drizzled. So acclimated had I become to my life in Asia that it was always startling for me to see a picture of myself towering over my fellow monks and the old village women who were daily fixtures at the monastery. Now, for nine days, I had squatted or sat or stretched out uncomfortably on the damp, straw-lined floor of the lurching wooden cart, not daring to stand up until I could plant my feet on Thai soil. Climbing down from the raft, I didn't care that we had run aground a few feet from shore and that mud sucked at my ankles. It felt good to stretch my aching legs, free at last from the victorious Pathet Lao.

Occasionally passing groups of Thai soldiers standing watch along the river, Ajahn Piyadhammo and I joined the silent procession of refugees, walking east along the winding road that led to Nong Khai, the Thai trading town that sat across the Mekong from the Laotian capital. Once there, Piyadhammo brought me to the abbot of a Buddhist monastery-college that occupied several blocks in the center of town. The abbot arranged through one of his lay supporters for me to take the express bus that went through Udorn and Roi Et to Ubon Ratchathani. From there, it would be easy to take a baht-bus to Warin Chamrap and a *sawngtao* the last few kilometers to Wat Pah Nirapai and Ajahn Po, my preceptor and first teacher. The old wooden ferryboats and water taxis coming from Vientiane were dangerously overloaded. From the checkpoint at the boat landing to the bus station and on to the train station at the edge of town, the usually quiet streets were teeming. Refugees without the proper papers were being rounded up by patrols of Thai soldiers and national policemen and loaded into trucks that would take them to camps where their fate would be turned over to men with large desks and inkpads and racks of rubber stamps.

Ajahn Piyadhammo walked with me to the bus station, where we found the Ubon bus was already filling up. It was surprisingly roomy and was equipped with air-conditioning, a luxury I hadn't enjoyed since I left the Air Force. I wanted to give my teacher a big American bear hug goodbye and knew I couldn't. Instead, I placed my hands together in the traditional Asian gesture of respect, bowed deeply, and gave him the most heartfelt *wai*

I was capable of before I climbed on board and settled into one of the few remaining seats.

I was beginning to relax when I caught sight of another larger-than-life *farang* heading my way. He was dressed in civvies, but his shaved head and the way he walked were ultramilitary, scary. Even after three years of purging my memories and purifying my mind and body, it was impossible to forget Tony Pope, "the Confessor," the CIA agent who operated deep in the mountain jungles of Laotian no-man's land. Now with sweat glistening on his massive forehead, he was closing in fast, his Yao-princess wife walking quickly behind him with their two young daughters in tow. His wife carried herself like a princess, even if she was from a primitive hill tribe, proudly wearing a black turban on her head and a long black tunic with a hand-embroidered apron in front. The girls dressed and carried themselves like their mother.

I suspected we would be sharing the air-conditioned express bus as far as Udorn, the old CIA headquarters for Thailand and Laos. A flash of fear welled up in me at the rush of memories—Harley and I brought in by his men and clothed and fed, only to discover we were toasting each other with a sacrament of human blood. Discovering the wooden bucket filled by his mercenary assassins with the ears of their victims. The pickle jars of shrunken enemy heads that lined the office wall of the plywood castle he shared with his Yao family.

He had been proud then, so totally consumed in his mission that he had never given a thought to the methods he used in his war against Communism. Tonight, climbing the steps at the front of the bus, he looked angry, betrayed, as if he wanted to find whoever was responsible for this final debacle in the collapse of Southeast Asia and personally put a bullet between the guilty party's eyes. He looked around, saw that the seats across from me were empty, and made his way back, putting his little girls in first and helping his wife slip in next to them. As I expected, his wife had stayed calm, almost serene, while enduring this latest ordeal, but I couldn't help noticing that even though the girls looked tired and a little scared, they, too, looked like princesses—so angelic it was hard to believe they were Pope's progeny. Without asking, he squeezed his burly body in next to me. After looking my monk's robes over carefully out of the corner of his eye, he asked, "You an American?"

"Canadian," I lied, sticking with the cover story I'd been using since I arrived in Laos.

"The only Buddhist monk I saw for ten years up the mountains came with the Chinese exiles serving in my militia. The Yao and Hmong hill tribes who did most of the fighting were strictly into spirit worship, but you look familiar."

"Actually, we met once. I was in the U.S. Air Force and my gunship was shot down. You called in a dust-off for me and my partner."

"I'll be damned. A Canadian coming to America instead of the other way around."

"I was young and bored to tears living in Kamloops. You must be glad to be getting out of Laos. Things have gotten a little rough."

"I'd still be up there if the Company hadn't pulled me out. My guys were self-sufficient. They hunted, raised their own crops. Just had to sell off a little opium to the Burmese and Chinese caravans, and they had enough ammunition to hold out until the U.S. elected a new congress and a president with enough guts to come back in here and straighten out this mess."

"Where are you headed?"

"Back to Udorn. That's where I settled after that damned *New York Times* reporter got wind of my operation and stirred up all the bleeding hearts in congress. I'd been training hill-tribe guerrillas for years, holding off a Pathet Lao army that smuggles in all the arms it wants directly from North Vietnam, but these son-of-a-bitch liberal congressmen seem to think you should fight a counterrevolution in the mountains of Laos following the fuckin' Queensberry Rules. Before I knew it, the Company asked me to take an early retirement and left a small Hmong army out to dry."

"What are you doing with your wife and daughters?"

"Getting them the hell out of Laos. I had to leave them behind when the CIA extracted me. Except her father's village got overrun, her father was executed, and they were stuck in a refugee camp outside Vientiane when I found them yesterday."

"Are you going back to the States?"

"Only if somebody pays me to put a bullet through Jane Fonda's head."

I caught a whiff of Jack Daniels on his breath. "What have you been doing in Udorn?"

"I'm a 'security consultant.' There are plenty of rich expatriate Laotians down there who want to go back up and clean things up, with or without American assistance. Say, you sure you were in the Air Force? You sure you weren't ever a friggin' *New York Times* reporter?"

I was overtaken with the irrational thought that Pope was going to blame me for his lost war. I slipped back into a kind of semi-madness, a fight-or-flight instinct taking over with flight as the only option, the same abject fear returning that shut off my rational mental processes over so much of my last year in the Air Force. Then, over and over, I had been trapped in a tin can that flew at night ten thousand feet above the Ho Chi Minh Trail. The bus's engine revved up, and I heard the whoosh of the front door closing. I slithered past Pope and hurried up to the driver, telling him in Thai that I was sick, that I had to get off, that he shouldn't wait for me.

I watched Pope glaring out the window at me as the bus pulled out into the street and sped away. Ajahn Piyadhammo was surprised to see me but seemed to accept my explanation that the bus was too luxurious, that I would rather take one of the dented "Orange Crush" local buses that ran along the Mekong to Nakhon Phanom. "Just in case I never come back to Laos, I want to look across the Mekong one more time."

I bid a final goodbye to Ajahn Piyadhammo, my teacher and protector for the last two and a half years, and to Laos, the country I loved and pitied so deeply. The local bus was not air-conditioned, and the seats did not recline; in fact, I could barely fit my legs into the back seat, the roomiest spot available. The windows were open, though, and the breeze felt fine as we drove for hours on a winding two-lane road that was better than any I had seen in war-ravaged Laos. I could sit there amazed at the ticket takers who gracefully hung out the doors, almost daring a bus or truck coming the other direction to catch them off guard and prove the theory of reincarnation. For hours I could reflect on the distant mountains—how rugged and beautiful they were from fifty miles away and how sturdy the hill tribes who lived there and the Pathet Lao and Hmong armies who fought there had to be. We stopped for the night at Ban Mai, a trading village that looked like the set for *Gunsmoke*, right down to the wooden sidewalks. I stayed in a small, run-down monastery and left on the first bus the next morning before the monks came back with their alms bowls from *pindabaht*.

The sun was high overhead when we reached the bus station on the outskirts of Nakhon Phanom. I was growing faint with hunger but accepted that chances were slim I would be able to find a meal before midday. When I learned that NKP's old Royal Thai Air Force base was six miles to the west, out in the country, I decided to walk instead to the center of town, where I stopped and stared at a large, poorly built, modern hotel, imagining how only recently it had been full of Americans—officers and civilian contractors—all on government business. I barely noticed when a kind middle-aged man started talking to me. I must have looked tired because he asked if I had come from Laos. He asked me if I ever came to Thailand before, and when I told him I used to be an American airman, his face lit up. "I used to be cook at Air Force base. Now I have restaurant my own. Come."

He brought me to the New Suan Mai, an exquisite *rahn-ahahn* in the northeast corner of town, down along the river, and was surprised but pleased when I told him I had heard of his restaurant. Colonel Strbik and Captain Rooker and Captain Rush had come here often during their exile in NKP, and I could see now why they mentioned it, why they used to sit here for hours on end. It had clean teak floors and Chinese pillars covered with golden dragons against a field of vermilion. The northeast side of the room was open, and across the river, like a tapestry, loomed the mountains of Laos—haunting, jagged jewels you wanted to hold in your hands, places where planes would go down with no survivors, sometimes without a trace at all.

Left alone at a table with an unobstructed view across the wide veranda, I gazed at the *Mae Nam Kong*, mother river of Southeast Asia, and before my weary eyes her clay-stained waters turned to blood. I heard Strbik and Rooker laughing behind me, but when I looked up, it was the owner and two members of his staff bringing me a plateful of steaming white rice and bowls of chicken and vegetable curries. I was embarrassed by the respect and awe with which the owner treated me. It seemed as if everyone on his staff wanted to have a chance to serve the American soldier who had become a *bhikkhu*. I wasn't sure I deserved their respect in view of the fact that my search for truth and serenity had brought me as much pain and confusion as insight. This morning, however, a bigger truth was clear to me. It was bringing the generous ex-cook happiness to earn merit at a time when for all we knew the North Vietnamese army might decide to walk across the Mekong in the coming hot season as easily as the grizzled rice farmer had carried me in his oxcart down the highway from Luang Prabang. My embarrassment was multiplied by the fact that even though my empty stomach ached, I scarcely seemed able to eat. Again the ex-cook understood without the need for words. He had seen a lot of people passing through NKP recently whose stomachs were shrunken with hunger.

I was able to sip some warm Chinese tea, which strengthened me and helped to restore my appetite. As I ate, I had a brief, silly hope that they might bring me ice cream, but I wasn't permitted to ask and it wasn't offered. When they were finished feeding me, the proud owner and his staff sat around and asked me where I was from in the States and told me about Thais they knew who had moved to Boston and L.A. and would be opening restaurants and whom I should look up. They asked me how long I had been in Thailand and how long I intended to stay a monk. I told them I didn't know. Did I have a *faen*? "A monk can't have a girlfriend," I tried to answer solemnly, but I blushed and continued with a smile, "There is a very nice young woman in Ubon, a schoolteacher, who maybe hopes I will not always be a monk."

They all smiled knowingly, especially the woman with the deep red, betel-nut-stained teeth who cooked. They asked me if I was staying long in Nakhon Phanom and seemed to understand when I said I wasn't. "Where was I going?" they asked. And when I told them I was returning to Ajahn Po at Wat Pah Nirapai, a hushed and reverent murmur fell over the room. A businessman came in with his entourage, and our little party had to come to an end. The owner went over to greet his new customers and called over a waiter to seat them. The tiny wisp of a cook went back to the kitchen, the other waiters went back to their stations, and my host took me outside to call a *sahmlaw*. He gave the driver an envelope and instructed him to take me to the air-con bus terminal.

The bus ride to Ubon was a luxury I had long forgotten but this time permitted myself with no Tony Pope in sight to spoil my journey. After three years of walking or riding battered pickup trucks and buses, this was like floating on a cushion of air. The engine ran as smoothly and quietly as a jetliner's, and the air-conditioning blew away a thin film of perspiration that had covered me since I left the ComDoc trailer for the last time three years earlier. I put my seat back and relaxed, recalling that the last time I had slept well was before the journey began, the night I had my dream of Pawnsiri. I slept now. And the bubbling mountain brook sang to me again. *"I'm wet,"* called the gentle voice.

It was the Second Coming and the Immaculate Conception. Miss Pawnsiri,
the proper schoolteacher, her smile as demure as jasmine, performing onstage in
a dusky nightclub in her secret Saturday evening life, swathed in a silk evening
gown while cooing dovesongs with marimbas, horns, and congas serenading
her softly in the background. Miss Pawnsiri—proper schoolteacher, student,
virgin—now naked under the volcanic waterfall, perfect sculpture, the female
David come to life, cool marble now dripping, the wet season in Thailand,
ripe mango, the Heart Sutta sung in monotone by a thousand monks on a
Tibetan mountaintop, the Queen of Butterflies spreading her wings, blinding
me with her light, enwrapping me in her warm cocoon. Everlasting mercy,
eternal darkness. The songs of angels. Apocalypse. Tranquility. Fire and rain.
The Dance of Life and Death. My last night in the Sangha. Time to return to
the world outside, unprotected. Time to become the protector.

My meditation teachers had taught me in many ways to "just observe"
the images that came up while meditating, to avoid trying to attach meaning
to these *nimittas*. But my dream consciousness told me this was not just a
fleeting image, this was a true vision I could trust: my future wife was calling.

"Chaat Nah"—Another Lifetime

When I awoke from my dreams of Pawnsiri and our smiling babies, the bus was slowing on the outskirts of Ubon. I felt a twinge of disappointment—the Big Buddha had passed by in my sleep. To my right, however, looming above the palms, were the inspiring white obelisks of Wat Nong Bua, stupas modeled after the venerated temple-shrine at Bodhgaya, India. Two old women sitting behind me asked the familiar *"Bai nai?"* When I told them I was going to Wat Pah Nirapai, their eyes lit up, pleased that another *farang* was bringing merit to their corner of Ubon Province. A hundred yards past the Ubon Hotel, the bus pulled to a stop. I could see from glancing down the alley that led to Prommaraj Road that the place had been patched up, but the bustling hotel where Woody Shahbazian once snatched victory from me on Talent Night was now run-down and sleepy and did not have an American in sight.

"*Na!*" said the two village women, following close behind me and pointing to the familiar mud-streaked white baht-bus that would cross the Mun River to the market in Warin. They waddled up to an unsuspecting high school student waiting at the bus stop. Before I realized what they were doing, they had drafted him to ride with me to Warin to make sure I found the correct *sawngtao* to drop me off at the dirt lane that led to Ajahn Po's forest monastery. They were about to buy my bus ticket for me, but I explained that I had to visit some friends in town first. The student was given new orders and walked with me as far as the intersection of Rajaboodt and Prommaraj roads, asking the familiar, respectful questions about where I was from, how old I was, how long I had been a monk, and where I had studied Thai. When we reached the corner, he asked, "Do you know the way from here to house your friend?"

Even though I wasn't sure, I told him "yes" and freed him to return to the bus stop. I said goodbye and turned in the direction of where Woodstock Music once stood, dreading as I had the morning of the fire that Vrisnei, Sommit, Chai, or someone else from their family had perished. Or that their businesses had gone bankrupt and the family moved away. I had been overwhelmed the last time I was here by the vast destruction wrought by the conflagration of the downtown commercial district. Now I was overwhelmed by an even more dramatic change that had taken place in my absence. Every shop and second-floor apartment as far as I could see for several blocks in both directions had been rebuilt or was in the last stages of reconstruction.

So much was new that as I walked, I couldn't help feeling like a ghost in an old black-and-white movie who could hear and see but couldn't be seen or heard himself. The smells and sounds of the market down by the river had not changed, but every shop and stall had. Only old people seemed to have survived. The packs of off-duty GIs were missing, as were their counterparts, the adorable schoolgirl sales clerks whom Khun Jim had trained to speak passable business English. The English language subscript on the street signs had been painted over, giving me a chilling sense of how much U.S. airmen were no longer wanted. In case the NVA ever came marching through, the locals were disappearing all traces of things American in what was once very much an American Air Force town.

A shrunken old woman walked by carrying two baskets of charcoal on a bamboo pole balanced across her shoulder. She looked like she had lived here in the Issan since the days when Ankhor kings ruled from the Indian Ocean to the South China Sea. "*Khaw toht, khrab,*" I asked her, "*Rahn Dontrii Woodstock yuu tiinii iik mai?*"

She gave me a blank look of mild surprise, wondering what strange language I was attempting to speak. I asked her a second time, slowly, and the veil that had clouded her eyes lifted. "*Yuu tiinawn,*" she answered, pointing several blocks down the street where virtually every building was in some stage of reconstruction, now three, four, even five stories high where once every shop uniformly supported only a second-floor apartment.

Chai was busy conferring with his foreman when I stepped inside. The new store was still in a state of disarray, but I instantly felt at home in a first-floor showroom filled with drums and other instruments from around the world. No matter that they were covered with plastic and that sawing and hammering was going on all around us. I could remember the single counter they used to occupy in their parents' old store.

When Chai glanced over at the door, his face lit up. "Prah Bren-dan!" he called.

"Khun Chai!" I replied. "*Sabai dii ruu?*"

"I'm well," he answered, and we both smiled and *waied*. "How are *you*? Two year ago, everybody decide you die in Laos—or else go back S-tate."

"I went *tudong* in Laos, then stayed in Luang Prabang. Before I left, I came by your old store, but there was nothing! I couldn't find your family. I thought everything was destroyed."

"Sommit and I put many thing in our truck during fire. We take to cousin's, come back, get more. We save many thing."

"How are your mother and father? I worried about them."

"They are well. They build store one block away."

"And Vrisnei?"

"She mar-ry and live in Korat with her hus-band. They run a photography studio. Sometime I work for them." He pulled a magazine from under the counter and blew off the sawdust before opening it up for me. "My pictures of Loy Kratong are in *Thai Airways Magazine*."

I looked through the pictures, amazed at my friends' success amid the reversals that the war had brought to so many others in their corner of the world. "These are good, Chai, *really* good." I handed back the magazine and looked around. "Everything is so different around here!"

"Even without the fire, there is always change. First, there was the war and prosperity for the merchants, and then peace and not so much prosperity and now maybe war again. Thailand is surrounded by unfriendly government. Have Communi't government in Prathet Lao and Kampuchea and Wietnam. Pamah have socialist government. Thai people don't want Communi't government. When Thai students come back from study in Moscow, they say '*Mai sanuk!*' There is no freedom! But many people here in Thailand angry with American government, also. After American War, nobody trust American government anymore. Too many refugee from Prathet Lao, Kampuchea, and Wietnam come here, live in camp."

He had grown deeply serious. Suddenly his smile returned. "But that not mean we don't like American *people*. Come, I will show you upstair before I take you see Sommit and my parent at Yoon On Store." On that cheerful note, he led me up three flights of stairs, pointing out along the way how the second floor would be divided into soundproof classrooms for the music school; how the third floor—thanks to a freight elevator—would be used as a warehouse, as a shipping center, and for storing a vast collection of sheet music; and finally, how the fourth floor would be used for studios—for rehearsals and recording, often for bands made up of Issan teenagers who couldn't afford to own instruments. From the fourth floor, Chai showed me the detached three-story apartment that Sommit was building in back for his wife and children.

After the pessimism of Chai's outlook for the region, which seemed to fatalistically assume that war was inevitable, I was amazed. "I thought you were afraid of the Vietnamese army," I said as we rode down the freight elevator.

"Thai diplomat very skillful," he replied laconically, leading me out the front door. We walked along the street, bustling in the late afternoon with construction workers, trucks, and heavy equipment still hard at work renovating the Thai-Sikh-Chinese business district. "They know that Lao and Kampuchean people don't like Wietnam either."

At his parents' store his father politely feigned remembering me, and his mother really did. Sommit stepped through a beaded curtain, smiling in his low-key way until he recognized me and his eyes brightened. "Prah Brendan!" He had put on some weight and aged pleasantly into a prosperous businessman. "Come!" he said, taking me back through the beaded curtains to a large, military-grade supply cabinet and swinging open the metal door. It was filled with American $33^{1}/_{3}$ rpm record albums, thousands of them, and he pointed out the hundreds I had personally smuggled him from the BX in exchange for the numerous favors he had been able to perform for me. Miraculously, Chai and Sommit had saved them from the fire. I asked what he intended to do with them, and the enterprising young businessman who brought Woodstock to Ubon and was in the process of building a palace to Thai pop music and rock 'n' roll confessed he had no idea.

"Why don't you start a radio station from the top of your new music store?"

Sommit smiled politely, sparing me the details of how impossible it was for a small businessman to open a commercial radio station in a country that, for all its freedom of travel and *sanuk* lifestyle, for all its fine food and entertainment, for all its freewheeling entrepreneurship at the local level, and for all its trappings of democracy and enlightened monarchy, was in the final analysis run by military men.

"Will you go back to Wat Pah Nirapai?" he asked.

"Actually, I think it may be time to disrobe."

"We're very surprise you stay a monk this long. Especially in Prathet Lao. For many Thai men, one Rains Retreat is enough."

"For many business people and government people, one Rains Retreat is *too much*," added Chai. We all laughed softly.

"Before I go to the monastery today..." My throat seemed to dry up and I found it difficult to continue. "I don't suppose the suitcase I left with you survived the—"

Chai had already disappeared up a narrow flight of stairs. I could hear him pull something from what sounded like an upper shelf and, in a moment, came back down with my beat-up leather valise. I opened it, took out a single change of clothes and my low-cut boots, and closed it back up. "May I leave this here one more night? I would like to stay at Wat Pah Nirapai tonight and turn in my robes tomorrow after the morning meal."

"No problem. We can take you in our van."

Their mother didn't speak much English but understood the gist of our discussion. She spoke to them in Chinese.

"Our mother say you travel much today. She ask if you want *ap nam* before you go to *wat.*"

"I would appreciate that very much, Khun Chai, Khun Sommit, Khun Mae."

Chai led me back through the beaded curtains and pointed to a door at the back of the storeroom. "Bathing room is over there," he said.

When I had finished washing away the day's trail dust and had folded my fresh change of civilian clothes to fit neatly in my ochre carrying bag, I followed Chai and Sommit down Thanon Luang toward the river. We turned into a narrow alley and stopped at the double doors of a two-story clapboard building that garaged several merchants' delivery vans and a couple of Toyota Crowns, a top-of-the-line luxury car on the Thai-Laotian frontier. Sommit swung open the garage doors and began to unlock the doors to their van. Chai, who had been so gracious and generous, seemed a little uncomfortable. "When you come back tomorrow—if you want to visit around Ubon, please to use my bicycle."

"That's very kind of you. Is that the one I left with you?"

Sommit stopped and looked on while Chai answered, "I afraid your bicycle is one thing that we could not save from fire." He made his way back to the corner and picked up something that looked like a tiny meteorite.

Bringing it over to me, he broke into a smile. "We keep it for you. Don't know why, but think maybe you want a souvenir."

On closer examination, I could see the meteorite was made of aluminum, rubber, and a small saddle's worth of leather. "This is my *bicycle*?" I laughed, turning it upside down and sideways. "It's *better* than a souvenir—it's our good luck charm! We're all very lucky. We've made it through war and fire, and we're all still here!" The three of us enjoyed the foolishness of it all before I was struck with a related but somewhat more serious idea. "There is one thing I would like to do before I go to the monastery. Could we make a short visit to Bungalow Ruam Chon Sawng?"

"No problem," said Sommit as he backed the van out and we climbed in.

Mama-sahn was sitting on her front stoop when we arrived a few minutes later, bra-less and mildly stoned on betel as always. Perpetually ancient and girlish, she smiled and *waied* when she saw me climb out of the van and walk through the front gate. "*Sawatdii*, Tahn Bren-dan!"

"*Sawatdii*, Mama-sahn! Bun-lii *yuu tiinii yang, khrab*? Does Bun-lii still live here?"

"*Mai yuu*," she answered, explaining in Thai that Bun-lii had gone back to her family's farm in Tahk.

"*Bai wai sahn prah puum, dai mai?*" I said, asking if it was okay to visit the spirit house at the end of the alley.

"*Dai*," she replied, smiling shamelessly, and I walked on.

The last of the Americans had long left Ruam Chon Sawng, and the once-roomy bungalows had been subdivided into tiny apartments that no gangly American could fit into without developing claustrophobia. The spirit house had changed little, though, which gave me a small measure of solace. I lit a joss stick and prayed to the *jao tii* who lived inside, thanking the spirits for my safe if difficult passage to Laos and my safe return. Thinking of all my friends who had once lived here or visited here and were gone forever, I felt my throat constrict. I stood there another moment in silence until the sound of children playing broke me out of my reverie. Not wanting to take any more advantage of Chai and Sommit's kindness, I walked back to the waiting van. "*Lagawn, Mama-sahn*."

"*Chohk dii*, Tahn Bren-dan. Good luck to you." They were the first words I had ever heard her say in English.

"Is there anything else you want to do in Ubon?" asked Sommit, putting the van in gear and making a couple of left turns to get us back to old Route 66.

"Not today," I replied. "But can you come back to the monastery tomorrow morning at ten o'clock?"

"We can," Chai said.

"And are you still holding some money for me?"

"We are."

"Will you have enough time to bring that with you?"

Chai and Sommit glanced at each other and nodded. Chai said, "We can."

"There's something I need to do before eleven, and I'll need your help."

"We happy to help," Sommit answered. Soon we were crossing the Warin Bridge and drove the rest of the way in Noble Silence. It had just started to get dark when we arrived at Wat Pah Nirapai. Chai slid open the side door of the van and let me out. "See you tomorrow, Tahn Bren-dan."

I thanked them and walked through the gate, continuing on towards Ajahn Po's *kuti*, where the monks usually gathered for tea at that time of the day. I was surprised to see Ajahn Pichit, the vice abbot, seated at the back of the screened area under Ajahn Po's residence in the place usually held by Ajahn Po himself. He was telling the assembled monks that he had just received a letter from Tahn Suñño, who was traveling in Burma. Unfolding it, he read:

The past nine months have been challenging but illuminating while visiting meditation temples in Thailand and Burma. Ajahn Maha Boowa, up north near Udorn, was as fierce as you would expect from someone who, like Ajahn Po, once wandered the tiger-infested jungles of Thailand and Laos with Ajahn Mun. Ajahn Jumnien is just the opposite—the embodiment of Loving-Kindness, even though he teaches in the politically unstable South. In Surat Thani, a little further north on the Gulf of Siam, Ajahn Buddhadasa has become ecumenical in his old age, incorporating elements of several branches of Buddhism, including Zen, into the grounds, the artworks he displays, and his teachings and writings at Wat Suan Mokkh. A female teacher named Ajahn Naeb works with new students at Wat Sraket, an oasis of quiet located in the heart of Bangkok.

Since coming to Burma, I have been fortunate to study with the highly respected lay meditation master, U Ba Khin. He has developed a technique of sweeping the body for ever-changing feelings and sensations—while holding several cabinet-level positions in the Burmese government. I am now beginning an intensive retreat at a large center run by another respected Burmese meditation master, Mahasi Sayadaw. I expect to be returning to the States in the next year, where I hope to compile a book about the twelve great teachers I have now studied with in Thailand and Burma and how these modern masters continue to transmit Dhamma that has been passed down orally for over 2,500 years. Now that my travels are coming to an end, it is clear that Ajahn Po will hold a place of honor at the front of the book when it is finished.

With Metta,
Suñño Bhikkhu

Ajahn Pichit put the letter down and addressed the monks directly. "Please enjoy the rest of your tea. We will meet for our evening chanting and meditation in one hour." When he noticed me sitting silently just inside the door, his eyes lit up and he said, "It look like one of our *tudong* monks has come back to us. Welcome, Tahn Santisekkho. Please have some tea, and then Tahn Anando will help you to find a *kuti*."

When the other monks and novices had left, I stayed behind to talk to Pichit and Anando. "Where is Ajahn Po?" I asked.

"I guess you haven't heard," Anando said. "Luang Paaw has had a stroke. He was in the hospital in Bangkok for a month, but there's nothing more they can do, so he's back here, being well cared for."

"He very tired and sleep a lot," said Ajahn Pichit. "He is still in his old room upstair, but it will be better if we take you to pay your respect in the morning after breakfast. Meanwhile, you must tell us about your travel. We were not sure for quite a while what happen to you, but finally, a monk from Luang Prabang pass through and talk about a Canadian monk staying at Wat Pah Pohn Pao. We did not correct him about nationality. But we hope that it was you."

"It was. I'm afraid I haven't been good about writing letters. And I spent much of my time on silent retreat. Please accept my apologies if I caused you any worries." I kept it simple and didn't mention my forged Canadian passport.

"Will you be staying with us permanently?" the vice abbot asked.

His kind nature made it more difficult than I expected for me to tell Ajahn Pichit that I wanted to stay one more night with the Sangha but that I planned to disrobe after *pindabaht* and a final morning meal together. "I hope you've considered your decision carefully," he replied.

"I have," I said, *waiing* deeply and walking outside with Anando.

"Come," said the former pilot, "I can give you a *kuti* not far from your old one so you won't get lost. Why did you stay away so long?"

"Wasn't it you who said I had a lot of *kamma* to work out?"

"A lot of us said that, Santisekkho." He found me a mat and a mosquito net in the storeroom behind the Dhamma hall, which I tucked under my arm, and then handed me a pillow—the one Pawnsiri had made for me three years earlier.

I thanked him and followed him along the narrow dirt path a short ways into the forest to the hut where I would stay for the night. I put my things inside and sat down on the porch. Anando joined me. "What happened to Ajahn Po?" I asked. "He was so strong! He had been in the jungle with Ajahn Mun in the days when there were still man-eating tigers stalking around. He seemed indestructible."

"And he also taught us that none of us are indestructible."

"Even so, didn't this catch any of you off guard?"

"In all honesty, it did. What we couldn't understand is why he still lives, his brilliant, witty mind almost like a sleepy little baby's while his body seems to be perfectly healthy. We knew Luang Paaw wouldn't approve—in fact, he might have forbidden it—but Suñño heard about an old monk in a nearby village who can travel back in time and see people's past lives. We were certain it's all a bunch of superstitious rubbish, and we'll tell Ajahn Po that if he ever happens to wake up. But we went to see the old monk anyway. He was quite a sight—missing most of his teeth and covered with tattoos. He said he knew we were coming and offered us one of his Camel cigarettes. We declined and watched while he smoked his. And then rather quickly, he went into a deep meditation that most people would call a trance, rocking a little instead of sitting totally still the way we are trained. And instead of the little smile on his face that we often get while meditating in a state of *samadhi*, his face seemed to sink into itself, almost the way a living person's face becomes a death mask just before they pass on. After a while, we could see his eyes moving rapidly back and forth, even though his lids were shut, and at one point his face twitched horribly. And then he became very still. When he opened his eyes, they seemed genuinely sad. It seemed like an eternity before he spoke. Finally, after drawing a deep breath, he told us that our esteemed abbot, Ajahn Po, had once been a great Chinese general who had won many victories, serving bravely under two kings. But in winning his victories, many innocent women and children died violent deaths. Rivers flowed with blood. Whole cities and miles of rice fields burned. Instead of peace, his victories brought famine and starvation. And for this, his *kamma* is to endure ten years of suffering in this lifetime, trapped alive inside his body."

"Wow," I said.

"That's exactly what *we* said. I don't know if I ever mentioned it to you, but many of Ajahn Po's followers through the years have been soldiers. One of our most generous benefactors is a Burmese arms merchant."

"I seem to remember a distinguished guest once having to stay in the smallest *kuti* and asking Ajahn Po, 'Why? After all I have given Wat Pah Nirapai—' And Ajahn Po answered, 'Because I want you to know how little you really need.'"

"That would be the one," Anando replied, smiling as he stood up. "And now, my fellow warrior-*bhikkhu*, shall we walk together to the Dhamma hall?"

Later, returning from the evening chanting, I decided to take a farewell walk along the old paths that wound through the woods of the monastery grounds. Moving slowly, I contemplated my many colorful friends and mentors, wondering which of those still living I would see again. And I reflected further on which of those I could talk to about my three years as a *bhikkhu* and realized I couldn't know until I saw them. I returned to the *kuti* and slept one last time on the grass mat with only a mosquito net to cover me in a room lit by a single candle.

The next morning I arose with the others at 3:00 a.m. After the familiar routine of chanting and meditation in the Dhamma hall, I went on *pindabaht* for a final time. Ajahn Pichit assigned me to the group led by Anando. Returning from my long pilgrimage, I had gained in seniority and now walked in the middle of the group, following several of the more experienced monks and leading a few junior monks and novices out the front gate. We walked barefoot along a path which turned into the dike that led through a grid of rain-irrigated rice fields and out to a road that took us to the hamlet of Ban Lok. As always, I was touched by the austere existence of the villagers, some already at work behind wooden plows pulled by water buffalo. Those on their way to the rice fields often stopped, slipped out of their sandals, and knelt at the side of the road to offer us food. I asked myself, as I had asked so often, *How is such generosity possible in people whose life is so hard?* Walking through the village, I observed once again how mothers and grandparents were teaching their young children to perform these simple acts of kindness, dishing rice or curry into each of our bowls as we walked past.

It seemed strange to gather in the Dhamma hall for the morning meal without Ajahn Po to lead us. Sitting on the low riser that ran the length of the far wall, he had always occupied the position of honor nearest the bronze Buddha at the front of the hall with the other monks sitting to his left in descending order of seniority. He couldn't have stood over five-and-a-half feet tall, and yet his presence always loomed large. To his credit, Ajahn Pichit held his place as acting abbot with great dignity, accepting individual offerings of food brought by lay supporters and passing the food on down the long line of monks and novices, who in turn passed what was left to the visitors themselves. He led the monks chanting the *anumodana*, blessing the laypeople for the generous support that made the existence of Wat Pah Nirapai possible. After we paused a moment to contemplate the food in our bowls, Ajahn Pichit rang his little bell and invited us to begin eating.

When the morning meal was over, I cleaned out my bowl and freshened up and found Anando, who took me to Ajahn Po's residence. Ajahn Pichit was waiting for us downstairs. "I will stay here while you go to pay your respect," he said. And then he warned me gently, "Don't be too shocked at the change in your preceptor. Remember, Luang Paaw is being well cared for."

We removed our sandals, and Anando led me up the stairs and through the open door into Ajahn Po's room. The monastic rules required the young and healthy to sleep on a grass mat, but the rules were flexible enough to permit a sick man the use of a hospital bed. My heart seemed to stop a moment at the sight of this small but powerful man, this lightning bolt of energy, this funny, earthy, most inspiring teacher of teachers, this General George Patton of monastics, now lying there helplessly, still as a sleeping baby, his arms stuck with wires and tubes. And yet, looking closely, I could see that this once-fierce forest monk was lying there in peace, the trace of a Buddha-like smile lighting up his face. His skin was smooth and seemed to glow. A young monk attended him, mopping his face and arms with a cool, damp cloth and then adjusting the valve on the drip.

"He seems to be able to hear us when we chant," said Anando. "He can't speak, but his face seems to light up a bit more."

"Shall we recite 'Going to the Three Refuges'?" I asked.

"Would you like to join us?" Anando asked the young monk.

We all knelt at the side of Ajahn Po's bed and, after bowing to him, sat in the lotus position, cross-legged with our spines straight. As I had done my first day visiting Wat Pah Nirapai and had continued to do every day thereafter, regardless of what monastery I was living at, we chanted, "*Namo tassa bhagavato arahato sammāsambuddhassa*"—"Homage to the Blessed One, the Noble One, the Perfectly Enlightened One"—repeating it twice more before continuing in Pali, "To the Buddha I go for refuge, To the Dhamma I go for refuge, To the Sangha I go for refuge." We repeated the passage in Pali for a second and then a third time before Anando led us in another chant, "Five Subjects for Frequent Recollection." Again, in deep, resonant Pali, the three-tone chanting reverberated through our bodies, giving the words heightened power:

> *I am of the nature to age. I have not gone beyond aging.*
> *I am of the nature to sicken. I have not gone beyond sickness.*
> *I am of the nature to die. I have not gone beyond dying.*

We continued:

> *All that is mine, beloved and pleasing, will become otherwise, will become separated from me.*
> *I am the owner of my kamma, heir to my kamma,*
> *Born of my kamma, related to my kamma, abide supported by my kamma.*
> *Whatsoever kamma I shall do—for good or for ill—*
> *Of all that I will be the heir.*
> *Thus we should frequently recollect.*

We prostrated ourselves before Luang Paaw and stood respectfully, gazing into his serene face that had indeed grown even more serene. I bowed my head and said a brief silent prayer, asking that he understand my need to return to the life of a householder as well as he had once understood my need to make a pilgrimage to Laos better than I understood it myself.

When we returned downstairs, Ajahn Pichit asked me to come with him and Anando to the *bot*, the ordination hall where he could witness my intention to disrobe. They sat near the altar at the front of the chapel, and I bowed before them. "Are you in a clear state of mind?" asked Ajahn Pichit.

"Yes, sir, I am."

"And are you of clear and firm intention?"

"Yes, sir, I am."

"You may proceed."

I answered for the last time as Santisekkho Bhikkhu, saying, "It is my wish to become a householder and lay follower of this Sangha and the worldwide Sangha of followers of the Lord Buddha. I am grateful to my generous teachers, fellow monks, and lay supporters here at Wat Pah Nirapai, at Wat Ph'a Yai where I was first taught the Dhamma, and at Wat Pah Pohn Pao in Luang Prabang for all that they have given me these past three years in both wisdom and in material support."

I bowed three times to the Buddha and three times to Ajahn Pichit, and with that humble gesture, my reverse ordination was over. Returning to my *kuti*, I removed my robes, hung them on a hook on the wall, and changed into my civilian clothes. I rolled up my grass mat and put the pillow, the mosquito net, and my well-worn alms bowl on top, offerings to the next monk in need who passed through. Before folding up my carrying bag, I reached into the bottom, pulled out my U.S. passport, the forged Canadian passport, and the tattered letter from Pawnsiri and slipped them carefully into my shirt pocket. Reaching in a final time, I found my grandfather's old penknife and dropped it into my pants pocket. Last, I took down the saffron robes, folded them neatly, and put them next to the alms bowl on the rolled-up mat.

My return to lay life complete, I stopped by the kitchen and checked the time: it was almost ten o'clock. Making sure I wasn't noticed, I dropped my Canadian passport into a bag of trash that was waiting to be hauled away, moved my American passport to the empty front pocket of my pants, and headed out. Leaving through a side gate, I was heartened to see Chai and Sommit waiting as they had promised in the unpaved visitors parking area. We *waied* and exchanged hellos. "Thank you so much for helping me out," I said. "I want to surprise the monks, and I can't do this myself." I paused a moment, purposely trying to build up a little suspense. "Do you know a place where we can get a big stainless steel drum of chocolate ice cream?"

Chai and Sommit laughed at first and then conferred with great animation in Chinese. Chai said to me, "Maybe near the big market in Warin. Otherwise, there is pastry shop in Ubon near post-telegraph office that also make ice cream for all the hotel and big *rahn-ahahn*. We should hurry if we want to be back before twelve o'clock."

We were lucky. My friends found the ice cream we needed in a large pastry shop hidden away in the shadows at the back of the Warin central market, the first place we stopped. I asked Chai if he brought the money from my bank account. He said he had, but when I asked that they use it to pay for the ice cream, they insisted on taking care of it themselves. "You need to save your money," Sommit said with a smile.

Back at Wat Pah Nirapai, I spotted Samai, the young novice I'd met on my first visit three years earlier, and asked him to take me to Ajahn Pichit. We found the abbot sitting in meditation on the front porch of his *kuti*. Looking up, he smiled and teased, "You've decided to come back already?"

"Not as a monk, Ajahn, but I have brought something I would like to offer to all the monks in the meditation hall. Please ask them to bring their alms bowls and spoons."

He instructed Samai to send several other novices around to deliver my message and then to go ring the temple bell. Everything had gone perfectly. It was just 11:00 a.m. when the bell began to sound, and soon the monks started to gather in the Dhamma hall, holding their alms bowls quizzically. Ajahn Po had been well-known for his strict one-meal-a-day discipline when we were in residence at the *wat*. Some, especially the younger monks and novices, were excited at an unexpected break from their daily routine. A couple of monks who had only recently taken up meditation and had to work hard to sustain their practice appeared to be mildly irritated, but they soon got caught up in the curiosity and excitement. When everyone had taken the same places on the riser along the side of the hall that they sat at for the morning meal, Sommit and Chai carried in the frost-covered stainless-steel cylinder. They had left their sandals at the entrance and bent low as they approached Ajahn Pichit, where I was already kneeling. They set the cylinder down next to me, unfastened the top, and then backed away, maintaining a posture of humility and respect. "Ajahn Pichit," I said, "please accept this offering of thanks to you and all the *bhikkhus* of Wat Pah Nirapai."

The abbot smiled broadly, surprised that he could be surprised, and said, "The *bhikkhus* of Wat Pah Nirapai thank you, Khun Brendan, for not forgetting them as you return to your new life as a householder."

He called up a young monk, a strong Issan farm boy, to carry the drum of ice cream down the line of seated monks. One of the old village women who supervised the kitchen handed the boy a serving spoon. As the young monk made his way down the line, gradually getting the hang of dishing out something harder and colder than curry and rice, I made three prostrations to Ajahn Pichit and slowly backed up several steps on my knees before I rose and paused a moment. When I *waied* to the assembled monks, who were waiting patiently for all to be served, I caught the eye of Tahn Anando. He gave me a little head nod, and I gave him a nod back, both of us smiling ever so subtly. The farm boy served himself and gave what was left to the old woman to take to her friends still lingering in the kitchen.

"Please enjoy this offering from a former monk," said Ajahn Pichit. And as they began eating mindfully, aware of anticipation as they scooped up ice cream with their spoons, aware of the sensation of sweetness and cold as it touched their lips, and aware of the taste as it melted in their mouths and slid down their throats, I caught another glance from Anando. I gave him what started as a *wai* and turned into an unobtrusive salute to the monk who had been a forward air controller in Laos and had rarely said a word about the experience of flying more than two hundred combat missions. I took a deep breath and walked out of the hall, stooped over in respect like Chai and Sommit. I met them outside, behind the Dhamma hall, and quietly we slipped away.

Along the way back to Warin, Khun Chai produced the canceled passbook from the Thai Farmers Bank and handed it to me with an envelope tucked inside filled with more than thirteen thousand baht. "This is the money you gave me before you left, plus a little interest. It not much, but this is enough to live on for a few month if you decide to stay in Bangkok."

I took it from him and thanked him.

"Where will you go?" he asked. "Back to America?"

"With a little luck, I'd like to stay in Ubon and teach."

Chai's face changed in a small way that most Americans would not have noticed. "USIS is gone, and the Peace Corps—they went to the North. Everybody think it too dangerous here. Too many VC come with the refugees. Too many North Vietnamese on the border. Many people afraid to have GIs here. Afraid the war will come here like it came to Lao and Kampuchea. Bangkok or Chiang Mai is better."

"Well, I'm not a GI anymore, but you're right, I suppose. In any case, I want to check in to the Ubon Hotel and relax for a day or two before I do anything. Maybe I'll buy *us* a big dish of chocolate ice cream."

We were passing through the busy streets of Warin and about to turn onto the road to the Warin-Ubon Bridge when Sommit surprised me. "You have *faen*, Khun Bren-dan?"

My smile gave me away. "Monks aren't supposed to have girlfriends, Khun Sommit. You know that better than I. But I have been wondering if you or Chai have heard from Miss Pawnsiri lately."

"Nothing since after the fire. We very busy with the store and she very busy at the college. Ubon get too big now, and she live at the other side of the town."

"You still like to use my bike for today?" Chai asked.

"I don't want to trouble you."

"No trouble! I must mind store anyway."

"You're too kind. Before I check in at the hotel, I would like to ride out to see the old Air Force base and maybe try to say hello to Khun Pawnsiri. We talked about putting a band together when I came back. Maybe we can use the studio at Woodstock Music to rehearse!"

Sommit replied, "My parents hear from her family that she now very busy with teaching, Khun Bren-dan. She used to come to store almost every week to buy sheet music, but now she never come." He turned up Thanon Luang and pulled into the alley that led to the clapboard garage. Chai unlocked the double doors. While Sommit parked the van, Chai took me to the back where he kept an old black English ten-speed. He dusted off the seat and checked the tires, which needed a few shots of air from the hand pump. When he finished, I gave him a friendly squeeze on his shoulder and thanked him. Saying goodbye to Chai and Sommit, I climbed on the bike and rode off toward Route 66 and the air base, leaving behind the ruins and rebuilding of the business district and entering what was becoming an even newer part of town. Turning right, I passed the Sanam Luang, the site of countless soccer matches located next to Wat Tung Sri Muang, the hub of Ubon's largest Buddhist festivals—and the start/finish line for the Big Buddha Bicycle Race. Both the bicycle and my body grunted and groaned from lack of use.

Pedaling north on Route 66 and looking more carefully than I had on the bus ride in, it was just as Chai had told me. The U.S. Information Service was gone, the airy white building with blue trim now a cafe, the outline of the letters "USIS" still faintly visible where they had been removed. The turnoff to Thanon Uparisawn, the road to the Royal Thai Air Force Base, was hardly recognizable. The Shell Oil station on the corner remained, but the tailor shops were gone, and the cafes that were still in business all had new names. Next door, where Maharaj Massage once stood—where once upon a time the girls all drove motorbikes and only went home with American officers— the doors and windows were boarded over while the interior was being converted into a budget hotel.

There was a sign on the opposite corner with pink and lavender letters, not very large, that read "Thai Airways Terminal." I followed it to the old gate, once lined with GIs waiting in flashy custom-made shirts and bell-bottomed pants for the one-baht bus ride to town, to paradise, to the true Eastern side of Eden, ripe mangoes by the bushel barrel, by the truckload, to be given away to the soldier who could produce an American apple.

I told the Thai Air Policeman at the gate that I needed to cash a traveler's check at the airline terminal. The guard towers on my left stood silent as I bicycled up the empty access road. On my right, I passed more than a mile of empty revetments that were once full of fighter-bombers—muscular F-105s and state-of-the-art F-4 Phantoms—their engines roaring as they came and went. All gone home. An A-37 flew overhead, and I hoped it was on a training mission because the North Vietnamese had brought plenty of shoulder-mounted Strela missiles with them into South Vietnam in 1972. A Strela had been enough to take down Spectre 544, and the word around Ubon Air Force Base at the time was that they had nailed so many ARVN A-37s that South Vietnamese Air Force pilots refused to fly.

At the turnoff to the old aeroport terminal where I first set foot in upcountry Thailand, I kept going straight. I had trouble recognizing the chapel where Chaplain Kirkgartner used to listen patiently to the ramblings of his lost tribe of hippie airmen and his boss, Colonel Pedigrew, used to preach to the officers who were trying to make the best of what they called "the only war we've got" to advance their careers. The cross had been taken down, and the eaves now swept upward in the classical lines of a Thai Buddhist temple.

The hospital still stood intact. The Little Pentagon had vanished. The Almighty BX, the picture many Thai farm girls had of what Nibbana must be like—now a concrete slab, a basketball court. The Officers' Club, the NCO Club, and the Airmen's Club had been folded up like the Little Pentagon and taken away, put in storage like the sets of a Hollywood movie. The airmen's swimming pool and patio beer garden sufficed for the Thai officers. The hootches where six GIs used to share bunks and lockers were now stuffed with the families and chickens and pigs of Thai airmen. I didn't see where the Thai pilots slept, but it was not in the air-conditioned trailers the Americans took with them. In the streets where young American airmen, most of whom looked like farm boys from Iowa, tossed footballs and baseballs a couple of years earlier, the children of the skeleton crew of Thais rode their second-hand bicycles and kicked worn-out soccer balls.

I talked to one Thai sergeant who had worked with the Americans since he was sixteen—fifteen years mastering jet engine maintenance. He was thirty-one and he looked fifty. He was still trim, but his hair was graying, and the wrinkles in the corners of his eyes were digging in deep. We didn't have to talk much about it. We both knew an A-37 was not an F-4 and that a Russian-built MiG-21 would squish it like a bug. Thailand's best hope was in skillful diplomacy, in absolutely not counting on the U.S. government, and in the probability that the North Vietnamese were tired and bled dry after taking the rest of Indochina.

I circled back to the main gate and cruised along on autopilot through the old neighborhoods to the west of the base. Niko's Massage Parlor was now a vegetarian restaurant, and the bowling alley on Highway 66, the road to Big Buddha, had become a supermarket. In fact, nothing on the road to Big Buddha looked the same. The old two-story shop-front apartments were replaced with airline ticket offices and department stores, and I passed a new hotel-restaurant-nightclub-massage complex that was bigger than the Ubon Hotel, the Hotel Tokyo, the Lotus Blossom, the Soul Sister, and Maharaj Massage put together, an entertainment conglomerate gone mad where Asian businessmen were spending real money.

Feeling a bit of trepidation, I made the turn that took me past the teachers college. I found the *rongphayaban* where Pawnsiri's older sister once worked as a nurse before she moved to Bangkok, and a few other things looked familiar, but I grew disorientated just the same riding through the narrow, unpaved alleys. The illusion that I had ever developed a cool heart, let alone been on a path to enlightenment, got a little shaky. "Damn!" I muttered, climbing off the bike and looking up and down the muddy *soy* in frustration, trying to get my bearings.

At that very moment, a young mother pulled up on a motor scooter, her little girl sitting in front of her straddling the gas tank, and asked if I was lost. "I'm afraid so," I answered in Thai. "Do you happen to know if a teacher named Khun Pawnsiri still lives around here?"

"I think I remember she live close by, sir," the woman replied. "Can you please to follow me?" She rode slowly so that I had no trouble keeping up, and sure enough, she led me to the front gate of Pawnsiri's old family compound. She glanced at my hair, which hadn't been shaved in a month and was starting to grow in. "You used to be monk?" she asked.

Embarrassed, I told her I had tried, although not too well. Apparently she had been unfazed by my cursing. "Very good for *farang* to be monk!" she said with a beautiful Thai smile. I had taken her several blocks out of her way on dusty back streets, and she hadn't thought anything of it, still smiling contentedly as she rode off with her baby.

If I had only gone a few blocks further up Route 66, I would have reached Pawnsiri's old bus stop and recognized the lane that led to my intended destination—and my destiny. Her father's house was still impressive, made of many planks of fine teak, protected from termites and floods by a concrete slab that supported the eight-foot posts, also made of concrete. There was a new house inside the compound, next to the gate, and I thought perhaps her older sister or brother had moved back. I could feel my heart pounding as I parked my borrowed bicycle and walked to the gate. It was locked, but I knocked anyway and called out, "*Khun Pawnsiri yuu tiinii mai?* Hello! Is Pawnsiri home?"

Nobody answered. I waited another moment, expecting the door to open. I continued waiting, and still nothing happened. The soft rumble of traffic coming from Route 66 and the low roar of another solitary A-37 taking off a mile to the east barely registered on my ears. The dream in Luang Prabang had seemed so certain, as had the little after-shock dream on the bus from Nakhon Phanom. I was totally unprepared for finding—what? Nothing? Even though my teachers had told us to beware of *nimittas*, I had chosen to believe this one. "*They can be true or not true, and you cannot tell the difference,*" I recalled Ajahn Po warning us in a Dhamma talk shortly before I left on *tudong*. Ajahn Saisamut had said almost the same thing during my first rains at Wat Pah Pohn Pao.

I climbed onto Chai's bicycle and started back into town. Passing the turnoff to the teachers college, I thought of Professor Natapong. Remembering his warmth and graciousness quickly cheered me up. *Surely a busy college professor who had taken the time to follow Pawnsiri's singing career would know where his ex-student was teaching*, I thought.

Pedaling across the campus, I couldn't help thinking how pleasant it would be to teach here if his offer was still open. It was Friday, unfortunately, and by the time I found his office, the department secretary told me he had already left for the weekend. I asked her if she happened to know the whereabouts of an old student of his named Pawnsiri.

"Professor Natapong has so many student," she replied a little warily.

"She is also a singer. The professor and I used to watch her perform." That only seemed to make her warier. "She also used to be a student of mine at AUA." I pulled the tattered aerogramme from my shirt pocket and glanced at the return address containing her long last name, something that was rarely used in Thailand other than situations like this. "Can you check your records for Pawnsiri Leemingsawat?" I asked, holding the address out for her to read herself.

"You might check at the Polytechnic High School, sir. I believe I sent her records to them a year or two ago."

I thanked her and was soon back on my bicycle, pedaling in the direction of the high school that I knew well from my nights teaching adult school English. I checked in at the front desk of the headmaster's office, this time mentioning straight away to the secretary that I had fond memories of teaching an AUA class at her school. She directed me to a biology classroom on the second floor in the back of the building. When I got close to Pawnsiri's room, I could hear her voice, just a little clearer and purer than the voices of other teachers and students that echoed through the school. The shutters to the windows of her classroom were open so that I could stand in the shadows on the second-floor balcony and watch her teach. It was beautiful to watch her in command of the classroom, moving confidently and gracefully from her desk to the chalkboard and back to her students. She clearly enjoyed being in front of her students as much as she used to enjoy singing in front of a night club audience, except she seemed to be more alive now, invigorated even more by her students' questions than by the applause of an audience of strangers. It was the last class of the day, and the moment the bell rang, the students sprang to their feet, gathered their notes and books, and swooped happily out of the classroom.

Pawnsiri was standing at her desk, putting papers into her briefcase when I knocked lightly on the open door. She stopped what she was doing and looked up, staring at me a moment, taking a few seconds to compute what this strange, tall, bald-headed *farang* was doing at her door in an obscure part of the Thai hinterlands. Suddenly she broke into a wide, warm smile. "Bren-dan!" she cried, rushing to the door.

At precisely the moment I thought she would throw her arms around me, she stopped. She looked up at me, her brown-onyx eyes wide and bright at first and then glistening with tears. She had suddenly slipped back in time, no longer a vigorous young educator commanding a classroom. Now she was again a worshipful schoolgirl. Without taking her eyes from mine, she touched her hands together in a heartfelt *wai* that Father Boyle would have sworn was a prayer of thanks and devotion. "I miss you so much! I so glad you come back. Everybody say you die in Lao—the same they say you die when your plane crash. You tell me you have much bad *kamma*," she said, starting to laugh. "Not true! You have much *good* luck!"

"Can we go somewhere and talk? Is the little *rahn-ahahn* near your bus stop still there?"

"Just a minute," she said. She ran back to her desk, stuffed the last of her papers into the briefcase, snapped it shut, and walked quickly past me to the door. "Okay, we can go!"

Monsoon rains started falling when we were halfway across campus. Running the rest of the way, we got to the little noodle shop just before the gentle rain turned into a deluge. We sat at our old table in the back, and she looked even more adorable to me, pushing away a few strands of wet hair that had blown across her face. Her eyes glistened with a hint of sadness. "Why you never write?"

"I did write."

"Really? Then why did I never get letter?"

"I don't understand. I did write. It took a long time to put my feelings into words…and to put those words down on paper. But I did write."

"It doesn't matter now—"

"I'm so sorry. Everything was more difficult than I imagined. Before I left Ubon, I had so many nightmares that I couldn't sleep, couldn't think. I had to go *tudong*. But it got worse. *Tii puukhau, phom dai klai pen bah-bah baw-baw noy*—in the mountains I went a little crazy. I don't remember how long it lasted exactly. At least a month. It got worse almost as soon as I left Pakse. I saw things and heard things, and I couldn't tell if they were real or if they were *nimittas*. Every night I was afraid and alone. Some nights the Vietnamese soldiers walked ten feet from where I tried to sleep. Many days and nights I went hungry. The rumors you heard were nearly true. Many times I thought I was going to die. Then I got to Luang Prabang and for a long time there was no war at all, at least near *us*. It was so peaceful that sometimes I thought I must be dead and I must be in heaven. Many times I thought about how much I just needed to rest. My mind and body both needed to rest. My body was exhausted, but still my mind raced around and around so madly it wouldn't let me sleep."

"Did you get letter I send to Wat Pah Nirapai?"

I pulled it out of my pocket. Fragile to begin with, now it was starting to disintegrate from the raindrops that had soaked through my shirt. "It took months to reach me at Wat Pah Pohn Pao. But when I read it, I was overwhelmed. You expressed so much feeling. I could never answer so much feeling with written words when I was feeling dead. It took a year to heal, but I finally wrote. When I didn't hear from you, I reminded myself that the airport was often closed and that Luang Prabang was still surrounded by war. There was supposed to be a truce, but both sides were moving troops around, often blocking the roads. It would have been easy for a letter to be lost, whether it was mine to you or your reply. But just two weeks ago I had a powerful dream—I heard you calling out to me in the night."

"I did call out to you—many time—from my dreams to your dreams."

"It was almost as if we didn't need letters to talk to each other across four hundred miles of mountains and river valleys."

"I dreamed about you night after night, but you never called back in my dreams."

"Can you forgive me?"

"I forgive you."

"Will you marry me?"

"I would like that very much. I wanted that more than anything in the world for more than a year—"

"For more than a year? And then what?"

"And now I cannot marry you."

"But why? I thought you said you forgive me."

"I do forgive you, and I care about you very much, Bren-dan. But—" Pawnsiri looked down a moment. "I have husband already," she said, slowly lifting her hand and showing me her wedding ring.

I winced. "*That* part was not in my dream." I struggled to take a breath, feeling like a vise had been tightened on my chest. "I don't know what to say… Except, I hope you are very happy with him."

She gave me a look that said she wasn't exactly happy. "He's a good man," she said, measuring her words. "Our family know each other for a long time."

"Do you have any children?"

"We have a little girl. My mother take care of our daughter for us while we work."

"And is your husband a teacher too?"

"He teach English at the district school in Wijittra Pittaya."

My eyes drifted off through the rain to the *sala* on the other side of the wide walkway where Pawnsiri and I had waited for her bus the last time we had been alone together. Today a solitary old woman waited in the shelter, holding a woven bag half-filled with groceries from the small market nearby.

"Where you stay?"

"I'm planning to stay at the Ubon hotel."

"Can we give you a ride? This is where I wait for my husband."

"Thanks, Pawnsiri, but your old friend Chai lent me his bicycle."

"How can you ride in the rain? We have a van. We can take you. No problem."

"I'll be okay. It's not that far, and the rain's starting to let up."

"What are your plan, Bren-dan?"

"My big plan was to see you. Now that I've found you, there's not much left to do. I'll have dinner tonight with Chai and Sommit. All that's left tomorrow is to go pay my respects to Prah Samrong at Wat Ph'a Yai. Tomorrow night I'll take the train to Bangkok."

"I would like you to meet Boonsom, my husband. I think you will like each other."

"I'd like to," I lied, "but I'd better get back before it starts raining hard again. I'm afraid Khun Chai is already worrying about me being gone too long."

I needed to go. Getting up quickly, I *waied* and walked off into the drizzly, gloomy afternoon. My feet felt like they were dragging a ball and chain as I sloshed along the wet pavement to the administration office, where I unlocked the bicycle and climbed on. A torrent of rain was falling again by the time I reached Route 66, which was flowing with a river of blood-red clay. Despite having fenders—unlike my old no-name racing bike—Chai's bike threw up a thin, steady spray from the runoff on the street, soaking through my clothing from below while the rain pounded me from above. I arrived wet and defeated at Woodstock Music to pick up the garage key from Chai.

"Don't worry about it," he said.

"We'll put it away in the morning," added Sommit.

"I'd like to check in at the Ubon Hotel. Will your parents mind if I pick up my suitcase?"

Chai answered, "We'll come with you. No more customer coming today in the rain."

"After you check in, we can take you to dinner," said Sommit.

"I wanted to take both of *you* to dinner."

Sommit smiled. "Save your money for Bangkok."

Soaked from head to toe, I picked up my valise at their parents' shop and walked with my friends the short distance to the hotel, hiding as best we could under Chai's umbrella while we dodged from awning to awning. Looking and feeling more like a stray dog than a human being when I checked in, I was glad my friends waited with me, smiling to reassure the desk clerk that I wasn't some wandering derelict before they rode the elevator to the rooftop restaurant to get a table for us. Up in my room, after setting my passport and my envelope of baht on the dresser to dry out, I took a long, steamy shower and changed into the only other shirt I owned.

The restaurant was almost empty when I got there. The view outside as the Ubon city lights began coming on at dusk was better than I remembered, maybe because there was little to obscure it—no clouds of cigarette smoke hanging in the air and no dolled-up women circulating around half-interested GIs. The aromas alone emanating from the passing trays of food were enough to get my mouth watering. Fortunately, Chai and Sommit had already ordered beef satay and spicy shrimp soup, which arrived for a first course just as I was sitting down. They had also ordered several curried dishes and a spicy Thai version of sweet-and-sour pork. They asked me what I wanted to add to our family-style banquet, and I quickly ordered *somtam*—Thai-style papaya salad—my bitter, sweet, spicy favorite from a few years earlier when I sat alone night after night at the end of the bar.

For the first time in three years, I took a drink, a Mekhong and soda that our waiter mixed for us at the table. It tasted better than good, which made me appreciate a little more just how much my Buddhist friends were giving up when they stayed on at tough forest monasteries like Wat Ph'a Yai, Wat Pah Nirapai, and Wat Pah Pohn Pao. The waiter left the ice bucket and the bottles there for us to freshen up our drinks whenever we pleased. Dinner was full of warm conversation and good cheer and ended with hope for all of us to have healthy, prosperous futures. When it was time to head down to my room, my friends insisted I take the half-empty bottle of Mekhong with me.

The moment I closed the door behind me I felt awful. I tried to meditate on the linoleum tile floor. Immediately my butt began to ache. I got up and pulled a pillow off the bed and tried again. It was back to day one, my mind racing everywhere in a desperate panic. Already I was missing the support of the Sangha. Even in the caves outside Luang Prabang, meditating alone, I felt support simply by wearing the robes. I brought my mind back to my breath, but soon my butt was bothering me again, this time growing numb from the *softness* of the pillow. My knees began to ache. I tried to focus loving-kindness on them, but instead of relieving the pain, new pain sprung up in my neck and my damaged left shoulder and wrist. And then I started to develop a headache. I gave up, deciding to wash out my muddy shirt and underwear. When I stood up, though, the half-empty bottle of Mekhong that sat on my dresser was looking me straight in the eye. I decided washing clothes could wait till I got to Bangkok and hung the soggy shirt over the tub to dry.

I tore the wrapper off a glass I found in the bathroom, set it on the dresser next to the bottle, and walked down the hall to the elevator landing for a bottle of Coke and some ice. Back in my room fixing the drink, I felt like I was meeting an old friend. I took a sip. It quenched my thirst, but I wanted to savor it. Stretching out on the bed, I continued savoring it as I slowly sipped some more. For a brief moment, I thought I heard Lek's throaty laugh echoing out in the hall. I toasted her and her little boy and her father, wherever they were on the Korat Plain, and before I knew it, the drink was gone. I hated to get back up, but the icy concoction tasted so good that I decided, or maybe the Mekhong decided for me, that I should make one more. By the time I finished that one, I was feeling so good I thought 8:00 p.m. might be a good time for a nap.

Not bothering to pull down the covers, I stretched out again, only to have a tourist brochure catch my eye. When I saw that it was written three-fourths in Thai, I decided to give myself a reading lesson, seeing how many of the strange Pali-based letters I could decipher, but the exercise quickly began to overtax the part of my brain that was still working. I don't know how long I had been sleeping when I heard the knocking on my door. I sat up with a start. Without bothering to button my shirt, I crossed the room drowsily and asked, "Who is it?"

"It's me," I heard a muffled female voice reply. "Open up the door."

I unhooked the chain, and there she stood—Miss Pawnsiri, who was now Mrs. Pawnsiri. She only took a single step into the room. "I can't stay long. My sister wait for me downstair. But I talk to Boonsom, my husband, and he agree. We want you to spend the day with us tomorrow. Can you wait until Sunday to go to Bangkok?"

"I suppose, but I really did want to see Prah Samrong before I go."

"We can take you there. Then we want to take you to a housewarming. Many of our friend will be there, maybe even Professor Natapong. Can you be ready at 10:00 a.m.?"

"Sure. Thanks." She was standing only a foot away. I could barely contain my need to touch her, to hold her.

"My sister gave me some interesting news today. Your letter did come to our house, but our parent hid it from me. Afraid you never come back to Ubon. Afraid I lose chance for marry Boonsom, afraid I wait too long for you and become too old for marry any-one. Only they were so wrong." She leaned in closer and whispered, "Because right now I still want to go with you."

"I *want* you to come with me."

"I want to sleep with you—right now."

"I *want* you to sleep with me—"

"*But we can't,*" we said together.

She shut the door and pushed me backwards until my calves hit the low Thai bed, and I landed on my backside with a thunk. "Why you take so long to write!" she said, all five feet two inches of her towering over me.

"I don't know exactly, but I couldn't. I tried to explain in the letter that you never received. I'll try again even though it's too late." I paused, struggling to collect my thoughts before I could continue.

"I was so full of anger and despair about the war—so much loss, so much waste. But as bad as the war was, the Big Buddha Bicycle Race was worse because it was *my* idea. My friends died and Thai pilots died. I had a *faen* before I met you, and *she* died. My *friends* killed her. Her brother was a terrorist who tried to kill *me*, and I thought he was my friend! I needed to tell you this, but I didn't know how. I needed time to grieve and to forgive myself, to understand why my *faen's* brother did this and why she didn't warn me. I tried to understand, tried to forgive, but I was numb, exhausted."

"We hear story about your *faen* and her brother. But I don' care. I only care about *you*, Bren-dan."

"Anger mixed with despair was such strong poison. I needed to sit for a long time to even begin to heal. But maybe I was a little arrogant, too. It took reflecting back on my entire life to see how cut off I am now. Painfully sensitive to my own feelings but too shut down to feel other people's pain— especially yours. Hearing that you were in pain because I wasn't there, I shut down even more. Maybe I thought you would always wait for me. Maybe I took it for granted that you would read my mind across four hundred miles of rivers and mountains and know I would come back, even though *I* didn't know when I was coming back. What I can see now is that healing from the war didn't heal me, it opened up the wounds of my childhood. How phony my family was, putting on a show for the world and tearing ourselves apart at home—physically sometimes, but emotional cuts went even deeper. I finally understood why my father was always complaining that I never smiled in our family photographs. I had learned to completely shut myself off, although I still can't answer whether or not that was by choice because maybe a child really has no choice.

"If the Communists hadn't come, who knows how much longer I might have stayed in Luang Prabang? Why did I love a *pu-ying jai dam* who would have ruined my life but shut down to you who offered me true love and commitment? Maybe this, too, is my *kamma*. Now that I can finally open up my heart to you, it's too late. But what I *can* do is tell you how sorry I am that you married a man you don't love. *Khaw toht. Khaw toht.*"

She sank to her knees in front of me. "I want to have your baby. I want to have your baby right this instant."

"Except we can't."

"Maybe Boonsom never know."

"He might get suspicious if it's a son—or a daughter—who grows up to be six feet tall."

"And I want to have your baby anyway. And you're right, I can't."

"You told me he's a good man."

"He's a very good man. And still, Bren-dan, I want to have your baby."

There was another knock at the door, which scared the hell out of me. Another female voice bled through, which at least ruled out the possibility of a jealous husband with a gun. *My God—Does Lek know I'm here? Did Mama-sahn send her a telegram?* Pawnsiri called back to the voice and looked up at me. "It my sis-ter. She worry we be late for movie." She stood up and walked over to the mirror that hung over the dresser, checking her makeup and straightening out her blouse. Her reflection made eye contact with me. "The movie we see— it's a love story," she said with a wry smile. "A sad, sad love story."

"You'll have to tell me all about it tomorrow," I said, walking over to the door and opening it for her. I gave her sister a polite little nod of my head and a *wai* as Pawnsiri swept past me.

"Until tomorrow," she said, and as bittersweet as it would be, the promise of one more day with Pawnsiri and her family and friends calmed me. My headache cleared up, and I could feel a relaxed smile on my face as I fell back to sleep.

In the morning, I had an American-style breakfast in the ground-floor café, the first time I had eaten eggs sunny-side up since I left the States. Pawnsiri and her husband joined me for a cup of sweet Thai coffee, and I quickly saw that she was right. I did enjoy meeting Boonsom, pleasantly surprised how much he reminded me of a new, improved *Thai* version of myself—at my funniest and warmest and most generous.

As we drove together to the Big Buddha Forest Monastery, I had to confess to myself that Pawnsiri was probably better off without me and without the mood swings and bouts of depression and incapacitating self-doubt I brought with me. How long would it have taken her to tire of talking baby-talk Thai to me while she was working five days a week and trying to raise a family? How soon would I have grown frustrated not being able to fully express the wanderings of my mind to her? How soon would I have grown weary of being admired without being understood?

Boonsom found a shady spot to park in the lot leading to the main gate, and we walked inside. After experiencing impermanence everywhere I had traveled the past few weeks, it was a relief to see how little the monastery at Big Buddha had changed. I lit a stick of incense, placed it in a sand-filled urn below the large, powerful form of the seated Buddha—Ph'a Yai—and said short prayers for Murray, Spitzer, and Sachs. I reflected a little longer on Prasert and wondered how Lek and Harley and Tom were surviving life's trials. I lit another stick of incense and prayed for Moonbeam Liscomb, my hero in so many ways, and for Pook, his adoring, adorable puppy-dog of a *tii-rahk*. I lit a third stick of incense and prayed longest of all for Tukada Maneewatana and her life that had been cut so short and for Pawnsiri Leemingsawat, whose new last name I didn't even know yet and whose life as mother, wife, and teacher was just beginning. She kneeled with her baby girl, not too far away, and I wondered what thoughts and feelings were passing through *her* mind and heart.

When I finished, I saw that by some lucky coincidence, Boonsom and Prah Samrong were talking together quietly in the shadow of a grove of trees. When I joined them, Samrong said, "Khun Boonsom tell me he was novice monk for many year when he was young so he can go to school at village *wat*. That was before they build government school in his district.

"He also tell me, Bren-dan, that you disrobe only a few day ago and that now you going back to United S-tate."

"I'll be leaving tomorrow, Tahn Samrong. But before I left, I wanted to thank you for being my first teacher. *Samadhi* and *vipassana*—concentration and insight—have helped me in many ways, but especially in letting go of the war. And thank you for sending me to Wat Pah Nirapai."

"I'm sorry to hear that Ajahn Po is not well."

"I'm thankful that I knew him when he was still strong. His Dhamma talks taught me a new way to look at life—and death," I said, *waiing* deeply to Prah Samrong and wishing him well in the future.

Not far from the monastery in the town of Amnat Charoen, we stopped for lunch at an open-air Chinese noodle shop, a welcome transition before we drove off to a housewarming full of strangers. On the way back to Ubon, Pawnsiri reminded me that the whole of Buddhist teaching as she had learned it as a child came down to: "Do good. Cause no harm. Purify the heart."

I wish my own meditations had been so simple, I thought.

The housewarming was taking place not too far from Pawnsiri's part of town, so it was only a slight detour dropping off their little girl to spend the afternoon with her grandmother. The host and hostess were friends of Boonsom and Pawnsiri's who were also teachers. They were moving into a small but comfortable home, larger than a traditional village hut but maintaining many of its elements, including a pitched roof and overhanging eaves. As Pawnsiri and Boonsom chatted with friends on our way in, I noticed how the house was raised on stilts, but like Pawnsiri's father's residence, the stilts were of reinforced concrete.

The air downstairs was filled with fragrant aromas from sizzling woks on portable charcoal braziers like the one Lek used to cook with on our porch at Ruam Chon Sawng, so much cooking going on that I had no idea where the permanent kitchen was tucked away. Upstairs we seated ourselves on a mat on the floor in the living room. All the furniture had been moved out and an altar with a Buddha image set up to the right of the door. The senior monk sat to the right of the altar, and eight more monks, in turn, sat to the right of him, all of them sitting in a semi-circle along the wall. Nine was the same propitious number of monks that had presided over Harley's funeral-wedding. And again from Harley and Mali's nuptials, I recognized the *sai sin* or sacred thread that had been draped around the outside perimeter of the yard and garden and run back in the window and around the right hand of the Buddha *rupa* before being passed to the abbot and his fellow monks. Pawnsiri whispered to me that its purpose was to keep away evil spirits.

Once the senior monk had consecrated the water in his alms bowl by carefully dripping in wax from a burning white candle, the assembly of monks began chanting in Pali and continued in deep, resonant tones for a half an hour or so, pleasant waves of energy coursing through my body, reminding me of the monks I used to listen to on retreat in the hills outside Luang Prabang and the younger assembly of monks led by Ajahn Saisamut at Wat Pah Pohn Pao. A few of the women came and went, still tending to the cooking downstairs, I suspected, but most of us, including the host and hostess, sat respectfully with our hands pressed together in a gesture of prayer. Halfway through the ceremony, I noticed Ajahn Natapong and his wife come in, sitting down unobtrusively in the back. When the chanting was over, the senior monk picked up a whisk, dipped it into the bowl of consecrated water, and sprinkled it over the householders and their guests, thereby blessing everyone, including the house itself. As the monks filed out, their leader anointed the front door with nine dots made from a white paste he had specially prepared for the occasion. The crowd dispersed slowly, with many old friends spotting each other and chatting for a moment, as we did with the Natapongs and several other of Pawnsiri and Boonsom's friends.

In the next room, the host and hostess stood together with a Brahman priest before a miniature white artificial tree, many pieces of *sai sin* tied to its branches, which sat on a small dining table. The priest was dressed in white and chanted in Hindi, doubling the couple's chances of chasing away evil spirits. All that appeared to be left to do in that department was putting up a spirit house. I only had a chance to glance at the shorter Hindu part of the proceedings before Ajahn Natapong, his wife, Boonsom, and Pawnsiri escorted me downstairs, where we spent the afternoon enjoying what seemed like an endless assortment of Thai delicacies heaped on steaming plates of rice. There was plenty of Mekhong and other beverages to go around, followed at last by mounds of fresh fruit and platters of cigarettes. Pawnsiri and Natapong's wife got up from time to time to help out in the kitchen, Boonsom and Natapong moved around occasionally to say hello to old friends, and I pretty much stayed in one place, enjoying the food and the warmth that pervaded the celebration. Times had changed, though, and Professor Natapong made no mention of his old offer of a teaching position.

While the others were eating dessert, I had to get up and stretch my legs, wandering off to the garden, which was fragrant with freshly planted roses that were already coming into bloom. "You know a Thai housewarming is very much like a Thai wedding," said Pawnsiri, slipping up behind me quietly.

"I noticed," I said, turning to face her and see if we were alone. "It reminded me a lot of when Harley and Mali got married up in Roi Et."

"All afternoon, I think about Miss Pawnsiri having housewarming with Khun Bren-dan."

"It's a lovely thought," I replied, forcing myself to smile.

"All afternoon, people who don't know us ask me if you my hus-band. Even Ajahn Natapong say, 'You know, before he become monk, I think maybe you and Khun Bren-dan get married someday.'"

"Sounds like the movie you saw last night. A sad, sad story."

"Bren-dan, do you *have* to go Bangkok tomorrow?"

"I think you already know the answer."

We stood there a moment, looking at each other, breathing in the perfumed air, drinking in the sight of each other one last time. "I guess we better go back for dessert," she said.

Saturday night back in my room, I was exhausted. I tried to meditate, but I felt drowsy and unfocused. I washed out my only two shirts and hung them in the bathroom to dry. New shoes would wait till I got to Bangkok; I would have to make do with my low-cut side-zipper boots, the BX's most fashionable four seasons back, and my trusty pair of flip-flop shower shoes that in Laos and Issan Thailand could pass equally well for work boots or formal wear. Thanks to the thirteen thousand baht that Chai had saved for me, there would be enough for a train ticket to Bangkok and a decent place to stay while I found a job teaching English. I needed to earn my passage home and not ask my parents for a handout. Maybe because I was afraid they wouldn't have a clue what to make of me after four years in Asia. And maybe because after four years in Asia I was having trouble remembering who my parents were. But I did remember that Dad had brought me up Depression-era Old School—*that* was ingrained deep inside me—and I wanted to stand on my own two feet. I fell asleep early that night. I was tired and slept deeply and did not dream.

Sunday morning, I boarded the mud-streaked baht-bus that would take me to the Warin train station for the last time. There were only a few people in line at the station when I bought my ticket for the early train to Bangkok. I wanted to watch the Thai countryside slide past me one more time and buy fresh pineapple and bananas and barbecued chicken from the old *mama-sahns* at the stops along the way. At the same time, I felt a deep sadness, knowing I was leaving Ubon with no expectation of ever coming back. I stood by myself out on the platform, leaning against a steel pillar a few feet away from the families that sat together on wooden benches waiting for the train to arrive so they could start boarding. I remembered standing in almost the same spot three and a half years earlier, waiting for Harley and our road trip to Thammasatstock. I was lost in those pleasant memories when out of the corner of my eye, I caught sight of Pawnsiri running toward me. "What are *you* doing here?" I asked. "I thought we said our goodbyes last night."

"I had to see you one last time. I had to see you get on this train, so I know you really leave."

My heart began beating strongly, and my chest swelled with emotion. "Where's your family?"

"They stay home. I had to see you alone."

I was more certain than ever—now that I had found her and seen her in the flesh and felt the love she still felt for me—that I loved Pawnsiri deeply. And at the same time, I feared that I would be haunted forever by the ghost of Tukada Maneewatana, cursed to love only someone I could not have. Or would *I* be the conundrum, hungry for love but unable to connect, to commit? Was there a lesson to be salvaged here? Even if this wasn't more deeply than I had ever loved anyone before, wasn't it deep enough? Wasn't the love I felt for Pawnsiri deep enough to raise a family and grow old together? I felt a sense of doom, fearing I would never love a woman this way again.

And in the end, it didn't matter. I couldn't express any of it, respecting Thai culture too much to hold Pawnsiri tightly the way I wanted to and smother her with kisses, drinking in her tears. I couldn't even touch her, as much as I ached for that touch.

"Why you stay away so long!" she cried. "Why you never write back when you didn't hear from me? Maybe my parent will miss that let-ter!"

"*Khaw toht, khaw toht, khaw toht.* I'm sorry. I should have tried again. Even if I didn't trust the mail service, I should have tried again. And again after that until I reached you."

"Do you know that for a year, I kissed your picture every night before I go to bed? Do you know that every night for a year, my pillow was soaked with tears that I cry for you? Sometime I dream about our band, making such beautiful music that everyone *ramwong*—young people and old people and little children can't help dancing with big smile on their face, our music so good."

"Should I stay? Maybe Boonsom wouldn't mind if we were just playing in a band—"

"How can my teacher be so stupid? I love you so much, other time I dream we have babies, beautiful babies, and I am so happy in my dream..."

"Pawnsiri, I'm so sorry." Tears pricked my eyes.

"I still think about leaving Boonsom. I will never love him as much as I love you."

"But he's a good man."

"He's such a good man that he *likes* you even though I think he know how I feel. I think he know my thoughts without I talk to him. After he was novice monk, he ordain as full monk for many year before he become a teacher. I think he know about us and have great compassion for us."

I tried to laugh it off. "Seems kind of unfair that a husband can have two wives in Thailand, but a wife can't have two husbands."

Her brows furrowed, and her eyes flashed in anger, sadness, and frustration. "How can my *ajahn* be so stupid?"

"Fate can be cruel, Pawnsiri. Fate brought us together. Fate sent me to Luang Prabang. I needed peace. I needed to atone for so much. So many people died. I needed time to heal. And now Fate has brought you a good husband and a baby, and we must never see each other again."

"*Chaat nah,*" she smiled, crying gently. "In this lifetime, I must stay with my husband, who is a good man, and raise my baby, who need to have her mother and father's love. Boonsom love Noy very much. How could I take her to America? How could I leave her here?"

And we knew there was no answer that could give our story a happy ending. We gazed into each other's eyes, our time together ticking away. "'*Chaat nah,*'" I said. "I don't think I know that expression."

"In our next lifetime, we will meet again. Somehow we will find each other."

The train had whistled, and the stationmaster had been making announcements over the PA that I had barely paid attention to. "Excuse me, sir?" the conductor asked politely. "Are you taking the Bangkok train?"

The last few passengers were hurrying to get on board. I picked up my valise and swung the strap over my shoulder. "*Chaat nah,*" I said, *waiing* deeply and turning away.

Climbing on and maneuvering quickly down the aisle, I was able to find a window seat at the back of second class. Pawnsiri hadn't moved. I waved and caught her eye. She gave me a tiny wave in return. And when I *waied*, she *waied* back and came over to my car. She put her fingers to the window, and I opened it and reached out and for the first and last time held her tiny hand—as soft and delicate as a rose petal—in mine. I could see that her gentle tears were still falling, and I wanted desperately to kiss them away and kiss her eyes and ears and neck and lips...and knew I never would. She smiled sadly and said, "Write to me."

"Do you really think that's a good idea?"

"Just to let me know you are okay. That you are back in the United States."

"I can do that. And I want to hear about your family."

"I want to come see you in America some day."

"Except you have a young husband and a family—who will need you for a long time."

The train began to move. She walked with me for a few steps, and then we had to let go. "I love you!" she called.

"I love you, too!"

"*Chaat nah,* Bren-dan!"

"*Chaat nah,* Pawnsiri!"

She said something else, but the train was gradually picking up speed, and whatever she said was lost in a muddle of engine noise, crashing couplers, shrieking whistles, and clanging bells. As the train began its journey west toward Si Saket and Surin, I watched Pawnsiri grow smaller and smaller in the morning mist until she became a speck in the Issan landscape and then a speck within a speck and she finally disappeared.

The train settled into a rhythmic click-clacking that rocked me comfortably, and for the rest of the day, I fell in and out of sleep. When

I awoke, I sat mesmerized, watching rice fields and small towns pass by in a blur. We passed Surin, and I remembered Jack Wu with his *National Geographic*-sized camera lenses, and Larry and Peung and Tom and Lek, laughing and in love. A few hours later we came to Korat, and I almost jumped off to search for Lek and her son and her sick father, and then I let the thought go. As the day went on, I discovered that I had no appetite, no desire to buy fresh fruit from the vendors who waited by the side of the tracks at each station. I wondered how long a Volkswagen Bug could survive abandoned along a shoulder of the Pacific Coast Highway. I nodded off to sleep but couldn't sleep. *Am I capable*, I wondered, *of carrying with me any truth I have discovered, or will I succumb to the material world once I am immersed in it again? Or is the Korat Plain, the Issan, the frontier of Laos and Thailand, now my true home?* I had survived my tour of duty, but I had no peace. I had a story to tell, but would anyone care? When the dust had settled, and the Communist liberation fronts of Laos, Vietnam, and Cambodia had made the difficult transition Marx never talked about from the euphoria of victory to the drudgery of governing, would my fate take me back to Asia?

After spending the next few months in Bangkok sitting all day in a dark corner of Lucy's Tiger Den drinking Mekhong and Coke and listening to Old China Hands telling cryptic war stories, after teaching nights and weekends at AUA-Bangkok, and after getting my paperwork in order with USC, I bought a one-way ticket to L.A. Out at Don Muang Airport, the mandolin solo on a Nitty Gritty Dirt Band song was playing over the PA. The sad strings gently opened up my heart, and I wondered how much longer Ajahn Po would be alive and if he could ever awaken from his sleep to take me back. Could a lapsed Irish Catholic buy indulgences from a living Buddhist master? Was the penance I did sufficient to absolve my sins? Did sin exist? Why did Buddhists call it defilement?

On the flight home, I felt as cool as dry ice, as numb as a cadaver at the thought of seeing friends and family I had left behind. Sitting in tourist class on the 747 heading back to the United States, I felt nothing, neither nostalgia nor excitement. I was heading into a time warp where the innocent, smiling natives could never become true Citizens of the World. Where scribed above the entrance to the USC film school was the legend: *Reality Ends Here.*

Where I yearned in vain for a second opinion from Dave Murray and Tom Wheeler, from Harley Baker and Moonbeam Liscomb, from Colonel Strbik and Ajahn Po, and from Tukada Maneewatana and Pawnsiri Leemingsawat on where *they* thought reality ended. Why did I fear spending the rest of my life alone, yearning for someone to talk to? Why did that fear refuse to die?

The End

Glossary

There is no direct transliteration of Thai—a tonal language with 44 consonants and 21 vowels—into English. The following, however, should give English-speaking readers a sense of its sounds and rhythms.

Frequently occurring vowels:

/**a** or **ah**/ = /ah/ as in aha; /**ai**/ = /y/ as in my; /**ae**/ = /ay/ as in say; /**ao**/ = /ow/ as in wow; /**aw**/ = /aw/ as in saw; /**ii**/ = /ee/ as in see; /**oh**/ = /oa/ as in oat; /**u**/ or /**uu**/=/oo/ as in shoot.

Frequently occurring consonants:

Except for proper nouns starting with /**Th**/ like Thailand and Thanon (street), the aspirated /**t**/ will be written as such, and the unaspirated t and d will both be written as /**d**/. Except for proper nouns starting with /**Ph**/ like Nakhon Phanom (city, Royal Thai AFB) and Phansa (Buddhist Lent), the aspirated /**p**/ will be written as such, and the unaspirated p and b will both be written as /**b**/. Finally, /**kh**/ = /k/; /**k**/ = /g/.

Noun and verb endings:

The Thai language does not have verb or noun endings like English. A noun or verb can be both singular and plural. When speaking informally, English speakers often form the plural of Thai nouns by adding 's', as in English (e.g., *wats*) and add English-style endings to verbs (e.g., *waiing*).

AAVS—Aerospace Audiovisual Service
ahimsa—doctrine of refraining from the taking of any life
ajahn, Ajahn— master Buddhist teacher, university professor
anatta—Buddha's fundamental insight that no permanent self or soul is embedded in existence
anicca—the impermanence of all things
anigarika—"homeless one," a pre-novice, still technically a layperson, who lives in a Buddhist monastery following the Eight Precepts
ap nam—(n. or v.) shower

Arri/Arriflex/Arri St—shorthand for the Arriflex St, a handheld 16mm movie camera, noisy but sturdy for combat photography

AUA—American University Alumni Association Language Center

ARVN—Army of the Republic of Vietnam (pro-American South Vietnamese soldiers)

"back in the World"—Black or hipster GI slang for "back home, back in the U.S., back to civilization"

bahng fai—bamboo rocket

baht—unit of Thai currency, traded twenty to the U.S. dollar in early 1970s; the fare on local Ubon buses

baisii—(Laotian/Issan Thai) traditional pre-Buddhist celebration of arrivals and departures

Beetle Bailey—American comic strip spoofing the U.S. Army that has run in thousands of newspapers including the *Pacific Stars and Stripes* since it was by created in 1950

bhikkhu—Buddhist term for monk

bot—ordination hall, a small temple within a Thai monastery where only men are permitted

bun—merit

bun bahng fai—making merit with rockets, a pre-Buddhist rain ritual later absorbed into the Visakha Bucha holiday

BX—Base Exchange, on-base department store for GIs and dependents only, source of tax-free imported goods like whiskey and cigarettes often traded on the black market

CBPO—Consolidated Base Personnel Office

chedi—structure containing relics (typically remains of monks or nuns) that is used as a place of meditation. In Thailand and Laos, often in the shape of an inverted bell with a path around it for ritual circumambulation

"*Chohk dii*"—(Thai) "Good luck (to you)"

CINCPAC—Commander-in-Chief Pacific (commander of all U.S. military forces in Asia and the Pacific)

ComDoc—Air Force shorthand for Combat Documentation, primary mission of Detachment 3, 601st Photo Squadron

Dhamma—(from ancient Pali) in Thai Buddhism: the teachings of the Buddha; in Thai culture: nature or the true nature of things. (similar to Sanskrit *dharma*)

"*Dii mahk!*"—Very good!

DOD—Department of Defence

DODCOCS—Pentagon computer school for field-grade officers (plumb billet for an enlisted man wanting to avoid combat)

domino theory-—belief that the fall of one country to communism could trigger a chain reaction, used by the U.S. government to justify intervention in Southeast Asia after WW II; capitalized: Leary's band

dukkha—suffering, discontent, anguish, stress experienced by all humans according to Buddhist teaching

FAA—Federal Aviation Administration

farang—Caucasian foreigner

flight—when applied to Air Force combat units, a formation consisting of 2–4 aircraft

geng mahk—very clever(ly)

GI—member of the U.S. armed forces, especially an enlisted man in the Army

glot—large umbrella with a cylinder of mosquito netting attached that *tudong* monks carry for shelter on pilgrimage

hong nam—bathroom (lit. "water room")

Issan—the northeast region of Thailand, drought-prone and poverty-stricken

Issan Liberation Front—composite of guerrilla units of the Communist Party of Thailand, the Thai United Patriotic Front, the Pathet Lao, and the North Vietnamese Army operating in Northern and Northeast Thailand, probing U.S. Air Force bases and firing at U.S. aircraft

jao tii—guardian spirits of a home

jai yen—cool heart and mind, a quality admired in Thai culture

jingjok—small house gecko, normally harmless

Jolly Green—large-capacity Sikorsky HH-3E rescue helicopter

kamma—(from ancient Pali) in Thai Buddhism: action and the consequence of that action, resulting from habitual impulse or volition; in Thai culture: actions that result in rebirth into the earthly realm and prevent attaining Nibbana. (similar to Sanskrit "karma" and "Nirvana")

kha—polite way for female to end sentence (akin to "sir" or "madam," see *khrab*)

khaopaht—fried rice

"*Khaw toht*"—Excuse me (lit. "Please hit me")

"*Khob khun mahk*"—Thank you very much

khrab—polite way for male to end sentence (akin to "sir" or "madam," see *kha*)

Khun; *khun*—Mr./Mrs./Miss; you (singular)

klong—drainage canals, often mixed with sewage

kuti—small hut where a monk from a forest monastery resides

"*Lagawn*"— (Thai and Laotian) Goodbye

lao lao—Laotian rice whiskey

lotus position—a cross-legged sitting meditation pose, either half (with one foot placed on the opposite thigh) or full (with each foot so placed)

Luang Paaw—"Venerable Father," term of address for senior monks that is both affectionate and respectful.

Mae Nam Kong—Mekong River

mahk—much/very

mai—no, not; at end of sentence it forms a question (e.g., "You're ready, no?")

mai sanuk—not festive (thus clashing with a pillar of Thai culture—fun!)

mama-sahn—GI pidgin for an older Asian woman managing a small, often shady, business

Mama-sahn—the wily old upcountry businesswoman who owns Leary's bungalow complex

metta—goodwill, loving-kindness in Buddhist teaching

mii krawp—crispy noodle appetizer

MIT—Massachusetts Institute of Technology

na?/!—sometimes meaningless syllable added for emphasis; there!

NCO—non-commissioned officer

Nibbana—Pali equivalent of Sanskrit "Nirvana"

nimitta—mental sign or image seen when meditating

nissaya—five-year apprenticeship served by a new monk under the guidance of an experienced bhikkhu before he is allowed to teach the Dhamma

NKP—Nakhon Phanom, a town and air base on the Thai side of Mekong River

NVA—North Vietnamese Army (highly trained regular soldiers)

OSI—Office of Special Investigations (U.S. Air Force)

Pacific Stars and Stripes—GI newspaper, by law "an authorized unofficial publication for the U.S. Armed Forces of the Pacific Command"

pah-tii—Thai form of borrowed English word "party"

papa-sahn—GI pidgin for an older Asian man managing a small, often shady, business

Papa-sahn—wily old drug dealer reached only by boat

pii—ghost

pii tai hong—restless, vengeful ghosts of those who died violent deaths

pindabaht—a daily alms round in the Theravada (Southeast Asian) tradition made by monks to collect food

"Pohp kan mai na khrab/kha"—Until I see you again

Prah—form of address for monk

psy-ops—psychological operations

pu-ying—Thai female

pu-ying jai dam—evil woman (lit. "black-hearted woman")

R&R—military slang for rest and recreation (*or* rest and relaxation *or* rest and recuperation)

rahn-ahahn—restaurant

ramwong—Thai folk dancing

revetment—barricade to shelter aircraft (from bomb fragments or strafing)

rongphayaban—hospital

RTAFB—Royal Thai Air Force Base

ruu?—short-form question word meaning "or not?"

"Sabaidii"—(Laotian) Hello/Goodbye; similar to *Sawatdii* in Thai

sahmlaw—bicycle-powered rickshaw (lit. "three wheels")

sahn prah puum—spirit house (shrine in shape of small Buddhist temple where joss sticks are burned and food offered)

sai sin—sacred white string

sala—a roofed, open-air shelter

SAM—Russian surface-to-air missiles capable of shooting down high-altitude B-52 bombers over Hanoi, used late in the Vietnam War on the Ho Chi Minh Trail against AC-130 gunships

samadhi—state of deep concentration or one-pointedness of mind attained in meditation

samsara—Buddhist belief in repeated cycles of birth, misery, and death caused by bad *kamma*

Sangha—the worldwide community of Buddhist monks, nuns, and enlightened laypeople; individual monastic communities

sanuk—festive

sapparoht—pineapple

"Sawatdii"—(Thai) Hello/Goodbye

sawngtao—passenger truck with facing benches on each side in back (lit. "two rows")

Siam—The Kingdom of Thailand's name before 1932 when it became a constitutional monarchy *sNorton Bird*—GI underground newspaper published at Norton AFB, CA

"*Sohk dii*"—(Laotian) Good luck

sutta—(from ancient Pali) in Thai Buddhism: one of the discourses of the Buddha that constitute the basic text of Buddhist scripture. (similar to Sanskrit sutra)

Tahn—respectful but familiar form of address for a monk (less formal than *Prah*)

TDY—Temporary Duty Assignment

tii—to/at/that (adj., adv., prep., common prefix)

tiinii—here

tiinawn—over there

tii-rahk—informally, girl or boyfriend; GI/bar-girl slang: to live together (lit. "loved one")

triple-A (or AAA)—anti-aircraft artillery

tudong—more rigorous rules of discipline permitted by the Buddha and followed by forest monks (including no handling of money, one meal a day); also applied by Thai Buddhists to a pilgrimage taken by forest monks (to go *tudong*)

Tukada—char. name (literally: doll)

USAF—United States Air Force

USC—University of Southern California

USIS—United States Information Service

VC—Viet Cong, Communist insurgents operating in South Vietnam

viharn—assembly hall where both monks and laypeople can gather for chanting, meditation and other Buddhist ceremonies

vipassana (Pali) or *wipassana* (Thai)—insight meditation, taught in Buddhist monasteries in South and Southeast Asia

Visakha Bucha—annual celebration of the Buddha's birth, enlightenment, and death

wai—prayer-like gesture of greeting or respect

wat, Wat—Thai Buddhist monastery

yuu—reside, located

Acknowledgments

In the Year of the Rabbit is a work of fiction. Poetic license has been taken. But I would like to thank the following writers and teachers for whatever cultural and historical authenticity this book contains: Jack Kornfield, whose writing and teaching opened many doors for me, Ajahn Buddhadasa, Ajahn Chah, Charles Agar, Dean Barrett, Capt Thomas D. Boettcher, Sarah Conover, Joe Cummings, Alan Dawson, Dieter Dengler, Ron Emmons, Col David Hackworth, Jane Hamilton-Merritt, John Hinds, Yupa Holzner, Stanley Karnow, Lutz Lehman, Alfred W. McCoy, Gen Bruce Palmer, Jr., Christopher Robbins, Richard A. Ruth, Denis Segaller, William Shawcross, Wallace Terry, Col Gerald H. Turley, Bill Weir, and Col Henry Zeybel. And the following publishers: Aerospace Publishing, Amaravati Publications (especially for translations of Buddhist chants), Arnow Press, Insight Guides, The International Labor Organization, Lonely Planet, Military Press, Moon Handbooks, Shambala Publications, Wikipedia, and the World Fellowship of Buddhists. And finally, the many Buddhist laypeople in Thailand, the United States, and England, whose generosity has made possible the publication of countless books available for free distribution at Buddhist monasteries in those countries.

And I would especially like to thank the following people: MSgt Larry Tener (USAF, ret.), a big-hearted warrior and friend forever; Susan Craig, for her continued encouragement; Ajahn Jayasaro; Ajahn Pasanno; Ajahn Sumedho; Ajahn Thanissaro (Phra Jeff); Capt John Harkin (USAir, ret.); Francis Kirby; Dorothy Little; Capt Bob Mueller, (USAir, ret.); LtCol Chris O'Grady (USAF, Ret.); Samai and Lumpian Pengjam; Anthony Posepny, an enigma and a legend; Jeanne Rosenberg; Jay and Nittaya Uhley; former Air Force Captain Duke Underwood, Shinzen Young; Susan Walsh; Joe Rumbaugh and Tong at Asia Vehicle Rental in Vientiane, Laos; Jim Centracchio and Peter Wood for their encyclopedic knowledge of Rock history; my high school English teacher, Rudy Spik, who pored over the first draft; Professor Irwin Blacker and editor Caitlin Alexander for challenging me to dig deep and make this a better book; Ken Silverman for getting me back on my bicycle; Steve Meyer and Writers Aloud; Rebecca Weldon and

Lee Thomas and Writers Without Borders; Bhikkhu Nirodho (Phra Charles), Harry Spring; Prof. Patrick Keeney and Prof. Michael Ray Fitzgerald for their close readings; Trasvin Jittidecharak, my publisher, and Kamolpaj Tosinthiti, her assistant, at Silkworm Books; and finally, my wife Nancy, for her insight, humor, and unwavering support.

About the Author

Terence A. Harkin earned a BA in English-American Literature from Brown University while spending weekends touring New England with rock bands that opened for the Yardbirds, the Critters, and Jimi Hendrix. After winning a CBS Fellowship for his screenwriting while completing an MFA at the University of Southern California, he went on to spend twenty-five years as a Hollywood cameraman. His credits include *The Goodbye Girl, The Legend of Billie Jean, Quincy, Designing Women, Seinfeld, Tracy Ullman, MASH,* and the miniseries of *From Here to Eternity.* His debut novel, *The Big Buddha Bicycle Race,* was listed as a Kirkus Top 100 Indie Novel of 2017. It continues to be ranked as a Top Ten Vietnam War book at Goodreads.com and won a Silver Medal in literary fiction from the Military Writers Society of America. The sequel, *In the Year of the Rabbit,* like *Big Buddha,* is set in Ubon, Thailand, where he served with Aerospace Audiovisual Service Detachment 3 during the Vietnam War. He is currently at work on a third novel, *Tinseltown Two-Step,* set in L.A. and Chiang Mai, Thailand, and the book to a musical, *Paint Your Dreams,* based on the music of Lisa Bouchelle.

Readers can contact Terence A. Harkin at his Web address: http://www.taharkin.net

CPSIA information can be obtained
at www.ICGtesting.com
Printed in the USA
BVHW080734220322
631815BV00003B/7